A WARRIOR OR A GENTLEMAN?

Images from earlier in the evening flooded her mind. Iain storming, pale and furious, into Lord William's study. Iain trying to punish her with his kisses. Iain making her tremble, his mouth upon her breasts.

But other images came to her mind as well. Iain grinning to his men as he walked, shackled, toward the whipping post. The reassuring strength in his eyes. His body tensing with agony at each stroke of the lash.

'Twas the price he'd willingly paid for her life, though she was but a stranger to him.

She'd thought him a barbarian at first, and she'd been right. But there was honor in him—honor that went soul deep—and courage as strong as the roots of a mountain. Honor and courage—if those weren't the traits of a gentleman, what were?

Surrender

PAMELA CLARE

LEISURE BOOKS NEW YORK CITY

A LEISURE BOOK®

March 2006

Published by

Dorchester Publishing Co., Inc.
200 Madison Avenue
New York, NY 10016

ISBN 0-8439-5488-4

The name "Leisure Books" and the stylized "L" with design are trademarks of Dorchester Publishing Co., Inc.

Printed in the United States of America.

Visit us on the web at www.dorchesterpub.com.

With love for my sons, Alec and Ben.
You will always be the best and most
important thing I have ever done.

ACKNOWLEDGMENTS

With special thanks to Catrìona Mary Mac Kirnan for giving Iain and his brothers their Scottish Gaelic voice.

Deep gratitude to Natasha Kern for her constant encouragement; Alicia Condon for her support and patience; and the staff at Dorchester Publishing for their hard work.

Personal thanks to: Michelle White, Timalyn O'Neill, Vickie McCloud, Sara Megibow, Karen Marie Moning, Dede & Wayne Laugesen, Kally Jo Surbeck, Amy Vandersall, Candice Voorhies, Scott Weiser and the women at Rebel Writer's Refuge. What would I do without you?

Surrender

Prologue

July 28, 1755
Albany on the Hudson River
The Colony of New-York

If Lord William Wentworth needed proof that he had come to the outermost edge of civilization, he need only look out his window. In the dusty street below, a man who looked as if he'd never bathed rutted with an even filthier whore, pounding into her from behind with the mindfulness of an animal. A dog relieved itself in the dirt a few feet away. Two painted Indians strode by, seemed not to notice the tupping pair.

William supposed he ought to find the display below revolting. Instead he felt mild amusement. He'd been in the Colonies for four months now, and thus far the inhabitants had not ceased to provide diversion—nor the vastness and beauty of the land to stir his blood.

Behind him, Lieutenant Cooke, the young officer assigned to him, struggled to excuse Braddock's recent devastating defeat. "The general had no experience fighting in such dense forest against so ruthless a foe, my lord. He expected the French and their allies to fight with honor, not shoot from the shadows like brigands."

"Did he not have Indian scouts and provincials of his own to advise him?" William spoke without turning from the window, his gaze fixed on the coarse activity below. The man had climaxed and was tucking himself back into his breeches.

"Aye, my lord." Lieutenant Cooke fell into an uncomfortable silence.

They had come to the unpleasant truth of it.

"Why did Braddock fail?"

The whore smoothed her tattered skirts, then turned to the man and held out a grimy hand for her fee.

"Please, my lord, the general is but weeks in the grave. It hardly seems polite—"

"I did not call you here to eulogize General Braddock but to analyze his defeat. If you wish to advance in rank and one day lead men into battle, you must learn from the strategic errors of others. Is that understood, Lieutenant?"

"Aye, my lord."

"Tell me, then. Why did Braddock fail?"

"He chose not to heed the advice of his provincials, and he offended his Indian fighters, many of whom abandoned him."

The man in the street, having eased the ache in his groin, apparently didn't wish to pay. He struck the whore across the face, knocking her to the ground.

"In sum, the general failed to recognize his own limitations." It was a mistake William was determined not to make. "Braddock was an arrogant fool who paid for his hubris with his life—and the lives of his men."

"Y-yes, my lord."

The whore struggled to her feet, a sagging breast threatening to fall free of her low bodice. She leapt for the man, teeth and claws bared.

"What must be done if His Majesty is to prevail in the struggle for this continent, Lieutenant?"

The man struck the whore again, and a knife appeared in his hand.

"W-we must learn to fight as the heathen fight, my lord."

"Or take into His Majesty's service those who do." William was so caught up in the tasteless little drama below that he scarce heard himself speak.

The man's arm cut an arc through the air. The whore jumped back, stepped on her hems, fell backwards with a shriek.

William was about to shout through the open window to interrupt imminent bloodshed, when a tall man—a trapper or frontiersman by the look of him—appeared out of nowhere. In the time it took William to blink, the trapper had subdued the man, dropped him to the ground and ripped the knife from his grasp.

William had never seen any man move that quickly. Was the trapper part Indian perhaps? His dark hair hung well past his shoulders. His skin was brown from the sun, and Indian designs decorated his forearms, but he was dressed like a European in leather breeches and a simple shirt of homespun. Well over six feet, he carried a bundle of furs and what appeared to be a broadsword on his back. Around its handle was bound a strip of plaid.

An exiled Highlander.

In one hand he held a rifle. A knife rested in its sheath at his left hip, a pistol at his right. A powder horn hung from his left shoulder, and around his waist was a leather pouch for flints and shot.

William watched as the Highlander—who had been joined by two other men so like him in dress and appearance that they could only be his brothers—sorted out the dispute and forced the man to pay.

Enraged, the man tossed a coin into the dirt.

The whore grabbed it, bit it, then fled.

Lieutenant Cooke appeared at William's side. "Is aught amiss, my lord? I'll have those miscreants driven beyond the palisade, if you wish."

William shook his head, smiled at the youthful look of disgust on Cooke's face. "Are you familiar with the Ranger Corps, Lieutenant?"

"Most certainly, my lord. The ranging companies served His Majesty well during Governor Shirley's War. Just the other day, General Johnson spoke of the need to outfit more such companies for this conflict."

In the street below, the Highlander helped the man he'd bested to his feet, handed him back his knife. But, outraged, the man lunged as if to plant his blade in the Highlander's heart. The Highlander neatly sidestepped the blow, a grin on his face, then kicked the man's legs out from under him, sending him sprawling.

"I'm in agreement with Johnson and have been charged with raising a company of Rangers to serve under my command at Fort Elizabeth. If I am to succeed, it is men like those I must persuade to join me."

Lieutenant Cooke frowned. "They look like a troublesome lot, ill suited to British military discipline, my lord. Good heavens, are those clan colors?"

William smiled. "I want to know who they are and what they're doing here in Albany. Track their every move, Lieutenant, but take care lest they discover you. Hire someone if you must, but come dawn, I would know all there is to know about those three Scots."

"I am your humble servant, my lord." The lieutenant bowed his head respectfully.

"You are dismissed." William turned away from the window and back toward his chessboard.

The pieces were set. It was time for a new game.

Iain MacKinnon fought to rein in his rage and followed the redcoat officer up the stairs, his movements made awkward by the heavy fetters around his ankles and wrists. Their shackles clinking, Morgan and Connor walked behind him, five soldiers with bayonets at their backs.

"We didna do it."

Connor sounded like a lad about to feel the sting of his father's belt strap. But the charge was murder. 'Twas far more than a beating they'd be in for if they failed to prove their innocence.

Iain and his brothers had been on their way out of town when a dozen redcoats had fallen on them and arrested them. Morgan and Connor had drawn their blades, ready to fight their way free, but Iain had stayed their hands.

"There's no sense dyin' over what is surely a mistake, lads," he'd told his younger brothers as the redcoats had shackled his wrists.

They'd been arrested before a mob of gawking townsfolk and then taken to the fort that stood on the hill. There they'd been made to wait in a dank cell, where they'd had plenty of time to discuss the charge and make certain none of them had killed anyone. After all, they'd each had more than a gill or two of whisky, and the night's events were a wee bit foggy.

Connor had said he'd spent his night between the thighs of bonnie Kally Vandall, consoling her over the loss of her much older husband. Iain and Morgan had whiled their hours away at Oldiah Cooper's tavern. Morgan had played at draughts and fondled the alewife's plump daughter until lust overcame him and he'd taken her upstairs for a good tupping. Iain had sat alone with his ale and thought of Jeannie, with her long honey-brown hair and big brown eyes.

When they got home again, Iain was going to wash, shave, put on his clean shirt and ride to Jeannie's father's farm to ask his permission to wed his daughter. Old Master Grant favored him above her other suitors, Iain knew. The MacKinnon farm was fruitful, the larder well stocked with corn, smoked turkey and venison, proving Iain's skill with plow and hunting rifle. Only the formalities stood in the way of his taking Jeannie to wife. With any luck, they'd be sharing a marriage bed by summer's end.

That was why he and his brothers had come to Albany. Iain had paid the gunsmith a visit in hopes that the smithy could make his mother's gold wedding band fit Jeannie's smaller hand. Iain had measured her finger with a bit of string and brought the string with him. The gunsmith had been happy to oblige and had taken in fee the small bit of gold he'd cut from the ring.

It was thoughts of Jeannie that had kept Iain from fighting when the redcoats had taken them. The last thing Grant would want for his daughter was a man in trouble with the accursed English. Iain would settle this misunderstanding. Then he'd get his brothers out of Albany and back to the farm.

The redcoat officer reached the top of the stairs and led them down a short hallway to the right. Why they'd been brought here and not to some kind of court Iain knew not, but he didn't like it. Something didn't feel right.

The officer stopped and knocked on the only door.

A voice from within—imperious and very English—bade them enter.

Iain found himself being shoved with his brothers into a large room filled with foppish chairs, silver candelabra and a great writing table of dark, gleaming wood. Portraits in gilded frames lined the walls. Toward the center of the room sat a young bewigged Englishman, his fingertips pressed together as he contemplated with furrowed brow the figures on a marble chessboard. The bronze gorget at his throat proclaimed him an officer, while the glittering ring on his finger bespoke nobility.

Iain bit back the instinctive loathing that swelled inside him, shot a warning glance to his brothers. 'Twas not the time for an airing of their grievances with the *Sassenach*.

The young officer who'd let them into the room gave a respectful bow. "They are here, my lord."

So he *was* a lord. And arrogant. He raised a finger for silence and continued to stare at the chessboard. After what seemed an eternity, he picked up a black pawn and moved it forward one space. Then he stood.

He was almost as tall as Iain, though of a lesser build. His skin was pale like that of a gentleman who disdained the sun, but his features were manly, even strong. His brows were dark, a sharp contrast to his white wig. Through cold gray eyes he gazed first at Connor, then Morgan. Then at last his gaze met Iain's, and he seemed to measure Iain as if weighing his soul.

Impatience whipped through Iain's belly. "I am Iain MacKinnon. These are my—"

The butt of a rifle slammed into his gut, drove the air from his lungs.

"You'll speak when spoken to!" the younger officer shouted in Iain's face.

"That's enough, Lieutenant." The lordling gave a dismissive flick of his wrist, then turned toward his writing table and poured himself a brandy. "I know much about you, Iain MacKinnon. These two men beside you are your brothers, Morgan and Connor. You arrived in New York as boys and grew up on the frontier, where you spent time among the heathen and learned to speak several Indian tongues. Your father, Lachlan MacKinnon, died three winters past; your mother, Elasaid Cameron, several years earlier. Your grandsire was Iain Og MacKinnon, barbarian lord of the MacKinnon clan and the Catholic traitor who helped the Young Pretender escape justice after my uncle's victory at Culloden."

My uncle's victory at Culloden.

Those final words struck Iain like a fist, made his gorge rise. MacKinnon blood had stained the moor red that terrible spring day, a mere foretaste of weeks of slaughter that had followed, slaughter ordered by one man: the Butcher of Cumberland, son of the *Sassenach* king.

Iain tried to picture Jeannie's face, fought to keep the hatred from his voice. "Then you are—"

The lordling turned to face him again, brandy in hand, an arrogant smile on his face. "Lord William Wentworth, third son of Robert Wentworth, Marquis of Rockingham, who is husband to Her Royal Highness Princess Amelia Sophia. My grandsire—well, no doubt you can deduce who he is."

Iain could.

Bloody King George.

A thousand curses passed through his mind—and with them a thousand questions. But only one mattered. "Why have you brought us here?"

Wentworth swirled his brandy, took a sip, swallowed. "From what I understand, you're soon to be convicted of murder and hanged."

Iain glanced over at his brothers, saw the look of disbelief on their faces. "We've no' been convicted, nor has there yet been a trial. The accusation is false. There's been some kind of mistake."

Connor's voice dripped with contempt. "What evidence do you have against us?"

Wentworth set his drink down, glared at Connor. "Sometime during the night, the three of you encountered and killed Henry Walsh—the man you grappled with yesterday afternoon outside my window."

"That's a bloody lie! We didna—" Connor's words became a grunt as a rifle butt struck his ribs once, twice.

Fists clenched, Iain took a step toward Wentworth. "Your men will no' strike him again, or I'll show you just how much *barbarian* blood runs in my veins!"

Wentworth nodded to the redcoat, who backed away from Connor. "I've already seen you fight. In fact, it's because of your *barbarian* blood, as you put it, that I'm prepared to offer you an . . . arrangement."

Iain felt the hair on the back of his neck rise. "What kind of arrangement?"

"I'll see to it personally that all charges against you and your brothers are suspended. In exchange, you'll take up the leadership of a Ranger unit under my command and fight for your Sovereign against the French and their Indian allies."

The idea was so absurd it almost made Iain laugh. "You're daft!"

"Am I? His Majesty needs men who know the land and the ways of the Indians, if he is to successfully pursue his interests on this continent. And without my help, you and your brothers will surely be hanged."

Iain felt his teeth grind. "What proof do you have against us?"

Wentworth gave a shrug. "Why, in addition to the dead body, any I choose to offer, of course."

And then Iain understood. Unless he agreed to fight for the British against the French, fellow Catholics and traditional allies of the Highland clans, the three of them would die for a crime they did not commit. No Englishman's court would take the word of a traitorous Catholic Highlander over that of their king's bloody grandson.

Blood rushed to Iain's head. " 'Tis slavery!"

Wentworth answered in a voice as cold as winter. " 'Tis your duty to serve your king, whether by your free will or not."

The room seemed to press in on Iain. He fought to keep his voice steady. "If I accept, what will become of my brothers?"

"Your brothers will be free to go as they please, while you will be given beating orders and funds sufficient to piece together and outfit a company of one hundred fifty men such as you judge fit for ranging service. You will report to me at Fort Elizabeth by August twenty-first and serve me until death release you or this war is ended. If you fail to appear or abandon your post, you will be shot for desertion and your brothers will be hanged for murder."

"Dinnae do it, Iain! Curse him!" Morgan then did exactly that, letting loose a stream of Gaelic that would have shocked Satan himself.

"I'm no' afraid to die." Connor's voice held quiet resignation. "Let them hang us! We willna be the first Highlanders murdered by English lies, nor the last."

Scarcely able to breathe, Iain considered the unbearable choice that had been thrust upon him—kill Frenchmen for the hated English, or die with his brothers in shame and agony.

But there was more at stake than that.

Jeannie. Sweet Jeannie.

Grant would not let his daughter wed a soldier. He wanted to settle her with a farmer, a man whose mind was bent on tilling the soil and raising a family, not fighting a war. If Iain took up his rifle and sword, she would surely be lost to him.

There was also the farm. It had been his father's dream to see it thrive and become the foundation for a revived Mac-Kinnon clan in the Americas. 'Twas unending, backbreaking labor, demanding both sweat and soul. If he fought for the English, his brothers would have to plant and harvest and fend off the forest without his help.

And then there was the matter of honor. If he served the British king, slayer of his kin, he would have none. What was a man without honor?

"What say you?" Wentworth watched him with that measuring gaze.

"Bugger him, Iain!"

"Dinnae do it! Let them hang us!"

Iain looked over at Morgan and Connor, felt the weight of his brothers' lives in his hands.

Then he closed his eyes, and sent a silent prayer skyward. *God forgi'e me.*

Chapter One

Inveraray, Scotland
September 14, 1757

Lady Anne Burness Campbell huddled in the corner of the dank gaol cell, shivering. Tears streamed down her already tearstained cheeks, though she did not notice them. Her eyes stared unseeing into the darkness, and she paid little heed to the rats that poked about in the stale straw. What did rats matter now?

Any moment the sheriff's men would come for her. They would drag her into the town square. They would brand her on the thumb, mark her for the rest of her life as a thief. Then they would send her over the sea in shame.

But she had stolen nothing. Nothing.

"O, Mamaidh!" Mother!

Her mother could not help her now. She'd died three weeks past, the breath choked from her body, her spirit shattered. Uncle Bain had claimed it was an accident, a terrible tragedy, but Annie had known better. She'd overheard the whisperings of servants, heard them speak of his unnatural appetites, his liking for the pain of others. She'd remembered the handful of people who'd died over the years, most of them young servant lads and lasses, their deaths explained away in like fashion. And then there was her mother's warning.

If aught should happen to me, tarry not, but take my jewels and what coin I have and flee this place. Make your way to Glasgow and seek out your father's old solicitor, Argus Seton. Dinnae trust your uncle Bain! I know you love him, but you cannae trust him! Do you understand, Annie?

Annie hadn't understood. Not then.

If only she'd known. If only her mother had told her. She'd have gotten them both away from him somehow. But her mother hadn't been able to bear the shame of Annie knowing, and now it was too late. Her mother was gone.

Annie's heart seemed to burst under the crushing weight of her grief, and she fought back a sob. How she longed to hear her mother's voice, to feel her mother's hand upon her hair, to see her sweet smile—simple tokens of a mother's love. Annie hadn't understood how precious they were until they had passed forever beyond her reach. How could she live without them?

She was alone.

Now she was to be branded and sent on a ship to a strange land—all at the hands of a man she'd loved and respected as a father.

'Twas like being swallowed by a nightmare.

Fear spread like a sickening poison through her belly. How badly would the hot iron hurt? Would she survive the journey? What sort of people would she be forced to serve?

Be brave, lass! Dinnae let your fear rattle you.

Her father's voice, words he'd spoken so long ago, came suddenly into her mind. She'd been five, and he'd been teaching her to ride her pony. But the pony had seemed so high off the ground, and she'd been sore afraid. Only the sound of his voice and the reassurance of his smile had kept her in the saddle that long hour. And when she'd learned to ride with skill and confidence, his praise had seemed like sunshine. It had been the happiest summer of her life.

Within the year, her father had died fighting for King George at Prestonpans, cleaved in two by a Jacobite claymore, her brothers cut down without mercy beside him—Robert, William, and Charles. Uncle Bain had fought beside them and, despite his own injuries, had protected their bodies with his claymore, spilling his own blood to spare them despoilment and earning a hero's honor for himself.

Annie had been six.

For a time, she and her mother had remained in their home. But her father, though an earl, had not been wealthy. Pressed by creditors, overwhelmed by grief, her mother had been forced to sell the estate and live with Uncle Bain, her brother by marriage. A marquis and widower with one grown son who spent his time in London, Uncle Bain had seemed to welcome them to his nearby estate with open arms. Only after her mother's death had Annie realized her uncle hadn't taken them in out of the kindness of his heart.

If only her father or brothers had lived. Everything would have been different. If her father had lived—

Footsteps.

They were coming.

Annie tried to swallow, but her mouth had gone dry. Her heart beat painfully in her breast. If she'd had anything in her belly, she might have been sick.

Be brave, lass!

She forced herself to stand on trembling legs, smoothed her skirts. Then she wiped the tears from her face. No matter what they did to her, she was still Lady Anne Burness Campbell.

The clanking of iron keys. The tumbling of the lock. The creaking of hinges.

A shaft of flickering light spilled into the cell, spread across both rats and straw as the door was pushed open wide and her two tormentors appeared. For three weeks she'd suffered their leering glances, listened to their vile blather, done her best to escape their grasping hands.

"Did ye miss me, lass?" The taller of the two, Fergus, gave her a repulsive smile and laughed. "Time tae come wi' us."

Wat, the shorter one, grabbed her roughly by the arm. "There's a gentleman come tae see ye."

"A gentleman?" Annie felt a spark of hope. Perhaps the sheriff had sent her letter to Argus Seton after all. Perhaps her father's old friend had come to prove that she was, indeed, Lady Anne Campbell and not some thieving servant wench as her uncle claimed. "Take me to him."

" 'Tak' me tae him.' " Fergus mimicked her words, held out a pair of shackles. "She's up and spake tae us as if we was her servant laddies come tae dae her biddin'."

"Can we no' humble her a bit wi' a fast tup in the straw? She'll no' speak thus tae us efter we've had her on her back."

Annie pretended their words did not touch her, as much for her own sake as to discourage them. She'd learned quickly that acting like a frightened virgin only fed their wickedness. She held out her wrists, felt the dreaded touch of cold iron against her skin as Fergus locked the shackles in place.

"We've no time for that just now, Wat." Fergus looked at her breasts, grinned. "Sorry tae disappoint ye, lass."

The two men pushed her out the door of her cell and down a narrow arched hallway where fat yellow candles flickered in iron sconces against walls of crumbling gray stone. From behind a dozen small arched doors like hers came sounds of human misery—moans, murmurs, a woman's wailing, curses, mad laughter—and Annie found herself wanting to run from this place, from the stench and the loneliness and the terror of it.

But perhaps she *was* leaving. She prayed with all her heart it was so. She tried to imagine who the gentleman might be, felt her heart lift. It had to be Master Seton. She'd written no one else. There was no one else.

A kindly man bowed from years of working over his ledgers, he would see to it that she was set free and the jewels restored to her, together with all the belongings she'd left behind in her uncle's hall when she'd fled. And then, when they were safely away from Inveraray, the first thing she would ask for was a hot bath and a soft bed. For three long weeks she'd had neither.

They came to another hallway, but instead of going up the stairs as they'd done when she'd been taken before the judge, they turned left toward stairs that descended into darkness.

Annie stopped, stared down the dark stone stairway, alarm creeping up her spine. "Wh-where are you takin' me?"

Fergus gave her a shove, almost sent her toppling. "Ye'll see soon enough, lassie."

With each step, Annie's doubt and dread grew. The public rooms of the gaol were upstairs, not below stairs. If her father's solicitor had come for her, surely he'd have been left to wait upon her above.

Be brave, lass!

But she didn't feel brave. By the time they reached the doorway at the bottom of the stairs, she was trembling again.

Fergus grabbed the iron handle, pushed the door open.

Uncle Bain.

Annie felt the blood rush from her head, felt herself sway on unsteady legs, her last hope shattered.

The man she'd once loved as a father stood before the fire in the middle of a room filled with devices whose purposes could only be cruelty. Wearing no wig and dressed only in his shirtsleeves, he looked disheveled, his face lined with fatigue as if he had been unable to sleep. His gaze was hard upon her, but he spoke to the guards. "Leave us."

Chuckling, Fergus and Wat forced her through the door, shut it behind her.

"I trust they haven't laid hands upon you, lass. I've paid them well." He looked so like her father—the same blue eyes, the same smile, the same square jaw. It had been easy to love him, easy to trust him. But he was nothing like her father. "Those stupid little men. They think I've come to ravish you. Is that what you think? Aye, I can see that it is. Would I do that to my brother's dear child, my own blood?"

Annie lifted her chin. "W-why have you come here?"

"Why, to give you one last chance, lamb. You need but say the word, and I'll have my carriage brought round. You'll be home by midday in your own chamber, sittin' in a hot bath before the fire with a warm cup of chocolate. I'll have cook make your favorite meal—partridge with sage stuffing, glazed pears, cakes—and tonight you'll sleep in your own bed."

The thought of her chamber with its treasures and comforts brought fresh tears to her eyes. Her books. The porcelain doll her father had given her for Christmas. The silver-handled brush that had belonged to her grandmother. The portrait of her parents newly wed. Her feather-soft bed. She could almost feel the hot water of the bath, smell the rose-scented soap, taste the partridge. She longed for home, longed to leave this place, longed for the nightmare to end.

Perhaps she *could* go with him. He would drop the charge against her, and she could act the part of the contrite and loving niece until another chance to escape came along. Aye, she could do that. There'd be no more rats, no brand, no ship carrying her across the sea.

A part of her longed to throw herself into his arms, to beg his forgiveness, to love him with all her heart, just as she once had. She longed to believe him, to forget her mother's words, to retreat into the life she knew.

Dinnae trust your uncle Bain! I know you love him, but you cannae trust him!

She forced herself to meet his gaze. "W-what promise can you give me that you willna harm me or seek out my bed?"

A look of revulsion crossed his face. "Who put such notions into your head, Annie? I have loved you, raised you as my own, treated you as a daughter. Have I ever harmed you?"

A lifetime of happy memories flashed through her mind. Uncle Bain bouncing her on his knee and telling her tales of ancient Scottish history. Uncle Bain buying her a blooded mare for her birthday. Uncle Bain teaching her to dance a quadrille.

Annie had taken a step toward him when another image

came into her mind: her mother lying dead, her cheeks stained with tears, deep purple bruises round her throat.

Annie looked into her uncle's face, a face she'd once held dear, and saw the animal that lurked beneath his skin. Then she heard herself laughing. "Have you ever harmed me? I am here, am I no'? Is it no' because of your lies that I am locked in wi' rats and filth and men who have more hands than wits and cannae keep a decent tongue in their mouths?"

"Och, Annie, forgive me! I was angry. After all I've done for you, I couldna bear it to know you'd left my home like a thief in secret. It willna happen again. If you wish to go to Glasgow, we shall go to Glasgow."

And Annie understood. She would never have another chance to escape him. He would guard her every step, watch her day and night. Where she went, he would go. She would be every bit as much a prisoner under his roof as she was here. It would only be a matter of time until she shared her mother's fate.

Horrified at the choice she must make, she could scarce speak. "Oh, uncle!"

A victorious grin spread across his face. "That's my Annie. You've learned your lesson, so let's be off home."

She shook her head, backed away from him. "Nay, I willna go wi' you."

For a moment he gaped at her as if astonished. Then his face grew cold. "You prefer to stay here and face what awaits you?"

Then she spoke the words she knew would seal her fate, words that terrified her, words she'd longed to hurl against him for three long weeks. "I-I saw you wi' my mother the night she died. Y-you killed her like you killed the others— for the sake of your own twisted pleasure!"

His nostrils flared, and a look of rage such as she'd never seen came over his face. He walked toward her slowly, menacingly. He reached out, took a lock of her hair, rubbed it between his fingers, his blue eyes cold. Then he laughed. "What would a prim little virgin know of pleasure?"

He stepped back from her and clapped his hands to bring Fergus and Wat back through the door. Then he strode to the fire and pulled out a branding iron Annie had not noticed before. "Bind her to the table. Bare her legs."

Panic surged through her, made her heart beat so hard she thought it might come apart. "Nay, please! Uncle, you cannae do this! I'm to be branded in public! In public!"

But her cries were drowned out by men's laughter.

Rough hands grabbed her, pulled her over to a wooden table. Despite her desperate struggles and screams, the men soon had her on her back, her skirts lifted to her hips, her legs held apart and bound fast, her drawers torn aside.

Her uncle approached the table, a queer look on his face. In his hand was the hot iron, the letter *T* at its end glowing orange.

"Nay, Uncle, please! For the love of your brother, dinnae—"

"You have no idea how much this pains me, Annie, but I cannae have you spreadin' lies." Then he stroked the sensitive flesh of her naked inner thigh. "Here, I think. It willna mar your beauty, but any man you try to love shall find it—and discard you."

"Nay, please!"

A hiss against her thigh.

Terrible, searing pain.

The sound of her own screams.

Chapter Two

March 20, 1758
Near Otter Creek
New York frontier

Instinct awoke him. Only men who wanted to wake up dead slept until dawn this deep in enemy territory. They were but one day's march south of Ticonderoga, too close to the French to take risks.

Iain MacKinnon opened his eyes, found himself staring into his brother Morgan's bewhiskered, sleeping face. On the other side of Morgan, Connor was still snoring.

Iain gave Morgan a jab. "Wake up."

Morgan's eyes opened, and he yawned.

"Och, hell, you stink!" Iain sat up.

"And you smell like a daisy." Morgan stretched, then shook Connor.

Iain ducked out of the lean-to they'd built last night, pulled his bearskin overcoat tightly around him and looked about. Several inches of new snow had fallen while they'd slept, and the air was cold. Grabbing his rifle, which stood primed, loaded and corked just inside the shelter, he headed off into the trees to take a piss.

Already his men were stirring. Some had packed their gear and now stomped about to warm themselves. After almost three years of fighting, rising early was their habit. Strong Scotsmen and stubborn Irish, they didn't need him to nag at them like some old fishwife.

'Twas their fourth day out on a routine scout up to Ticonderoga. Their mission was simple—determine how many troops the French were sheltering, observe the fort's supply lines and mark any changes made to the fort itself since their last scout. Clearly, the redcoat generals were planning to attack the fort come summer.

"MacKinnon."

"Dougie."

"*Dia dhuit*, Mack." *God be with you.*

"*Dia dhuit fhein*, Cam." *And with you.*

Iain relieved himself, listened to the sounds of camp coming quietly awake. He couldn't deny the pride he felt in his Rangers, in their woodcraft, their marksmanship, their ability to survive. There were no better fighters in the Colonies, no men better suited to the challenge of this war. 'Twas an honor to lead them, an honor to fight beside them. If it came to it, 'twould be an honor to die beside them.

Still, no amount of pride could vanquish the remorse Iain felt for the men he'd lost or the Catholic blood he'd spilled. The French had always been the Highlanders' truest allies, the English their most reviled enemies. To kill French Catholics for the German Protestant who ruled over Britain seemed an abomination.

This was not the life he had wanted. It was not the life he had chosen. It had been forced upon him by that whoreson of an English lord. In truth, Iain was little more than a bondsman, a servant whose job it was to fight at his master's command. No matter that they called him "Major" and "Ranger." Wentworth had forced him to fight for Britain at the point of a gun. His brothers, unwilling to let him face danger alone, had joined him as his officers. And so they had all been ensnared.

For nigh three years, Iain and his Rangers had done as Wentworth asked of them, harrying the French at every turn, confusing their plans, dogging them through bog and forest. They'd faced the enemy in battles that had left scores of good men dead and sent countless Frenchmen and Indians to hell. They'd done things to stay alive no civilized man could comprehend. Sometimes he wondered if they still deserved to be called men.

He'd always imagined that by the age of eight-and-twenty he'd be settled with a wife at his side and bairns at his knee. In his mind he'd seen fields of ripening corn, chickens that scattered at his sons' and daughters' feet, fattened cattle and hogs, an orchard of juicy apples, stacks of sweet hay drying in the sun. He'd pictured teaching his sons to hunt and track, watching his daughters grow into womanhood under his wife's gentle hand, perhaps living to see his children have children of their own.

He'd always imagined he'd marry Jeannie.

He'd certainly never imagined this.

Ahead in the darkness, a sentry called out the sign. "King George's codpiece."

A familiar voice returned the countersign. "Empty."

Iain tied the fall of his breeches, watched Captain Joseph approach. "*Aquai.*" *Hello, old friend.*

White teeth flashed in the darkness. "*Aquai.* Is this bunch of old women rested?"

Iain grinned. "Aye. And those weakling children you call warriors?"

"They're ready enough."

The two walked back into camp, planning their strategy for the day. Iain and his Rangers would take the lead and scout to the rendezvous point, while Captain Joseph and his men would take the rear and watch for any French force that tried to sweep down upon them from Ticonderoga.

Iain trusted Joseph as a brother and knew Joseph and his men would fight to the death beside him if necessary. He'd known Joseph since he was a lad of sixteen. Joseph and his father had approached the MacKinnon farm one autumn afternoon, bringing gifts of corn and dried venison that had helped Iain and his family endure that first hard winter in their new home. Though the sight of Indians on her doorstep had terrified Iain's mother, a fast friendship had been struck between his family and the neighboring Muhheconneok, or Mohican, people, many of whom were Christian—though not of the one true Church, as Iain's father had pointed out many times.

Iain and Joseph had become men together, had earned their warrior marks side by side. And although Iain knew it had pained his father to see his three sons become more like the Muhheconneok with each passing day, what they had learned from their Indian neighbors had kept them all alive and enabled the farm to thrive.

"We'll see you at the rendezvous tonight." Joseph put a hand on Iain's shoulder, grinned. "Let us know if you need to stop and rest. Perhaps my men can carry your gear for you."

"Take care that you don't get lost in the woods, friend. If you do—"

From afar came the sound of gunfire.

* * *

Annie watched the milk squirt into the tin bucket, grateful for the warmth of the cow's teats against her chilled fingers. After three months of daily practice, she was able to do the milking quickly without losing a single precious drop. Mistress Hawes would have no reason to take a strap to her now.

Not that her mistress needed a reason to strike her. No matter how hard Annie tried, she could not seem to please her. Mistress Hawes found fault with everything Annie said or did. She even claimed to know what Annie was thinking.

"Ye be thinkin' yer ower guid tae be servin' the likes o' us, do ye no', lassie?" she'd said last night when she'd found Annie rubbing her sore, chapped hands with a bit of rabbit fat she'd scraped out of the cookpot.

"Nay, mistress!" Annie had answered.

But her words hadn't come fast enough to stop her mistress from rapping her knuckles with a wooden spoon. Annie had been sorely tempted to grab the spoon from Mistress Hawes's hands and throw it in the hearth fire.

'Twas a boon that Mistress Hawes was now heavy with child. Annie was quicker and more agile than she and was learning to guess her temper. More than once Annie had been able to avoid being struck by hurrying to a safe distance. But Mistress Hawes would not be with child much longer. And Annie could do nothing to stay Master Hawes's hand if he took a notion to punish her for some imagined sin or misdeed. Though he rarely struck her, each blow from his hand rattled bone.

Though Uncle Bain struck his servants upon occasion, Annie had never done so, nor had her mother or father. A few of their servants had been with the family for generations—the fact of which they boasted with pride. Betsy, who'd been Annie's lady's maid since Annie was old enough to wear stays, had been more a friend and confidant than a hireling. But after a few months of servitude, Annie couldn't help wondering whether Betsy had felt the same friendship or whether she'd found serving Annie to be a hateful chore. Did she miss Annie as much as Annie missed her?

The weight of Annie's misfortune pressed in on her, compounded by grief, regret, desolation. Could she endure fourteen long years of this?

Last night, she'd dreamt she was safe in her father's hall in Rothesay. They'd all been there: her father and mother, Robert, William and Charles. They'd been preparing the main hall for Christmas, hanging mistletoe and holly, laughing and singing. She'd felt so warm and happy, as if the past seven months of her life had never happened.

"Stay wi' me," she'd told the others, suddenly afraid they might leave her.

Her father had reached out and taken her hand. "We're always wi' you, Annie."

Yet too soon she'd opened her eyes to find herself alone, lying on a straw pallet beneath a crude ceiling of hewn logs, nothing left of her dream but a bittersweet ache.

Tears stung her eyes, blurring udder, milk and bucket. Wary of being caught weeping—it would surely lead to another beating—Annie wiped the tears from her cheeks with the sleeve of her coarse woolen gown. It was not really her gown, of course. Mistress Hawes, seeing that Annie's gown and petticoats were much finer than her own, had demanded that Annie switch with her the day Master Hawes had purchased Annie's indenture. She'd taken Annie's coat, her gloves and her boots, as well, and forced Annie to wear her crude wooden brogues.

" 'Tis nae fittin' that ye be wearin' such a goun an' yer mistress be wearin' auld woolsey."

It didn't matter that Mistress Hawes was taller than Annie, nor that her shoulders were wider and her feet larger. Mistress Hawes had demanded that Annie remove her clothing that instant. Annie's only consolation was the knowledge that her boots pinched Mistress Hawes's toes.

'Twas strange to think that gown, borrowed from Betsy the night she'd tried to flee her uncle's home, should be seen as finery. It was by far the humblest, least lovely gown Annie had ever worn. After all, her goal had been to disguise herself until she'd made her way to Glasgow. With her mother's jewels sewn into the hems of her petticoats, she'd fled in the dark of night but made it only as far as the main road before her uncle had caught her.

Now she wore the brand of a thief, a mark of shame seared into her skin in a hidden place, a place it had pleased her uncle to maim. Transported far from home, she was the property of another until fourteen years should pass or death should claim her. 'Twas her punishment for defying her uncle, for knowing the vile truth about him.

Annie stood and set the pail aside, careful not to spill the milk. She untied the cow, let it wander back to its wee calf, then carried fresh hay and oats to the horses. When she'd first arrived, she hadn't known a thing about caring for cows or plucking down from a goose or cooking ashcakes. Yet such things were now her life.

It wasn't the hard work she minded, nor even the rough means of living. Nor was it the vastness of the wilderness, the war with the French, the fear of marauding Indians, or the haunting howls of wolves at night, though at first these things had frightened her. She would gladly have accepted all such hardships to evade her uncle.

It was the loss of freedom that grieved her—and the certain knowledge that she would never marry, never raise children of her own. By the time she was free again, she'd be thirty-two, far beyond marriageable age. No man would find her desirable then.

And then there was the brand. What man would want to take a marked woman—a supposed convicted thief—to be his wife and the mother of his children?

Any man you try to love shall find it—and discard you.

It would accomplish nothing to protest her innocence.

She knew from bitter experience that no one would believe her.

Fighting the despair she felt whenever she allowed her mind to wander down this path, Annie picked up the milk pail and had taken but three steps toward the barn door when she heard Mistress Hawes scream. Her first thought was that the time of her mistress's travail had come. Then she heard a sound that stopped her heart.

A dozen wild, shrieking cries.

Indians!

The air rushed from her lungs; her pulse was like thunder in her ears.

Gunshots. More screams—bloodcurdling and agonized.

And Annie knew. Her master and mistress were dying—or dead.

She was alone.

Panic turned her blood to ice. She stood in the middle of the barn as if frozen, unable to breathe, staring at the half-open barn door, expecting death to charge toward her at any moment. She'd heard the stories, tales of rape, torture and butchery that made quick death seem a blessing. But she didn't want to die.

It was the smell of smoke that roused her.

They were burning the cabin. Nay, not just the cabin. Tendrils of smoke curled through the cracks in the barn walls, followed by sharp tongues of flame.

The horses whinnied in alarm, reared. The cow and calf bawled.

An idea only half formed in her mind, Annie dropped the milk bucket, freed first the cow and its calf, then the horses. Driven by instinct, the animals pushed through the barn and out the door.

Annie knew it was her only chance. Praying the animals would distract the attackers, she ripped the greased parchment out of the back window, lifted herself over the sill and fell to the snowy ground below, her heart slamming in her breast.

From the other side of the barn by the cabin came cruel whoops of victory. Above her, gray smoke rolled into the early morning sky. Before her lay a snowy field—and beyond it the dark line of the forest.

She leapt to her feet and ran, only one thought on her mind—survival.

The wooden brogues, too large for her feet, made her stumble. She kicked them off, lifted the gown and dashed barefooted toward the safety of the trees, heedless of the snow's icy chill. She'd just reached the forest when an arrow whizzed past her cheek.

They'd seen her!

A scream stuck in her throat, she darted blindly among the trees, driven by raw terror, with no idea where she was going. Branches slashed at her skin, tore at her gown and her hair. Sharp stones and tree roots, hidden by the snow, cut at her bare feet, stubbed her toes, sought to trip her. The dark gloom of the forest closed in around her, made it hard to see.

Her lungs ached for want of breath. The muscles in her legs burned. Her bruised feet throbbed. But still she ran. She ran until it seemed her heart would burst, until her legs felt like lead, until her breath came in sobs.

And they followed.

She could hear them laughing behind her, shouting to one another in French and some strange heathen tongue. They were running her down, hunting her like a pack of dogs, and they were enjoying it. They were predators, and she nothing but prey.

Tears streamed down her cheeks, tears of fear, of desperation, of anger. She did not want to die like this—alone in a strange land, her body fodder for wild animals. Her mind had just latched onto the words of a prayer when the ground seemed to disappear beneath her.

Down she fell, over ice and jagged rock, until she found herself lying on her belly beside a frozen creek, her face in the snow. Stunned, she lay for a moment, confused, out of breath, almost unable to move.

And then she heard it. Someone breathing hard.

She lifted her face, looked up the steep embankment, saw an Indian man. His head was bare save for a feathered scalp lock, and his dark face was striped with red and black. Dressed in painted animal hides, he stared down at her, lips stretched in a cruel smile, then shouted back to his companions with words she did not understand.

Horror spread through her like venom, turning her stomach, leaving her mouth dry as kindling. She could see in his eyes that he planned to kill her. But not straightaway.

Shivering from cold, from fear, from pain, Annie forced herself onto her hands and knees and looked into his dark eyes. She heard herself speak, her words a hiss from between clenched teeth. "You dinnae have me yet!"

She stood, willing her unsteady legs to hold her. She would not die lying helplessly on the ground like a wounded animal.

On the embankment above, four more Indians and one French soldier appeared. The one who'd found her made his way down the steep slope, a hatchet in his hand.

Her strength all but spent, she reached down, picked up a rock, backed away from him, waiting for the right moment.

But his companions had seen. They shouted down what must have been a warning, for he looked at her closed hand and laughed.

The rock hit him squarely in the mouth, turning his mocking grin to blood.

For a moment he gaped at her as if in surprise, then he spat out a tooth, his eyes filling with rage. In the time it took Annie to take a single step backwards, he'd closed the distance between them, his hatchet raised.

She had just enough time to wonder if she'd find her family waiting for her in heaven before pain exploded against her skull.

Chapter Three

Iain watched from the cover of the forest, anger grinding in his gut, as the tall Abenaki moved in on his victim.

The young woman, her body bruised and bleeding from her tumble, forced herself onto her hands and knees, her tangled golden hair dragging in the snow. "You dinnae have me yet!"

Something twisted in Iain's chest at her soft Scottish burr, at her feminine courage, at her desperate desire to live. She didn't have a prayer.

Poor, brave lass.

Iain and his men had broken camp and moved quickly through the forest to discover the source of the gunfire, Captain Joseph and his men guarding their flank. They'd known a party of French and Abenaki was nearby, but they'd had no idea how close, until this lass had spilled out of the forest like some pagan tree spirit, blood-hungry warriors behind her.

Now she stood barefooted, shivering in the snow in her shapeless gray gown, hair the color of sunlight hanging in a tangle to her hips. She reached down and grabbed a rock.

"Beware of this one," one of the Abenaki shouted down to his friend with a grin. "She has a stone, and she wants to use it on your thick skull."

Iain found himself raising his rifle to his shoulder and cocking it.

Morgan pulled the rifle down. "Iain, are you daft? You ken our orders. It's best no' to watch. There's naugh' you can do for her. Come away."

As with any scouting mission, he and his men were supposed to move in secret through the forest and engage the enemy only when ambushed. They were to take no prisoners unless ordered to do so. Nor were they to join in any battles they might encounter along the way, not even to protect British frontier families. Stealth was their chief aim.

Iain had given his word to obey Wentworth, and he had kept it. But Iain had his rules, too. MacKinnon's Rangers took no scalps. They wore no uniforms. They killed no servants of the Church. Nor did they make war on women and children. From where Iain crouched among the trees, he could see no difference between allowing the Abenaki to kill the lass and killing her himself.

Iain jerked his rifle from his brother's grasp just in time to see her hurl the stone into the Abenaki's face—and felt savage delight when she struck her target. "To hell with Wentworth! I cannae sit idly by and let them rip her to pieces!"

"I grieve for the lass, too, but you risk too much! You'll endanger the men, and Wentworth will have you flogged!"

"Let him." Iain raised his rifle again, but he was too late.

The warrior struck her in the temple with the back of his tomahawk, and she fell like a broken doll to the snow.

Iain knew a moment of sharp regret before he realized she was not dead.

Even as the Abenaki warrior reached beneath his breechclout to free himself, she moaned, rolled onto her belly and struggled to crawl away.

The warrior planted his moccasin in the middle of her back, held her down, while his friends clambered down the rocky slope—vultures eager for a taste of her young body.

Bloodlust pounded through Iain's veins. They would all die. "Morgan, take the men and go. Make for the rendezvous point, but dinnae wait for me. If I am no' there by dawn, keep movin', aye? Complete the mission no matter what happens to me. I would not have Wentworth blame you."

Morgan's face showed he did not understand. "I ken why you're doin' this. She reminds you of Jeannie! But Jeannie's dead, Iain, and you cannae help her now!"

Iain ignored the jolt of pain triggered by Morgan's words. He'd been a hundred miles away when a war party had attacked Grant's farm and slaughtered every living thing—man, woman and beast. By the time he'd returned, Jeannie had been two weeks in her grave, her new husband beside her.

No, he couldn't help Jeannie. But he could help this poor lass, whoever she was.

Connor, breathless from running, squatted down beside them. "There's a force of about three hundred French and Abenaki a mile east of here. This must be their scoutin' party. They've burned out a farmstead about a mile to the north, slaughtered and scalped the man and his good wife—and she far gone with child. Captain Joseph and his men are keepin' an eye on the main company of the French to make certain they dinnae surprise us."

Then Connor paused. "What in God's name are you doin', Iain?"

Morgan answered, "He's gone daft."

Iain ignored them, aimed the rifle at the Abenaki's cold heart. "Morgan, get the men out of here. You're in command now."

"Let us at least fight beside you! There are six of them and one—!"

"I said go! That's an order, captain!"

"Blast it, Iain! This is mad!" Morgan swore, hesitated for a moment, then moved silently off to do as he'd been ordered.

It was Connor's turn to be defiant. "Have you lost your bleedin' mind? Wentworth will have your balls for breakfast, and you'll call the main body of the French down on our heads! Good men—men who've followed you since the beginning—will die!"

Connor spoke truly. The sounds of fighting and the disappearance of their scouting party would lead the French here, and they'd be able to track Iain and his men through many miles of forest, all the long way back to Fort Elizabeth. The mission itself would be at stake. Was one woman's life worth that much risk?

All Iain had to do was turn away. Follow orders. Let the

Frenchman and the Abenaki have her. He'd seen death before, watched his men die, even left the dying to fend for themselves when duty had demanded it. Why, then, could he not leave her?

The lass tried to roll over, kicked, and screamed when the warrior began to lift her skirts from behind.

"Curse me for a fool, but I cannae abandon her. This is of my choosin'. Leave me to it! I'll rendezvous wi' you if I can. Go! Now!" Iain waited until Connor had disappeared into the trees behind him, whispered his clan's motto.

"Audentes fortuna iuvat." Fortune assists the daring.

Then he squeezed the trigger.

The ball pierced the Abenaki's chest, and he fell lifeless beside the struggling woman.

Iain dropped his rifle, pulled his pistol free, aimed and fired, sending the Frenchman sprawling.

With no time to reload and the element of surprise lost, Iain rushed from the cover of the forest, a war cry on his lips, a tomahawk in one hand, a knife in the other.

Startled but ready to fight, the four remaining Abenaki held their ground, answered his cry with cries of their own.

Iain hurled his tomahawk and caught the nearest one in the chest. He heard something whistling through the air and ducked to the right to avoid a war club. Then he spun about and sank his knife deep into the belly of the man who'd tried to strike him.

He heard snow crunching behind him, pulled his knife free, whirled and threw it just as a blast from a rifle rang out. The warrior fell to the ground, Iain's knife in his shoulder and a bullet wound in his throat, proof Iain's brothers hadn't followed orders but were watching over him like a couple of bloody hens. He'd kick them squarely in the arse later. But for now he had other problems.

Left only with his claymore, Iain reached behind his head, drew it from his tumpline pack and adjusted its familiar weight in his hands.

The lone survivor, a young Abenaki barely old enough to go to war, stared at him and his long blade, terror on his painted face. "Mack-in-non?"

Iain answered in Abenaki. *"Oho, MacKinnon nia."* Aye, I am MacKinnon.

The young warrior's eyes grew wide, and he stared at Iain as if seeing an evil spirit come to life. For a moment, he looked as though he would turn to flee. Then he raised his chin, tightened his grip on his knife, and charged.

He died with Iain's blade buried deep in his chest.

Iain pulled his sword free, wiped it clean on the young Abenaki's leather shirt, then turned toward the woman.

Hurt and no doubt terrified, she had crawled beneath some nearby undergrowth. Like a wild thing, she had gone to ground. Blood flowed freely from the wound on her temple where she'd been struck. Her feet, too, were bleeding.

He strode over to her, sword still in hand, knelt beside the bushes, and reached for her. "Come, lass, it's over now."

But rather than taking the hand he offered, she scooted deeper into the underbrush. "N-nay! Nay!"

Iain felt a stab of annoyance. "I just finished savin' your life, woman! You've no cause to fear me."

Then he saw her eyes. Her pupils were wide, and she seemed to look through him. He'd seen that look in men's eyes before. She was hurt, in shock, and weak with cold.

He thrust his sword into the snow, yanked his tumpline pack over his head, and slipped out of his bearskin overcoat. Then he dropped to his knees, reached into the bushes, grabbed her around the waist and carefully pulled her to him. He needed to warm her or she would die.

"Nay!" she cried out, a desperate, anguished plea, and fought him with surprising strength, kicking, hitting, twisting in his arms.

But she was injured and a woman and much smaller than he. He forced her into his coat, then held her fast against him, whispering repeatedly into her ear, "You're safe now, lass. I willna hurt you."

He knew the exact moment when her mind heard him. Her body went limp. Her head sank against his chest, and she shivered. "I-I'm s-so c-cold!"

He pulled the bearskin overcoat tightly around her. "My coat will warm you. Rest here while I scout us a path. I willna go far."

But she had already fainted.

Annie was having the strangest dream. It seemed she was riding on the back of a great bear. He was not a fearsome bear, and he made no move to devour her. Instead he bore her along through endless reaches of forest, keeping her warm with his soft, thick fur.

Sometimes it seemed the bear became a man. With a bonnie face and fierce blue eyes, he whispered to her, gave her water to drink and held snow to her temple where her head ached so horribly. She wanted to ask this man his name, to ask him about the bear, to ask what had happened to her, but she couldn't seem to form the words.

And so, lost in her dreams, she drifted.

Iain adjusted the weight of the woman on his back, pulled the tumpline down to the broadest part of his chest.

She whimpered in her sleep.

He was certain the constant pressure of the rope across her back hurt her, but it needed to be tight to hold her in place. If the war party caught up with them, he would need to run for cover. For her to fall from his back at such a moment would surely mean death for both of them.

He slipped his hands beneath her thighs to support her legs, checked to make certain his overcoat still covered her, then stood and made his way down the snow-covered hillside. The day had warmed considerably since the morn, and the snow was soft and gave way beneath his snowshoes. He still wore them backwards and needed to be heedful of each step, lest he trip and plunge them both downhill.

While she had lain unconscious at the site of the attack, he'd taken what they needed from the men he'd killed—powder, shot and an extra set of knives and pistols for himself; a pair of leather leggings and fur-lined moccasins for her. Then he'd cleaned his sword, knife and tomahawk and primed and loaded the firearms. After he'd tied the leggings around her calves and slipped the warm moccasins onto her bleeding and nearly frozen feet, he'd scouted the area around the forest and quickly come up with a plan.

He'd stomped over the site of the battle in his snowshoes to confuse anyone who might try to guess numbers. Then he'd headed off at a run through the forest in the opposite direction from that which he planned to travel. When he reached the edge of a nearby cliff, he'd stopped on one foot, so as to imitate a man in midstride. He'd pulled himself into a tree, put his snowshoes on backwards and carefully lowered himself into his own tracks. He'd backtracked to her side in that fashion, hoping the Abenaki would follow his trail and conclude that he'd run off the cliff or, if they were superstitious, that he'd turned into a great bird and taken flight.

Then he'd used the tumpline to hold her on his back as he'd done many times with wounded men. Wrapped in his greatcoat and pressed against the warmth of his back, she'd soon quit shivering and had seemed to fall into a deep sleep. As much as he'd wanted to treat her injuries, chiefly the cut on her temple, their survival depended on keeping ahead of the Abenaki.

Fortunately she was a much lighter burden than any of his Rangers, so she didn't slow him down. She was a sight bonnier, and she smelled better, too. What was her name? How old was she? Her face was youthful and fair, but her body was soft with a woman's curves, and her courage spoke of strength beyond that of a mere child.

You dinnae have me yet!

She had stared her own death in the face and defied it. Many a grown man would have wept and begged.

Iain would do all he could to make certain her bravery was not in vain. He had resolved to travel through the night, bearing her all the way if necessary. Although the main body of the French would likely pursue his men, the Abenaki would be after blood. They would send a war party after him, hoping to catch him and take him back to their village so the women could assuage their grief over their lost sons, husbands, and fathers by torturing the man who'd killed them. Still, it was unlikely their thirst for vengeance would drive them to forgo meals and sleep. If Iain's ruse with his snowshoes had worked, he'd gained perhaps an hour on them. By walking through the night and the following day, he hoped to stretch that lead to several hours.

The hunter could afford to rest. The hunted could not.

Above his head, a raven took flight from the branches of a tall pine, its wings all but silent on the wind. He stopped, listened, heard nothing other than the chatter of birds.

But the Abenaki were out there. He could feel them.

The enemy was not Iain's only worry. 'Twas yet a three-day journey back to Fort Elizabeth, and he carried provisions for only one person, most of the company's provisions being packed away and tied onto sleighs. The cornmeal in his pouch was enough to fill his belly when he was pressed and had no time to hunt, but he was used to deprivation. He knew how to ignore hunger pangs, how to force mile after mile from his body without sustenance. It was certain she did not.

And then there were his Rangers. They knew the land around Lake George better than any group of men alive, white or Indian. They were hardy, trained to endure, trained to fight, trained to survive. But they were outnumbered two to one. If the French managed to outflank them and set up an ambuscade, they would suffer grievous losses. And their deaths would be on Iain's head. If anything were to happen to Morgan or Connor . . .

He'd had most of a day to consider his own actions. He'd

defied Wentworth's orders, endangered his brothers, his men and the mission, all for one woman. There would be hell to pay when he reached the fort—provided he did, indeed, reach the fort. And yet, he could not bring himself to regret what he'd done.

You dinnae have me yet!

She'd wanted so desperately to live, had fought ferociously to save herself. Had he left her to suffer rape and a torturous death, her screams would have haunted him forever. 'Twas enough to be haunted by the faces of the men he'd slain.

Oh, aye, he supposed her plight had put him in mind of Jeannie, and it was true that some part of Iain had never quit grieving for Jeannie or for the life he might have had. But well he knew this lass was not Jeannie.

It came down to this: The lass had needed him, and he would no longer have been able to call himself a man had he turned his back on her and let her be ravished and slaughtered, no matter what his orders.

He reached the base of the hill, crossed a frozen creek and then followed it east toward Lake George, ignoring the ache in his shoulders. He'd abandoned the idea of meeting his brothers at the rendezvous point. He didn't want to lead the Abenaki war party in their direction, nor did he care to risk an encounter with the main body of the French. For the sake of his men and for his own sake, he was on his own.

But he was not without a strategy. He and his men had hidden four whaleboats at the mouth of this creek last December when the lake had frozen over. Though there was little chance the boats had remained undiscovered and intact these many months, it was worth the lost time and effort to make certain. He'd preserve his strength, leave less of a trail for the Abenaki to follow and make better speed toward the fort if they were to travel by boat at night and rest ashore during the day. 'Twould be easier on the lass, as well.

To be sure, traveling in the dark on the lake brought its own risks.

Chapter Four

'Twas the pain that roused Annie. Like cold hellfire, something burned her feet. And then she felt it—a man lifting her skirts, his hands on her calves.

A spark of memory.

The Indian man with the hatchet. He was trying to . . .

Fear surged through her, brought her fully awake. She screamed, kicked blindly at him, felt her heel drive into his groin.

"Och, Jesus!" He groaned in pain.

She fought the dizziness that threatened to suck her down, tried to get to her feet.

But he was stronger, faster and very angry. In a blink, he'd thrown his body over hers, pinned her on her back and clasped his hand over her mouth to silence her. Then he pressed his forehead against hers and whispered, his voice tight with pain, "Kickin' a man in the stones is a strange way to thank him for savin' your life, lass!"

As he spoke, Annie became aware of three things. The first was his Highland burr. He was no Indian. The second was the color of his eyes. Blue they were, like a mountain loch, and full of fury. The third was his body. Raw and braw, the length of it pressed against her, his strength seeming to burn through her woolen gown. She found it strangely hard to breathe.

"Holy mother of—!" The man groaned again, breath hissing through clenched teeth. "I ken what it must have seemed like for you to wake and find me wi' my hands on you, but I was no' tryin' to dishonor you. In fact, I'm tryin' to keep you alive. And if you're as smart a lass as I think you are, you willna scream again. There's an Indian war party not far behind us bent on vengeance, and unless you want to lead them straight here, you'd best be silent, aye?"

She nodded, heart still pounding.

Slowly, he released her and sat back on his heels. "Now lie still and let me tend your wounds."

He was a strapping man, tall and almost twice her weight. His hair, thick and dark as midnight, hung unbound almost to his waist. He was dressed in leather breeches and a shirt of homespun, its sleeves rolled up to the elbow. Strange markings decorated his forearms and wrists, black lines and geometric shapes. A small wooden cross hung about his neck on a leather thong. And his face—bonnie it was, yet also manly. His square jaw was covered with a dark growth of whiskers. His nose was straight, apart from a small widening where it had apparently once been broken. A small scar above his left brow gave him a slightly sinister look. Only his lips, which were unusually full, and his eyelashes, which were oddly long for a man, softened his otherwise starkly male features.

Then something caught her eye. A claymore. It stood, blade thrust into the ground, beside his gear. Tied around its handle was a strip of a Highland tartan. 'Twas against the law to flaunt clan colors, and they marked him for what he was— the member of a traitorous clan, the son of Jacobites, a barbarian. Alarm shivered up her spine. "Y-you're a MacKinnon."

The words were out before she could stop them.

A hint of fire in his eyes, he glanced up at her. "If that displeases you, lass, I can leave you here for the next savior who comes along."

She didn't need him to tell her there would be no other. She tried to sweeten her tongue. "I-I'm grateful for your help."

She sat up slowly, her head throbbing. Her gaze was drawn to the strange markings on his arms. Aye, he was a barbarian—like the men who had killed her father and brothers.

She dared not trust him.

She had no choice but to trust him.

Her life depended upon him.

He reached into a small clay jar, scooped something onto his finger, then rubbed it onto a cut on her right ankle. It stung like fire.

She gasped at the pain, tried to slap his hand away. "What are you doin'?"

He caught her wrist, touched the salve to another cut. " 'Tis a salve that will keep your wounds from festerin'."

"Oooh, mercy! It burns! What is in it?"

He grinned. "I dinnae ken. 'Tis a remedy made by the old grannies of the Muhheconneok people. Try though I might to get those old women to yield their secrets, they tell me I am only a man and that I should fetch more meat and ask fewer questions."

Muhhec . . . The word he'd just spoken seemed impossible, like something that ought to have gotten stuck in his throat and yet had not. "You have friends among the Indians?"

"Aye, my brothers and I have lived as friends with the Muhheconneok from the time we came to this land. We learned much from them, lived with them and fight beside them. Now, shall I put this on you, or would you rather do it yourself?"

The brand! Had he seen it?

She quickly pushed her skirts down over her knees. "I-I'll do it."

He thrust the jar of salve into her hands, then stood. "Be sure to put it on every cut. We've a long journey ahead of us, aye? I cannae have you fallin' ill wi' fever."

She sniffed the salve, not sure she could trust this strange concoction or the man who'd given it to her, and she smelled something akin to turpentine. She was about to ask him what he meant by a long journey, when she caught sight of her own feet. Black and blue they were, swollen and covered with scratches and deep cuts. Her legs were also scratched and bruised, though not as badly. It looked as though she'd run through broken glass.

Without warning, the full weight of what had happened pressed in on her, sounds and images filling her mind. Agonized screams. Her flight through the forest. Falling down the embankment. The Indian man's mocking leer. The rock. The raised hatchet.

She touched a hand to her left temple, winced at the pain, felt something sticky. When she drew her fingers away, she saw blood. "Oh, mercy . . ."

The forest seemed to spin. Her stomach pitched and rolled. Her body shook.

She fought to draw air into her lungs, leapt to her aching feet, stumbled headlong toward the nearest tree.

Strong arms shot out of nowhere and lowered her to the ground. "Where in God's name do you think you're goin'?"

"Please! I'm goin' to be sick!" Her stomach lurched.

"Then be sick here, lassie. You are no' fit to be dashin' off like this."

She had no choice now and lost the meager contents of her stomach in the snow while he held back her hair. When it was over, she felt shaky and weak and utterly humiliated.

But she remembered. She remembered the gunfire and the Indian man who'd been about to rape her falling dead beside her. The sounds of fighting, of dying. A man with a sword.

He truly had saved her life.

She took a deep breath, tried to steady herself. "The others . . . back at the cabin? They're . . . d-dead?"

"Aye. My regrets for your sorrow, lass." His voice was deep, gentle.

She bore Master and Mistress Hawes no affection, but to think they'd come to such an end, and their innocent, un-born child with them, brought tears to her eyes—and the gnawing pain of guilt to her belly. "I was in the barn. I-I heard them screamin', and I . . . I ran. I should have tried to save them. I should have stood beside them."

"You'd have been killed, too. There is no shame in tryin' to live another day."

She shook her head, felt tears spill onto her cheeks. "I was afraid. I ran. *I left them.*"

"You've no cause to punish yourself. I dinnae ken when I've seen so brave a lass. When the time came, you fought wi' courage that would do a man proud." His words were soothing, a balm.

"D-did you find them? Did you bury them?"

"My men found them, but there was no time to bury them. I'm sorry."

In disbelief and fury, she glared at him. "We cannae leave them to be eaten by animals! 'Tis uncivilized, heartless!"

He gave a harsh laugh. "You're a long way from civilization."

Sick with remorse and furious, she tried to stand. "I must go back! 'Tis my duty!"

A muscle in his jaw clenched. He gripped her arms and gave her a little shake. "Your duty now is to survive! There's naugh' you can do for your kin except pray for their souls. Besides, their bodies lie a good day's march from here, and there's an Abenaki war party out for our blood."

Kin? He thought Master and Mistress Hawes were her kin? She almost laughed.

And then, slowly, it became clear to her.

Her master and mistress were dead, and her indenture papers had surely burned with the cabin. There was no one around who knew she was a convict, no one who knew she was bound by a fourteen-year indenture. Only the sheriff who'd registered Master Hawes's purchase of her, the captain who'd brought her over and the others who'd been transported with her would recognize her. But they were a handful of people on a vast continent and far away.

She was free.

The realization left her stunned.

Could it be that easy? Could she simply walk out of the forest and begin a new life? Could she take back at least part of the future that had been stolen from her? Could she escape the misery her uncle had planned for her?

"What's your name, lass?"

She'd been so lost in her thoughts that his question startled her. She opened her mouth to answer, caught herself. She could no longer be Lady Anne Burness Campbell or even Annie Campbell. "Annie Burns."

Shame assailed her. She'd never lied before, not like this. But was it really so grave a sin if it helped to unmake a worse lie, a grave injustice? Was she wrong to reclaim the freedom that had been taken from her if it meant being dishonest? She did not know.

"Do you have family nearby? A husband or brother perhaps?"

"Nay. They . . . were the last." She closed her eyes, sickened by her own words. She was lying to him and did not deserve his sympathy.

" 'S duilichinn orm gun do dh'fhuladh thu." *I regret that you should suffer.*

The soft, sweet sound of Gaelic made her throat tight and brought fresh tears to her eyes. She struggled to rein in her warring emotions, and for a moment they sat in silence.

"I'm Iain MacKinnon, Miss Burns. If you'll tend to your wounds, I'll get the boat ready. 'Tis almost sunset, and we've tarried overlong as it is." He glanced about as if looking for signs of trouble, then rose and strode through the trees.

"Where are you takin' me?" She wiped the tears from her face, tried to think of the days to come, not the past. She looked at her surroundings for the first time and saw they sat in the middle of a small clearing. Through the forest to her left she could see what looked like a lake, but she saw no boat.

"Fort Elizabeth. 'Tis a hard two or three days' journey from here, depending on what befalls us." He reached what appeared to be a mound and began to brush the snow aside as if digging for something. "We'll make better time on the water, and it will be easier on you. You willna soon want to walk on those feet, aye?"

Fighting the pricking of her conscience, she forced her mind to the task at hand. She dabbed a finger into the salve, found a particularly deep scratch on her left shin, and rubbed the salve onto it. She gasped and bit back a moan, shocked by the intense burn. The burning slowly faded and became a tingle. She took more salve, held her breath, dabbed another cut. Once she knew to expect the pain, it became easier to bear.

She tried to distract herself with conversation, asking questions from between gritted teeth. "How is it you happened to find me this mornin'? Do you have a farm nearby?"

Now he seemed to be tossing aside undergrowth and branches he'd uncovered, revealing the dark, wet earth beneath. "Let's just say you almost found me."

She got the feeling he was trying not to answer her. "Where are we?"

"On the eastern shore of Lake George south of Ticonderoga."

His words meant little to her. "How did we get here?"

"I walked wi' you on my back."

Stunned, she gaped at him. "The whole way?"

"You are no' so heavy, lass. I've carried grown men before and over much greater distances."

The extent of what he'd done amazed her. Not only had he fought uneven odds to save her life—she remembered counting five Indians and one Frenchman—but he'd borne her as a burden through miles of forest.

Her mind flashed on her dream. *The bear.*

She set the salve aside, smoothed her skirts over her legs and looked up at him. "Master MacKinnon, I . . . I'm sorry I kicked you."

He bent down, grabbed what looked like a bit of dirty rope, but did not bother to look her way. "You're forgiven. But dinnae do it again. I've no desire to live as a monk."

She felt her cheeks flush at his words. "What I'm tryin' to say is . . . What in heaven's name are you doin'?"

"Gettin' our boat ready." He pulled on the rope, which seemed to run into the earthen mound, and the mound shifted. It was no earthen mound, but a piece of earth-covered canvas. And beneath it were four small boats. Made of cedar, they were flipped upside down.

Annie watched as Master MacKinnon ran his hands over their hulls, as if inspecting every inch, then lifted one onto its side, carefully tipped it over onto its keel and began to inspect the inside. Three sets of oars were lashed to the benches. She was about to ask him if these were his boats when she saw the words MAJ. MACKINNON painted on the bow.

She looked up at him again, remembered his words.

My men found them.

Was he some kind of military commander? If so, it helped to explain how he'd been able to fight so many men and survive. But where was his uniform? And where were his men?

She didn't realize she'd spoken her questions aloud until he answered.

"I'm Major Iain MacKinnon, in command of MacKinnon's Rangers. We dinnae wear uniforms except as each man sees fit. As for my men"—his gaze shifted to the dark forest behind her—"they're out there somewhere, fightin' to get home."

She stared at him, felt she was seeing him for the first time. "You're a Ranger?"

"Aye." He didn't seem particularly proud of it.

She'd heard of the Rangers, of course. Master Hawes had spoken of them many times, insisting to his wife that if it were not for Robert Rogers and the many companies of Rangers, this war would already be lost. To hear him speak, one might think Rangers were invincible. She'd thought his words nothing but tall tales, but watching Major MacKinnon, knowing what he had done for her this day, she began to wonder if the stories might be true.

"I've heard it said 'tis a great honor to serve in one of the king's ranging companies."

His head jerked up, and he glared at her, his gaze hard and piercing. "I dinnae fight for Britain, and the Hanoverian is no' my king."

Shocked, she could only stare at him, his traitorous words

and the harsh tone of his voice like a slap across the face. Only the knowledge that her life depended upon him kept her tongue still. Aware he was watching her, she struggled to cover her response and plucked another question from the air. "W-why are you no wi' your men?"

In his eyes she saw the answer.

He wasn't with his men because of her.

Iain pushed the whaleboat over the mud and into the water. A thin layer of ice still rimmed the lake, but the boat was heavy and sturdy enough to break through it. With one last shove, it floated free.

He held fast the line, tied it off on a nearby tree, and then set to work wrapping two sets of oars in cloth and setting one in its gunwales. The other he laid in the bottom of the boat. When the boat was ready, he turned back to get his gear. 'Twas time they left this place. They'd already been here too long. If the Abenaki had tracked him, they could not be far off.

It was fortunate she was conscious. A few hours ago, he'd wondered if she'd ever wake again. Now she was clear-headed enough to ask questions—some of them vexing.

He hadn't missed the way her face had flushed with anger when he'd disowned Britain and its German king. She'd said her name was Burns. He tried to remember what he knew about minor Highland septs—her speech was that of the Highlands, and he knew she'd understood him when he'd spoken Gaelic to her. But it had been many long years since he'd studied the clans. Did he perhaps have a wee loyalist on his hands?

Iain tried to dwell on that mildly annoying likelihood and not her loveliness. He could not allow himself to be distracted by her silky golden hair. Or her heart-shaped face, with its high cheekbones. Or her apple green eyes with their long, smoky lashes. Or her creamy white skin, so pale and soft. Or the lush swell of her breasts. Or those sweet rosy lips. If he did, he'd end up with his hair hanging from an Abenaki lodge pole and his scalped head on a French pike.

Besides, there were many miles to go between this place and Fort Elizabeth. He couldn't endure having a hard cock the entire way.

He found her where he'd left her, sitting in the clearing wrapped in his bearskin overcoat. Swallowed up by the overlarge fur, she looked small and helpless. He could tell by the way her gaze searched the trees that the approach of night scared her. But to her credit she kept quiet.

She spotted him, relief at war with wariness on her face.

She still didn't trust him.

The realization annoyed him, even as he understood it. Hadn't he proved himself to her when he'd saved her life?

He thrust his irritation aside, knelt down beside her to pack his gear together. "Put on the leggings and the moccasins. You'll need them. Have you finished wi' the salve?"

She wrestled with one of the leggings, seemed to be trying to put it on without lifting her skirts—an impossible task. "Aye."

"Nay, you forgot one." Iain took his water skin and poured a bit of water onto his neckerchief. Then he pressed it to her temple.

She winced.

"Hold still." He carefully washed the congealed blood from her face and hairline. But the Abenaki's tomahawk had split her skin open, and it oozed blood still. She needed stitching. "I'm afraid it calls for sewin', lass."

"Wh-what?" Her eyes flew wide.

"I'll be quick. I've done it many times before." He quickly dug though his gear and prepared a needle and thread.

"Nay! You willna sew upon me!" She stared at the needle in his hands.

"Are you afraid?"

Her chin came up. "Nay. But you are no' a surgeon."

"By the time we reach the fort, the wound will have

closed so the surgeon cannae stitch it cleanly." He handed her his flask of rum. "Take a drink. It will strengthen you."

Glaring at him, she accepted the flask, pulled the cork, drank deeply, then coughed and gasped. "Mercy!"

Iain bit back a chuckle. "Rest your head in my lap, lass."

She glowered at him, but she did as he asked. "I am no' afraid."

Suddenly Iain felt all thumbs. He was used to stitching the ugsome, furry faces of ruddy, stinking men, not the tender white skin of lovely young women. He turned her head just so, then ducked the needle beneath her skin and pulled it through.

A hiss of breath escaped her, but she did not cry out.

He pulled the stitch tight, tied a knot, heard her gasp again. He found himself wanting once again to kill the bastard who'd struck her—more slowly this time. "I dinnae wish to hurt you, lass."

" 'Tis no' . . . so bad."

He worked as fast as he could, wishing it were some Ranger's hairy arse he were jabbing with his needle. But beyond the occasional gasp, she made no sound. " 'Tis done. But now I need to put some salve on it."

She nodded, a sheen of sweat on her forehead, her face pale.

Iain put the needle and thread away, retrieved the little jar, scooped salve onto his finger. "Take my other hand, lass."

She hesitated. Then her small, cold fingers mingled with his.

The contact burned him. He couldn't stop himself from caressing the silk of her hand with his thumb. "Are you ready?"

She nodded.

Quickly, he dabbed the salve over the cut, worked it into the skin.

She whimpered, squeezed his hand, bit her lip, then lay still, her eyes closed.

Iain fought the urge to caress her cheek. " 'Tis finished, Miss Burns."

"Th-thank you. But I dinnae . . . feel so good . . . just now."

Neither did Iain. There seemed to be no breath in his lungs. He helped her to sit, then stood. "I'm going to stow my gear in the boat. Be ready to go when I return."

Iain checked his weapons, packed his gear together, then carried it to the boat, trying to clear his mind of her. The sun had set, leaving just a hint of rose on the western horizon. The moon would be near new, making it hard for him to spot danger tonight. Fortunately the darkness would make it hard for danger to spot them, as well.

He turned and strode quickly back toward the little clearing. He needed to destroy the other three boats, and then they'd be off. He'd gone but a few feet when the raucous cries of ravens rang out from the trees five hundred yards north of the clearing. Then the forest fell silent.

The Abenaki.

He ran.

Chapter Five

Annie gingerly touched the stitches on her temple. They were small and evenly spaced. Almost dainty. It hadn't hurt too badly. Certainly it wasn't the worst pain she'd ever felt. Nothing could compare to the agony of red-hot iron burning itself deeply into tender flesh.

Barbarian though he might be, Master MacKinnon seemed to have gone out of his way not to cause her pain. He'd even held her hand. Such a big hand. It had completely enclosed hers, made hers seem tiny by comparison. Big and yet strangely gentle. He'd caressed her with the callused pad of his thumb. Of course, he'd only been trying to comfort her. Nothing more. But somehow she'd felt more aware of that simple touch than any before it.

He's a MacKinnon, Annie. Dinnae be forgettin' that.

He confused her, left her feeling unsettled. He was a big man, a rough man, a man who lived by the sword. But he'd saved her life, shown her kindness, even compassion. He fought as the leader of a Ranger company. Yet his words were those of a traitor. There was something about him that frightened her, and yet . . . something drew her to him, as well.

I dinnae fight for Britain, lass, and the Hanoverian is no' my king.

Men like him had turned against their Sovereign. Men like him had caused a war and brought bloodshed to Britain. Men like him had slain her father and her brothers and left them dead upon the cold ground.

Men like him. But not him.

He'd been but a child at the time, just as she had been.

Unsure what to think or feel, she slid her legs into the leather leggings. Did Indian women wear these? What strange garments they were. Then it dawned on her that, had she been wearing them this morning, she'd not have gotten scratched and cut on her legs.

She had just slipped the second moccasin on when the major rushed into the clearing, pistols drawn.

"Run! To the boat! Now!"

Heart thrashing in her breast, she leapt up, but the pain in her feet and her head was excruciating and she found herself on her hands and knees, dizzy and fighting to stay conscious.

She heard a gunshot and a loud blast like a cannon and screamed. She looked up to see fire and smoke rising from what moments ago had been a boat. Bits of wood rained down around her.

"Go, Annie!" The major threw something onto the hull of the last remaining boat, pointed his other pistol, fired at it.

Another blast and a rain of splintered wood.

Then from behind her came a familiar, terrible sound.
War cries.

She forced herself to her feet, took two agonizing steps, then felt herself being scooped off the ground. She wrapped her arms around the major's neck, hardly daring to breathe as he ran through the trees toward the lake.

Ahead through the gloom, she could see the boat bobbing gently in the water.

He ran into the water, dropped her in the little craft, then turned back to loose the line. "Row!"

She scrambled over the benches to the oars, grabbed them, dipped them into the water and pulled. But the boat went the wrong way and hit ground. "Oh, mercy!"

"Oh, for God's—!" He threw the line into the boat, thrust his shoulder into the bow and pushed it out into the lake, running in the water until it reached his hips. "Row! The other way!"

Almost sick with panic, Annie reversed what she'd done before and felt the boat pull away from the shoreline. She rowed with all her strength.

The major leapt in. "Get down! Behind me!"

She let go of the oars, dropped into the belly of the boat, felt it jerk as he dug at the water with powerful strokes. She had no idea how far out into the lake they'd come, when she heard a burst of gunfire, followed by the dull thud of lead against wood. She bit back a scream, prayed the boat would not sink.

She heard Iain curse, looked up to see blood blossom red against the sleeve of his shirt. But he kept rowing, the muscles of his back and shoulders straining as the boat moved through the water.

"Are you hurt, lass?" He glanced at her over his shoulder, still rowing hard.

"Nay." She looked up at his bleeding arm. "But you've been shot!"

" 'Tis nothing—only a nick. It can wait until morn. Stay down!"

For a moment there was no sound but the oars slicing through water.

More gunshots, but they sounded farther away now.

And then a single deep voice cried out from the shore, "Mack-in-non! *Saba,* Mack-in-non!"

Through the last of the light, Annie could just make out a handful of figures, Indians like those she'd seen this morning, watching them from the shore, flintlocks in hand.

Death's clammy fingers had reached for her twice today.

And twice she had evaded their grasp—but only because of the major.

"Tell me, Miss Burns. Have you never rowed a boat before?"

"Nay, major. I'm sor—"

"Dinnae call me that."

"Is it no' the proper form of address?"

"Call me MacKinnon or Mack or Iain or whatever you like, but no' 'major.' "

"Aye . . . Iain." It felt awkward to use his Christian name. "And you may call me Annie." Then she remembered he already had.

"Can you load and fire a pistol, Annie?"

"Nay." There was more. She thought he should know, given that they were on a lake. "And I cannae swim."

She heard him swear. "You've no' been out here long, have you, lass?"

She felt strangely ashamed, though she had no cause to. 'Twas not her fault she'd never learned to shoot guns or row boats or wrestle bears. The life she'd come from had not demanded such things. "Three months."

He gave a rather impolite snort. "Your lessons start tomorrow. Now get some sleep."

But she couldn't resist asking, "What did he shout to you, that Indian on the shore?"

For a moment he said nothing. "It was his way of saying he'd find me tomorrow."

A cold chill ran up her spine.

* * *

Iain kept up the rhythm of his rowing and watched the woman who slept, exhausted, at his feet. It was nearing dawn, and he would have to wake her soon. But not yet.

Though her face was tranquil in sleep, the horror she'd lived through showed clearly enough. One of her eyes had blackened, and her temple was swollen and badly bruised, as well. Stitches puckered her skin. She would have a scar—nothing could be done to stop it.

He felt the slow burn of rage in his stomach. 'Twas surely among the worst of sins to make war on women and children. Men were not men who sought to destroy the heart of innocence or to slay life at its beginning.

She shifted in her sleep, turning her face away from him, exposing the white column of her throat. The bearskin coat slipped open to reveal the soft swell of one breast.

It hit Iain with the force of a fist.

Raw, aching lust.

He'd been trying to ignore it ever since she awoke. But here in the dark with only himself and the night for company, there was no point in denying it. He wanted her. He wanted to stow the oars, scoop her up in his arms and kiss her to wakefulness. Then he would taste her creamy skin, feel the weight of her breasts in his hands and bury himself in her tight heat, bringing them both pleasure until neither one of them could bear more.

Was she yet untouched? He remembered her repeated attempts to cover her legs with her skirts and guessed she was. Though it didn't matter to him whether her maidenhead was intact or not, he liked the idea of being the man to initiate her into sex, of being the first man to suckle her, the first to penetrate her, the first to make her cry out in climax.

Even with her black eye and her bruises, she was one of the loveliest lasses he'd ever seen. But it was more than that. There was something different about her, something that set her apart. She was courageous. She was strong. She was intelligent—even if she couldn't row a blasted boat or swim or load a weapon.

She didn't know how to curse very well either—something that would surely be remedied if she spent any time in Ranger camp.

Oh, mercy!

Mercy certainly wasn't what the Abenaki'd had in mind.

It had been close—far too close. Iain ought to have followed his gut instinct and left without taking time to sew her wound. It could have waited until morning. But he'd allowed himself to get caught up in her, to be distracted by her, by those eyes. And the two of them had almost paid the price.

What the bloody hell was wrong with him? Since he'd first seen her, he'd defied his orders, deserted his men, endangered his mission and come close to allowing a war party he *knew* was behind him to move in for the kill.

Perhaps he'd simply gone without a woman for too long.

It had been two months since he and his brothers had visited Stockbridge, where young Muhheconneok women had welcomed them into their beds. There had been no shame in this mutual exchange of pleasure. Despite the tiresome preaching of that Puritan Jonathan Edwards, shame was not the Muhheconneok way when it came to such things. 'Twas a pleasant way to spend the cold winter nights, nothing more.

Iain's first taste of sex had come at the hands of Rebecca Aupauteunk, Joseph's elder sister. Iain had been seventeen. She'd been at least twenty-five and skilled beyond his boyish imaginings. He'd learned how to please a woman from her, just as he'd learned to track and fight from her brother. Since then, there'd always been a Muhheconneok woman keen to bed him, and, except for when he'd been wooing Jeannie, he'd been more than happy to oblige.

Had he not been bound to this war, he might have taken a black-eyed lass from Stockbridge to wife. But he had nothing to offer a woman—not a home, not even a name.

Ever since Wentworth had used the threat of the gallows to coerce him into fighting this bloody war, the MacKinnon name had lain under a shadow, and the farm had languished in neglect. Fields once ripe with corn now lay fallow and overrun by brush and saplings. The livestock had long ago been sold to the British to feed the army, and the larder was empty. The cabin and barn had been burned by a war party last summer and would need to be rebuilt. Although he and his brothers did what they could whenever Wentworth gave them leave, it was going to take them years to reclaim and rebuild what had once been a thriving farmstead.

It had been his father's dream to see his sons turn the farm into a new homeland for the MacKinnon clan. Instead, Iain had overseen its demise and the besmirching of the MacKinnon name.

Nothing to offer a woman.

He glanced down at Annie again, and he wondered what kind of life awaited her now. Her kin had been slain, her home destroyed. Where would she go? Who would provide for her? Who would protect her?

The only thing Iain knew for certain was that it could not be him.

And that's why you need to keep your breeches tied and your hands to yourself, you randy bastard.

He glanced over his shoulder at the eastern horizon, saw the faintest hint of dawn.

'Twas time.

He pulled in the oars, sat beside her, drew her into his arms.

Annie was so tired. Someone was trying to wake her. But her entire body ached, and she needed so desperately to sleep. She let herself sink deeper into darkness and dreams.

And it was a good dream. A man was kissing her, his lips full and hot against hers. He kissed her gently at first, brushing his lips over hers as if to tease her. Then he took her mouth with his, and pulled her against him.

Her lips tingled, and she found herself kissing him back, wanting more, reaching for him.

"Oh, Annie, I knew you would taste sweet."

It was the Highlander. Major MacKinnon. Iain. He was kissing her, and she wanted him to keep kissing her. 'Twas, after all, only a dream.

His mouth closed over hers again, and his tongue traced the line of her lips, parted them and thrust—

Annie's eyes flew open, and she might have screamed had her tongue not been entwined with his. She meant to push him away, to slap him soundly, but her arms were already wrapped around his neck, her fingers clutched in his hair.

'Twas he who ended the kiss.

He clamped a hand over her mouth, held a finger to his lips. Even in the darkness she could see the intensity of his gaze.

She heard the gentle lapping of water, felt a rocking beneath her and remembered.

The boat. The lake. The attack.

Her heart, already racing, lurched in her breast.

He leaned close, whispered in her ear. " 'Tis almost dawn. We must go ashore and hide the boat. We are goin' in blind, wi' no idea who might be encamped there. Be silent. Do exactly as I tell you, aye?"

She nodded.

"Sit up. Keep a sharp eye. Listen. But no matter what, dinnae make a sound." He released her, then, moving silently, he sat back on the bench and slipped the oars quietly into the water.

Her outrage at his boldness momentarily forgotten, Annie slowly sat, peered forward into the inky blackness, but saw nothing beyond the prow. How did he know where they were or which direction to row? The stars, perhaps? But stars could not help him see sharp rocks or know where it was safe to land. What if he rowed straight up to an Indian encampment or blundered into a pack of wolves?

She glanced back at him, saw a look of concentration on his face, his brow furrowed. He was listening. And so she listened, too.

At first all she could hear was the pounding of her own heart. But then, gradually, the night revealed itself.

The whisper of oars in water.

The hoot of an owl.

A creaking sound.

The lapping of water against . . . something. Was that the shore?

She looked up at Iain, realized he'd heard it, too. He pulled the oars in, let the boat glide, his gaze focused straight ahead.

And then out of the darkness—a cough.

Annie gasped. The cough sounded as if someone were standing just beyond the prow.

The boat jerked backwards, Iain already rowing away fast and hard.

One stroke. Two. Three.

"Qu'est-ce que c'est?" An angry whisper.

And she knew. With her gasp, she'd given them away.

Chapter Six

Her blood froze. Unable to move, unable to breathe, she sat and listened as another voice joined the first. She did not speak French, did not understand them, but she knew they'd heard her.

Gradually the whispers faded, and Annie let out a shaky breath.

And then a light pierced the darkness. It came from where they had been moments ago, and it revealed the figure of a man standing not on the shore, but on the deck of a large ship. He wore a French uniform and held up a lantern.

Iain whispered in her ear. "Easy, lass. He's a fool. He cannae see us wi' that light blindin' his eyes."

Annie turned and glanced at Iain's face, saw there a look

of determination, not the fear that assailed her. How could he remain so calm? Did nothing frighten him? They had almost collided with a French ship!

Mercy!

Trembling, she huddled deeper into his coat, the darkness pressing in on her with dangers she could not see. She'd known the frontier was perilous, but she'd no idea how brutal or dangerous until yesterday. How did the common people endure this constant fear, this constant peril? She supposed most faced each day as it came, did what they had to do to stay alive.

And so must she.

Lulled by the rocking of the boat and the renewed silence, her fear began to lessen, and she found herself remembering her dream. Only it hadn't been a dream. It had been real. Iain MacKinnon had taken her into his arms while she lay sleeping and had kissed her.

He had kissed her!

What was she to think of that? He had saved her life, but did he now expect to profit from it? Was he the sort of man to demand payment in kind for helping a woman in need? Her uncle had been that sort of man.

Well, she would not trade her virtue for safety. She would rather be left out here alone in the wild than made to serve a man's lust. And as soon as it was safe for her confront him, she'd tell him just what she thought of his actions. It had not been proper of him. It had not been right. It had not been honorable.

It had been . . . astonishing.

Annie had never been kissed before. She hadn't imagined it could be so . . . stirring. She found herself touching her own lips, remembering the way they'd seemed to burn and tingle when pressed against his. She remembered more: the rasp of his beard against her skin, the velvet glide of his tongue against hers, the way her very blood had seemed to quicken.

Her gaze was drawn to his face.

He was watching the faint glow on the eastern horizon.

And she understood. If the sun rose while they were still on the lake, the men on the ship would spot them.

His muscles aching with fatigue, Iain rowed harder. Dawn was but moments away, and then they would be visible. They were nearing the other shore now. He'd planned to cross the lake and camp on the western side. It would have put the lake between them and that Abenaki war party—not an insurmountable barrier, as the Abenaki probably had canoes somewhere, but enough to slow them down.

Of course, the Abenaki had no idea whether he'd crossed over or not—that was part of the reason for traveling by night. But if he didn't get this boat to shore before the first rays of light hit the lake, anyone who was watching would be able to see them. That included not only the war party, but also the French on that ship and anyone else with a view of the water.

Annie sat stiff-backed, her eyes searching the darkness, his overcoat bundled around her. Her surprised gasp had nearly given them away. 'Twould have earned any Ranger a stiff punishment. But she was not a Ranger, and he had no desire to punish her. He'd much rather go back to kissing her.

He'd tried to wake her with words and a gentle shake, but she'd been so deeply asleep she hadn't responded. And so he'd done what he'd been thinking of doing all night—he'd kissed her. He'd meant to take just a taste, but he'd found her too sweet to resist and had taken more. And although his kiss at first had not roused her, it had certainly *aroused* her.

Her lips had grown warm and pliant, and she'd begun to kiss him back, arching softly into him, meeting his mouth with hers. 'Twas clear kissing was new to her, but still he'd been taken aback by her responsiveness. If she was that passionate in her sleep, what would she be like in the heat of desire?

Mother of God, he couldn't afford to think about that, especially not now. He'd been a witless idiot to kiss her. He had at least one more day alone with her in the wild and would pay a cruel price if he woke in himself a hunger that could not be sated.

Ahead in the distance he heard the lapping of water against shoreline.

"Quiet, lass. No' a sound!"

She nodded, determination and fear playing across her face.

Already there was enough light that he could see the water's edge and the dark shapes of trees beyond it. Against that backdrop, something moved.

He drew in the oars, lifted his rifle, cocked it. Then he let out a breath of relief. Five does had come down to the water's edge to drink. There were no war parties encamped here.

Annie watched as he tied off the boat, then came back for her. He set her down at the base of a tall cedar and strode back to the boat. Then he reached over the bow and, as the first rays of light hit the lake, slowly dragged the little craft into the shadows.

By the time he'd concealed the boat, Annie was aching for breakfast. She hadn't eaten since the night before the attack. But if she'd expected him to unpack a cook pot and boil them some creamy porridge and perhaps a blessed cup of tea, she was mistaken. Rather than unpacking, he put on his snowshoes, picked up his gear and trudged over to her.

"Put this on." He dropped his tumpline pack with its heavy broadsword behind her.

Though she'd never worn a tumpline before, she'd seen Master Hawes do so. She took the thick, beaded band and drew it over her head. But it had been made for shoulders much broader than her own and fell to her waist.

"Like this." He bent down and lifted the band over one shoulder so that it stretched diagonally across her chest from shoulder to hip. Then he adjusted the heavy bundle at her back and took her hands. "Can you stand?"

Confused as to why she was carrying his heavy gear while he carried nothing, she accepted his hands, gritted her teeth and let him pull her to her feet. The pain was terrible, and she bit back a moan. "I'm sorry . . . but I fear I cannae walk!"

"I dinnae mean for you to walk. Stand but a blink." He turned his back to her, then knelt down. "Wrap your arms around my neck, lass."

He meant to bear her again.

She bent down, slipped her arms around him, felt him begin to stand.

Then all at once, he reached down and scooped his arms beneath her knees and lifted her until her thighs wrapped around his hips. 'Twas awkward and more than a wee bit embarrassing to be pressed up against him like this, her gown hitched almost up to her hips, her legs embracing him thus. Was this how he'd carried her before?

"Mercy!"

He chuckled, a deep sound that rumbled in his chest. "Hold on tight."

"Are we no' goin' to make camp?"

"Aye, but no' so near the water." With no further explanation, he turned away from the lake and began to hike uphill, leaving the boat behind.

He did not seem hindered by her weight on his back, but moved almost silently, picking a clean path up the hillside, his gaze focused ahead. His breathing was slow, his heartbeat strong and steady beneath her palms.

Pressed so close like this, she could feel the hard planes and valleys of his muscles bunching and shifting as he walked. It seemed so intimate to feel the workings of his body, to be pressed against the heat of his skin, to be wrapped around him. He smelled of pine, leather and sweat, a strangely pleasing combination. And though she labored not at all, she found her own heart beating faster.

Why had he kissed her? Would he try to do it again?

She must not let him. She'd lost everything to protect her virtue. Now it was all she had. She would not trade it to some barbarian Highlander for his protection.

But more than that, she could not chance his finding her

brand and turning her over to the sheriff. She had an opportunity for a new life now. 'Twas nothing like the life she'd lost, but at least she was free. She would not risk her freedom for anything.

The sun was well up by the time he stopped, lowered her to the ground and took his gear from her shoulders. They had come to a sheltered clearing near the top of a hill. On one side stood an outcropping of rocks, on the other a steep ravine. To the east below them stretched an immense forest. Downhill through the trees to the west was the lake, its surface glittering in the sunlight.

She watched, fascinated, as he quickly cut branches from nearby trees with his hatchet and used them to create a wee lean-to, in which he laid a pallet of pine boughs. Then he pulled out his water skin, drank deeply and handed the skin to her.

The water was icy cold and tasted strange.

He grinned. "Ginger root. It helps to ward off scurvy."

At the mention of scurvy—perhaps the water was to blame—her stomach growled so loudly that had an enemy been near, it would have given them away. Annie pressed a hand to her belly, felt her cheeks flush crimson.

He reached inside his pack and tossed a leather pouch into her lap. "Take as much as can fill your hand, chew it and swallow it with water. It will swell in your belly and make you feel less hungry. I'm going to have a look at that ship."

She opened the pouch, saw only parched cornmeal inside. Ravenous, she took a handful and put it in her mouth. 'Twas not unlike eating . . . sand. She ground the dry, crushed kernels between her teeth, then washed them down her throat. This was breakfast?

She tried not to think of eggs, bacon and bread with butter. Or bowls of thick porridge. Or pots of hot tea with milk and honey. Or clotted cream. Or fresh strawberries. Or any of the things she'd been accustomed to eat for breakfast in Scotland.

She tried—and failed.

When she finished, she found Iain lying on his belly a few feet away and looking through a spying glass to the lake beyond. For a moment he was silent, training the glass this way and that. Then he spoke. "Come, lass. I want you to see this."

She crawled on her hands and knees to where he lay. She'd never used a spying glass before, and he had to show her.

"No, the other way. That's it. Do you see them?"

Amazed, she found herself staring at the surface of the water far below as if it were just before her. She shifted the glass but a little and found herself staring at the opposite shore. If she moved it again, she could see where they'd come ashore far below. "See who?"

"Here, let me." Iain put his arm around her to hold the glass, pressed his beard-roughened cheek to hers, guided the glass for her.

And then she saw.

Not just one French ship, but four.

Annie nearly let the spying glass slip from her fingers; the danger they'd been in was suddenly horrifyingly clear to her. For a moment, she could say nothing. "What would they have done to us?"

He took the glass from her hands. "If they didna shoot us outright, they'd have taken us prisoner and interrogated us both. If their captain was an honorable man, he'd have protected you from his men until you could be traded back to the redcoats for a French prisoner. If not, I suspect they'd have passed you around like a flask of rum. After that, lass, I dinnae think it would much have mattered."

A wave of nausea rolled through her belly, and she wondered what kind of man this Highlander was that he could speak of such horrors so calmly. "What would they have done wi' you?"

"They'd have tried to break me, to pry secrets from my mind. Then they'd have given me to the Abenaki, who would have tortured me to death wi' great delight and merriment."

The images his words conjured sickened her, and it pained her to think she'd come close to repaying his kindness with such suffering and horror. "I'm sorry, Iain. In my foolishness, I almost cost you your life."

He held the glass to his eye once more. When he lowered it, his blue eyes were hard, his voice cold. "If you were a Ranger, you'd be punished. You could have cost us *both* our lives. But you are no' a Ranger, nor even a soldier, nor are you used to livin' on the frontier."

A frisson of fear shot through her. "Wh-what will you do?"

"I've a mind to take a strap to your backside, Annie Burns."

Annie was too infuriated to speak. Take a strap to her backside like Mistress Hawes? She was not a child! Nor was she his to do with as he saw fit! She hadn't yet found her tongue when he took her chin between his fingers.

There was no mistaking the threatening edge in his voice. "Hear me, lass. I risked more than you ken to save your life! If you wish to get out of this alive, *you will obey me!* You will do exactly as I say at all times! Rarely does the frontier give second chances!"

Leaning so close to her, Iain was strangely tempted to seal his rebuke with a kiss. The taste of her was yet on his tongue, and he could still feel the soft surrender of her lips beneath his. But their plight was grave, and he could not afford to think with his cock. He released her.

He could see she was furious with him—and more than a little afraid. Good. If he frightened her now, it might well save both their lives later.

She lifted her chin, fear in her eyes. " 'Twas no' my intent to disobey you. I was startled. I am truly sorry. You saved my life more than once, and I would rather you'd never found me than see you suffer on my account. I will obey you in all things—save one."

Her last words took him by surprise. He thought he'd made himself clear. "And what would that be?"

She took a breath as if to steady herself, then looked him straight in the eye. "I willna trade my virtue for survival. If that is the price for your aid and protection, then I ask you to leave me here."

He felt a surge of temper at this insult—perhaps because it struck too near the path his thoughts had been taking. He leaned in closer, his voice sounding harsh even to his own ears. "I've asked for your obedience, no' your maidenhead! And make no mistake—on your own, you'd be dead within the week!"

She blanched at his words, but her chin stayed high. "Why did you kiss me?"

Because I couldna stop myself. "I needed to wake you and was afraid you'd cry out in alarm. Havin' my mouth over yours was but a way to keep you quiet."

Now she looked angry. "You could have done that wi' your hand!"

There was no denying that, so he said the first thing that came to mind. "Why did you kiss me back?"

A rosy blush stole into her cheeks, and she looked away from him, seeming suddenly young and vulnerable, like a spring flower that had just been trodden upon.

You're a bastard, MacKinnon. The lass has been through hell.

He stopped himself from brushing a strand of golden hair from her cheek. "You've no cause to fear such dishonor at my hands, lass. I'll ask nothing of you beyond your obedience."

She met his gaze, her green eyes clouded by doubt. "And I will do my best no' to fail you again."

Iain stood, lifted her into his arms and carried her toward the pallet, trying not to hate himself.

Annie fought to sort out her jumbled emotions. She'd been reprimanded—and she'd deserved it. This was not the forest around Rothesay, after all, but the Colonial frontier. Her carelessness might have gotten them both killed. He was right to be angry with her.

But was she not also right to be angry with him? He'd threatened to take a strap to her as if she were his slave or a wayward child! 'Twas one thing to endure such abuse from Master and Mistress Hawes, for they had owned her and no matter how much she'd hated it, such had been their right by law. But she was not one of the major's Rangers. She was not subject to his discipline.

And then there was the kiss. She'd been asleep, and he had taken advantage of that to steal a kiss. She did not believe for a moment this was how Rangers woke one another as a rule. Then again, he had done nothing more.

Why did you kiss me back?

'Twas a question she could not answer, and it troubled her all the more.

He set her down on the pallet, which was surprisingly soft and springy, then began removing his gear. He pulled off his powder horn, slipped one knife from its sheath at his hip and another from somewhere behind his back. Then he reached for his sword and removed his pistols. But the pouch at his waist remained as it was. "I'd say we gained twelve hours on them overnight. I'll give us half of that to sleep. Then we start your lessons."

"Lessons?"

"Aye. It's time you learned to load a firearm. If you're to be wi' me in the wild, then you'd best learn to be useful. 'Tis for your own sake." He set his weapons down in one corner of the little shelter. Then, much to Annie's dismay, he lay down beside her. "Take off the coat."

Confused, but having just agreed to obey him, she did as he asked.

He drew it over himself as if it were a blanket and held one side up for her. "Come, Annie."

Did he expect her to lie near him? There was room in the small shelter for some space between them. "But—!"

"Och, for God's sake, lass!" He reached out, took her about the waist, and pulled her against him. Then he tucked the overcoat snugly beneath her chin. "Go to sleep!"

She felt surrounded by him. Her bottom pressed against his hard thighs, her back against his chest. His arm, with its corded muscles and strange markings, encircled her waist, and his breath ruffled her hair. His scent mingled with that of the freshly cut pine boughs. She had never been so close to a man before. She could not sleep like this!

But even as her mind protested, her eyelids grew heavy. And as she drifted to sleep, she realized Iain had somehow managed to bear her on his back all day yesterday and row a boat all through the night. He'd had no sleep at all.

Chapter Seven

Annie felt warm and snug. Floating between slumber and wakefulness, she drew closer to the warmth surrounding her. She felt the steady thrum of a heartbeat against her cheek, the rise and fall of someone breathing. She smelled freshly cut pine and leather and man.

Her eyes flew open. She froze.

She lay beneath his bearskin overcoat, her face pressed against his chest, her head resting on the hard bulge of his upper arm. His other arm encircled her, held her close. Their legs lay in a tangle, his hard thigh tucked intimately between hers, her leg draped over his, her skirts rucked up to her hips.

She lay still for a moment, her pulse skittering. She did not wish to wake him. Not only did he need his sleep, but she would die of mortification if he were to discover the two of them entwined like this. Besides, she needed to see to personal matters, and that would be so much easier to do if he were asleep.

She withdrew the arm she'd draped about his waist and tried to lift her head, only to discover that her hair was trapped beneath him. She grasped her locks with one hand, slowly pulled them free. Then she began to wriggle carefully backwards. But his thigh was tucked so tightly between hers that she could not move without her most private flesh rubbing against it.

She froze. Tried again. Stopped, and then tried again.

The friction alarmed her, sent a jolt of heat deep into her belly. Distressed, she gave up trying to not to wake him and scooted quickly away from him and out from under the bearskin overcoat.

Miraculously, he did not wake. His eyes were still closed, his lashes dark against his sun-browned skin, his breathing slow and steady. No doubt the rigors of the past two days had left him deeply weary.

Annie crawled out of the lean-to and found herself beneath a wide, blue sky. The sun had traveled far across the heavens, making it late afternoon. Birds sang in the branches of trees. The snow was melting. A breeze murmured through the tops of the trees, carrying the scent of pine and snow and damp earth. Although there was still a chill in the air, spring was almost come.

But the peacefulness of the moment was not to be trusted. She need only look at herself to know that. Her gown was torn and bloodied, her hair a tangled mass. Her feet were still horribly sore. And although she could not see her face, she could feel the deep gash Iain had stitched together and knew she was badly bruised.

She looked at the man who had saved her life. Oh, aye, he was bonnie, though he was in need of both a bath and a barber. She'd never seen a man with such long hair before. Civilized and refined, the men in her father's circle kept their hair short and wore fine, powdered wigs. They would never have let the sun bake their skin until it was brown like an Indian's, nor would they have worn animal hides or etched themselves with strange markings.

Nor would they have been able to fight off six attackers and carry you all day.

Even as her mind made the unwelcome comparison, the gentlemen she'd known, whose faces she'd once found handsome, seemed suddenly foppish, pampered and soft. Not like Iain MacKinnon. Even in his sleep, his vigor and manliness were plain to see.

Realizing she was staring, she forced herself slowly to her feet and, biting back a moan, willed herself to walk off into the trees, footstep by agonizing footstep.

Iain listened to her hesitant steps, to the catch of breath in her throat and knew she was in pain. He had to admire her fortitude. For a lass, she showed great spirit.

He'd been dozing for a while now, unwilling to wake her. He'd sensed the instant she was fully awake because she'd held her breath for a moment. He'd feigned sleep, amused by her silly, skittish attempts to disentangle her body from his—until all her wriggling and writhing had caused his blood to run hot and turned his cock to stone. When her sex had rubbed innocently against his thigh and the contact had startled her, as clearly it had, it had taken all his will not to reach down, grab her rounded bottom and show her just what such friction could do for a woman.

She had been heaven to hold, even in his sleep. She'd felt small in his arms, her body soft in all the right places. He'd had to remind himself more than once that he could neither bed her nor woo her. He had nothing to offer her until this accursed war was over and his farm was restored. He doubted a flower as fair as she would remain unplucked until then, and he knew better than to ask any woman to wait.

Hadn't he asked Jeannie to wait? Aye, he had—and she'd endured all of three months before marrying another man. A farmer come lately from Ulster, the man she'd chosen hadn't had the skill to keep himself and his wife alive. Now the two of them bided in earth together.

Annie would likely be some man's wife within the year. And what a lucky bastard her husband would be, for Annie was a lass of deep passion—responsive, spirited, hot blooded. Of that much Iain was certain.

He sat up, feeling more than a little surly. He needed release—that was all. He needed five minutes by himself or a night in Stockbridge, and then he'd be able to quit thinking about her. Unfortunately, he'd get neither any time soon.

He tossed off the bearskin overcoat, felt a nipping pain in his shoulder.

The gunshot wound. He'd been so exhausted, he'd forgotten all about it.

He pulled his shirt over his head, felt it pull where the cloth stuck fast to dried blood. The ball had cut a path across his skin, but not so deep that it was worrisome. He poured water onto his neckerchief and wiped the blood away.

He heard her limping footsteps, looked up to find her at the edge of the clearing leaning against a tree, her face ashen and lined with pain. Still in a foul temper, he dropped the cloth, stomped over to her and lifted her into his arms, his tone of voice more gruff than he intended. "All you need do is ask, Annie."

"You cannae bear me as a burden forever."

"You'll heal soon enough." He set her down on the pallet, sat next to her, and then reached for the salve. He spread the burning ointment on his shoulder, grateful it gave him something to think about other than the woman beside him.

When she didn't speak, he looked up to find her looking desperately ill at ease. He thought he knew the cause, and he couldn't resist baiting her. "Did you sleep well, lass?"

She looked at the sky, but her face flushed pink. "Aye."

"Did the heat of my body keep you warm?"

She looked at the forested valley below them and nodded. Pink became scarlet.

"I'm glad. Did my arm make a good pillow?"

Her gaze flew to his, horror in her eyes. Then her gaze fell to his chest. Her eyes grew wide, and she quickly looked away.

So she found the sight of him without a shirt troubling, did she? For some reason, Iain liked that, and his bad temper began to fade. Holding back a grin, he held up a strip of clean cloth. "Can you help me wi' this, lass? I cannae tie a dressing on my arm one-handed."

Annie tried to keep her mortification from showing on her face. He knew. *He knew!* He knew she'd lain with her head on his arm. Which meant he probably knew how their bodies had pressed together.

Trying not to look at him, she scooted closer to him, took the cloth from his hands, then moved to her knees. "We may be forced to bend the rules of decency for survival's sake, but you might at least feign that you're as unhappy wi' the circumstances as I am."

"But I am no' unhappy, Annie. Most nights I sleep wi' my brothers. You smell better than they do."

"Perhaps you all ought to try bathing. I've heard soap and water . . ." The angry wound on his shoulder stopped her retort. A lead ball had carved a groove in his flesh, not terribly deep but surely painful. It was her fault. Had she rowed in the right direction, he might not have been hit.

Suddenly she felt like a thoughtless, silly child. Lives had been lost, and she was fretting over sharing a pallet with him. She wrapped the cloth carefully around his arm. "Does it hurt?"

"Nay. 'Tis little more than a scratch."

Her fingers brushed his smooth, warm skin as she worked, each touch making her breath catch. His arm was so different from hers, hard and sculpted and so thick at the top she would not have been able to circle it with her two hands. The mysterious black designs that decorated his forearms traveled up his skin, ending in bands of strange shapes that wrapped around the widest part of his upper arms.

"I-I dinnae wish to cause you pain."

He chuckled. "No need to fret, lass."

But fret she did. She had never seen a man without his shirt before, and the sight was more than a little disturbing. Planes and ridges of muscle. Flat nipples the color of red wine. Skin almost as brown as the wooden cross that hung against his chest. A scattering of dark curls that tapered down the center of his belly and disappeared beneath the buckskin of his breeches. Rough and raw though he might be, he was also quite braw and . . . beautiful.

Strange warmth spread though her belly, left her feeling flustered. Barely able to think, she fastened the cloth in place with a small knot. Then, before she knew what she was about, she touched her fingertips to the band of markings on his left arm, traced them. A row of spirals. Lines that zigged and zagged. Triangles. And what looked like—

"Bear claws. I was adopted into the Muchquauh, the Bear Clan, of the Muhheconneok people when I reached manhood." Iain watched her face as her fingers moved slowly over his skin, her touch leaving a trail of fire.

She looked up at him, clearly surprised. "Adopted?"

"Aye, lass. The grannies got so tired of my bein' forever at their fires eatin' their food that they decided to make me part of the family so they could quit treatin' me like a guest and send me out to fish."

That made her smile.

"Did it hurt?" Her fingers continued their innocent exploration of his skin.

"Aye, it did, for a fact. But no' near as much as the tongue-lashing I got from my father when he saw." Iain wondered how words managed to find their way past his lips. He could scarce think, much less speak. "He feared the symbols would turn me into a heathen."

Her fingers reached the sensitive skin of his inner wrist, and she lifted her gaze once more to his. And he saw in her eyes that her curiosity was not entirely innocent. So, she felt it, too—this pull between them.

She jerked her hand away. "Forgi'e me. 'Twas no' right of me to touch you like that."

Feeling cheerful despite the unsatisfied heat in his blood, he caught her hand, raised it to his lips and watched her eyes darken. Oh, aye, she felt it, too. " 'Tis only natural for you to be curious, lass. Now let's have somethin' to eat."

* * *

Annie tried again. She placed the heavy rifle at half cock, then opened the pan by pushing the frizzen forward. Next she poured a bit of black powder into the pan and closed it.

Her stomach growled. She felt her cheeks flaming red and looked up to see Iain with a grin on his face. "How do you Rangers stay so big and strong eatin' naught but dried cornmeal?"

His grin grew wider. " 'Tis only when harried or on a forced march that we eat so little. I promise you'll dine on better fare at the fort, lass. Load your weapon."

She poured a bit of powder down the long muzzle, a task that required her to get up on her knees and reach high. Then she grabbed a ball, dropped it into the muzzle and drove it to the bottom with the very long rod. Last, she slipped the rod back into its stock—this time without hitting Iain.

"Well done." Iain took the rifle, put the cock to rest, and put a cork in its muzzle. "What would you do next?"

"Cock it, aim and fire." She was surprised to find his praise meant something to her. " 'Tis no' so hard as I thought."

He chuckled. "Nay, 'tis no' hard to load a weapon when you're sittin' in a patch of sunshine wi' the wee birdies singin' in the trees. 'Tis somethin' very different to load and reload under fire wi' the screams of the dyin' around you."

Annie saw the laughter fade from his eyes, felt a shiver chase up her spine. "I hadna thought of that. It must be terrible."

"It is war." He set the rifle aside, stretched out on his side, his weight propped up on one elbow. Fortunately, he'd donned his shirt again, or she'd not have been able to speak. " 'Tis a cool head, sharp aim and the skill to reload quickly that keep a man alive at such times."

He'd said it was only natural for her to be curious, and she was—about him. 'Twas the first time in many long months she'd really spoken with anyone. Master and Mistress Hawes had never had words to spare for her unless it was to scold her or to preach their dour notions of the Bible. It felt so good just to talk with someone.

"Have you seen many battles?"

His gaze searched the dark line of trees at the edge of the clearing. "A fair few."

"How fast can you reload?"

"Pray to God you never have cause to find out, lass." He reached for his water skin, squirted liquid into his mouth, handed it to her. "Talk of war is no' fittin' for a woman."

She drank, plugged the water skin, then handed it back to him. "And yet women die in war and their children wi' them. Why hide the truth of it from us?"

She thought of Mistress Hawes and her unborn child, felt another surge of remorse.

For a moment he said nothing; then he reached over and traced a line down her cheek with his finger. "When a man looks into a woman's eyes, lass, he doesna want to see the horrors he has kent written there. He wants to see joy and warmth and some measure of innocence. 'Tis the natural duty and desire of a man to protect his woman and children from the world's bitterness."

For some reason, his words brought tears to her eyes. She blinked them back and hoped he had not seen. "H-how long have you been here in America?"

"You've a gabbie tongue of a sudden." He measured her with his gaze. "We left Skye in 'forty-six."

"After Culloden." If she could have pulled the words back, she would have.

For a moment he said nothing, his gaze seeming to pierce her. "Aye, lass, after Culloden. And after that butcher Cumberland and his pawn Argyll had ridden the clans down and killed every man wi' a sword and many women and children besides."

"That is no' true! Argyll wouldna kill wom—!"

In one motion, he sat up, pressed his face close to hers, his eyes blue fire. "The armies of Cumberland and Argyll forced women to watch as their men and sons were slaughtered like cattle. Then they raped and slew them—grandmothers, wives, young lassies."

His words were lies. They had to be. The men of her clan would not kill innocent women and children. Trembling with anger, she fought to keep her voice steady, tried to remember that her life depended upon this man. "Did you see it wi' your own eyes, or are these the bitter tales told by those who lost the war and wished to malign the victors?"

"I was a stripling lad then, no' yet strong enough to wield a claymore, but that didna hinder them from tryin' to run me through as they did many of my friends and cousins. 'Twas my grandfather who stopped them, who traded his life for mine. But they didna have the decency to fight him and let him die with honor. Instead they locked him on a stinking prison ship and took away his lands. Aye, I saw it, lass, and I tell you Cumberland could teach the Indians a thing or two about brutality!"

My grandfather. Locked him on a prison ship. Took away his lands.

And Annie understood. Iain wasn't just a MacKinnon. He was the grandson and namesake of *The* MacKinnon—the chieftain of the MacKinnon clan.

No wonder he loathed King George. 'Twas in his blood.

Just as loyalty to Britain was in hers.

"Why do you fight for the king if you feel no love for him?"

"I was given a choice between dyin' at the end of a noose or fightin'."

She felt a hitch of fear in her belly. "S-so you are a convict."

He laughed. "A Catholic Scot need no' be guilty to be hanged. Nay, lass. My brothers and I were falsely accused of murderin' a man and given the choice of facin' trial already condemned or fightin' for Britain."

Murder.

The word sent chills up her spine and reminded her how little she knew about the man who had saved her. Was he capable of killing? Aye, for certain. But murder?

"I can see the doubt in your eyes, Annie, but you've no cause to fear me. The murder charge was but a plot to force us into service. We murdered no one."

Silence stretched sharp-edged and cumbersome between them.

Pulse still racing, she looked up, found him watching her through impenetrable eyes. She sought for a way to guide their talk back into safer waters. "D-do you miss it? Do you miss Scotland?"

He shrugged his broad shoulders. "Sometimes I miss the water, the smell of the sea, the rise of the Cuillin Mountains. I miss my clansmen. I miss our village ceilidhs wi' their songs and dancin', the heather in the hills. But I've been here for almost half my life. For me, the Highlands of Skye are but a memory. And you, lassie, where are you from?"

He asked the question as if it were no more than mere conversation, but she was not so easily fooled. She hesitated.

He swore under his breath. "Do you think me heartless, Annie? I dinnae care where your loyalties lie. I'd no' abandon a wee woman alone in the wilderness were she the daughter of Argyll himself."

She looked into his eyes, saw he meant what he said.

"I'm from Rothesay, near . . ." Suddenly she found it impossible to speak. In her mind, she saw the sun rising bright over Wemyss Bay, smelled the mingled scents of field and shore, and heard the cries of the gulls as they soared over the water toward the sea. But it was lost to her. Like her father, her brothers and her mother, Scotland was gone.

Hot tears sprang to her eyes, spilled onto her cheeks, her heart aching with such grief that she was certain she could not bear it. She fought it back, subdued it.

He sat up, took off his neckerchief, dabbed gently at her tears. "Why did you come here?"

"My mother . . . died, and there was no one left. I had nothing, no home, no family."

"Except here."

Here? *Master and Mistress Hawes*. Guilt gnawed at her, and she could not look him in the eyes. "Aye."

"How long have you been in the Colonies?"

"Four months." *Four long, lonely months.*

" 'Tis no wonder you miss Scotland. You've no' had the kindest welcome, and now you've lost the last of your kin."

"Aye." She felt ill, and tears burned her eyes afresh. She did not deserve his kindness or his compassion. She had run, leaving Master and Mistress Hawes to face death alone. And she had once again lied to him.

"I see on your face that you still blame yourself, lass." He leaned in close, ran his thumb down her cheek. "There's nothing you could have done for them."

She wanted to tell him. She wanted to tell him the truth, the whole sordid tale. She wanted to feel clean again. If it were true that he, too, had been falsely accused of a crime, perhaps he would believe her. Yet, if he didn't believe her and turned her over to the sheriff, she'd find herself sold again, perhaps to an even crueler master or mistress. She could not take that risk. "Please, I cannae . . ."

He nodded. "Lie back and rest. I'll watch over you. We leave at sunset."

Annie lay down on the pallet of pine boughs, let him draw the bearskin overcoat up to her chin. But it was long ere she drifted to sleep.

Chapter Eight

Iain cleaned his rifle and pistols and watched the lass sleep, his mind full of her.

He had no doubt now that her kin had been loyalists during the '45. She'd said she was from Rothesay. If his memory did not mislead him, Rothesay was in Campbell country, on the Isle of Bute. 'Twas likely the men of her family had fought beside their laird at Culloden, spilling Scottish blood on Scottish soil.

Her ignorance of the savagery that had followed Culloden had infuriated him, and yet he could not fault her for it. She'd have been no more than a bairn at the time, a wee lassie bouncing on her father's knee. 'Twas unlikely the men of Rothesay had tarnished their triumphant return by telling their wives and daughters how they'd raped and murdered their way through the Highlands.

She stirred in her sleep, her brow troubled as if with a bad dream.

He reached out and caressed her cheek. His touch seemed to calm her, and a strange feeling of protectiveness swelled in his chest.

The frontier was hard on women—that much was certain. Hunger, sickness and bloodshed each took their toll. Any woman who survived these might yet perish in childbed or die from the grief of burying too many bairns. 'Twas an unforgiving land that gave beauty and gentleness no quarter.

Yet it seemed to him Annie was more out of place in the wilderness than most women. Though she was courageous and strong and had fought hard to save her own life, he could not deny there was something oddish about her.

When he'd rubbed the salve onto her feet, he'd found them strangely smooth and uncallused. It seemed she'd never gone barefoot a day in her life, as impossible as such a thing might be.

And her hands. Though chapped, they bore only fresh calluses, as if she rarely did a lick of work. He'd held one, stroked it, felt the silk of her touch upon his skin.

Nor was the tone of her speech what he might expect from a poor Highland lassie. 'Twas more primsie, like that of a woman who'd had the benefit of some teaching.

Yet her ill-fitting woolen gown, poorly made and threadbare, was the sort he'd expect the poorest crofter's wife to wear.

Aye, there was something oddish about her.

But that was not for him to fathom. Once he got her safely to the fort, she'd no longer be his concern. He'd face whatever penance was due him for defying orders, then put her—and the mounting need he felt for her—behind him. Wentworth would likely send her on to Albany with the next dispatch. Then she'd have to make her way as best she could.

Iain wrapped the cleaning cloth around the ramrod of the last pistol, thrust it down the barrel, trying not to think of Annie alone in Albany. 'Twas a rough town full of hard men who would think nothing of deceiving her, using her and leaving her in the streets. But there was little he could do to ease her path once they left the forest. He was not a free man.

He glanced at the western horizon, guessed he had an hour of daylight yet. He needed to watch the lake, see if he could spot any war parties or ships on the water. He also needed to scout the site around their camp to make certain no enemies had been prowling about or lay in ambush. Then, with the last rays of sunlight to guide them, they'd set out once more.

If all went well, tonight would be their last night on the lake. Their journey would take them to the lake's southern shore. From there, they'd be forced to continue on foot after some hours' rest. He would not chance the road to Fort Elizabeth in the darkness. 'Twould be the most dangerous leg of their journey.

He began to pack his gear, reluctant to wake her just yet.

"Bind her to the table. Bare her legs."

"Nay, Uncle, please! For the love of your brother, dinnae—"

The glowing iron.

His hateful caress against her inner thigh.

"Here, I think . . . Any man you try to love shall find it—and discard you."

"Nay, please!"

Horrible burning pain.

Her own screams.

Annie struck at the man who held her fast, a sob trapped in her throat. "Nay!"

"Shhh, lass. 'Tis but a dream."

"Nay, please!" Disoriented, the claws of her nightmare still dragging at her, she opened her eyes and found herself in the Highlander's arms. "I-Iain?"

"Aye, lass. You're safe." He held her close, stroked her hair, his voice a soothing rumble in his chest. "I'll no' let any man harm you—no' while there is still breath in my body."

Her mouth slick with the taste of horror, her body trembling, she clung to him. He felt strong and warm, something steady in a world gone mad. Slowly her trembling subsided, the lingering fog of her nightmare dissolving in the refuge of his strong embrace.

"I . . . I'm sorry." Feeling suddenly awkward, she lifted her head from his chest and looked away from him. The last time he'd held her like that, he'd kissed her.

His hands cupped her cheeks and he forced her to meet his gaze. There was no reproach in his eyes, only concern. His thumbs wiped away tears she'd not known she'd shed. "You've no cause to be sorry. There is no shame in a bad dream."

The way he said it gave her pause, and she found herself wondering. "Do you have them—nightmares?"

His eyes filled with shadows, and he looked off into the forest. "Aye, lass. Aye."

Then he stood, and she saw he wore his gear, everything but his tumpline pack. "Are we goin'?"

"No' quite yet. I'll scout around camp and down by the boat first. Then I'll come back for you." He pulled a pistol from the waist of his breeches, turned the barrel away from her and then held it out to her. "If you should hear gunfire, hide up among those rocks. If I survive, I'll be back for you. If no' . . ."

Icy fingers clutched at her stomach as she took the pistol

from him and felt its deadly weight in her hand. It hadn't oc-
curred to her that he might be killed and leave her alone in
this wilderness. Suddenly her uncle's malice seemed far-
away and trifling. "Can I no' come wi' you? If they kill you, I'll
perish anyway, from hunger if naught else."

He seemed to consider this, then shook his head. "Nay,
lass. Stay here. Bide a wee. I'll be back afore you can miss
me."

Then he strode silently down the hill and left her alone.

Time seemed to creep by as she waited, the sun dipping
lower on the horizon. She huddled deeper into the bearskin
coat, drew back into the lean-to, the silence of the forest and
the twilight seeming to press in upon her.

He would come back. He *must* come back.

She looked at the pistol in her hand, felt a shiver creep up
her spine that had nothing to do with the chill in the air.
How far away her old life of comfort seemed, how strange
and terrifying this new one. If the time came, would she be
able to pull the trigger and kill a man?

She thought of the Indian who'd struck her, the one she'd
hit with the rock.

Aye, she could kill.

She tried to shift the direction of her thoughts, found herself running through the steps of loading a pistol, practicing
them in her mind.

*'Tis no' hard to load a weapon when you're sittin' in a
patch of sunshine wi' the wee birdies singin' in the trees. 'Tis
somethin' very different to load and reload under fire wi' the
screams of the dyin' around you.*

Nor did it seem so easy in the twilight, surrounded by the
furtive noises of the forest.

And then it struck her. She ought to prepare herself. She
ought to have powder and shot ready in case she needed to
reload. Surely he'd left both for her in his pack.

She reached for it, searched through it for a spare powder
horn and shot.

A small tin bucket. A clasp knife. A fork. A small horn of

salt. A tin cup. A flask of rum. A tin plate. The jar of salve. Cloth for bandages. A sliver of lye soap in a cloth. Candles. Needle and thread. A bit of ginger wrapped in parchment. But no powder and no shot.

She felt a surge of anger. Why teach her to reload if he did not give her the means to do so? She would ask him just that when he returned. He *would* return.

Her stomach rumbled. She was hungry and thirsty. Though she could not in good conscience eat another handful of cornmeal, as he was rationing it for both of them, she could at least slake her thirst. She looked for the water-skin, and when she didn't find it realized he must have taken it with him. Hesitantly, she reached for the flask of rum, remembering how it had burned her throat. She un-corked it, sniffed it, and then brought it to her lips.

"Annie, no!"

She gasped, nearly dropped the flask, saw Iain rush to-ward her from out of the trees.

"Christ, woman, what in God's bloody name do you think you're doin'?" He dropped to his knees before her, jerked the flask from her hands, corked it. "Did you drink from this? Annie, tell me!"

She shook her head. "N-nay!"

Iain felt a warm rush of relief—and a surge of anger. He fought the desire to throttle her. "What in the name of the Almighty are you doin' searchin' through my gear?"

"I-I was looking for powder and shot, and I got thirsty!"

"Do you ken what this is?"

She lifted her chin. "Rum."

"Aye, it's rum. Poisoned rum! The good rum's in the flask I keep on me. If you'd taken so much as a swallow of this, you'd be dyin', and there'd be naugh' I could do to stop it!"

She blanched, and her eyes grew wide. "P-poisoned rum? Why—?"

"If I'm captured, whoever takes me prisoner will surely ransack my gear just like you did." He saw an embarrassed flush creep into her cheeks. "If I'm lucky, they'll pass the flask around and die before they can kill me or get me back to their camp."

"Mercy!"

When he'd seen the flask against her lips, he'd felt a moment of sheer terror. To think what would have happened if he'd have come but a moment later . . .

He tossed the waterskin into her lap. "Drink, blast it! Then we go."

"You might have told me." She grabbed the skin, pulled out the stopper, drank.

Still furious, he rammed the flask back into his pack. "I didna think you'd go creepin' through my pack like a thief!"

She thrust the waterskin at him, and her face turned scarlet. "I am no thief!"

The pricking of his conscience told him she was right. He ought to have warned her. But he wasn't used to being in the wild with anyone who wasn't a Ranger. In truth, he'd all but forgotten the bloody flask was there. It was on the tip of his tongue to tell her this, but he was still angry—angry with her for giving him such a shock, angry with himself for failing to warn her.

"You take more lookin' after than a bairn."

A look of hurt crossed her face. Then she did something he did not expect. She crawled out of the lean-to, stood and, with halting footsteps, walked off down the hill.

Iain walked beside Annie, one eye on the forest, the other on her. He hadn't thought she'd make it this far. He knew from her ashen face and her uneven breathing that each step hurt terribly. He tried to dismiss the voice in his head that told him this was his fault. 'Twas her silly female pride that demanded she walk on her battered feet, not him.

The ground grew steeper, the snow slick and icy from thawing and freezing again. He was about to tell her to watch her step, when she slipped.

He caught her about the waist. "Careful, lass. 'Tis steep and slippery from here. Perhaps you should take my hand."

For a moment she sagged against him. Then she pulled away and, ignoring him, used trunks of trees and saplings to steady herself as she continued down the hill.

"Bloody stubborn wench!" he swore under his breath.

Annie heard him swear, knew he was angry with her. But he could go jump off the nearest cliff. He'd called her a thief—or so near as made no difference! But she had taken nothing. If he'd left her with powder and shot, she'd not have gone near his pack. And how was she to know the rum was poisoned? He ought to have told her! He ought to have apologized instead of raising his voice at her and scolding her like a child.

You take more lookin' after than a bairn.

She was not a child! If she needed his help, it was only because she was in the middle of an unfamiliar land and injured. If she were at home in Rothesay, she'd not need him for anything.

Because you'd have servants to do it all for you, Annie.

She reached for the next tree branch, tried to ignore the irksome voice in her mind and the horrible pain in her feet. She couldn't help that she was of noble birth and knew nothing of this way of life. She was here only because men like Iain had killed her father and brothers, destroying her life and leaving her and her mother subject to her uncle's cruelty.

Men like Iain. But no' Iain.

He had saved her life. He'd kept her safe, shown her kindness, given her comfort. And if he'd also cursed her king and accused her kin of atrocities?

Then they raped and slew them—grandmothers, wives, young lassies.

Annie leaned against a tree, clenched her teeth to keep from moaning. She looked out, feeling almost dizzy, and saw the water still a good distance below them.

"Lass, for God's sake! Why do you torture yourself when I am willin' to bear you?"

Clinging to her anger, she took another step.

Then a hand clamped hard over her mouth, and strong arms dragged her to the ground. His body was on top of hers, his hips pressing into the small of her back, his chest against her shoulders.

He whispered against her temple, "No' a sound."

Dread coursing through her, she nodded.

He took his hand from her mouth, and she heard the quiet cock of his rifle.

Then she saw.

Out on the lake a stone's throw from the shore, four small boats glided silently through the water, each carrying five or six painted Indian warriors. They looked much like the one who had struck her, and each carried a flintlock of some kind. They watched the shore as if searching for something.

The boat!

It lay upside down in the underbrush not far from the shore. If they found it . . .

The pounding of her heart was so loud, she was surprised they could not hear it. She squeezed her eyes shut, pressed her face to the snow, tried not to breathe.

Soft lips touched her temple, whispered almost silently. "Easy, Annie."

She opened her eyes, saw that the boats were almost even with them now. The warriors gazed intently at the shore, their heads turning this way and that. Then one lifted his eyes to the hillside. He seemed to look right at her, his gaze sliding over her like a shadow.

She felt Iain's body tense.

One of them spoke, and for a moment she was certain they'd seen the boat. But they made no move to come ashore, and with agonizing slowness they glided up the lake and out of sight.

She let out the breath she'd been holding, felt Iain's weight shift from her.

Without warning, strong arms turned her to face him. Blue eyes bored into her. "I'm bearin' you the rest of the way to the boat, and I'll no' hear a word against it."

* * *

'Twas an hour before dawn when they reached the southern shore of Lake George. Though weary from hours of rowing and six days in the wild, Iain could not yet rest. He did his best to conceal the boat, then lifted Annie onto his back and carried her a short distance inland to await the dawn. He found a sheltered spot on the leeward side of a large boulder, then set her down and left her with his pistol while he scouted the vicinity. When he was certain no enemies were encamped nearby, he returned to find her sitting wide-eyed in the darkness, pistol cocked and in hand.

She jumped. "Did you hear that?"

Around them were only the sounds of the sleeping forest—the wind in the trees, the distant howl of wolves, the lap of water against sand and stone.

"Hear what?" His words sounded bad-tempered, even to his own ears.

"It sounded like a scream."

"Och, that. 'Twas a catamount." He'd been short with her tonight, though he couldn't say why. He'd gone back and forth all night between wanting to shout at her and wanting to drag her against him and kiss her witless. Like a bow strung too tightly, he felt ready to snap.

Then he saw the fear on her face. He knelt down before her, brushed a strand of hair from her face, forced the anger from his voice. "Dinnae let it trouble you, lass. 'Tis far distant from this place and means us no harm. Come. It's time for sleep."

Chapter Nine

It seemed to Annie she'd just fallen asleep when Iain nudged her awake again. Her body achy, her mind dulled by fatigue and hunger, she sat up and saw that it was not long past dawn. Had she ever been this tired? What she wouldn't give for just one more hour of sleep! Or a hot bath. Or porridge and a cup of tea.

How could Iain look so alert and vigorous when she felt listless and painfully weary? They were alive only because of his labors. 'Twas he who'd borne her through the forest on his back, he who'd rowed the boat through two dark nights, he who'd kept watch while she'd slept. 'Twas he who should be worn with fatigue.

Humbled by her own weakness, she sat up straighter, tried to force the cobwebs from her mind. The least she could do was to press herself as hard as he pressed himself and to endure without complaint. She was no squeamish, spiritless lass, and although she might not have been born to this rugged life, she had her wits and at least some courage.

If she'd understood him, they had most of a day's journey before them over land to Fort Elizabeth. She could endure one more day.

Iain handed her the leather pouch of cornmeal. "Bide here a wee."

Then he headed off toward the lake with the tin bucket in his hand.

She took a handful of cornmeal, chewed it, and washed it into her empty stomach with a mouthful of cold water from his waterskin.

It had been a long night. Wary after their encounter with the French ships the night before and determined not to fail Iain again, she'd made certain to stay awake and had watched the darkness glide past, reluctant even to breathe.

Yet he'd seemed angry, his voice gruff the few times he'd spoken, his face hard. Perhaps he was in a temper over the things she'd said earlier about Culloden and the war. Or maybe he was still vexed with her for giving them away to the French on the ship. Or perhaps it was the poisoned rum, though that certainly had not been her fault.

You take more lookin' after than a bairn.

She'd wanted to be helpful and had offered to take up the other set of oars and row, but he'd shaken his head.

"A pair of oars in your hands would make a bloody din."

She'd felt ashamed to know he was likely right. And so the perilous, long watch of the night had passed in frosty silence, with Annie feeling useless and angry and afraid.

Oh, how he confused her! One moment he held her and comforted her to help her nightmares pass. The next he belittled her, humiliated her.

At least he hadn't kissed her again.

Why hadn't he kissed her again?

Each time she thought of it, her heart seemed to trip. The hot feel of his lips against hers. The scorching shock of his tongue in her mouth. The hard press of his body.

Oh, Annie, I knew you would taste sweet.

The memory of his words made her breath catch in her throat, and she realized she'd taken pleasure in it. She'd taken pleasure in his kiss.

Even as the truth of it came to her, she rejected it. She'd been asleep and caught up in a dream when he'd stolen that kiss from her. 'Twas a trick of her dream that she'd enjoyed it. How could she, who'd been raised a lady, find any pleasure in kissing a traitor, a rough Ranger, a Highland barbarian?

She looked up and saw the man who bedeviled her thoughts walking toward her. The shadow of beard on his chin had grown thicker and darker, and his black hair still hung long and unbound, lending him a wild appearance. His shirt had come open at the throat, revealing a wedge of dark curls. She remembered what he'd looked like without his shirt, how it had felt to be held against that chest, and her breath caught again.

He moved almost silently, his motions sure, agile and smooth despite his size. He was, she realized, quite graceful. The very idea surprised her. Male grace was a quality she'd never thought of beyond the ballroom; either a man could dance a quadrille with skill and without stepping on her feet, or he could not. But here was another kind of grace altogether—an untrained grace, an instinctive grace, an animal grace.

He set the bucket down before her, then knelt beside his pack and took out the soap and cloth she'd seen yesterday, together with the little jar of salve. "The cold water will soothe your feet. Wash them if you like and put on more salve."

Surprised by his thoughtfulness, Annie took the cloth from his hand. "Thank you."

"Be quick about it. I'm goin' scoutin'." He rose and strode silently into the forest.

She felt the water with her fingers, found it ice cold. She removed the moccasins, exposing her battered feet. Then she dipped the cloth in the water, squeezed it out and rubbed the soap against it. Although she had every intention of washing her feet, she found herself pressing the cloth to her face instead.

She almost moaned. It felt wonderful. The cold water made her skin tingle, washed away the grime, brought her back to life. Careful not to waste a drop, she washed her face, then her throat, water running in icy rivulets down her neck and beneath her gown. Next, she washed her feet and ankles.

But it wasn't enough.

She glanced about her to make certain Iain was nowhere near. Then she knelt, let the bearskin coat fall to the ground and slipped her gown and shift down her shoulders to her waist. All she needed was a few moments.

She'd never been naked in the open air like this, and a part of her could scarce believe she was doing something so reckless. She dipped the cloth into the bucket, squeezed it, then stared in astonishment at her own body. Purple bruises, caused by her tumble down the embankment, stained her skin. One of her breasts was scratched, and there was an angry red welt above her right hip. Death had made its mark on her.

She shivered.

Eager to put it all behind her, she washed quickly, first her breasts and belly, then her arms and shoulders. The breeze raised bumps on her wet skin, but the cold water soothed her bruises. As dirt and mud and dried blood washed away, she began to feel like herself again.

"You'd tempt a saint, lass. But I am no' a saint."

Annie gasped and covered her breasts with her arms.

He stood not ten feet away, the butt of his rifle resting on the ground, his hand around the barrel, his gaze sliding blatantly over her.

"Y-you ought no' be watchin'!"

"You ought no' be naked."

Iain was surprised he could speak. At his first sight of her kneeling bare-breasted and wet-skinned, the breath had rushed from his lungs. His thoughts had scattered like ashes in a gust of wind. He'd found himself rooted to the spot, his cock painfully hard, his anger and frustration from the past few days merging into sharp sexual need.

Even scratched and bruised, she was bonnie. Her cheeks glowed pink with shame, her apple-green eyes wide with a maid's innocent wariness. Her breasts were round and full, their rosy tips pinched from the cold. Her skin was creamy, her shoulders soft and curved.

Iain had been raised to treat women gently, but he did not feel gentle just now. His mother's Viking blood burned in him, ancient and hot, urging him to fist his hands in Annie's hair and bear her onto her back, to claim her in the most primitive way a man could, to plant his seed inside her again and again, whether she consented or no.

One arm still shielding her breasts, she fumbled for her shift and gown.

"Leave them off."

She stared up at him, clearly alarmed, and reached again for her gown.

"I said leave them." He closed the distance between them, knelt down beside her, only one thought on his mind: He had to touch her.

Her breathing was ragged, and she trembled. Her eyes were huge and round.

He reached out, took her wrists in his hands, and drew them one at a time to his lips, exposing her. "Dinnae hide your loveliness from me, lass."

Then he feasted on the sight of her. Her creamy breasts rose and fell with each rapid breath, their weight enough to fill his hands. Her puckered nipples looked as if a man had already sucked them to tight, wet peaks. One was marred by an angry red scratch. Behind her breastbone, her heartbeat fluttered like that of a wild bird.

Desire lanced through him, sent a bolt of heat to his already aching groin, made it hard for him to breathe. He wanted to cup the weight of her breasts in his hands, to taste her, to draw her nipples into his mouth and tease them with his tongue and teeth.

He ducked down, pressed his lips to the scratch, kissed it.

She gasped, and her body jerked as if his lips had been a brand. "P-please dinnae—"

Lust roared in his ears like the raging thrum of a heartbeat. His cock strained against the leather of his breeches, claiming the right to mate. "You've naugh' to fear from me, Annie."

'Twas an outright lie. If she knew what he was thinking, she'd likely slap him soundly—or scream and run.

You're a bastard, MacKinnon. Can you no' see the lass is an innocent and sore afraid?

Fighting to defeat his need for her, he released her wrists, picked up the cloth and dipped it in the bucket. "Turn 'round. I'll wash your back."

Covering her breasts again, she seemed to hesitate, then did as he asked.

He squeezed out the cloth, lifted the heavy weight of her tangled hair over her shoulder and pressed the wet cloth to her skin. He heard her tiny intake of breath, felt her shiver, saw the rapid beating of her pulse against the column of her throat. And the fire inside him grew hotter.

Slowly he ran the cloth over her silky skin, mindful of her bruises, his hand guiding the cloth over the soft angles of her back to the gentle swell of her hips below. Then he saw.

Beneath the deep purple bruises caused by her fall were the fading yellow marks left by what could only be a leather strap. Someone had beaten her—repeatedly.

Cold fury doused the heat in his blood, left him feeling disgust for himself. The poor lass was bruised and battered—and not for the first time—and all he could think of was having his will with her. The kiss was to blame. He'd allowed himself to take one taste of her, had found her more delectable than he'd imagined, and now he wanted more.

'Tis your own fault your breeches are tight, MacKinnon, you gobshite.

But hadn't he vowed not to let any man harm her?

Aye, he had.

If he couldn't protect her from himself, he couldn't protect her at all.

He set the cloth aside, lifted her gown to her shoulders. "Here, lass. Cover yourself. It's past time we left this place."

Annie held on to Iain's broad shoulders as he carried her through the forest, his words ominous in her mind.

"The Abenaki ken where we're goin', Annie," he'd warned her. "We lost them along the lake, so their best chance of catchin' us is to seek out our trail now or to wait in ambush along the road to Fort Elizabeth. This is the most treacherous leg of our journey. You must be silent."

The charred ruins of the fort they'd passed—a monument to death—proved they now tread a dangerous path. Iain had called the place Fort William Henry and had stayed well clear of it, keeping to the shadows. "It fell last summer and many men, women and children wi' it."

Strange it was for Annie to think that last summer when the fort had been burning, she'd been living in comfort in her uncle's hall, blind to his depravity and to her mother's suffering, and all but unaware of the conflict in America. She'd not have been able to imagine what lay ahead of her—her mother's death, her uncle's cruelty, the terrors of war in a harsh new world.

Master Hawes had once told Annie a man never hears the arrow that kills him, and in this vast land, she could understand how that might be true. The forest seemed to loom above her and around her, each hill, each stand of trees, each ravine and outcropping of rocks full of terrible possibility. Out there, somewhere, death was stalking them.

Something moved in the shadows. A fox.

A tree branch bobbed and swayed. A pair of squirrels.

For a time, Annie forgot how distressing—and stirring—it had been to have Iain's gaze hot upon her bare breasts. She forgot the way the look in his eyes had made her heartbeat falter. She forgot the strange warmth that had spread through her belly when he'd kissed the sensitive skin of her inner wrists. She forgot the way her skin had tingled at his touch when he'd washed her back. As Iain slowly picked a path through the undergrowth, uphill and down, over snow and ice and rock, she could think only of survival.

It must have been midmorning when he stopped near a small creek to refill the waterskin. He lowered her to the ground and lifted the weight of his tumpline pack from her shoulders. There were beads of sweat on his forehead, and she knew it couldn't be easy for him to carry her through such rough terrain over so many miles.

"If you need to see to yourself, now is the time. But dinnae go far." He knelt down beside the creek, held the waterskin beneath a hole in the ice to fill it.

Annie wandered with painful steps a short distance away from the creek and took care of her private needs. Then she walked back as quickly as she could. She sat next to Iain, watched him take a long drink from the waterskin, her gaze focused on the shifting muscles of his throat.

He wiped his mouth on his sleeve. "Are you thirsty? Drink now, and I'll refill it. I dinnae want to have to stop again."

She took the waterskin and had just begun to drink when she heard it—a distant popping sound that could only be . . .

Gunfire.

In a heartbeat, Iain was on his feet, his brow furrowed in concentration as he listened. Then he closed his eyes, exhaled, and for a moment a look of deep weariness or remorse crossed his face.

"Iain? What is it?"

"My men. My brothers. They're under attack."

Iain moved as quickly as he could, heading due south toward the fort. He did not want the battle to overtake them, lest Annie find herself in the midst of fighting. The gunfire had ceased for a time, only to begin again, closer this time. Then it had stopped again. He didn't need to be with his men to know what was afoot. He'd drilled them himself, knew every ploy, every trick, every scheme they might use in battle.

He could see it in his mind.

They'd been outnumbered, else they would not have been retreating toward the fort so quickly. They'd formed a circle to keep themselves from being outflanked and had then laid murderous fire upon the French and their Abenaki allies. When the French lines had broken, the Rangers had fallen back, hurrying toward the fort.

But the French lines had re-formed and advanced once more. And so his men had drawn into a circle again, each switching with the man beside him to shoot and reload so the enemy was constantly under fire. But what had happened next?

The silence told Iain nothing.

Had the French claimed the victory? Or had the French lines faltered again, leaving his men to retreat through the forest once more?

Those weren't the only questions that troubled his mind. How many good men had been killed? How many were struggling through the forest wounded, who might yet lose their limbs or lives? How many had been taken prisoner and now awaited brutal and agonizing deaths at the hands of their captors? And what of Morgan and Connor?

Iain had known this might happen. He'd known their mission might be endangered. He'd known he might well lose men, perhaps even his brothers. And still he'd defied orders. He would have to live with the bloody cost of his decision forever.

Yet he did not regret saving Annie's life.

He felt her upon his back, warm and soft and alive, and that feeling of protectiveness again surged from his gut. She did not deserve what had befallen her. He could no more have watched her die than he could have slain her with his own hands.

Not for the first time he wondered who had beaten her. Was it the man Connor had found dead in the snow—her kin? It must have been. There was no one else.

Annie did not seem the submissive sort of woman who would abide a beating without fighting back. Then again, if they were her only kin, perhaps she'd felt she had to endure whatever the man had thrust upon her or risk losing the roof over her head. If such were the way of it, then Iain was grateful the bastard was dead. Men who beat women didn't deserve the life their mothers gave them.

A doe sprang from the shadows, interrupting his thoughts and forcing his mind back to the moment. He could not allow himself to become distracted. The ground had grown steep and rocky, offering an enemy many places to hide. He had just spotted a jutting prow of rock, one his men had used to ambush the French in the past, when the gunfire began afresh.

And this time it was almost on top of them.

Chapter Ten

Iain ran uphill toward the prow of rock, as the forest not far behind them exploded with rifle fire and shouting. He needed to find cover for Annie. Then he would take position and fight.

The slope was steep and icy, and his snowshoes slipped as he ran. He ignored the burning in his legs, forced himself to run harder.

Behind them the shouts and shooting drew nearer.

He reached the jutting wall of rock, leapt behind it and helped Annie from his back.

Her face was pale, her eyes wide, but she did not yield to panic despite the battle that now drew perilously close.

"Keep your head down, lass." He lifted the tumpline pack from her shoulders, then took her by the hand, bent low and led her uphill.

What appeared to be a prow of rock on one side was a low rock wall on the other. Only down by its sharp bow, where the earth had washed away completely, leaving the stone exposed, was there room for a man to stand up straight without being seen. 'Twas what made it such a perfect place for an ambush. Unassailable from the north, its south side offered a man a place where he was concealed and yet could spot and shoot his enemies with ease.

Iain settled Annie in a small crevice, handed her a pistol, powder and shot. "Stay down. Dinnae fire until he's afore you, and then shoot to kill. Do you hear me, Annie?"

She nodded, the same look of frightened courage on her face that he'd seen when she'd faced down the Abenaki. She clasped his hand. "Be careful, Iain!"

Iain wasn't sure why he did it. Perhaps the madness of battle was already upon him. Perhaps her fear and resolve touched something inside him. Perhaps he simply *wanted* to do it.

He fisted his hand in her hair, ducked down and kissed her.

Annie had known he was going to kiss her the moment before he did it, and still the heat of his lips surprised her. It lasted for only a heartbeat, but in that moment Annie forgot to be afraid.

He pulled back from her, stroked her cheek and gave her a lopsided grin. "I didna ken you cared, lass."

Then he was gone, creeping beside the rock wall on his belly until he was a dozen feet or so away from her. He looked out over the wall for a moment, his expression grave. Then he lay on his belly again and turned his gaze to her.

"There are French and Abenaki below us. They're trying to get 'round my men. They dinnae ken we're here, so I should be able to pick them off like ducks on a pond. But if they feel pressed, they might seek shelter here. If they do, stay hidden, aye?"

"Aye."

Was he daft? Did he truly think she'd rush out and try to fight French soldiers?

But he had already turned away from her and was once again peering over the rock. He raised the rifle to his shoulder, cocked it, aimed and seemed to wait. Then he whispered something that sounded like Latin—and fired.

The blast startled her, made her jump.

"Easy, Annie." He had flipped onto his back and was already reloading, his hands moving quickly over the weapon. Then he flipped over onto his belly, cocked the rifle, and fired again. His motions were practiced and smooth, the actions of a man who'd fought many battles.

Annie watched, both terrified and fascinated, as he reloaded and fired with speed that ought to have been impossible, flipping from his belly to his back and to his belly again. As if drawn by some dark enchantment, she sat up taller and slowly turned to look over the wall. Beyond the bottom of the hill, the snow was grisly with blood. French soldiers lay dead upon the ground, the bodies of Indians beside them. Many dozens of others hid behind trees, their backs to the rock wall, their weapons aimed into the darkness of the forest. Distracted by the near constant fire of Iain's men, they clearly had no notion Iain was behind them.

Iain fired again, and another man fell.

Blood. The reek of gunpowder. Cries of pain.

"For the love of God, Annie, get down!"

She sank back down, feeling queasy. She did not want to see.

Iain aimed for an officer, fired.

The man pitched forward onto his face and lay still.

Iain reloaded, counting the seconds. He'd been trying to match the fire of his men, timing his shots with theirs so as not to give away his position. He rolled onto his belly, aimed and watched the French lines break.

Panicked soldiers, deprived of their leader, turned to retreat and stumbled over the bodies of their fallen compatriots. And still Iain's men kept up their fire, holding their positions and picking off the frightened French as they fled for cover.

"Aye, boys, that's the way." Iain aimed at a tall Abenaki, fired, reloaded.

But even as he felt pride and relief at the Rangers' imminent victory, he knew he and Annie were now in mortal danger. The French and Abenaki were running up the hill toward the cover of the rock wall.

'Twas what he had feared.

He crept on his belly to where Annie sat, huddled in his coat, the horror of war upon her face. 'Twas a horror he had hoped to spare her, but there was naught he could do about it now.

He drew his claymore over his head and freed the strip of MacKinnon plaid that had always decorated the pommel. "The lines have broken, but the French are fleeing our way. Bide here, lass. Be silent! Dinnae use the pistol unless you must! If augh' should happen to me, wait until my men over-take you and show them this. My brothers will guide you to safety."

He pressed the bit of woolen tartan into her palm and closed her fingers around it.

She looked up at him, surprise and dread on her pretty face. "Iain—!"

Something stirred inside him to learn that she feared for him. He pressed a finger to her lips. "Shhh, lass!"

Then he thrust his sword back into his pack and turned away from her. Slinging his rifle over his shoulder, he dragged himself forward, using his forearms, until the wall of rock was high enough that he could sit. He grabbed his rifle, cocked it, aimed.

He did not have to wait long. The first of the retreating French appeared at the end of the wall almost at once.

He fired.

A soldier fell to the ground, a look of confusion in his eyes as the light left them.

Iain tossed the rifle aside, drew his pistols, and charged.

Annie watched in horror as Iain ran toward the stream of French survivors. Two men fell as he fired his pistols, another when he struck with his hatchet. But there were so many of them and only one of him. Where were his men?

She looked back over the wall, saw only French and Indians, and some detached part of her realized she and Iain might well perish in this fight.

She did not want to die. She did not want Iain to die.

At the bottom of the hill, Iain had drawn his claymore. Although some of the French had fled away from the wall into the forest or farther up the hill, others turned on him, the only obstacle between them and cover.

Iain had placed himself between her and the enemy. He would remain there until the French were defeated—or until he fell.

Unwilling to watch but unable to turn away, Annie saw a French soldier try to spear Iain with his bayonet, only to fall, his chest cleaved open. Another raised a pistol but lost his arm. Yet another fell, his bowels spilled onto the snow.

Annie knew what a Highlander with a claymore could do, but she had never thought to witness the brutality of it. It sickened her, terrified her. But as Iain swung the deadly blade yet again, she knew he was shedding blood for her sake. He was fighting to save her life—again.

More French soldiers pressed toward him, driven forward by shots fired by the Rangers still concealed in the forest. One soldier passed Iain, then turned and raised his rifle. But Iain did not seem to see him. His back was turned, his blade clashing with another soldier's bayonet.

Before she realized what she was doing, Annie found herself on her feet, gliding as if by some spell down the hill, the pistol gripped in her hands. The French soldier saw her just before she pulled the trigger, his eyes widening in surprise.

Two things seemed to happen at once: The pistol leapt in her grasp, and the soldier fell to the ground, writhing.

Stunned by what she'd just done, Annie stared at the weapon that smoked in her hands, at the man who now lay still in the snow.

What happened next, Annie could not say.

A bloodcurdling cry rose from the forest, as if the forest were possessed of demons. Rough men poured out of the shadows, driving the French before them. And Iain was there, bearing her to the ground, his body a shield, his weight heavy upon her.

Iain heard Morgan shouting orders to the men behind him, recognized Connor's victory shout. But even as he offered a prayer of gratitude for his brothers' lives, his hands searched Annie's trembling body for wounds.

"Is the lass hurt?" Morgan knelt down beside him. "I saw what she did. I had the bastard in my sights when she fired."

"What she did was defy my orders for a second time, and she'll be lucky if I dinnae flay her alive for it!" Iain pulled Annie to a sitting position, fear for her safety turning to blazing fury. "Blast it, Annie! I told you to stay where you were! You're bloody lucky you were no' shot!"

Her gaze met his, her green eyes glazed and filled with shadows. "I-Iain?"

Iain understood those shadows only too well. She was in shock. She had witnessed the full horror of war. Worse, she had killed a man. Like a young soldier after his first battle, she was struggling to cope. 'Twas an anguish no woman should have to bear.

His rage broke like the tide against the shore, and before he could think, he pulled her hard against him, held her, stroked her hair. "You foolish, brave woman! Why do you no' obey me?"

"What the bloody hell is he doin'?" Connor asked from somewhere behind them.

Morgan answered, "I think he's punishin' her."

"If he tries this on the men, they'll mutiny."

They reached the fort in the early afternoon, with Captain Joseph's men behind them. Iain sent Morgan into the fort to make a full report to Wentworth, while he bore Annie across the bateau bridge to the island that served as Ranger camp. She'd been silent since the battle, and he knew she was near the end of her endurance.

He carried her through the door to his cabin, sat her on a wooden chair before the fire, then sent one of his men after a hot meal and another after water and the wooden wash-tub used in the laundry.

"The washtub?" Killy gaped at him in disbelief. "You've a mind to do a bit of laundry?"

"Nay, for God's sake! 'Tis for a bath for the lass."

Killy's eyebrows rose until they disappeared beneath the brim of his Scotch bonnet, and the corners of his mouth twitched. "Aye, Mack."

The man he'd sent for food returned first, carrying a basket of biscuits and butter and a large tin plate heaped with slices of boiled beef, sizzling pork sausages and boiled potatoes.

The smell made Iain's mouth water and his stomach rumble. "Set it on the table, and go feed yourself, Cam."

"Aye, Mack." Cam's gaze fell admiringly on Annie, lingering a bit too long for Iain's sake. "Poor lass."

"Sergeant?" Iain resisted the urge to grab the younger man by the shoulders and throw him out of the cabin.

Cam set the food down, then hurried out the door.

Iain walked over to Annie, pulled the bearskin coat from her shoulders. "Come, lass. Time for a hot meal."

Annie felt as if she were drifting through a world of shadows. She knew they'd outdistanced the battered French. She knew they'd reached the fort safely. But it all seemed far away, as if it were happening in someone else's life—or perhaps a dream. There'd been shooting and dead men lying upon the snow. And she had killed a soldier.

'Twas the smell of food that roused her.

It had been three days since she'd eaten anything but cornmeal. She felt Iain guide her to the table and stared at what seemed a feast—boiled beef, browned sausages, bread, butter, potatoes. Before she could catch herself, she grabbed a piece of bread and a sausage and began to eat greedily.

It tasted like heaven.

Iain sat beside her, touched a hand to her shoulder. "Slowly, lass. You'll make yourself sick else."

'Twas only then Annie realized she was eating with her fingers and gobbling her food like an animal. "Forgi'e me."

He slid a tin fork across the table. "There's naugh' to forgi'e. Here."

They shared the meal in silence, she eating with a fork and he with a knife, until Annie could not swallow another bite. 'Twas much sooner than she'd expected.

"Your belly has withered a bit," he explained. "You'll be hungrier in the morn. Now let's get you a bath, and then you can sleep."

A bath sounded heavenly, but she was so tired. She watched through heavy eyelids as a scarred old Ranger carried a wooden washtub through the door, then filled it with buckets of steaming water.

"Annie?" Iain's voice woke her.

She hadn't realized she'd drifted off.

"Your bath is ready, lass. There's soap on the chair and some linen for you to dry yourself. I'm goin' out. Take your time. Put out the latch string when you're finished."

He turned to go.

She reached out, grasped his hand. "Thank you, Iain. For savin' my life. For this kindness. For all of it."

He took her hand, bent to kiss it, then was gone.

Annie shed the moccasins and leggings first, then her gown and chemise. She sank into the hot water with a sigh.

It was finally over.

The news took Lord William utterly by surprise.

"They have returned, my lord, and they have with them a young woman. Captain MacKinnon was somewhat vague on the major's actions, but it seems Major MacKinnon rescued the young woman, by all accounts a Scottish rustic, from ravishment and slaughter at the hand of the enemy."

William studied the pieces on his chessboard without truly seeing them, while Lieutenant Cooke related to him the rest of Morgan MacKinnon's report.

The Rangers had reached Ticonderoga and observed the fort from the nearby summit of Rattlesnake Mountain. They'd watched as sixteen bateaux filled with gunpowder and other ordnance had been unloaded and had spotted forty-three Wyandot Indians entering the fort. They'd estimated the troop strength at some seven hundred French and Canadian partisans and again as many Indians.

But on the first morning of their return journey, they'd come across a group of French and Abenaki scouts that had attacked a frontier family and were about to rape and slay its lone survivor—a young woman.

"Captain MacKinnon claims the woman was fleeing and all but stumbled into their camp, necessitating action. Because she was wounded in the attack, the major sent his men ahead without him and reportedly carried her on his back the entire way here, if one can believe such a thing."

William had no difficulty believing it. He'd seen these Rangers in action and knew them to be uncommonly robust and capable of extraordinary physical feats. "Were they pursued?"

"Aye, my lord." Lieutenant Cooke cleared his throat, a sure sign he was about to deliver news he feared William would find displeasing. "A force of three hundred French and Indians harried them to within a few miles of our gates. Under Captain MacKinnon's command, the Rangers fought off three assaults, the last of which broke the enemy's will. The Captain estimates French losses to be nearly one hundred thirty."

William had no difficulty believing this either. "Our losses?"

Lieutenant Cooke cleared his throat again. "Four, my lord. Nine wounded, two gravely."

"Where are Major MacKinnon and this woman?"

"They arrived with the rest of the corps, my lord. Captain MacKinnon said he and the men overtook the major several miles from the fort."

"How did the major manage to get ahead of his own men while carrying a wounded woman on his back?"

"Captain MacKinnon did not explain that, my lord."

"Where is the major now?"

"Seeing to his wounded, my lord."

William rose, strode to his window, pondered what he'd just been told.

William wholeheartedly believed the Rangers were essential in winning this war. It took a savage to defeat a savage, and the colonies were rife with such men. America nurtured the human detritus of Europe's civilized nations. Lesser sons of lesser sons. Heretics. Petty adventurers. Bondsmen. Convicts.

Among the Rangers, the MacKinnon brothers were perhaps the best fighting men he'd ever seen—headstrong Highland Gaels who'd been raised in part by Indians. They knew the New York frontier like few others, and there were no better marksmen in the world. 'Twas their great delight to shoot at marks for sport even when not at war.

It was because of their skill that he tolerated their insolence. In truth, he'd found their treasonous insults—and their uncompromising hatred of him and his family—quite refreshing. No one had dared to call him a "wee German princeling" before he'd met Iain MacKinnon.

William prided himself on his understanding of human nature. He derived great pleasure from watching people struggle with their lives, and then make completely foreseeable decisions. He enjoyed measuring people's minds and abilities and observing as they rose—or sank—to meet his expectations. He found it quite diverting to use what he knew about people to predict and even manipulate their actions.

But he could not have predicted this.

Apart from treasonous speech, Major MacKinnon was as dedicated a commander as any military leader could hope to find. William trusted him—aye, he trusted him—to lead his men through the direst of straits with a clear mind. He trusted him to carry out his mission without fail. He trusted him to put military objectives ahead of personal ones. For three years MacKinnon had done just that.

But stopping to rescue this woman and abandoning his men constituted a grave breach of discipline. It wasn't something William could ignore. At best, it meant MacKinnon had gotten randy and earned a sound flogging. At worst, it signified desertion and mutiny and was punishable by death.

William turned to his lieutenant. "Have Major MacKinnon report to me at once. And bring the woman. I would see the Scottish flower who inspired our major to risk the gallows."

Chapter Eleven

Iain looked down at Lachlan Fraser's unconscious face, ran the names through his mind, each like a knife to his chest.

Peter. Robert Wallace. Robert Grant. Gordie. Jonny Harden.

Loyal men and true—all dead. First four, now five.

Before nightfall, Lachlan would be joining them.

A painful weariness crept over Iain. This was his doing. Every one of them might yet be alive had he not forsaken his mission. And then there were the wounded.

Young Brendan might lose his leg. Conall had bad powder burns on his belly—a shot had ignited his powder horn—and he might yet perish. Andrew had been struck on the head and hadn't awoken.

The rest, thank God, would recover.

"Mack!" Brendan called him from across the hospital.

Iain touched his hand to Lachlan's forehead, whispered a prayer to the Virgin Mother, crossed himself, then threaded his way past empty beds to Brendan's side. "Rest easy, lad."

"Is the lassie safe? Did you get her back alive?" Brendan's freckled face was wet with sweat, his eyes bright with fever. "I hear she's fine and bonnie."

"Aye." Iain thought of her sleeping in his cabin. He wasn't sure he liked the idea of his men talking about her. "And, aye, she is."

"I'm glad you did it, Mack." The boy shivered. "W-why are we fightin' if no' to keep our women s-safe?"

Iain pulled the blanket up under the boy's chin. "Morgan tells me you fought like a true Scotsman."

Brendan's face glowed with a warrior's pride. "I am no' afraid of the French."

But Iain could see fear in the lad's eyes. He placed a reassuring hand upon the boy's shoulder, forced a smile onto his face. "Rest, laddie."

"Mack, if they take my leg, w-will you be here wi' me?" The boy shivered again. "I'll be braver if you're here."

Iain nodded. "If it comes to that, I'll be right beside you."

"Thanks, Mack." A look of gratitude spread across the lad's face. "God bless you!"

"And you." Iain stood and strode out of the hospital, suddenly needing air in his lungs.

What special sort of hell had he crafted for himself? To see the consequences of his actions, to carry on his hands the blood of men who'd trusted him, to regret their deaths and yet to be sure he'd do nothing differently if given a second chance—'twas a burning torment.

Iain had taken no more than a few steps when he met Connor, who motioned him to the side of the hospital, gnawing on a piece of salt pork.

"Wentworth has sent for you. Cooke claims he's goin' to see you hang."

"Cooke is a bletherin' fool. He likes to stretch a tale. It makes him feel important."

"And what if you're wrong and that bastard truly wants to see you hang? Cooke says Wentworth is callin' what you did desertion."

Iain hadn't imagined Wentworth would go so far. Then again, it should not surprise him. Hadn't Wentworth proved his twisted sense of justice when he'd forced Iain and his brothers to fight this accursed war? "If he wants to hang me, he has to try me in a court martial first."

"The men willna stand for it. To a man, they're ready to help you escape, if you must. You need but say the word."

"I cannae do that." He clapped a hand on Connor's shoulder. "You and Morgan and the men—you all would pay the price."

Connor cursed under his breath. "This is all on account of her. If it hadna been—"

Iain found himself clutching the front of his brother's shirt, hissing in his face. "Watch your tongue, lad! Annie is no' to blame for any of this, and I willna hear you speak ill of her! She is an innocent!"

'Twas the strange look on Connor's face that stopped Iain. Stunned by the force of his own rage, he released his brother, stepped back.

"I meant her no insult, but too many good men have died for her already. I wouldna see you dancin' in the four winds for her sake."

"No one is goin' to hang." Iain had something he needed to do. "Can you and the men distract Cooke for a couple of hours so he cannae summon me?"

"That bumptious half-wit?" Connor grinned. "Aye—wi' pleasure."

There was one other thing. "And Connor, promise me that if augh' should befall me, you and Morgan will watch over Annie and see her safely settled off the frontier."

Connor hesitated, his brow furrowed, his blue eyes full of doubt.

"Promise me."

"Does she mean so much to you?" Connor's gaze seemed to measure him. "Aye, Iain, I give you my word. We'll watch after your lass."

"She is no' my lass." Iain glared at him, then strode off toward the sutler's.

From behind him came his brother's voice. "Now who's full of blether?"

When Iain reached the cabin he found her sound asleep, the strip of MacKinnon plaid in her hand. There was a time in his people's history when that would have meant something, when his colors would have laid a claim upon her.

Your lass.

That's what Connor had called her. But she did not belong to him. He was not free to wed. Wentworth had seen to it that he and his brothers were bound to Fort Elizabeth un-

108   Pamela Clare

til war's end, and Iain could not ask any woman to tie herself to a man who, like as not, would leave her a widow—and any child she bore him fatherless.

Nay, she was not his. She would be leaving the fort soon, on her way to Albany to start a new life. He would be staying here.

She lay on his bed, covered by his bearskin overcoat, her hair still wet. Only when he saw her tattered gown and chemise on the floor did he realize she was naked. She must have been so tired she'd crawled from the washtub straight onto his bed, forgetting her clothes. Or perhaps she'd felt clean and had not been able to force herself back into the filthy garments.

He added more wood to the fire, picked up the tattered bits of wool and linen and threw them onto the flames. She would no longer need them. He had seen to that.

He was not a wealthy man. His family had been stripped of riches before being exiled. Once the grandson of a powerful chieftain, he now carried his worldly goods on his back and dreamed not of holdings and halls, but of rich, dark earth that crumbled in his hands in the spring and yielded a bountiful harvest in the fall. But he also drew a major's pay and, as he rarely spent his coin, it had grown to a small but respectable sum.

He opened the canvas bag and took out the goods he'd bought from the sutler and his sons. A wooden comb for Annie's hair. Two shifts of soft, white cotton. Cotton stockings with silk garters. Linen petticoats. Stays. A linen gown of deep green and pink stripes, and another of broad pink and ivory stripes. A cloak of soft gray wool. Shoes that seemed impossibly small. Ribbons for her hair.

He'd never bought women's clothing before. His only experience with what woman wore—all those skirts and strange undergarments—came from undressing them. But Stockbridge women did not wear all of this frippery. The sutler had been the one to tell him what was needed and to guess at Annie's size. Of course, there was very little women's clothing to be found at the fort, only what officers' wives had traded or left behind. He hoped these garments would fit her.

Iain stacked the clothing on the table where she'd see it when she woke. Then for a moment he simply watched her sleep, unsettled emotion stirring inside him. He knew she was exhausted. She'd barely been awake enough to eat or bathe. He hoped her dreams would be free of troubles. She'd endured a lifetime's worth of horrors these past days. Nor had her life before been easy, judging from the bruises on her back.

Outside he could hear shouts, and he knew his men were making mischief in an effort to keep Cooke at bay. Quickly, he took off his clothes. Then he grabbed his razor and stepped into the cold bathwater. Wentworth was waiting.

Snug beneath the fur, Annie slept. She did not wake when Iain bent down to kiss her cheek. She did not wake when Morgan and Connor barricaded the door to the cabin to keep Lieutenant Cooke from disturbing her. She did not wake when the two brothers entered to check on her and stoke the fire.

Nor did she dream.

Iain glanced over at a furious Cooke, who stood dripping wet in white wig and uniform—the result of some unfortunate mishap with the bateaux bridge that had sent him plunging into the chilly Hudson—and tried not to grin. His men had done their work well.

Wentworth sat in a gilded chair in front of his writing table, one arm lifted to flaunt the ivory lace at his wrist, his uniform immaculate, every hair of his powdered wig in place. His cold gray eyes bored into Iain. He was quieter than Iain had ever seen him, and that meant he was angrier than Iain had ever known him to be.

"Thus far, Major, I have heard little to my pleasure. You freely admit you disobeyed my orders?"

"Aye, Your Gracefulness."

Wentworth stood and walked toward him with slow, measured steps, his heels clicking on the waxed wooden floor. "Have you forgotten there's a rather high price on your head? The enemy is waiting quite breathlessly for you to make a mistake."

"Nay, I have no' forgotten."

"Did you realize that by opening fire you'd be alerting the French to your whereabouts?"

"Any idiot of a private would ken that."

"Did you consider that men under your command might be killed as a result of so rash a decision?"

"Aye, though I prayed they wouldna."

"Your prayers were apparently not enough." Wentworth's nostrils flared and he leaned forward until his face was inches from Iain's. Then he spoke, his voice quiet, every word articulated and precise. "Five men have died thus far, and the lives of two still hang by a thread. They lost their lives because the man they trusted to lead them brought a force of three hundred—"

"I ken why they died!" Iain's temper snapped. "I will live wi' that anguish for the rest of my life! But you were no' there! You didna see her spill out of the forest at my feet! You didna watch her fightin' wi' all she had to stay alive! If I'd have left her to be raped and murdered, I'd no' be able to live wi' myself!"

"Can you live with the unnecessary deaths of your men?"

"If I must, aye. They were trained Rangers, men accustomed to war. At least they had a fightin' chance."

"Did it not occur to you that the Crown might view this woman as expendable, while your highly trained Rangers were not?"

"I dinnae weigh human lives in so cold a fashion as the bloody Crown."

"War demands sacrifice, Major MacKinnon."

"Dinnae try to tell me the cost of war, pretty wee prince! While you sit in here wi' your brandy and warm fire, my men and I live and breathe war! Hang me if you wish! Flay the skin off my back! But I could no more have left her to be murdered than I could have killed her myself!"

Wentworth's nostrils flared again, then he strode slowly over to his window, his hands clasped behind his back.

"Very well, Major. Tomorrow at dawn you shall be taken from the guardhouse to Ranger Camp, where you shall be flogged to the count of one hundred lashes." Then he glanced over at Cooke. "Put him in irons."

Annie awoke feeling befuddled and very, very hungry, the strip of Iain's plaid in her hand. Hadn't she given it back to him? She'd certainly meant to. She sat up, glanced about, tried to remember where she was. A claymore rested on hooks above the door. Snowshoes hung beside tools on the far wall. A rifle stood in the corner and on the mantle a crucifix.

Iain's cabin. She was in Ranger camp at Fort Elizabeth. Outside the window of greased parchment it was growing dark. Evening already?

A strong fire burned in the fireplace, proof that Iain had been there recently. She looked down at the bed, realized the blankets had not been turned down, nor was there any other hollow in the blankets save the one she'd made. She had slept alone.

Then she realized with a shock that beneath the bearskin she was naked. What had happened to her gown and shift? She crawled to the foot of the bed and searched for her gown around the washtub, but it was no longer there. She glanced about the room, but could not find it. Then she saw the table.

With a delighted gasp, she leapt from the bed. Pain in her feet nearly made her legs buckle. She winced and then hobbled across the small cabin, careful to keep the coat wrapped round her. There on the rough-hewn table were stockings and a clean white shift and petticoats and two gowns of lovely colors. Though they were made of simple linen and cotton, they were at that moment the most beautiful garments she'd ever seen.

She glanced over at the door, saw the latchstring was out. She quickly pulled it in for privacy. Then she let the fur fall from her shoulders and began to dress, feeling an excitement she hadn't known for months.

The stockings fit perfectly. The shift and petticoats also fit well. She had trouble lacing the stays by herself, and when she did succeed in drawing them tight, the whalebone pressed painfully against her bruises. Still, she hadn't worn stays since Mistress Hawes had stolen her clothing, and for once she felt properly dressed.

She ran her hands over the two gowns, chose the one with the slender green and pink stripes, then slipped it on. Feeling almost giddy, she smoothed her skirts, adjusted the sleeves of her shift so they hung properly, then looked down at herself. Besides the bodice, which was a bit tight, the gown fit as if it had been made for her.

How had he come by such lovely things out here? How was she ever going to thank him? She had no coin with which to pay him, nor anything to trade. Perhaps he had mending she could do. Or perhaps she could clean for him. She had no talent for cooking.

Then her gaze fell upon the wood comb, and tears pricked her eyes. She picked it up, ran her fingers over the delicate carving in the handle, and then combed away her tangles.

She'd just braided a ribbon into her hair when someone knocked on the door.

"Miss Burns. It's Captain Morgan MacKinnon, Major MacKinnon's brother. If you're awake, I would speak wi' you."

Hesitantly, she opened the door and saw a man who resembled Iain so closely that there was no mistaking him for kin. Tall like Iain, Morgan MacKinnon had the same blue eyes and dark hair, but his hair was a bit shorter and pulled back in a leather thong. "Wentworth wishes to speak wi' you."

"Where is Iain?"

Morgan ducked through the doorway, propped the door open, then dropped into a chair, his face troubled. His eyes, when he looked at her, held no warmth. "Iain took a terrible risk in savin' your life. Did he tell you that, lass?"

Annie sat and smoothed her skirts, feeling a strange sense of foreboding. "Nay."

A voice came from the doorway. "Five of his men are now dead and eight lie wounded because he chose to save you instead of doin' his duty."

"Did you have to say it like that, Connor?"

A man who might have been Iain's twin ducked through the door. "She ought to ken the truth of it."

Confused, Annie felt her stomach sink. "Please. I dinnae understand."

It was Morgan who explained what had happened. He told her how she'd toppled down the embankment, nearly landing at their feet. He told her how the Rangers had been under orders not to risk their mission by intervening in other battles, but to move silently through the forest. He told her how Iain, unable to turn his back on her and yet knowing three hundred French were nearby, had ignored those orders and saved her, tipping off the French to their position. He told her how the French had pursued them relentlessly, leaving too many of their fellow Rangers dead.

Connor glared at her. "And now they're goin' to flog him for it—a hundred strokes."

"Wh-what?" The blood rushed from her head. "They cannae do this!"

Connor crossed his arms over his chest. "Aye, by Satan, they can!"

A muscle twitched in Morgan's jaw. "They have Iain in irons in the guardhouse, and tomorrow at sunrise, they'll tie him to the whipping post and flay him."

Trembling with rage and afraid for Iain, Annie found herself on her feet. "Then 'tis good your commander wishes to speak wi' me, for I would surely speak wi' him. Once he hears all Iain did for me, he'll be moved to mercy."

Morgan stood, thrust his chair aside. "Wentworth doesna ken the meanin' of mercy, lass, but you're welcome to try."

Annie spotted her moccasins on the floor, slipped her sore feet into them, and then wrapped herself in the gray cloak. "Take me to him."

She walked as quickly as she could out of the cabin—then stopped. Rough men surrounded her—Rangers and Indians. A few of them she recognized. Most she did not. They stared at her, their faces grim, and she wondered if they blamed her for Iain's plight and the deaths of their comrades.

The grizzled man who'd carried in the washtub stepped forward, gave her a grin. His voice bore the lilt of Ireland. "Killy's the name, miss. Don't be lettin' this lot of stupid Scots trouble you. Have you ne'er seen a pretty woman before, you louts?"

A voice came from somewhere in the throng. "No' one so bonnie as this."

From behind her, she heard the low growl of Connor's voice. "Put your eyes back in your head, Dougie, or I'll feed them to the fishes."

Morgan stepped forward, raised his voice to the crowd. "The lass is goin' to speak wi' Wentworth to see what can be done."

Heads nodded, and the men gave way.

As Morgan and Connor guided her through the crowd, Annie did not feel the heat of their eyes upon her. Her thoughts were on Iain.

Was he cold and hungry? She remembered only too well her weeks in gaol—the rats, the moldy bread, the darkness, the bone-chilling cold.

Was he afraid? The pain of so many strokes would be unbearable, far worse than a single act of branding. He might even die.

Did he regret saving her life? Surely, he must. He'd lost

men, and now he was to face the public humiliation and agony of flogging.

Would the commander listen? Aye, he would. He must.

She would make him listen.

Chapter Twelve

Iain's brothers led her past beehive-shaped ovens and rows of wee cabins toward a great river that shone like a ribbon of silver in the twilight. On the other side stood Fort Elizabeth, the beautiful red and white crosses of the Union flag unfurled against the sky. A lump formed in Annie's throat at the sight of it—a symbol of home.

Two Rangers stood watch over the bridge. They nodded to Morgan and Connor—and stared at Annie. As she neared the river, Annie realized it was not a true bridge but many boats tied side by side and covered with planks that had been lashed together like a raft. At least a hundred feet across, it bobbed on the water.

"Mercy!" She stopped and stared. "I cannae swim."

Morgan tucked his arm through hers. "We willna let you fall in, lass."

"And if you do, we'll call Cam to fetch you out." Connor chuckled. " 'Twas he who fished Cooke out. If I live to be a hundred, Morgan, I swear I'll ne'er see so laughable a sight as that."

Annie scarce heard their banter; her attention was focused on the floating bridge.

Dinnae be a coward, Annie!

Fighting her trepidation, Annie took first one step and then another, holding tightly onto Morgan's arm. The row of boats sank slightly beneath her footsteps; the water, flowing in a great rushing current beneath her, made her dizzy.

"Dinnae look down if it frightens you." Morgan spoke to her as if she were a child.

You take more lookin' after than a bairn.

Annie lifted her gaze to the opposite shore, forced herself to walk with untroubled steps.

Beneath her, the torrent raged.

Another step and another and another.

'Twas with great relief she at last found herself on the other side.

Before her loomed the great earthen ramparts of Fort Elizabeth. Morgan and Connor led her past the gawking British soldiers who guarded this side of the bridge and through a seeming labyrinth of high walls. Inside the first set of walls, hundreds of canvas tents stood in tidy rows, lit from within so they seemed to glow. Inside the second set of walls was an empty stretch of ground sundered by a deep ditch that was spanned by a single wooden bridge. Beyond the bridge rose the high ramparts of the fort itself, from which soldiers and cannon peered out at her, dark silhouettes against the darkening sky.

A few of the soldiers called to her, their words boorish and indecent.

She pulled the cloak more tightly around herself.

Morgan took her arm once more. "They will no' harm you as long as you're wi' us."

"I'll cut out their bloody tongues." Connor glared up at them. "The whoresons wouldna dare speak so if she were a *Sassenach* officer's lass."

Sassenach. It was a word Annie had rarely heard growing up. The Argyll Campbell clan had close ties with England and with the Crown, and *Sassenach* was a word of rebellion, a word of hatred. It made her feel uncomfortable to hear it spoken now.

But the leering glances of the British soldiers made her uncomfortable, too. Men had never treated her with anything but courtesy—until Uncle Bain had denied her and cast her into gaol. Now it seemed men were always raking her with their eyes and saying vile things. Was this how common-born women were treated all the time? God forbid!

They passed through the gate into the fort itself. Wooden barracks two stories high stretched along the fort's four walls, leaving the center open like a large town square. One building stood out from the others. It was smaller than the rest, but it had glass windows and two stone chimneys. A pair of soldiers flanked its doorway, their muskets tipped with bayonets.

'Twas before those two soldiers Morgan and Connor led her.

"His Worship wants to see the lass." Morgan released her. "She's here."

Annie gaped at him, shocked by the disrespect in Morgan's voice.

The two soldiers glowered at him with eyes that told Annie such open contempt was nothing new.

Then one of them spoke, his accent clearly English. "Your brother's finally going to pay the price for his insolence. Are you next, Captain?"

Connor took a step forward, but Morgan restrained him. "Our brother is about to pay the price for bein' a man—somethin' the likes of you couldna understand."

For a moment the four men glared at one another in silence, and Annie could feel that words had brought them nigh to fighting.

She stepped forward. "Why do you argue? Are you no' on the same side in this war?"

'Twas Morgan who answered. "No' by choice."

The soldier who'd spoken shifted his angry gaze to Annie. "Wait here."

She watched the soldier disappear through the door, her stomach suddenly ajitter. Would this colonel blame her for Iain's disobedience or the deaths of his men?

Morgan seemed to read her thoughts. "Dinnae let him daunt you."

Annie took a deep breath, resolved not to be frightened. No matter that the colonel would see her only as a poor frontier lass. Inside her skin, she was still Lady Anne.

The soldier opened the door and bade her enter. "Through there, miss."

"We ken the way." Morgan strode in before her.

She lifted her chin, smoothed her skirts and followed him. Connor walked behind her.

Paintings hung from plastered walls in gilted frames. Thick carpets woven in the Orient clothed the waxed wooden floor in hues of claret, black and gold. Graceful white tapers burned in silver candelabra upon tables of polished wood.

Almost at once she felt more at ease, as if she'd stepped through a magic portal from the frontier, untamed and strange, into the world she knew. Surely the man who lived here was a gentleman and would listen to her. Surely he could be moved to compassion.

She followed Morgan into the next room to find three men in their waistcoats seated before a fire, glasses of brandy in their hands. Two looked over at her, curiosity about her turning to open contempt when they saw Morgan and Connor.

The third man gazed down at a marble chessboard, his face in shadow, his hands clasped together, his forefingers pressed to a point against his lips. Fine lace decorated his throat and wrists. A diamond glittered on his finger. Though he wore only his waistcoat, every detail of his uniform was neat, every hair in his white, powdered wig perfectly in place.

He raised a finger for silence and continued to stare at the chessboard.

Conner grumbled. "Och, Jesus."

After several minutes' contemplation, the colonel picked up the white bishop and moved it forward. Then he turned to face her.

Breath fled her body, and the floor seemed to tilt beneath her feet.

Wentworth.

Colonel Wentworth.

Lord William Wentworth.

Friend to Argyll. Nephew to the Duke of Cumberland. Grandson to His Majesty.

Before she could catch herself, Annie sank into a formal curtsy, her head bowed. "M-my lord."

She rose on unsteady legs to find him watching her, one dark eyebrow raised, his gaze inscrutable. "And you are?"

Dinnae be foolish, Annie! He doesna recognize you!

How could he? She'd been a lass of twelve summers last time he'd seen her. They'd met when he'd passed a stormy night with Uncle Bain on his way to visit Argyll. Lord William had been twenty or thereabouts and had scarce paid any heed to her, despite her mother's vexing efforts to win his interest. After all, he was the son of royalty, she a penniless earl's daughter. But that had been six years ago and half a world away.

She struggled to pull her thoughts together. As a man who'd once met her—and a man of great influence—he might believe her and be able to help her reclaim her name, return to Scotland and seek justice for her mother. Yet, as a friend of her uncle's, he might just as easily side with Uncle Bain and be done with her.

Was he her friend, or was he a danger to her?

Perhaps it was the cold glint in his gray eyes or the memory of him laughing over cognac with Uncle Bain, but some part of her refused to reveal herself.

She prayed she had not already roused his suspicions. "Annie Burns, my lord."

"I understand you owe your life to Major MacKinnon, Miss Burns." He sat again, but did not motion for her or Morgan or Connor to join him. "Please explain how this came to be."

And so Annie told Lord William how she'd just finished milking the cow, when she'd heard screams and gunshots and realized her sister and brother-by-marriage—she'd almost said "master and mistress"—were dead. She told him how she'd untied the animals, hoping they would divert the attackers, then climbed out the parchment window and fled barefooted through the forest. But by the time she reached the part of the tale where she'd fallen down the embankment, she was trembling from head to foot. Her words faltered.

"Please continue, Miss Burns."

Annie saw the tall Abenaki before her, saw the look in his eyes, knew what he was going to do to her, what they were all going to do to her.

"Can you no' see the lass is terrified?" Morgan's voice called her back from the darkness of her memories. "You've heard all there is to tell from Iain and from us. What need is there to force her to relive such horror?"

Lord William's gaze bored into her. "I need not share my reasons with you, Captain. Continue, Miss Burns."

Annie clutched her hands in the folds of her skirts, forced herself to speak. "I-I knew they were going to . . . hurt me and kill me. So I forced myself to stand, took a stone in my hand, and I threw it at him."

"At whom?"

"The tall Indian. I hit him in the mouth. Then he struck me wi' his hatchet." She raised her fingers to the stitches on her temple, still trembling. "After that I remember but little."

"You have no memory of Major MacKinnon fighting off your attackers?"

" 'Tis but broken images—gunshots, the sounds of fightin'. And the claymore. I remember seein' a man wi' a claymore."

"How many gunshots?"

She tried to remember. "Two or three—I cannae say for certain."

For a moment, Colonel Wentworth said nothing, but watched her as if to measure her.

Her conscience weighed heavily upon her, and she found it hard not to fidget. She'd just lied to the king's grandson! Should her lie be discovered and he not find it in his heart to pardon her, they would put her in the stocks and cut off her ears—or worse!

"Do you have kin elsewhere in the Colonies?"

"Nay, my lord."

"Is there anyone I might notify in Scotland on your behalf?"

"Thank you, my lord, but nay. There is no one." No one she could trust.

Colonel Wentworth nodded. "Another mouth for His Majesty to feed. Very well, Miss Burns. We shall have to decide what to do with you some other time. You may go."

Stunned to find herself dismissed so easily, she curtsied again. She had not come here to talk about herself. "Please, Colonel, might I speak?"

His brow furrowed, and he frowned. "Very well."

"I have heard Major MacKinnon is to suffer the lash for savin' me."

"He is being punished for willful disobedience that resulted in the deaths of five of his men, not specifically for saving your life. Though I see his plight distresses you, it is not your affair."

"Oh, but it is!" Annie felt all eyes in the room upon her. "I am deeply sorry for the deaths of his men, and I have no words to assuage such a grievous loss. But whatever else he might have done, Major MacKinnon treated me honorably."

It was the truth—apart from two stolen kisses and his heated glances.

The frown did not leave his face, so Annie tried to explain. "He risked his life for mine time and again, and I cannae bear to think of him sufferin' on my account. I owe him my life."

The two officers sitting nearby chuckled indulgently as if she'd just said something childlike and amusing.

Colonel Wentworth looked at her as he might an annoying bairn. "Miss Burns, you are a woman and young, so I do not expect you to understand when I tell you that Major MacKinnon's duty was to his men, not to you. As regrettable as your death might have been, the objectives of the Crown place the lives of fighting men first. Though the frontier can be repopulated, once lost it will be nearly impossible to regain."

His words were a slap across her face, and she felt heat rush into her cheeks. Her voice quavered. "I thought it was the job of the Crown and of the British Army to safeguard His Majesty's subjects, not sacrifice them like pawns for land!"

Colonel Wentworth stood, his expression unruffled. Though he was not as tall as Iain and his brothers, still he towered over her. His voice was as calm and cold as a frozen lake. "Clearly you do not comprehend the nature of warfare. I punish Major MacKinnon because I must in order to maintain military discipline. Major MacKinnon knew the risk he was taking when he chose to disobey my orders. Now he must pay the price."

Feeling sick for Iain, Annie met Colonel Wentworth's hard gaze and sank to her knees. "I beseech you, my lord! Are there no words I might speak to move you to mercy on his behalf? Is Britain so besieged by enemies that there is no room in justice for compassion?"

She felt Morgan move up behind her and heard the warning tone in his voice. *"Thoir an aire, a dh'Annaidh."* *Take care, Annie.*

The room fell silent save the crackling of the fire.

"Lieutenant Cooke, clear the room. Everyone out but Miss Burns."

"Aye, Colonel." A young officer leapt to his feet, set aside his brandy and herded Morgan and Connor toward the door.

"I promised my brother we'd watch over her," Connor protested. "We cannae leave her."

"I give you my word that the fair Miss Burns shall not be harmed, Captain."

Morgan gave a cruel laugh. "Your word? Since when has your word meant augh' to a MacKinnon?"

But the colonel's mind was fixed, and Annie quickly found herself alone with him—this man who might help her reclaim her life or who might just as easily return her to servitude, or worse, to her uncle.

William studied the young woman who knelt before him, her eyes downcast, her braid hanging like a river of gold almost to the floor. 'Twas not hard to see why Major MacKinnon had risked his mission to save her. She was spirited and uncommonly lovely, even black and blue with bruises. Her beauty had warmed the blood of every man in the room, including—if William were honest—his. Her skin was fair, her features refined, her body lush. Poor Cooke had stared at her décolletage as if he'd never seen the swell of a woman's breasts before.

But there was something about her that gave William pause. It was not her devotion to Major MacKinnon or her distress over his impending punishment. William would expect any woman rescued from such a brutal attack to act in like manner toward her rescuer. Women were, as a rule, meek souls and could not be expected to understand politics or warfare.

No, it was her manner that drew his attention. The last time he'd seen a woman curtsy like that, he'd been in Williamsburg at the governor's mansion. And though her speech was clearly Scottish, it was not the heavy accent he'd expect from an illiterate villager. In fact, her choice of words indicated a level of education that ought to have been beyond her family's means.

Then there was the way she had reacted when she'd first seen him. The blood had drained from her face, and he'd thought for a moment she would faint. Then she had called him by his courtesy title—"my lord"—a title of which she should know nothing.

Clearly she recognized him from somewhere. Ought he to recognize her?

"Rise, Miss Burns." William was surprised to find that her pleading gesture made him feel uncomfortable. "What would you have me do?"

She remained on her knees. "Please, my lord, spare him

the lash, I pray you, and suffer me to take him food and a blanket tonight!"

"You ask much." William found himself wondering what had happened out there in the forest. How far would she go for Major MacKinnon? There was one way to find out. He reached down, clasped her cold fingers, drew her to her feet. "I give you leave to take him food, water and a blanket. As for the rest—what are you prepared to offer me in exchange for leniency toward the major?"

Annie could not believe what she was hearing. She'd thought Colonel Wentworth a man of honor. Was he asking for her virtue? "Wh-what would you have me do, m-my lord?"

His gaze bored into her. "If I cut the number of lashes in half, would you be willing to offer me the pleasure of your company tomorrow evening?"

The pleasure of your company.

Annie felt dizzy, sick, her mind racing. Hadn't she fled her uncle's hall to preserve her virtue? Hadn't she suffered gaol and branding and exile rather than surrender her virginity to any man's misuse? Could she now yield her maidenhead to Lord William, knowing that lying with him would strip her of her innocence and reveal her brand, leaving her subject to his whim?

If she refused Lord William, she could walk away with her virtue intact, knowing she had done all she could honorably do for Iain's sake. Iain would suffer the terrible punishment that Lord William, not she, had decreed for him. And she could go on living as Annie Burns.

But then she thought of Master and Mistress Hawes and the lies she'd told Iain. She remembered Iain's kindness, the way he'd kept her warm at night. She remembered the feel of his skin beneath her fingers, the hot shock of his kiss. She remembered how he'd willingly offered up his life to save hers when the French had attacked.

If augh' should happen to me, wait until my men overtake you and show them this.

She owed him the very breath in her body.

How can you think of building a new life on lies and the suffering of one who risked everything for you, Annie?

And so Annie weighed the terrible choice before her—refuse Lord William and abandon Iain to one hundred lashes and perhaps even death, or surrender her virtue and risk her freedom to see Iain's punishment cut in half.

Tears pricked her eyes, and she glared at Lord William, seeing him anew. "H-how can you pretend to enforce justice when you wreak wrongs upon the world? You are no' an honorable man!"

Lord William seemed to measure her with his cold gaze. "Ah. So the answer is no."

"Nay, my lord." Her voice threatened to fail her. "The answer is . . . yes."

Chapter Thirteen

Iain leaned back against the wall of the cage they'd put him in and stared into the darkness. As soon as he was able, he would write letters to the families of the men he'd lost. He always did. The letters would not make any widow's grief one whit easier to bear. Nor would the act of writing the letters soothe Iain's conscience. But his men deserved this much—that those who loved them should learn they'd died as men.

His stomach growled, and he wished for a moment he'd had the foresight to tuck his pouch of cornmeal in his breeches. But it was no matter. He'd soon have greater discomforts to cope with than hunger. One hundred strokes were enough to do real harm to a man.

Was she still sleeping? He remembered how she'd looked when he'd left her, naked beneath his bearskin, her wet hair lying against his pillow, her lashes dark against her bruised cheeks. Her stitches were healing well and would need to be removed in a few days. When he was in the hospital being patched together tomorrow, he would have to remember to ask the surgeon to see to her.

He had no idea how long it would take him to heal, but once he was on his feet again, he'd do all he could to see Annie safely settled off the frontier in Albany or perhaps in Stockbridge. Rebecca would take her in if Iain asked her to. Iain could help support Annie by bringing venison, turkey and fish.

He could do no more for her than that. The summer campaigns were fast approaching, and much remained to be done in preparation. Wentworth was about as likely to grant him leave as he was to grow a human heart. But if she were still unmarried by war's end . . .

What the bloody hell are you thinkin', MacKinnon?

He was thinking of bedding her.

Nay, 'twas more than that. He was thinking of wooing her. Och, for God's sake! He was thinking of marrying her.

Are you mad, MacKinnon? You barely ken the lass!

Even as he rejected the notion, some part of him decided it was not so daft as it seemed. They were both from the Highlands. She was bonnie, strong and spirited, qualities she would surely pass to her children, while he had the skill to protect her, provide for her—and show her what the passion in her Scottish blood was for.

Aye, but she was a Protestant and came from loyalist roots, while he was Catholic and sprang from a clan that had stood by the Stuarts. Law forbade them from marrying. Then there was the fact that he was bound to this war until its end. And had a price on his head. And was without a roof to shelter her.

A lass would be silly to pass up such a match, MacKinnon. Bloody grand idea.

He kicked at the straw in aggravation, felt the heavy tug of the iron on his ankles.

Nay, Annie was not for him, and the sooner he made peace with that fact, the better off he'd be. He would not be free to love any woman until war's end.

And what if it's too late, you hapless bastard? What if you've already fallen for her?

Iain quashed that voice like a pesky insect.

From beyond the door, he heard Connor's voice. He got to his feet and, dragging his fetters with him, pressed against the iron bars to listen.

Then the door opened, and Connor himself appeared, carrying a lighted lamp.

"I've only a few moments. Morgan is right behind me wi' your lass."

Iain opened his mouth to tell Connor that Annie was not his and never would be, but that was not what came out. "Annie's comin' here?"

"She's come to coddle you wi' a warm meal and a soft blanket."

Iain found himself fighting to hide a stupid grin. "I could do wi' a bite just now. I dinnae suppose Wentworth agreed to this."

"Aye, he did."

Then Connor told him how Annie had been distraught to hear he was going to be flogged and had demanded to speak with Wentworth, unaware Wentworth had been trying to question her all day. Connor told him how she'd borne up well under Wentworth's scrutiny, even contradicting him and challenging his notions of justice.

"Then she said, 'I thought it was the job of the Crown and of the British Army to safeguard His Majesty's subjects, no' sacrifice them like pawns for land!' Och, he was angry wi' her, and she didna seem to see it! She has a pretty way with words, your lass does."

Iain's grin faded as he thought of Annie grappling with the man he most hated. He didn't like her being anywhere near Wentworth. "She is clever and has courage, but he will cast her out if she defies him."

Connor's face grew troubled. "I think it would be best if she were quickly settled in her new home and gone from this place."

Iain felt anger kindle in his gut. "You and Morgan dinnae like her. I can see it in the way you look at her."

"Nay, 'tis no' so. She is brave and bonnie and has a good heart. But I fear what may become of you if she stays. When Jeannie—"

"This has nothin' to do wi' Jeannie!"

Connor didn't look convinced. "I didna come to argue wi' you, but to tell you what has happened. When Wentworth at first refused to lessen your punishment, Annie sank to her knees and begged him to show you mercy."

It took a moment for Connor's words to sink in. "She did what?"

"Aye, she sank to her knees and begged him to spare you. I saw it wi' my own eyes. The lass cares for you, she does."

It sickened Iain to think of Annie on her knees before any man, let alone Wentworth. Knowing she'd done it for his sake only made his rage keener. "She shouldna have done that. I want nothing from that bastard, especially not his mercy!"

"Would you shut your gob and let a man speak? Wentworth threw everyone out of the room save Annie, and they spoke together for a goodly length of time. When she came out, she would no' speak wi' us except to say that Wentworth had cut your punishment to fifty lashes. And Iain—she was pale as a ghost."

Anger became foreboding. "Och, nay, Annie! He might own me, but I wouldna see him enslave her. What devil's bargain has he forced upon her?"

"I dinnae ken, but I fear for her." Connor's voice dropped to a whisper, and he cast a glance toward the door. "There's more. When she first laid eyes on Wentworth, the blood drained from her face. White as death she was—and shakin'. Then she curtsied as fine as any lady at court and called him 'my lord.' I'd swear she kent him and was sore afraid when she saw him."

Iain stared at his brother, tried to make sense of his words. "That cannae be."

"Are you so certain? What do you really ken about her, Iain?"

Had he not himself found her oddish and wondered about her? Iain brushed the question aside. "Did Wentworth show any sign that he kent her?"

"Nay, but who can tell? The bastard doesna let his thoughts show."

"Keep a close watch on her, Connor. Send her away with Joseph if you must. Wentworth would think naugh' of destroyin' her if it amused him."

" 'Tis no' just him you need to worry about, but every randy bastard in the fort. She's had more offers for a quick tumble in the past hour than a whore in a pub full of drunken sailors newly home from the sea."

Iain pressed his face against the bars, spoke through gritted teeth, wishing to hell he weren't locked up. "You tell them I'll slit any man who dishonors her from brow to balls, and that includes Wentworth! While she is here, she is under my protection!"

Even as the sound of his threat died away, Iain could hear Morgan and Annie outside the guardhouse door.

"We'll spread the word."

Then the door creaked open, and Annie stepped inside.

Iain felt his breath leave him.

Her hair, no longer matted and tangled, hung in a glistening braid over her shoulder and down the front of her cloak. Her eyes were wide and flashed green even in the weak light of Connor's lamp. She wore one of the gowns he'd bought for her, and from what he could see, it fit her well—perhaps too well—revealing feminine beauty her shapeless gray gown had hidden. Under one arm, she carried a blanket, over the other a basket covered by a cloth. On her bonnie face was a look of anguish.

Did she suffer out of concern for him—or because of Wentworth?

A redcoat stuck his head through the door. "One at a time! One at a time! The colonel doesn't trust you to be in here all at once. It's the girl's turn. You two—out!"

"I'm worried for you, Iain." Conner set down the lamp and walked away.

And Iain knew his brother wasn't speaking solely of tomorrow's flogging.

Annie glanced anxiously about. She'd expected to find rats scurrying at her feet, but the guardhouse was nothing like the gaol in Inveraray. There were no screams, no cries of misery and despair. It smelled not of human waste and rot and mold, but of pine. Its walls were not of cold, damp stone but wooden planks. Its puncheon floor was clean, apart from scattered straw. Three cells were empty. In the fourth stood Iain.

For a moment, she forgot why she'd come. She forgot the basket on her arm, the blanket in her grasp. She forgot the horror that awaited him tomorrow.

He had shaved away the dark stubble of his beard, leaving his face smooth and stunningly bonnie. His hair still hung unbound and long, but there was a gleam about it, and she knew he'd washed it. He wore a shirt of dark blue and white check that fell open at his throat to reveal dark curls and a hint of muscle. And though he still wore leather breeches, these were clean and without leggings—nothing but butter-soft buckskin from his hips to his moccasins.

She met his gaze, saw anger in his eyes. She could not blame him for it. He had saved her life, and because of it he was going to suffer.

Then the guard spoke, startling her. She'd forgotten he was there. "Get back in the corner, Major, and I'll open the door so she can set your supper inside."

"If I had it in mind to escape, you fool, I'd already be far from here." Iain stepped backward into the far corner, his chains dragging heavily across the wooden floor.

The sound of the key in the lock sent a shiver up Annie's spine.

Can we no' humble her a bit wi' a fast tup in the straw?

She fought to quell her sense of dread, forced those memories aside. 'Twas not she who was locked up, but Iain.

"Set it down on the floor, miss, and step out again."

Aware of Iain's gaze upon her, Annie did as the guard asked, leaving the basket of food and the blanket just inside the cell door.

The door shut with a clang, made her jump.

She smoothed her skirts, tried to mask her uneasiness. "I would speak wi' the major alone. Please leave us."

The guard grinned, raked her with his gaze. "So that's how it is. Are you sure you wouldn't rather have me lock you in with 'im? For a week's ration of rum, I'll—"

"Watch your tongue if you want to keep it." Iain spoke softly, but the menace in his voice was clear. "I willna always be in chains."

The guard paled, then turned and left, closing the door behind him.

For a moment the only sound was the clinking of Iain's shackles as he came to meet her. He grasped an iron bar in each hand and looked down at her, his brow furrowed. "My thanks for the supper, Annie, but you shouldna be in here alone wi' me. 'Twill only give the men reason to tittle."

"I-I thought you might be cold and hungry."

"So I was, but I willna have you dishonor yourself for my sake." There was an edge to his voice.

"I dinnae care what such men think. Their tongues are as filthy as their hides!"

"Would you have them say I tupped you in the guard-house like a flea-bitten whore?"

His crude words shocked her, made her face burn. She looked down at her hands. "You're angry. I dinnae blame you. I wouldna blame you if you hated the very sight of me. After all you did for me, to think you shall suffer—"

"Och, Annie! I am angry wi' you, but no' because I'm to be flogged. That is no' your doin', but Wentworth's. I'm angry because you demeaned yourself by gettin' on your knees before that bastard! Aye, Connor told me, and I was bloody fashed to hear it!"

Taken aback, Annie stared up at him. How could he be angry with her? Hadn't she gotten on her knees for his sake? "I was but tryin' to help the man who helped me."

His eyes were hard as slate, and a muscle clenched in his jaw. "I didna save your life so you could cheapen it! And now I would ken the truth, Annie. What is the cost of Wentworth's mercy?"

How did he know?

She shook her head, took a step back.

A hand shot out from between the bars, grasped her wrist in an iron grip. "Tell me!"

She felt her cheeks flame with both anger and humiliation. She'd said nothing to Iain's brothers of her agreement with Lord William, and she'd not expected Iain to know of it. Trapped, she sought for words, but he was quicker.

"You dinnae have to answer. I can see it in your eyes. For the love of Christ, Annie! Why?" His face was a mask of cold fury.

Annie felt herself on the brink of tears. "I cannae bear to think of your sufferin'!"

Iain heard the despair in her voice. He rested his forehead against cold iron, closed his eyes, tried to rein in his rage. "You will go with my brothers to Wentworth, and you will tell him you've had a change of heart. All will be as it was before."

She shook her head. "Nay, I cannae."

He pulled her against the bars, shouted, "Do it, Annie, or so help me God—"

She jerked her arm free, rubbed it, and he realized he'd hurt her.

"I am no' yours to order about, Iain MacKinnon! Do you no' understand? I wouldna be able to live wi' myself if I didna do all I can to spare you!"

" 'Tis you who dinnae understand, lass. I'd have gone to the whipping post gladly and taken each one of a hundred strokes wi'out complaint, knowin' you were safe and untouched. 'Twas a price I was willin' to pay. But now what does my pain buy? I'll have scars upon my back just the same, but you'll be Wentworth's whore!"

For a moment, she looked as if she'd been struck, tears glistening in her eyes. Then she did something he could not have foreseen. She reached inside her bodice and pulled the strip of his plaid out from between her breasts. "I-I wanted you to have this. I thought it might bring you strength."

Iain watched, bereft of speech, as she pressed the bit of wool into his palm, closed his fingers around it and pressed her lips to the back of his hand.

"God be wi' you, Iain MacKinnon."

Before he could find his tongue, she had fled.

"They've uprooted the whipping post and are threatening to toss it in the river, my lord." Lieutenant Cooke's young face was red with indignation.

William sipped a cup of tea, considered what damage he might inflict with his white knight, and mulled over this new development.

Full of rum, the Rangers had grown restless just after midnight, demanding their major be pardoned and released. William had immediately sent troops across the bateau bridge to warn them that any insurrection would be dealt with swiftly and severely. They'd responded by playing forbidden tunes on those infernal pipes of theirs, until the entire fort was roused from sleep and the Regulars were demanding to march out and face them in battle.

Now, apparently, the Rangers thought to stop Major MacKinnon's sentence from being carried out by getting rid of the whipping post.

William supposed that made sense to a drunken mind. "Where are Major MacKinnon's captain and lieutenant?"

"Captain MacKinnon has gone to dissuade the Stockbridge Indians from abandoning the fort in protest over the flogging, while Lieutenant MacKinnon is reportedly keeping watch on Miss Burns and trying to settle the men."

William pressed his fingers to his temples, feeling the beginning of a headache. So the Stockbridge were in rebellion, as well. He ought to have anticipated this. Their allegiance to the MacKinnon brothers was fierce, as they considered the three Highlanders kin. William hoped Captain MacKinnon would prevail upon them to remain loyal to the Crown. Their skills had proven to be invaluable, on par with those of the Rangers.

"Turn the cannon atop the Flag Bastion toward Ranger camp. Fire three six-pound rounds over their heads. Let's see if we can't sober them up. Then impose an immediate curfew for both Rangers and Regulars. Anyone not on duty who is found out of his quarters will join Major MacKinnon at the whipping post—once it is standing again."

"Aye, my lord." Lieutenant Cooke gave a perfunctory bow, but did not turn to carry out William's orders.

William looked up from the chessboard, met the younger man's gaze. "What is it, Lieutenant?"

"Why do his men defend him when he cost five of their companions their lives?"

"Loyalty, Lieutenant. Loyalty."

Doubt still showed on Cooke's young face. "Aye, my lord."

Iain had heard the shouts and curses and had realized the men were drunk and rioting. Then he'd heard McHugh's pipes—and he'd kent the situation was grim. He'd cursed, paced his cell, and cursed some more. What in the bloody hell were Morgan and Connor doing? And what of Annie? Were they watching over her?

Then the cannon had fired—three six-pounders.

Now there was silence.

He hated being caged, hated feeling helpless. If he were free, he'd be able to knock some sense into his men's drunken skulls and stop the mayhem. He'd be able to make certain Annie was safe. He'd be able to confront Wentworth.

He'd asked to speak with the bastard a half dozen times, planning to demand his full sentence be restored and Annie be released from any vow. But Wentworth had, of course, ignored him. Why would Wentworth give up rights to Annie's sweet body in exchange for the lesser pleasure of leaving more stripes upon Iain's back?

The thought of Wentworth touching her enraged Iain to the point of violence. He would stop it. Somehow he would stop it.

And then it came to him. What if Annie wanted to share Wentworth's bed? Hadn't Connor said she'd seemed to know Wentworth and had even curtsied to him?

But he also said she seemed to fear him, you lummox. Why would she want to lie wi' him if she's afraid of him?

Iain sat, stared at the strip of plaid in his hand and rubbed his thumb over the coarse wool, his thoughts crowded by anger and doubt. Unable to sleep and with nothing else to do, he waited for dawn.

Chapter Fourteen

Annie stared into the fire, exhausted from the long, sleepless night, her emotions raw and confused. 'Twas not the enraged shouts that had upset her, though the cannon had surely given her a fright. With Connor keeping a close watch on her, she'd known she was in no real danger.

Nay, it was the sunrise she feared—and what would come with it. She would have dreaded this flogging even were Iain a stranger. She'd never been able to bear it when Uncle Bain punished his servants and had at times aided them in hiding their transgressions. Nor was she one who liked to stare when their carriage passed some poor soul suffering in the pillory.

But Iain was not some faceless stranger, and her heart ached for what he must soon endure. He had saved her life with skill and daring few men possessed. And though at first he'd seemed to her little more than an exiled Highland barbarian—a shockingly bonnie one—she had seen such kindness in him as to change her mind. For he possessed many of the noble qualities she'd been reared to look for in a gentleman, while Lord William, by ordering this flogging and then using her concern for Iain to compel her into his bed, reminded her of her uncle—nobleman on the outside, barbarian within.

'Twas as if her world had once again been tilted on its edge.

So much had happened these past four days. It seemed a lifetime ago that she had slept before Master and Mistress Hawes's hearth in the vastness of the forest. Now they were dead, and Annie, who hadn't told a lie in her life, had become a queen of deception—and bargained away her maidenhead.

Meanwhile the man who had risked his life to save hers was about to pay for his kindness with terrible pain. Already the first bloody fingers of dawn reached above the dark outline of the forest. It would not be long.

Had he slept? Was he afraid?

Did he condemn her?

Now what does my pain buy? I'll have scars upon my back just the same, but you'll be Wentworth's whore.

Iain's words had haunted her thoughts all night, and she'd found herself wondering whether he was right. Would she have done better by him to let him bear the full brunt of his punishment even at the risk of death? Was she wrong to try to ease his torment by enduring dishonor herself?

He certainly thought so. But he didn't know what she knew. He didn't know she had lied to him about Master and Mistress Hawes. He didn't know she lived under penalty of indenture. He didn't know she was an Argyll Campbell.

He didn't know the woman he was protecting wasn't real.

Annie Burns was not real.

But why can she no' become real?

Had she not suffered enough as a result of Uncle Bain's

betrayal? Had not her uncle's greater lies already stripped her of all that was hers—her home, her possessions, her name? Why could she not take back her life, claiming a new name and forging a new life in exchange for the one that had been stolen?

Her rebellious thoughts gave her hope—but they did not soothe her conscience.

Yet one thing she knew she must do. She must learn to make her own way in the world. She could not be dependent upon others for her survival, nor could she wait for them to set her life aright. As soon as Iain was healed, she would make her way to New York City or to Philadelphia and find work as a seamstress or a lady's maid. She would start again.

And if Wentworth should get you with child?

A cold shudder ran through her. Though he was a handsome man and of royal blood, she could not bear the idea of lying with him and feeling his hands upon her. The thought of him kissing her as Iain had kissed her left her feeling nauseated and afraid.

And what of your brand? If he should find it—

A knock on the door made her jump.

Dread was like cold iron in her belly as she rose, crossed the small room and opened the door.

Connor stood there, his face grim. "Come. It's time."

In the distance, she heard the rhythmic beating of drums.

Annie shook her head, stepped back. "I cannae—"

"Aye, you can, and you will." He forced his way past her, grabbed her cloak and thrust it in her face, his voice gruff. "You will do him the honor of witnessin' his sacrifice if I have to drag you kickin' and screamin' every foot of the way!"

Was that how they saw it? If she watched Iain suffer, would he and his men feel she had shown him respect? How strangely these frontiersmen thought!

She could not do this. She did not want to do this.

She nodded. "If I can give him any comfort by bein' there, then I must."

She slipped into her cloak and moccasins and followed

Connor out into the chilly March morning. The sky was palest blue tinged with pink to the east. A breeze carried aloft the mingled scents of wood smoke and frying salt pork. Dogs nosed about here and there for scraps. Yet Annie noticed none of it; the day seemed cold and dark and empty.

By the time she and Connor reached the western side of the cabins, the Rangers had already turned out in ranks. Though she could not say they stood neatly at attention like British Regulars, they had managed to form lines and seemed alert, despite a night of drinking and rampaging. They turned their heads to look at her as she passed.

Her step faltered.

"They mean you no harm." His hand resting against her lower back, Connor guided her off to one side where Morgan stood.

Morgan looked down at her, his face grave. "Morn', lass."

Connor gave a grunt of disgust. "Look at them—the *Sassenach* vultures!"

Annie followed the direction of Connor's gaze, saw the ramparts of Fort Elizabeth crowded with curious soldiers who had come to point and watch. She felt a surge of rage at their callousness. How could anyone find pleasure or humor in this?

Morgan spat on the ground. "They've been waitin' for this day for a long time—a chance to see Iain MacKinnon brought low."

Annie wanted to ask Morgan why this was so, but her gaze happened upon the whipping post, and her stomach fell to the ground. It stood before them, hewn from the trunk of some unlucky tree, a band of iron affixed on each side to restrain the wrists of the man being flogged.

"Mercy!"

"You've come to the wrong place for that, lass." Morgan gave a cruel laugh.

The sound of drums grew louder, drowned out the twittering of birds.

Then Annie saw him.

Just crossing the bridge, he walked in the center of an escort, his wrists and ankles shackled, soldiers both before and after him, their bayonets glinting in the early morning light. Behind the soldiers came a young drummer, then Lieutenant Cooke and last of all Lord William, who had his own escort. The soldiers marched with stiff formality, but Iain walked as if he were out for a morning stroll, his lazy stride hindered only slightly by his bonds.

The feeling of dread inside Annie grew as they drew near.

The relentless *rat-a-tat-tat* of the drum. The plodding tramp of boots on frozen ground. The clinking of fetters, of brass buckles, of sabers in sheaths.

The escort reached the lines of Rangers, marched through their center.

Iain spoke to his men, a grin on his face. "Morn', boys. I heard you had a bit of a collieshangie in the night. Sorry to wake you so early."

His words were met with guffaws and a dozen shouts of "Morn', Mack" and "Sorry you couldna be there" and more than a few Gaelic curses aimed at Lord William, whose face remained as impassive as marble.

And then Iain was before her, his gaze upon her.

She looked into his eyes, saw he was still angry with her, watched his anger soften.

Without warning, he lifted his shackled wrists over her head and pulled her hard against him, claiming her in an almost brutal kiss. His fingers fisted in her hair and forced her head back, while his tongue plundered her mouth, taking advantage of her surprised gasp to thrust deep. It was no gentle kiss, but a kiss meant to claim her, to mark her before the other men.

And mark her it did—to her soul.

Then as suddenly as he had seized her, he released her, his voice a ragged whisper in her ear. "I willna let you do this, Annie! Dinnae make yourself his slave! Let me take the pain I have earned, and dinnae interfere!"

Before Annie could think or speak a word to him, rough

hands pushed him onward, leaving her shaken, fingers pressed to her bruised and tingling lips.

She watched, her emotions in turmoil, as the escort reached the whipping post, removed the shackles that bound Iain's wrists, and then ordered him to remove his shirt. This Iain did in one motion, pulling it over his head and dropping it to the cold ground. Then he turned to face the post, pulled his long hair to the side to expose his muscled back and stretched out his arms so the soldiers could lock his wrists in place.

Then Lieutenant Cooke began to read aloud. "Major Iain MacKinnon, you are hereby ordered to receive fifty strokes of the lash for willfully—"

"We all ken why I'm here, Cooke, for God's sake."

Howls of laughter from the Rangers.

Then Iain looked over his shoulder at her. "But 'tis one hundred strokes, no' fifty."

Red in the face, Lieutenant Cooke looked at the orders in his hands, then looked to Lord William for guidance.

And Lord William looked at Annie. "Miss Burns, I cannot now seem to recall—was it fifty lashes or one hundred?"

And she knew Lord William was letting her decide, forcing her to make an impossible, terrible choice once again.

She swallowed, felt the heat of every man's gaze upon her, then looked at Iain.

I'd have gone to the whipping post gladly and taken each one of a hundred strokes wi'out complaint, knowin' you were safe and untouched. 'Twas a price I was willin' to pay.

His gaze was steady, reassuring, insistent.

Holding on to the strength she saw in his eyes, she searched for her voice, feeling like a traitor. "One hundred."

His lips curved in a smile so warm it broke Annie's heart.

"So it was." Lord William nodded to Lieutenant Cooke.

Cooke motioned to another soldier, who stepped forward, whip in hand. He raised it, tested it in the air, snapping it with a sickening crack. Then he turned toward Iain.

Chills of horror raced along Annie's spine. "Nay!"

She found herself rushing forward, only to feel Morgan's arms shoot out to restrain her. "Nay, lassie! You cannae do more for him than you've done. Be strong!"

The first crack of the whip against Iain's bare skin turned her knees to water, and she'd have sunk to the earth had Morgan not already held her fast. Through her tears, she saw Iain's body stiffen with pain, saw a ribbon of red well up on his skin. Then came another terrible crack and another and another.

It hurt far more than Iain had imagined, each blow a shock to both mind and body. He fought not to cry out, unwilling to give Wentworth the satisfaction of breaking him, and bent his mind around thoughts of Annie.

Annie, desperate and alone, fighting the Abenaki.

Annie rowing the boat the wrong way, her eyes wide with terror.

Annie asleep in his arms, her body soft and warm.

Annie bare to the waist, her breasts wet, her rosy nipples puckered from cold.

Annie firing his pistol at the French soldier.

After thirty strokes, Iain lost count. After some dozen more, he felt dizzy, sick, his mind dazed from agony. After still more, he found himself leaning against the whipping post for support, his legs barely able to hold his weight.

Mother of God!

Blood ran down his back, hot and wet. Sweat stung his eyes. His breath came in shudders, his lungs straining to fill before the next stroke forced the air from him again. But still the blows did not stop.

He reach for Annie with his mind, wrapped his thoughts around her, fought the agony that threatened to strip him of strength, of will, of pride.

Annie!

Another stroke. And another. And another.

Then dimly he became aware that soldiers were unbinding his wrists.

It was finally over.

And then he knew only darkness.

Annie reached over and touched her hand to Iain's brow, grateful to find it still cool. The surgeon, a bespectacled older man with bushy white eyebrows and a large red nose, had warned her infection now posed the gravest danger.

"Sometimes they die of shock, but Major MacKinnon is heartier than most," Dr. Blake had told her as he'd washed the blood off Iain's back. "He'll no doubt recover fully."

As bad as it had looked from a distance, Iain's back looked even worse up close. Annie had been appalled to see how horribly the whip had torn his flesh. She could not fathom how badly it must have hurt, and as she'd watched Dr. Blake bandage Iain, she'd wished she'd stuck with her first choice and spared Iain the remaining fifty strokes, no matter what Lord William might have demanded of her.

The surgeon had tried to send her away, but Annie had refused to go, insisting she could help. Only when he'd realized she could read—she'd read aloud the label on a jar of medicine he'd had in hand—did he relent and allow her to stay.

"You might be of some assistance," he'd said.

Twice Iain had awoken, his brow furrowed with pain, and twice she had spooned broth and laudanum between his lips, though he had tried to refuse the latter.

"Nay, Annie. Poppy . . . will dull my mind. I must get back . . . on my feet."

She had stroked his hair, forced herself to smile. "You daftie. Sleep now."

And sleep he did.

Annie tried to make herself useful by sweeping the floor, rolling strips of linen into bandages and grinding dried plants into powder with a pestle, while Dr. Blake talked of the war and saw to his patients. One had shot himself in the foot. Another had a fever. Two were Rangers who'd been injured in the battle with the French. And then there was Iain.

Though she tried to listen politely to the doctor's tales, she couldn't keep her thoughts from drifting. Images of Iain bound to the whipping post, the lash striking his already bloodied back again and again, leapt unbidden into her mind, leaving her shaken. So much pain. And yet he hadn't made a sound.

And then there was the kiss. She could still feel the scorching press of his lips against hers, the invasion of his tongue, the twist of his fingers in her hair. And she found herself hoping he would kiss her again one day. Perhaps she was just overtired. She hadn't slept a wink last night, after all. Nor had she been herself these past few days. So much had happened.

She had just finished grinding some kind of tree bark—willow bark for fevers, the doctor had said—when a lad who until then had lain in a fevered sleep spoke to her.

"Are you the major's lassie?" Young he was, no older than Annie herself, with freckles and blond hair.

The major's lassie.

Annie wasn't sure how to answer. "Major MacKinnon saved my life."

"You are bonnie." A grin brightened the lad's pale face. "He said you were bonnie."

Iain had spoken of her and said she was bonnie? "Are you a Ranger?"

"Private Brendan Kinney of MacKinnon's Rangers, miss." His pride was clear to see.

While Dr. Blake examined Private Kinney's leg and gave him medicine to ease his fever, Annie listened to him tell how he'd been wounded.

" 'Twas in the first attack, miss. We heard the major fire his shots and knew they'd be after us. They laid on us hard—three hundred French or more. But we fought them back wi' Morgan and Connor to guide us. They caught me wi' a ball when I went for better cover."

Five of his men are now dead and eight lie wounded because he chose to save you instead of doin' his duty.

Connor's words came back to her, and at last she understood.

"You're very brave, Private Kinney, and I am sore grieved you were hurt."

"Dinnae let it worry you, miss. I'm glad Mack saved your life."

She swallowed the lump in her throat and glanced over at Iain, who still slept deeply. "Shall I read to you, Private Kinney?"

Iain was floating, Annie's voice flowing around him like warm honey. She was telling a story. It was a story he knew because it involved him. 'Twas the story of his attack on the Abenaki village.

" '—having marched many leagues through deep snows and frozen forests empty of game, and facing blizzards that stopped their progress, they were forced to boil their belts and leggings else starve.' Did you truly eat your belts, Private Kinney?"

"Aye, miss, and worse, but I willna speak of it to a lassie."

" 'After five-and-twenty days of such torments, they came upon the village, which they entered at dawn, having purposed to slay such warriors as they found there. In his account of the expedition to Colonel William Wentworth, Major MacKinnon reported finding more than one thousand scalps, including those of women and children, raised on poles above the lodges.' Mercy!"

That wasn't the whole tale, but only the tame version that had run in the *Boston Gazette*. How had she come by it? Was he dreaming? His mind foggy with laudanum, Iain tried to make sense of it, but soon he was drifting again.

It was pain that finally woke him—that, and Connor's irksome voice.

"Can you hear me, Iain?"

"Aye, you bloody idiot. You're shoutin' in my ear!" His

mouth was dry as sand and tasted of laudanum, but the drug had long since worn off. His back hurt like hell.

"How do you feel?" That was Morgan.

"Like the skin has been ripped off my back wi' grapplin' hooks." Iain lifted his head, saw his two brothers sitting beside him.

Connor glanced down at Iain's bandaged back. "Near enough. Sweet Jesus, Iain! I hope I never see anything like that again!"

"That makes two of us," Morgan agreed. "You held up well—a hundred lashes and no' a sound. The men are right proud, they are. And I'm certain Annie is, too."

Iain remembered the stricken look on Annie's face as she'd watched him walk to the whipping post. "You shouldna ha' made her watch."

" 'Twas hard on her, but she's a strong lass." Morgan handed Iain his waterskin. "She never took her eyes from you, Iain, but stood there weepin', pretty as a poem."

Connor grinned. "I think half the men would gladly have taken your place if only she'd have wept like that for them."

Iain drank, then looked about for Annie, certain he'd heard her voice but a moment ago, but he did not see her. "Where is she?"

Morgan and Connor exchanged a glance that had alarm coursing through Iain's veins.

"Where is she?" Iain tried to sit, found himself on his belly again, borne down by pain so terrible it left him dizzy.

Morgan spoke first. "There is naugh' you can do, Iain. You must regain your strength."

"Blast it! Where is she?" But Iain thought he knew the answer.

Connor met his gaze. "He took her."

Iain slammed his fist into the canvas of his pallet. "Why did you no' watch over her?"

"Wentworth punished the entire company for last night's

rumpus by settin' us to fell trees along the road. We've been hard at it all day wi' no chance to look after you or her."

Iain had told Wentworth exactly what would become of him if he touched her. The moment they'd taken Iain out of his cell, he'd confronted the bastard and made it clear to him that he'd best leave Annie alone, no matter what she had agreed to in her fear.

"Touch her, and 'tis your balls will be flyin' from yonder flagpole," Iain had warned him that morning as they'd lined up to march him to the whipping post. "She's under the protection of the MacKinnon Clan."

He'd thought Wentworth had understood. But the whoreson had given him his hundred lashes, then gotten both him and his brothers out of the way and gone after Annie anyway.

Rage cleared the last of the laudanum from his mind, and, gritting his teeth against overwhelming pain, he slowly sat. Dizziness assailed him, but soon his bare feet were flat on the floor. He looked down, saw thick bandages wrapped around him—but no shirt. "Where are my bloody moccasins and shirt?"

Morgan put a hand on his shoulder to restrain him. "You're no' fit for this, Iain!"

Iain knocked his hand aside. "Dinnae you try to stop me!"

Connor stood, shook his head. "Do what you will, but the good doctor says his men came for her three hours ago. Iain, it's too late! Whatever Wentworth wanted from her, he's taken by now—many times over."

Chapter Fifteen

Annie pretended to study the chessboard, well aware Lord William was watching her with those cold gray eyes of his. She struggled to feign interest in the game, her mind worn with worry for Iain and dulled by wine, her body aching from lack of sleep. How did he suppose she could give one jot or tittle about chess?

Lord William had already taken her rook and both of her knights and was bearing down upon her with his bishops and his queen. She moved her bishop, deliberately leaving her king and queen vulnerable, wanting the evening to end so she could return to the hospital and Iain.

It was strange to think that in another time and another place she'd have found Lord William bonnie—the ideal match and woefully beyond her reach. But as he sat before her planning his next move, she found it almost impossible to hide her rage and revulsion.

He'd sent for her just before sunset. Stunned, she'd been about to object when she'd remembered he was the fort's commander and could do as he liked. Expecting the worst, she'd been shocked when he'd led her not to his bedroom, but to his dinner table.

"Miss Burns, please tell me you didn't think I brought you here for some indecent purpose." He'd looked down at her disapprovingly, spoken in a superior, chiding voice. "Aye, I can see from the fear on your face that's exactly what you were thinking. But I wish only the pleasure of your company over dinner."

Her relief had been headier than the strongest wine.

"That might not have been the wisest move, Miss Burns," Lieutenant Cooke advised her now.

She looked up at him, pretended confusion. " 'Tis a tricky game. I dinnae know how anyone can keep all the rules in mind at one time."

Lord William's gaze was now on the board. "With practice, Miss Burns—with practice."

He moved his queen boldly forward, and Annie saw his mistake.

Whether it was from wine or lack of sleep, Annie took up her rook and captured his queen. Blood rushed to her head as she realized what she'd done.

Lord William's measuring gaze cornered hers, and for a

moment she felt like a fly looking into the spider's eyes.

But Lieutenant Cooke was beside himself. "Oh, very good, Miss Burns! Brilliantly played! See, you can learn the rules!"

His enthusiasm was at once so sincere and amusing that Annie couldn't help smiling.

That was how Iain found her—playing chess with Wentworth and surrounded by his officers, her golden braid hanging over her shoulder, a smile upon her face. He had not expected to find her enjoying herself. Hot rage burned in his gut, overcoming his pain and lingering dizziness.

"You wait until she's wi'out protection, and then you take her. The price was paid, Wentworth. You had no right!"

"Iain!" The blood leeched from Annie's face.

Everyone but Wentworth gaped at him in surprise, which swiftly became outrage.

"Now see here, Major!" Cooke spluttered, leaping to his feet. "No one seeks to dishonor Miss Burns!"

Iain heard the two redcoats who'd been guarding the door approach from behind. They'd regained their feet faster than he'd imagined. Clearly he was weaker than he realized.

"My apologies, Colonel. We tried to stop him, but he—"

"Major MacKinnon. What an unexpected pleasure." Wentworth dismissed the redcoats with a flick of his lace-clad wrist. "Won't you join us?"

"Nay, I willna bloody join you." Then he looked into Annie's wide eyes and switched to Gaelic. *"Tiùgainn leam, a dh'Annaidh!"* Come away, Annie!

She stood as if to obey, then turned her gaze to Wentworth.

This time Iain spoke English so Wentworth would understand. "You dinnae need his consent, for God's sake! You are no' bound to him."

Still she hesitated. "Iain, I—"

"Nor is she bound to you, major." Wentworth stood, took her hand, bowed over it, touched it to his lips. "You are free to go with him, if that is what you wish, Miss Burns. Thank you for a most enjoyable evening. I can't remember the last time anyone has even come close to besting me."

If Iain had had any doubts as to Wentworth's intentions toward Annie, those doubts vanished. He could smell the heat in Wentworth's blood from across the room.

Disgust rose in Iain's throat. He strode forward, forced Cooke out of his way with a glance, then took Annie by the arm and pulled her after him.

She followed without struggle, harrying him with questions. "Are you daft? What are you doin' out of bed? Why do you risk Lord William's wrath again?"

The sound of Wentworth's Christian name on her lips pushed him to the brink. *"Uist!"*

"Iain, he didna touch me!"

Morgan blocked his path. "Dinnae take your rage out on the lass. This was no' by her choice."

But Iain could think only of the smile he'd seen on her face. She'd looked willing enough. "Move aside."

He pushed past his brother, his strength sustained by raw anger. Ignoring her protests, he led her out of the fort, across the bridge, past his startled men to his cabin. Then he pulled her through the door and barred it behind him.

"Iain, please! You are no' yourself!"

Later he would not be able to say why he did it. Perhaps he was out of his mind from pain. Or mad with jealousy. He'd wanted to berate her, to rage at her, to throttle her. Instead, he found himself kissing her, marking inch by soft inch the lush territory another man had tried to claim from him.

Annie had hoped he would kiss her again, but not like this. Not out of anger. Not when he was so badly hurt. She turned her head away, pushed her hands against his chest, tried to free herself from his iron grip. "Please, Iain! You can barely stand!"

He took her chin in one hand, forced her to meet his gaze, his eyes as dark as midnight. "Did he kiss you like this?"

"He didna—!" She tried to answer.

But Iain thrust his tongue into her mouth, cut off her words.

The sweet delight of it drove all else from her mind, and for a moment she lost herself in him, in the burning crush of his lips, in the hot glide of tongue against tongue. A fluttering warmth rose from deep in her belly, and she could not help kissing him back, meeting him stroke for stroke, pressing herself against him, her body seeking something from his.

Then, remembering, she tried to pull away from him. "Iain, you shouldna be—"

But he twisted his hands in her hair, forced her head back, and laid bare the column of her throat. "Did he taste you like this?"

His teeth and tongue nipped and licked the sensitive skin beneath her ear, making her skin tingle, sending a sultry shiver of pleasure down her spine.

She moaned, clung to him, her hands fisted in his shirt. "He didna . . . he didna touch me at all!"

Without warning she was falling, being borne back onto his bed, his weight upon her. She felt a trill of alarm, but it melted under the onslaught of his lips and teeth and tongue.

"Did he touch you like this?" He captured her wrists in one big hand and pinioned them above her head. Then he yanked down her bodice, freed her breasts and began to suckle her.

"Mercy!"

Oh, God, but it felt good! His tongue licked fire against her nipples. His lips drew them to taut points that ached and burned. His teeth grazed and pinched them, making her gasp. Heat flared in her belly, turned to liquid between her thighs. She heard herself whimper, felt herself arch against him, and knew she could not resist him.

Iain heard her soft moans and felt her writhe with desire beneath him as he spent his rage on her flesh. But as the sweet taste of her soothed his anger, pain and exhaustion set in. And finally her words pierced his mind.

He didna touch me at all.

Wentworth had not tried to seduce her?

With that realization came an understanding of what he had just done.

He lifted his head, looked into Annie's green eyes and hated himself for the uncertainty he saw there. "Forgi'e me, lass!"

But ere darkness could claim him, he discerned another emotion in her eyes—desire.

Her body trembling with unfamiliar sensations, Annie felt Iain's head relax against her bared breast, heard the slow, steady sound of his breathing and knew he was utterly spent.

But so was she, and before the heat in her blood had cooled, she was fast asleep.

William closed his eyes as the pleasure of climax overtook him, and imagined it was Miss Burns's slick heat that gripped his cock. He thrust hard into his hand to finish it—once, twice, three times. Then he lay still for a moment, felt his body ease.

He reached for a cloth and wiped away his seed, which lay in pools of creamy white against his abdomen. He would have rather left it deep inside Miss Burns, but he'd long ago promised himself he'd not squander his wealth by spawning a brigade of bastards as his older brother had done. He'd not be able to call himself honorable if he allowed his get to starve on the streets, but he did not wish to take coin or property from his legitimate issue in order to support his by-blows.

Not that he was a monk—far from it. But he preferred to take his pleasure with a married woman who could blame her condition on her husband and add another blessing to his household, rather than looking to William for support. If the woman were already with child, so much the better. He couldn't plant a field that had already been sown.

Despite his vow to himself, he'd found it unusually difficult to proceed with his original plan tonight and *not* take Miss Burns to his bed. Knowing she'd come to him assuming he would rape her had been more than a little arousing. But he preferred a willing woman to an unwilling conquest, and Miss Burns had been deeply unhappy at the thought of lying in his bed.

For the moment.

William stood, crossed the room naked, and added more wood to the fire. Then he poured himself a cognac, savoring its aroma as the snifter slowly warmed in his hand.

He'd bet a chest of Spanish silver she was untouched. Annie Burns radiated the ripe innocence of a virgin bride. As to why MacKinnon had not plucked her yet—that William could only credit to MacKinnon's exaggerated Scottish sense of honor. William understood him well enough to know MacKinnon wouldn't debauch a woman he'd taken under his protection—at least not until he'd fought a long and arduous battle with himself.

Given the way he'd kissed her before his flogging—staking his claim to her before every man in the fort—he was already deep into that battle. William would enjoy watching him lose, just as he'd enjoyed watching MacKinnon charge into his home like an angry bull this evening. That the man could still stand on his feet after one hundred lashes was nothing short of astonishing. Iain MacKinnon had the endurance of stone.

William sipped his cognac, his mind drifting back to Miss Burns—if that was truly her name. As he'd watched her tonight, he'd grown more certain he'd seen her before—and that she was not who she said she was.

He'd set out the bait so as not to make her wary, then watched her respond. Though she'd wanted him to believe she did not possess refined table manners, he'd seen her shift her fork more than once from a proper hold to an improper one. Then, when he'd offered to pour her dessert wine, she'd reached immediately for the correct glass. And although she'd feigned ignorance of chess and had played poorly, her last move had been quite clever, taking him unawares.

In that moment when she'd captured his queen, her mask had dropped. Her gaze had met his, her eyes reflecting not a baseborn peasant's ignorance, but a well-bred young woman's intelligence—and more than a little panic. She'd slipped, and she'd known it.

But why would any young woman as fair and defenseless as she turn her back on privilege and choose to live a life of deprivation and hardship on the frontier? What was she running from? What was she hiding?

William smiled to himself, anticipating a fine game of wits. He was going to enjoy discovering Miss Burns's secrets—one by one.

Someone was pounding on the door.

At first Annie thought it a dream. She ignored it, tried to roll over and keep sleeping, but a heavy weight pinned her down.

Drowsy, she opened her eyes and gasped.

Iain lay atop her, asleep, his head upon her still-bare breast.

"Iain, open up, or we'll break the door down!" 'Twas Morgan.

In a panic lest Iain's brothers see her like this, she tried to slip out from beneath him without waking him, but it was too late.

He lifted his head, his brow furrowed with pain and irritation, and shouted toward the door. "Bide one bloody moment!"

She felt her face burn as his gaze met hers. "I'll let him in if you . . . if you can move."

A faint smile played across his pale face as he realized what he'd been lying upon, and he kissed her nipple. "A man couldna ask for a softer or finer pillow."

He gritted his teeth, raised himself off her, and sat on the edge of the bed.

The heat of a blush in her cheeks, she rose quickly, adjusted her gown and hurried to open the door.

"Thank you, Annie." Morgan strode through the door, followed by Connor.

And an Indian.

Annie's thoughts scattered as he strode toward her. Though some part of her knew he must be a friend of the MacKinnon brothers, she could not stop the panic that welled up inside her at the sight of him.

He was almost as tall as Iain, his hair long, straight and black as midnight and his skin dark and tanned. Apart from the bronze gorget that hung from his throat and the thin band of colorful beads that encircled his forehead, he wore only a leather breechclout with leggings, and seemed to Annie to be nearly naked. Markings like Iain's decorated the brown skin of his arms, chest and belly, but there was no paint on his face.

Morgan laid a reassuring hand on her arm. "Sorry, Joseph, but the lass has ne'er seen an Indian who wasna tryin' to kill her."

The Indian met her gaze with eyes as dark as night. Then he smiled, flashing white teeth. "So you're what all this trouble is about."

Chapter Sixteen

Annie looked first at the cloth and jar of fresh salve in her hand and then at Iain's raw, torn back, dreading what she must do. She knew how badly this concoction burned and couldn't imagine putting it on wounds as deep as Iain's. She did not want to cause him suffering, but she refused to let him grow sickly with fever.

Outside, a fiddle sang out the strains of a jig as the

Rangers settled down with their nightly ration of rum, but she scarce heard it.

"Are you ready, lass?" Morgan lay across Iain's legs so he would not thrash about and hurt someone.

Connor and Joseph each held an arm.

Iain was clearly furious, cursing Morgan. "You *neach dìolain,* I dinnae need to be held down! *Deog am fallus bhàrr tiadhain duine mhairbh!*"

The first part translated to "bastard," while the second seemed to suggest Morgan should suck the sweat off a dead man's . . . testicles.

"Aye, I'm ready." She dipped the cloth into the salve, then took a deep breath. "Forgi'e me, Iain."

Quickly, she spread the burning ointment across his back, starting at his shoulders and working her way down his flayed skin. She bent her mind upon her work, tried to ignore the way his body immediately tensed and arched beneath her hands, tried not to hear his groans.

But groans quickly turned to profanity. "Och, Christ!"

"Don't tell me you think this hurts." It was Joseph who jested with him.

Iain answered in kind, his voice forced between gritted teeth. "No more than . . . the touch of a feather. Holy Mary!"

Images from earlier in the evening flooded her mind. Iain storming, pale and furious, into Lord William's study. Iain trying to punish her with his kisses. Iain making her tremble, his mouth upon her breasts.

But other images came to her mind as well. Iain grinning to his men as he walked, shackled, toward the whipping post. The reassuring strength in his eyes. His body tensing with agony at each stroke of the lash.

'Twas the price he'd willingly paid for her life, though she was but a stranger to him.

She'd thought him a barbarian at first, and she'd been right. But there was honor in him—honor that went soul deep—and courage as strong as the roots of a mountain.

Honor and courage—if those weren't the traits of a gentleman, what were?

By the time she had finished rubbing the salve into his wounds, he was blessedly unconscious. Quickly she bandaged him, then she sat on the edge of his pallet, her legs suddenly unwilling to hold her, her hands trembling, her lungs bereft of breath.

She heard Morgan's voice as if it came from far away. "That's a good lass."

"You've the touch of a healer." That was Joseph.

"That ought to cure him—if it doesna kill him." Connor placed his big hand upon her shoulder, gave her a squeeze. "Our thanks."

Outside, the fiddle played on.

Still shaking, Annie looked at the jar in her hand and thought of the two Rangers still in the hospital. And she wondered.

Iain heard the honeyed sound of her voice.

Annie was humming.

He opened his eyes, found himself lying on his belly on his own bed. His back hurt horribly, and he felt weak as a newborn cub. His mouth once again tasted of laudanum, and he thought he remembered Annie coaxing him into swallowing a spoonful last night when he'd been half asleep, his mind clouded by pain.

Groggy from the tincture, he lifted his head, searched her out, found her sitting at his table stitching upon something.

His shirt.

There was naught wrong with it. Och, a wee tear under one arm. And at the left elbow. And that slash at the hem where he'd caught it while sheathing his blade. 'Twas not yet tattered enough to require sewing. Still, the sight of her mending something of his—such a wifely thing to do—stirred some forgotten longing inside him.

As if she sensed him watching her, she stopped humming

and looked up from her work. "You're awake. Are you thirsty?"

"Aye." His voice sounded like gravel.

She set her sewing aside, came to sit beside him, his tin cup in her hands. She held it to his lips and felt his forehead for fever with a cool, soft hand.

He drank every sweet drop. "More."

Twice more he drained the cup before his thirst was quenched.

"Lieutenant Cooke was here earlier to see you moved back to the hospital. Killy held him at bay until your brothers drove him off."

"Good. I'll no' be goin' back there but to check on my men." He glanced at the parchment window, saw it was well past dawn. He needed to get onto his feet and back to his duties. "If you'd hand me my shirt, lass, I'll be risin'."

She stood, put his shirt behind her back. "You'll be doin' no such thing, Iain MacKinnon. You're to stay in bed and rest."

He felt a spark of irritation. "Wentworth's orders?"

"Nay. Mine."

He glared at her. "I am no' an invalid."

She raised a single eyebrow. "You are no' fit to be rangin' about."

Gritting his teeth against the pain, he sat. "A wee lassie like you cannae stop me."

She backed up against the door as if to block it. "You willna leave this cabin. I'll tie you to your bed if I must."

He chuckled, amused by the idea of her even trying to restrain him. "Does the notion of tyin' me down excite you, lass?"

The color drained from her face, and her eyes grew wide.

'Twas more than a virgin's modesty. For a moment there was real fear on her face.

"Annie?"

Then, as if it had never been there, the fear vanished, and

she glared at him. "Lie down, or I'll fetch Joseph and your brothers to come sit on you again."

Letting the matter go for the moment, he glared back. "Very well. But if I'm to be a prisoner, who shall keep me company, feed me, and see to my needs?"

She lifted her chin. "As 'tis for my sake you're sufferin', I shall."

He tried not to look pleased.

"Lift your arms." Annie knelt before him, forcing herself to keep her gaze upon the roll of linen in her hands as she wrapped Iain's wounds in clean bandages. She did not want to notice his flat nipples. Or the dark curls on his chest. Or the way his muscles shifted as he moved. "Does this hurt?"

He sat on the edge of the bed, his dark hair pulled over one shoulder. "Do what you must, and dinnae fret."

Trying very hard not to cause him pain, she passed the roll behind his back—an action that required her to lean in close to him until her cheek almost pressed against his chest—then pulled it round to the front again. She could sense his gaze upon her, feel the warmth of his body, hear each slow, deep breath he drew.

Had she ever been as aware of any other man?

Nay. Never.

For a week she had cared for him, feeding him meals Killy brought from the kitchens, making him cups of strengthening tea, urging him to at least take laudanum at night so he could sleep free of pain. To pass the time, she'd mended his clothing and cleaned his cabin, leaving his side only briefly each day to tend his men in the hospital. At night, she'd slept on a pallet, warm before his fire.

And though he was badly injured and she knew he suffered, she had the sense he was enjoying it all. Perhaps it was the way his gaze seemed to follow her. Or the male satisfaction on his face. Or the deep purr in his voice when he spoke to her.

Still, he had not touched her, not like he had that night,

and a part of her was disappointed. She hadn't forgotten the hot taste of his tongue in her mouth or the feel of his kiss upon her breasts. In truth, she thought of it far too often. And every time she did, her belly grew tight and her blood hot.

'Twas maddening.

She passed the bandage roll behind his back again, taking care not to look into his eyes. As she drew it tight and tied it off, she felt him stiffen. "If you'd let me give you laudanum during the day, this wouldna hurt."

He grazed her cheek with his knuckles, leaving a trail of fire on her skin. "There are more important things than cheating pain, lass. I willna render myself weak and witless when I should be awake."

She knew he was thinking of Lord William. But she felt certain Lord William was not seeking to bed her. The look of haughty disdain on his face when she'd misunderstood his intent that night told her as much.

Please tell me you didn't think I brought you here for some indecent purpose.

Yet Iain seemed to think Lord William might carry her away.

It wasn't that Annie trusted Lord William or thought him honorable. She'd seen how he liked to play with people's lives when he'd tried to lure her into his bed in exchange for showing Iain mercy—and then had forced her to rethink her decision with Iain's men watching. But he'd already had his chance to defile her, and he'd acted as if the idea offended him. Surely any curiosity he'd felt regarding her was waning by now. If her taking his queen in that impulsive and reckless move hadn't roused his suspicions, nothing would.

"You force yourself to suffer needlessly, Iain. Lord William is no' comin' for me today, or ever. I am naught but an annoyance to him."

He took her chin firmly in his grasp and forced her to meet his gaze. There was anger in his eyes—and a dark edge of warning in his voice. "Listen to me, Annie. Stay far away from him. He is a deceiver and will stop at naugh' to take what he wants. And he wants you. You are an innocent and cannae see it, so you must be guided by me. I ken him and his devious ways better than most men."

Annie heard Iain's words but found herself staring at his lips, wishing for all the world he would kiss her. "You hate him because he is English."

Iain watched her eyes darken, watched her gaze drop to his mouth, and he knew she wanted him to kiss her. He'd been fighting the urge to do just that for seven long days, pain helping to dull his desire. He willed his body not to respond now, for he knew he must tell her. For her sake, she must be told what kind of man Wentworth was.

"Nay, Annie, I dinnae hate him for bein' English. I hate him for makin' me his slave."

And so he told her how he and his brothers had gone in to Albany so he could prepare his mother's ring for Jeannie's finger. He told her how he'd aided a whore he'd seen being beaten on the street while, unbeknownst to him, Wentworth watched from his window above. He told her how the man he'd bested had been found dead in the street the next morning and how he and his brothers had been falsely accused of killing him. He told her how, after sitting in gaol for several hours, they'd been led in chains before Wentworth, who had offered Iain a devil's bargain—command a company of Rangers and fight for the British, or die on the gallows with his brothers beside him.

"Morgan and Connor would no' see me go to war wi'out them to guard my back, and so they signed on, leaving our farm to fall into ruin. Every day since then, I have done Wentworth's bidding, ending other men's lives to save my own."

He felt Annie's fingertips caress his cheek, met her gaze, found her eyes soft with a woman's compassion. Then she spoke words he'd once said to comfort her. "There is no shame in tryin' to live another day. Is there no one who will listen—Lord William's commanding officer? The colony's governor?"

"Who will believe a Catholic Scot over their king's own grandson? Nay, lass."

She rose from her knees and sat beside him on the bed, her hands buried in the folds of her skirts, her face troubled. "And Jeannie. D-did you marry her?"

He chuckled at her poorly concealed curiosity—and was surprised to find that her question caused him no anguish. "Nay, we were never wed. Her father didna wish her to marry a soldier—or a man in trouble with the English. I asked her to wait until war's end, when my name would be restored, and she said she would. But within three months, she'd taken a farmer lad from Ulster as her husband. They were killed a few months later by a war party."

She laid her hand upon his arm, and he saw tears glisten in her eyes. "I am so sorry, Iain. Lord William is, indeed, a hard and hateful man to have stolen so much from you. You must spend each day wonderin' what your life might have been like, thinkin' of children you might have fathered, if only . . ."

It shook him that she understood him so deeply. But as he sat beside her, surrounded by her scent and the warmth of her concern, he found he could no longer remember Jeannie's face.

He brushed the braid from her shoulder, slipped his arm round her waist, and pulled her across his lap.

She gasped, looked up at him with startled eyes.

He ran his thumb over the fullness of her lower lip. "All I'm wonderin' today, *mo leannan,* is how I've gone so long wi'out doin' this."

Then he took her lips with his.

With a whimper, Annie gave herself up to his kiss, welcoming the sweet invasion of his tongue, melting into the hard wall of his chest. Heat licked through her, flared deep in her belly, leaving her weak, reckless, breathless. "Iain!"

He growled, took the kiss deeper, ravished her mouth, until her lips tingled and ached and there was nothing in her world but him. The sharp stubble of his beard. The hard curve of his shoulders. The spicy male scent of him.

She knew she should end it, for she could not lie with him. But she hadn't the will. Not when his lips strayed to the swells of her breasts. Not when he loosed her bodice, baring her tight, eager nipples to his hungry mouth. Not when his hand slipped around her hip to cup and squeeze her bum. Not until she felt him grab her skirts and lift them in impatient fistfuls.

"N-nay! Iain, stop!" She pushed his hand away. "I cannae!"

With a moan, he pressed his forehead to hers, his eyes squeezed shut as if in agony, his breathing ragged. "Och, Annie, a man could die for want of you!"

Her body shaking, she lay cradled in his arms, searching for an excuse. "M-my maidenhead is all I have to give a man. I-I cannae . . ."

He shook his head, his forehead still pressed against hers, his lashes dark against his cheeks. "You are far more than your maidenhead, Annie, but you dinnae need to explain. I have nothin' to offer a woman, and you deserve the love and protection of a husband. I wouldna send you to your marriage bed feelin' shame."

But it was his sweet understanding that shamed her. For the truth was not that she was clinging to her virginity, but rather to the tatters of a lie.

Annie lay awake that night, her body burning almost as much as her conscience. She should have told him. She should have told Iain the truth. If anyone would understand and believe her, surely he would. So why had she said nothing?

Certainly, he knew what it was like to be falsely accused of a crime. He knew what it was like to have his life taken from him and overturned. He knew what it was like to be forced unjustly to serve another.

But there was more to her plight than that.

You're an Argyll Campbell, Annie.

To tell him the truth, she would have to tell him her name. There wasn't a Catholic Scot alive who didn't hate the Argyll Campbells.

Would he forgive her? Or would he hate her?

Did it matter?

After all he'd done for her, Iain deserved to know the truth.

But did she have the courage to tell him?

Major MacKinnon refused to return to the hospital. Within a week, he refused to stay in bed, whereupon his men greeted him as if he were a conquering hero.

"As I said, he has the endurance of stone." William sipped his cognac as he listened to Lieutenant Cooke's report.

"Dr. Blake, who was profuse in his praise, said Miss Burns cared for the major quite competently, freeing him to see to his other patients." There was an amusing note of pride in Cooke's voice. "The doctor said she also helped tend the two Rangers still in the hospital and shows a natural skill for nursing the sick. Apparently she can read just as well as he can."

William had already heard this from Dr. Blake himself and had found it remarkable and yet somehow not surprising at all. Miss Burns was a young woman of uncommon ability. Not common at all. "Now that the major is on his feet again, perhaps it's time I decided what to do with the lovely Miss Burns. She claims to have no family and no place to go. Yet we have regulations here at Fort Elizabeth."

"No women in the fort apart from officers' wives and . . . er, camp followers, sir."

"Quite correct." William considered the courses of action open to him and found each more amusing than the last. "Summon both the major and Miss Burns to dine with us tomorrow evening."

"I am your servant, my lord." Lieutenant Cooke saluted smartly and was gone.

William took another sip and then smiled. Tomorrow evening was going to be every bit as enjoyable as a challenging game of chess. Perhaps even more so. For tomorrow evening he would face two opponents—the enigmatic and beautiful Miss Burns and the formidable and volatile Major MacKinnon.

"You'll take my cabin. I'll move in wi' Morgan for now." A part of Iain couldn't believe he was saying this, not when he wanted so desperately to be in bed with her.

Need for her consumed him, destroying his sleep, leaving him ill-tempered. Her femininity assailed him, pulled at him from across the room, called to him even when she was sleeping. With his pain no longer strong enough to distract him, how long would it be before his lust for her overthrew his honor?

She stood before his hearth, looking up at him from beneath sooty lashes, light from the fire sparking gold in her hair. "That is kind of you, Iain, but I dinnae want to put you out of your home. I've already been trouble enough. Dr. Blake said I could stay in the storeroom at the hospital until Lord William arranges for me to be taken back east."

"Nay, lass. You'll be safer here. These men are under my command. No' a one of them would dare to touch you, and if I order them to guard you wi' their lives, they will."

She glanced away, her face troubled. "I would have no more Rangers perish for my sake. I've brought death and suffering enough already. I'll stay at the hospital, where I'm no bother."

He wanted to tell her that none of that was her fault. Any debt she owed the Rangers she'd repaid many times over with her care not only of him, but of Brendan, who'd kept his leg and was now strong enough to hobble about on oxter staffs, and Conall, whose fever had finally broken.

"You'll stay here. You are no' safe so near Wentworth."

She touched a hand to his arm. "I know Lord William is a cruel man, but he is no' after getting' me into his bed, Iain. I'm certain he doesna spare a single thought for me."

How could she be so blind?

"Then why has he asked you to dine wi' him again?"

"He's asked us *both* to dine wi' him. Lieutenant Cooke said he wishes to discuss what's to be done wi' me."

"You dinnae ken him as I do. You'll stay in Ranger camp where my men and I can watch over you."

She gave him a beseeching look. "Why do you wish me to stay here in your cabin when we both know what might happen if I do?"

Her words struck with the force of a blow, and he understood. "You trust Wentworth to keep his hands off you more than you trust me, aye?"

She glared at him. "That is no' what I said!"

"Och, it is." It did nothing to blunt his anger that he doubted himself as much as she did. "But hear this! You are no' home in Rothesay, but on the American frontier in the midst of a war. You are under my protection and, therefore, under the force of my command. If I say you shall stay in my cabin, then, by God, you'll do just that, and I'll no' hear another word!"

Chapter Seventeen

Annie woke the next morning feeling truly rested for the first time in what seemed like ages, having slept on a bed and not on the floor. She glanced toward the parchment window, saw the faint glow of dawn. Outside, she could hear the Rangers already at work. From the fort in the distance came the sound of drums as Regulars marched over the parade grounds at morning muster.

Annie rose, added the last bit of wood to the fire, then poured water into a large wooden bowl and washed her face. Next she combed the tangles from her hair and tied it back with a pink ribbon. Then she changed into a clean shift and put on the other gown Iain had bought for her, the one with broad pink and ivory stripes. It fit as well as the first, though it was cut lower in the bodice. If she'd had a kerchief or shawl, she'd have covered herself for modesty's sake, but lacking either, she put on her cloak, took up the water pail, and stepped out into the morning.

The breeze was warm with just a hint of spring, and the eastern sky glowed pink with the promise of a new day. Had it not been for a lingering sadness and frustration at Iain's overbearing manner, she might have felt truly happy. Last night he'd acted as if she were one of his men, callously ordering her about until she'd been tempted to salute.

Did he truly think he had the right to command her? What had she done to merit his rage? Why did he insist on her remaining in his cabin when they both knew where that would lead?

She still hadn't found the courage to tell him the truth. Several times it had been on the tip of her tongue, but the moment had not yet seemed right for it. And just last night she'd heard Dougie play his fiddle and sing a song about rebellion, cursing her clan for traitors and lamenting the defeat of the Highlands.

Couldn't she be Annie Burns forever?

She stood for a moment on the cabin's doorstep, looking about at her new world. Though she'd been at the fort for more than a week now, she'd spent most of it in Iain's cabin or Dr. Blake's hospital and had been too worried about Iain to take any notice of her surroundings.

Around her the camp bustled. Near the kitchens, several men chopped and stacked firewood. Others sat before their cabins and repaired snowshoes or stitched leather into belts and leggings and moccasins. Still others cleaned their weapons. In the distance, she saw several on the river fishing, while two more crossed the bateau bridge, carrying a slain deer on a pole between them.

Then she saw them—Indian lodges. Rounded and covered with mats of tree bark or reeds, they stood on the north end of the island not far beyond the rows of Ranger cabins.

There must have been thirty of them—shelter for Joseph's warriors, Annie realized. Never had she heard of white men and Indians living so close together, and a frisson of fear chased itself down her spine. But she remembered the kindness in Joseph's eyes, the deep concern he'd shown for Iain, the way he'd called him "brother."

I was adopted into the Muchquauh, the Bear Clan, of the Muhheconneok people when I reached manhood. The grannies got so tired of my bein' forever at their fires eatin' their food that they decided to make me part of the family so they could quit treatin' me like a guest and send me out to fish.

Joseph's people were not just allies of the British, but kin to Iain and his brothers. They would not harm her.

She shut the door to Iain's cabin behind her and set out for the river. She needed to fetch water for washing and more wood for the fire. She hoped to wash her gown and shift and perhaps get a hot bath and some breakfast. Then she would visit Brendan and Conall as she had promised them.

She'd taken but a few steps when she saw several Rangers, some of whom she recognized and some of whom she did not, striding toward her. Startled, she froze.

"Bugger off, the lot of you!" Killy appeared from behind one of the cabins and dismissed the others with an impatient wave of his hand. "No pretty woman should have to suffer the company of Scots when there's an Irishman at hand."

In the sunlight and up close, Annie got her first real look at him. He was not much taller than she, thin and sinewy, his head topped by the same blue Scotch bonnet he always wore. His skin was red and leathery, and he seemed to be made of scars. One circled his neck, as if he'd been garroted. Another ran down his right cheek, tugging at the corner of his mouth. A dark circle on his left hand could only have come from a lead ball. But the smile on his face was bright and cheerful.

"Good morn', Killy."

"A good mornin' to you! Is there somethin' you're after, miss?"

"I had hoped to fetch water and the washtub for laundry and perhaps a bath."

"Another one?" He winked and took the pail from her. Then he turned to the handful of Rangers who still stood there, watching. "Did you not hear her, you pack of half-wits? Robert, bring wood, and stack it high. Dougie, carry water from the river until she tells you to stop. McHugh, get to the kitchens and fetch a breakfast fit for this fair creature. I shall carry the washtub. Well, boys, don't be keepin' her waitin'!"

The men nearly bumped into one another in their haste to do as they'd been told.

Charmed and amused, Annie couldn't help smiling. "They're a helpful lot."

"They're lazy as hounds, but they're grateful to you, miss. Morgan and Connor told us all you've done for Mack—aye, and for Brendan and Conall, too. If there's aught you need, just ask a Ranger."

When Iain saw her, she was sitting on a chair just outside his cabin, sipping something from a cup. She might as well have been seated on a throne. A dozen or so of his men sat on their haunches around her, staring up at her with adoring eyes, so enthralled they did not see him and made no effort to get back to their duties.

Iain could scarce blame them. Holy Mary, she was bonnie, her golden hair tied back in a ribbon, her skin like cream in the morning light. He'd spent a restless night thinking of her, tossing about on his makeshift pallet of pine boughs until Morgan had all but ordered him out of the cabin.

Och, for the love of God, Iain! If you want her so badly, then bed her or wed her! But dinnae keep me awake wi' your randy tossin' about!

Bed her or wed her.

Would that he could.

Killy was amusing her with the story of how he'd come to be in America. It was Killy's favorite story to tell. "Thinkin' me dead, they cut me from the gallows and threw me in a wooden box. Imagine their fright when on the way to the churchyard I started hollerin' and a-screamin' to get out!"

His tale was greeted by hoots of laughter from the men, a gasp from Annie.

"Mercy!" She held slender fingers to her lips, her green eyes wide in amazement. "Oh, Killy! They truly hanged you?"

Killy bared his scarred neck. "Aye, they did. But I'm one Irishman they could not kill."

"Did they not take you back to the gallows and try again?"

"Nay, miss. The vicar decided it was an act of God that spared my life, so they put me on a leaky ship and sent me here."

Cam grinned. "'Twas more likely an act of the Devil. He judged your soul too black for hell and spat you out!"

More laughter.

But Iain had seen enough. "It's a good thing the war is over, isn't it, boys? Otherwise, you might have chores to do."

Instantly his men were on their feet, and a few of them had the good sense to scatter.

"Mack." Killy faced him, not a trace of shame on his scarred face. "Good to see you up and about. The boys and I were seein' to it she had water and firewood to last the day."

Iain glanced at the wood pile, saw it was high enough to last until the Second Coming. He fought to keep his temper in check. "When 'tis your duty to dote on Miss Burns, I'll tell you."

"There's no need to get cankersome. A good day to you, miss." Killy gave Annie a tug of his forelock and sauntered off, whistling.

Iain glared after him. "Bloody Irish!"

"Why are you so cross wi' them? They were only tryin' to be helpful."

Iain looked down into Annie's furious and lovely face. But anger already had the best of him. "We're in the midst of a war, Annie. I cannae have my men distracted from their duty by a pretty set of petticoats."

She gave an outraged gasp. "A pretty set of . . . ! Is that what I am to you?"

He might have taken those words back had he not looked down at that moment and seen the bodice of her gown—or what little there was of it.

The vigor that had animated his tongue seemed to drain southward to his cock. His mouth opened, but nothing came out, while his erection stood at spirited attention.

"I've done naught to deserve your wrath, Major MacKinnon, and I willna stand here and bear your insults!" In a flounce of pink-striped skirts, she vanished inside, slammed the door to his own cabin in his face, and drew the string in.

"You cannae keep me out, Annie!"

Her quavering voice answered him, and he knew she was in tears. "Then b-break the d-door down like the b-barbarian I always thought you were!"

Barbarian? She thought him a barbarian?

And because he knew he was frightfully close to proving he was exactly that, he turned his back on his own cabin and strode away.

Annie spent her afternoon reading to Conall and the other patients and helping Dr. Blake, who had to leave several times to tend to a "camp follower." She was not certain what sort of military rank that was, but she'd felt both touched and pleased when Dr. Blake told her he was leaving his other patients in her hands.

"Have you heard, Miss Burns?" Conall asked as she wrestled with the pages of a newspaper. "They're sendin' me to Albany."

She looked over at him, surprised. "Albany? Why?"

"The doctor says I'm strong enough to travel and that I'll heal better there."

She smiled, happy for his good news. "Shall I write to you?"

"There will be no need, miss. Why, have you no' heard? You're comin' wi' me." His face lit up with a grin.

She felt her stomach sink.

Albany.

She could not go to Albany. Master Hawes had registered her indenture there. If the sheriff saw her, he would surely recognize her.

She willed herself to stay calm. "Where did you hear this, Conall?"

"Why, from Dr. Blake, of course. He says Wentworth has to send you on to Albany sooner or later, so he might as well send you wi' me."

Now she knew why Lord William wanted to see her. "I'd hoped to go to New York."

"Well, then, it's settled!" Conall's smile grew brighter. "The road to New York starts in Albany."

William couldn't remember ever having been more amused.

His dinner guests had arrived barely speaking to one another. Miss Burns, whose bruises were healed and who looked lovelier than he remembered, was pretending to be a wee crofter lass while ignoring the man for whom she'd so recently fallen to her knees. Major MacKinnon, meanwhile, sat in brooding silence, glowering at everyone, but most especially at the woman for whom he'd risked his life and taken one hundred lashes.

Clearly their lust for one another was stronger than William had imagined—and yet unsatisfied. Why that should please him, he did not know, unless some part of him wished Miss Burns for himself. And if he did? He certainly wasn't the only man to feel that way.

William's officers, who completed the evening's delightful dramatis personae, were so besotted with Miss Burns that they were blind to the jealous rage they fueled in the man who sat beside her. Lieutenant Cooke, in particular, seemed to want to court danger, leaning close to Miss Burns, laying his hand over hers, inviting her to tour the battlements with him—an outlandish offer William would have to rescind.

From where William sat, it was not a question of whether

the evening would devolve into tempers and perhaps even violence, but rather a question of when.

"My favorite of Master Shakespeare's plays is *Romeo and Juliet*, in which Juliet takes poison, and grief-stricken Romeo slays himself with his dagger in her tomb," offered Lieutenant Cooke, apparently unaware that a crofter's daughter could hardly be expected to have a refined appreciation of the plays of William Shakespeare.

Miss Burns smiled. " 'Tis Romeo who takes poison and Juliet who slays herself with his dagger when she finds no poison left for her."

William did not miss the fleeting look of surprise on Major MacKinnon's face or the way the major's gaze seemed to measure the woman beside him. So MacKinnon was aware of the inconsistencies in her manner, as well.

Lieutenant Cooke frowned. "Oh, yes, I believe you're right, Miss Burns. How could I have confused the two?"

" 'Tis likely you're thinkin' of the drug she takes to feign death."

Cooke smiled. "Ah, yes. Of course."

"Your acquaintance with literature is most impressive, Miss Burns." William saw wariness cloud her eyes and knew she'd just realized she'd made another mistake. "The doctor tells us you read with every bit as much skill as he."

"Oh, Dr. Blake speaks most highly of you." Lieutenant Cooke beamed. "Just this morning he told me how grateful he was for your assistance of late."

"He is too kind." She worried her lower lip, her pretty face seeming suddenly troubled. Then she met William's gaze. "My lord, might I speak on the subject of my future, for it touches on my work at Dr. Blake's hospital."

William saw Major MacKinnon's body stiffen. "Certainly, Miss Burns."

"I wish to remain at Fort Elizabeth. I find—"

"Are you daft! This place is no' fittin' for a lass. You'll go to Albany, and soon!" Major MacKinnon hadn't spoken two words all night. His outburst now startled everyone—and pleased William immensely.

"I don't believe she was addressing you, Major." William cast the major a reproving glance before settling his gaze on Miss Burns. "However, I'm afraid in this instance I must agree with the major, Miss Burns. We are at war, and Fort Elizabeth is but miles away from an enemy that would freeze your marrow. Besides, what could you do here to compensate His Majesty for his care of you?"

She seemed nervous and was clearly trying not to look at the major. "I had hoped Dr. Blake might permit me to work for him, Colonel. He did tell Lieutenant Cooke he was grateful for—"

The major gave a snort. "And what will you do, Annie, the first time you have to hold a screamin' man down so the doctor can cut off his leg—or the first time a soldier returns from battle wi' his skull blown open and his entrails draggin' on the earth?"

She paled slightly, but did not back down. "I didna say it would be easy, my lord, but I should like to try."

William saw the cold fury in the major's eyes, watched him take a swallow of wine, and felt the thrill of treading on dangerous ground. "I find your proposal most interesting, Miss Burns. However, there is another problem. My own rules prohibit women at Fort Elizabeth, except for officers' wives or camp followers."

She looked perplexed. "Camp followers are women?"

The major gave another snort, this time spewing wine across the tablecloth. "Aye, they're women."

"Perhaps I can be a camp follower and learn to do what they do."

William thought his officers would choke to death on their laughter, so valiantly did they try to hold it back.

But the major didn't bother to spare Miss Burns's feelings. He guffawed. "Och, I've no doubt you could learn, lass, and be quite skilled at it."

Lieutenant Cooke thrust back his chair and stood. "Take back those words, Major! I will not sit by while you dishonor Miss Burns!"

"Sit down, lad, and shut your bloody gob!" A muscle clenched in the major's jaw.

Apparently judging survival the better part of valor, the lieutenant slowly resumed his seat, his face as red as his uniform.

Miss Burns turned her gaze to William, her stunning green eyes filled with confusion—and apprehension. "P-please, my lord, what are camp followers?"

Delighted at the precarious way things were unfolding, William started to answer, but the major beat him to it.

"They're whores, lass. They service the men."

Miss Burns's face turned a charming shade of scarlet. "Mercy!"

"One of the vices of any army, I'm afraid." If William could have barred prostitutes from the fort without facing a mutiny, he would have. They carried disease and bred depravity.

"So I can stay at the fort only if I marry an officer or sell myself to your men." Her voice quavered slightly. "That doesna seem fair."

William could tell she was angry, but at whom—him or Major MacKinnon?

Enchanted by her innocence, William couldn't resist. "There's rather more to the rules, I'm afraid. In order to protect my men, any unmarried woman hoping to remain at the fort must first be examined for the . . . and et cetera."

When she didn't comprehend this commonly accepted polite way of referring to the deadly disease, Lieutenant Cooke leaned forward and whispered, "The pox, miss."

But the major, ever tactful, blared it out. "Syphilis, lass."

Her face turned an even deeper shade of crimson.

"I must admit I've never been in this predicament before, Miss Burns. I shall have to think on it before I make a decision. Perhaps if you can offer proof of your virtue or find a husband . . ." William let his voice trail off, held up his hand to silence his officers' outraged objections.

"H-how does one offer such proof?"

The major met William's gaze, his eyes filled with undisguised hatred. "You lie on your back, while the doctor tosses up your skirts and spreads your thighs to see if your maidenhead is intact."

Miss Burns was on her feet, the expression of utter shock on her face surely proof enough for every man at the table that she was still a virgin. She was visibly shaken and trembling, and William was surprised to find himself almost regretting having pushed matters this far.

She met his gaze, lifted her chin. "I am no' a whore, my lord, nor will I bare myself in so shameful a fashion to anyone!"

Chapter Eighteen

Annie threw her napkin on the table, then turned and fled down the hall, out the door and into the night, heedless of men's stares and the tears that spilled down her cheeks. Chased by her own fears, feeling trapped, angry, panicked, she ran.

They were going to send her to Albany! She couldn't go back there! She couldn't risk losing her newly found freedom. Nor could she spread her thighs for the doctor lest he see her brand. If he discovered her secret, she'd be left with no choice but to trust Lord William with the truth, and Lord William would surely contact her uncle. And then God save her!

"Annie!"

She heard Iain call for her, picked up her skirts and ran faster.

How could she ever have thought him honorable? The

man was an ill-mannered beast! When he hadn't sought to wound her with his boorish silence, he'd done his best to disgrace and humiliate her!

"Annie, for God's sake!"

Out the first gate she ran, across the wooden bridge, through the breech in the second wall and past the rows of canvas tents.

"Blast it, Annie!" He was not far behind her now.

She knew she could not escape him, but she did not care. She ran even faster, driven by hurt and rage and desperation. Through the outer wall she ran and toward the bateau bridge.

Strong arms shot out, caught her, held her fast. "Satan's arse, lass! What the bloody hell has gotten into you!"

"What has gotten into me? You're the one who behaved like an animal!" She kicked and struggled to free herself, but her strength was no match for his.

"Do you enjoy playin' the coquette to Wentworth's officers? Are you hopin' to ensnare one? To them you're naugh' but a poor bonnie Highland lass, no matter how hard you try to fit in at their table! They'll bed you, lass, but there's no' a one of them will take you to wife!"

"How can you—? Oooh! Let . . . go . . . of . . . me!" Beyond fury, she redoubled her struggles. She felt him turn her in his arms and found herself pinned against him, looking up into angry eyes as dark as midnight.

And then he was kissing her.

Or she was kissing him.

The torrent of emotion inside her became a flood of reckless need. She had to taste him, had to feel him. She fisted her hands in his long hair to pull him closer, invaded his mouth with her tongue, even as he invaded hers.

He groaned, a deep, male sound that rumbled in his chest, then crushed her against him, lifting her off her feet. His lips were soft, hot, demanding, his body breathtakingly hard. Awareness shuddered through her, kindling her blood, setting her on fire.

Whistles. Shouts.

"Bend her over, Highlander!"

Crude words, bellowed from the ramparts, pierced the fog of her desire.

Och, I've no doubt you could learn, lass, and be quite skilled at it.

Annie wrenched herself from his arms and slapped him across the face as hard as she could. "You brute!"

His gaze hard upon her, he rubbed his cheek. "What are you after, Annie?"

"That's the sixth kiss you've stolen from me!"

"So you're keepin' a tally, are you, lass?" He grinned. "Forgi'e me for saying so, but it seems to me you stole that one right back! Or was that someone else's tongue in my mouth?"

Heat suffused her cheeks. "Ooh, you despicable swine!"

"That's a fine thing to call a man who saved your life!"

"At least Lieutenant Cooke is a gentleman!"

His eyes narrowed. "While I'm a barbarian, aye?"

Realizing what she'd said and seeing the fury on his face, she turned and dashed onto the bateau bridge. She'd taken but a few steps when the back of her hems caught on one of the boards, then ripped, sending her hurtling into the dark, rushing water.

The icy torrent swallowed her, cut off her scream.

Panicked and shocked by the staggering cold, she kicked, flailed with her arms, tried to get her head above water. But the current was too strong. As if the river were a living thing, it tossed her about, dragged her to the bottom and pushed her over stones, binding her skirts about her legs.

She forced her panic aside, ignored the burning of her lungs, and struggled to remove the heavy weight of her skirts, determined to stay alive until Iain could help her. But when she opened her eyes, she saw only swirling darkness.

No one can help you down here, Annie. The river is too swift, and he cannae see you.

Strangely, the thought did not frighten her. Already her

mind seemed sluggish, the world around her silent apart from the frantic thrumming of her heart. The water was cold, so cold her bones ached and her limbs grew stiff.

Was this what it was like to die?

With her last strength, she touched her feet to the rocky riverbed, bent her knees and pushed off.

Iain had seen her trip and was already running toward her when the river claimed her. "Dear God, Annie!"

He drew a deep breath and plunged after her into the frigid water. He'd swum plenty of rivers and knew to expect the heart-stopping cold and the violence of the current. What he hadn't foreseen was the utter darkness. Deprived of sunlight, the depths of the river were black as ink.

He could see nothing.

He surfaced, drew air into his lungs, searched around him for any sign of golden hair or pink-striped skirts. Seeing naught but rushing water, he took another deep breath and dove, letting the current push him along. She'd been in the water only seconds longer than he. Wherever the river had carried her, it would surely carry him. He searched for her until he thought his lungs would burst, but still he saw nothing.

Fear colder than the frigid water swept through him.

He took another deep breath and dove again.

Annie!

Her name was an anguished shout in his mind.

He knew he had only moments. If panic and lack of breath hadn't already killed her, the icy chill surely would. Even he, used to the elements as he was, could not take much more of the frigid water.

Then something like lace brushed over the fingers of his right hand. He grabbed it in his fist and realized it was not lace but hair.

He fought the current, kicked hard, forced himself deeper, holding fast to her long strands. And there she was, below him, sinking like a fallen angel toward the very bottom, borne down by the sodden weight of her gown.

Live, Annie! Mother of God, let her live!

He caught her about the waist and felt a heady rush of relief when her cold hand closed weakly and clumsily over his. She was still alive!

With renewed strength he kicked for the surface.

It seemed an eternity before he got their heads above water, each second bringing her closer to death. Iain gulped precious air into his lungs, heard Annie cough and gasp and cough again, the sound sweet to his ears. Aching from cold, he let the water carry them, using his free arm like a rudder and guiding them toward the river's edge.

His men lined the bank, and several ran out into the frigid water to help.

"Bloody hell, Mack!"

"I'll be buggered! He found her!"

"Is she breathin'?"

Amid the excited shouts, he heard Morgan's voice. "I've got her, Iain. Come here, Annie, sweet. We'll warm you."

Reluctantly, Iain released her shivering body, felt her precious weight lift from his arms. He tried to speak through chattering teeth, managed only two words. "S-sweat l-lodge."

"Aye. Joseph already has the fires goin'."

Strong arms pulled him to his feet, helped him up the sandy riverbank. He found it strangely hard to walk, his limbs rigid and clumsy, his body shaking violently. Someone put a blanket around his shoulders and thrust a flask of rum into his hands.

Nearby, Connor shouted, "McHugh, take your boys and find out what the bloody hell tripped her! I want it fixed before someone else falls in!"

Iain drank deeply from the flask, felt the rum burn a path to his stomach, then stumbled after Morgan toward Joseph's camp, his gaze never leaving the sodden striped skirts that spilled over his brother's arm.

* * *

"Wake up, *a leannan*." It was Iain again.

But Annie was so tired. "Let me be!"

"If I let you sleep, you'll die. Open your eyes and drink." His voice was stern, and he held something warm to her lips.

She sipped, swallowed, grimacing at the bitter taste.

From close beside her came a loud hissing sound, like soup boiling over onto hearthstones—once, twice, thrice, four times.

She willed herself to open her eyes—and saw utter darkness. "Iain!"

Strong arms held her closer. "Dinnae be afraid, lass. You're in Joseph's sweat lodge."

"I cannae see you!"

"Nor can I see you, for the flaps are down. But there's no more cause to fear the darkness of the lodge than there is the darkness of your mother's womb. 'Tis here Joseph and his warriors come to pray. He is pourin' water on heated stones to warm us."

"But I am no' cold."

"You're so cold you cannae feel it, but soon you will start to shiver. Now drink. We must warm you in every way we can—and quickly."

Iain was right. Soon she began to shiver uncontrollably and her body to ache as the river's chill worked its way out of her. She moaned through chattering teeth, drank when Iain told her to drink, took comfort in his strength.

She had no idea how much time had passed, but as she breathed in the hot, steamy air, her shivering began to subside and her mind to clear. Little by little, she became aware that Joseph was nearby, singing and beating on a drum, his words in a language she could not understand. Iain was singing with him, his voice deep and warm. She sat in Iain's lap, cradled in his arms, her head against his shoulder, the two of them wrapped in a soft, thick fur.

They were pressed skin to skin—and they were naked.

Perhaps it was the magic of Joseph's song, the ancient

rhythm of the drum, or the freedom of the concealing dark, but Annie did not feel afraid. As if in a dream, she lifted her hand, pressed it to Iain's bare chest, felt his heart leap at her touch, then slid her palm over his sweat-slick skin.

His muscles tensed, but he did not stop her, nor did his song falter.

Emboldened, she felt the heavy planes of his chest, the flat velvet of his nipples, the soft rasp of his chest hair, her fingers bumping his little wooden cross along the way. But it wasn't enough. As if with a mind of their own, her hands savored the iron curve of his shoulders, the muscles of his arms, the healing flesh of his back.

His breath came faster now, and he seemed to be forgetting the words. Something hard pressed against her hip—his sex.

Had she done that to him?

His lips caressed her temple, and he whispered, "You've warmed my blood, *a leannan*. Now 'tis my turn to warm yours."

She felt a flutter in her stomach at his words. Unable to see him, able only to feel, she waited, uncertain what he would do. But she did not wait long.

Slowly, so slowly, his hand brushed over her hip, smoothed circles over her belly, stroked her ribcage, seeking out her curves and hollows. Then it moved to caress the sensitive underside of her breasts, his callused fingers drawing tingles from her skin, sending sparks skittering through her belly.

She felt her nipples tighten as if eager for his touch, and knew she desired him.

This Highland barbarian. This Ranger. Iain.

A loud hiss. A burst of steam against hot stone.

He took the full weight of one breast in his hand, caught an aching nipple between his fingers, stretched it, plucked it. Something inside her clenched, as if he had plucked it, too, and honeyed heat pooled between her thighs. She moaned and pressed her breast deeper into his palm, wanting more, needing more.

And he obliged her, molding her breasts, shaping them, brushing her nipples with his callused palm, now quickly, now slowly, until her breasts felt swollen and heavy and the bliss was unbearable. But he wasn't finished.

Annie felt him thrust the fur aside, exposing her bare skin to the thick, hot, moist air. Steam beaded against her breasts, ran in rivulets down her belly to her damp curls below. Then his mouth closed over one nipple, and with lips and tongue and teeth he suckled her.

The delight of it had her breath coming in pants. Here in the dark, in the burning heat, she reveled in it, twining her fingers through his thick, wet hair, pressing him closer, arching to feed him more of herself.

He took what she offered, drawing her more deeply into his mouth, the tugging of his lips and tongue against her nipples a sweet torment, the heat between her thighs a throbbing ache.

Water hit hot rocks, the loud hiss covering Annie's whimpers.

Then his hand skimmed across the wet skin of her belly, over her hip, down to her damp curls. He whispered in her ear, "Open for me, lass. Let me bring you release."

Her brand!

Annie caught his wrist, squeezed her thighs together, and tried to pull his hand away, alarm dampening her desire. "N-nay!"

He nuzzled her earlobe. "*Uist, a leannan!* I can pleasure you wi'out takin' your innocence. You burn. I can feel it. Let me free you from this need."

Ignoring her grip on his wrist, he cupped her sex and pressed the heel of his hand in slow, deep circles against her woman's mound, unleashing deep, staggering pleasure inside her. Then his mouth returned to her breast, his tongue teasing her nipples, sucking, licking, tasting.

More water. A scorching hiss. Steam.

Annie was lost. Her body trembled, overwhelmed with sensation. Something was building inside her—something wondrous and primal and more than a little frightening. She buried her face against the hot, damp skin of his chest, her fingers digging into the muscles of his shoulders, her breathing ragged.

"Dinnae fight it, lass. Come for me." His voice was husky, strained.

She felt him part her, felt a thick finger glide gently between her slick folds to circle and stroke her most sensitive flesh. The bliss of it stunned her, and in a heartbeat she found herself hovering on some unfamiliar and terrifying edge.

She clung to him, tried to keep from falling, but he was relentless. His finger, slick and wet, slid over her again and again, driving her closer to the brink. For a moment, the heat inside her burned bright as gold—then it exploded. Molten ecstasy seared through her, pleasure so intense it seemed to shake her apart. But instead of falling, she was flying, up and up and up to a place beyond sunlight, beyond starlight.

She arched in his arms, cried out. "Iain!"

He silenced her cries with his mouth, his hand never ceasing its rhythm until she lay, astonished and quivering, against him.

Still hard and burning with unspent passion, Iain held her trembling body, kissed her forehead, stroked her wet hair. She felt so precious in his arms, so perfect, and he thanked God, the Virgin, Jesus, and every saint who was listening— not to mention a few Muhheconneok spirits—for the miracle that had enabled him to find her in the rushing torrent. If her hair hadn't caught upon his fingers . . .

He didn't want to think about that, not now when she lay alive and warm and languid in his arms. God's blood, she was a passionate lass! She responded to his touch like the strings of a fiddle sang to the stroke of a bow. Strangely, it didn't matter to him that he was still hard as stone. Making her come had proved more than satisfying.

He doubted Joseph's sweat lodge had ever been used in this way, and he wondered if his friend would be offended.

He was certain Joseph had heard her cries. If his actions had been disrespectful, Iain would make amends, performing whatever labor or purification rite his Stockbridge brother demanded.

Iain hadn't set out to pleasure her. When they'd entered the lodge, his only thought had been to keep her alive—and to survive himself. But then the steam had warmed their blood, and she'd begun to explore him, her innocent touch more arousing than the practiced caresses of the most experienced lover. He'd found himself wanting to give her that which no man had given her before—sexual pleasure. Now, no matter what happened, he would always be the first man to have brought her to her peak. For some reason, that mattered to him.

Joseph was singing the bear song now, the last song he would sing before ending the ceremony and opening the flaps. Iain was about to join him in the words, when she spoke.

"I knew you would find me." Her voice was soft like sleep.

He wanted to confess that he had not been so certain, that for terrible long moments he'd feared her lost. But a pang of guilt assailed him. She'd been running from him. "We must teach you to swim."

"I tried to remove my skirts so I wouldna sink, but my fingers were clumsy from cold."

"Aye, I saw. You're a clever lass, for certain, and very brave." The thought of her alone in the raging water, struggling with her gown, waiting for help that very nearly had not reached her made his chest ache.

"I'm sorry I struck you."

He'd forgotten about that. " 'Tis no matter. 'Twas likely I deserved it."

"You mocked me wi' vile words."

Something twisted in his gut. He ignored it. If he'd upset her, it was for her own good. As long as she stayed at the fort she was in danger—from Wentworth, who'd clearly taken an impure interest in her; from the soldiers, who would use her cruelly if they could; from the war, which was nowhere near its end; and most especially from him.

He kissed her hair. "I didna mock you, Annie. I told you the truth. You dinnae belong on the frontier, and Wentworth is a damned fool and a madman if he lets you linger here."

"I willna go to Albany. I cannae go to Albany."

There was a note of fear in her voice, and Iain wondered why she should dread the place. " 'Tis a rough town, aye, but far safer than your sister's cabin."

"I cannae go there. Please dinnae send me there."

"What frightens you, Annie?"

She seemed to hesitate. " 'Tis no' safe for me. Please dinnae ask me more."

Galled that she did not trust him, he answered more harshly than he'd intended. "You'll go where I deem you safe."

She stiffened in his arms. "I am safe here."

"Nay, Annie. You're right about me. I am a barbarian. If you stay, 'tis only a matter of time before I come to your bed and steal far more than a kiss. You ken it as well as I. Aye, I can feel it in the way your heart is beatin'. If you stay here, you and I will lie together—as sure as the sun rises."

Chapter Nineteen

Annie pulled weeds from the dark soil, careful not to dislodge the delicate chamomile seedlings. Dr. Blake had set her to work in the little herb garden behind the hospital. 'Twas here he grew the herbs and other plants needed for his poultices and tinctures—at least the ones that grew in this clime. Hidden behind a high wooden fence that kept soldiers from stealing the precious plants—or trampling them underfoot—it was perhaps the only place in the fort where Annie could enjoy the sunshine away from the prying eyes of men.

Lord William had not yet decided her fate. He'd sent Conall off to Albany without her, the entire question of her future set aside as he waited upon General Abercrombie, who had arrived unannounced more than a fortnight ago with a sizeable escort, setting the fort astir with parades, drills and inspections. Although the Regulars seemed excited to show their skill before their general, the Rangers didn't bother to hide their disdain, calling him Mrs. Nanny Crombie for his inability to make decisions.

"Nanny Crombie is a curse upon this army," Killy had told her. "He's no more a warrior than I am the pope."

But if the Rangers loathed General Abercrombie, the general seemed fascinated by them, touring their camp, watching each day's drill, even calling upon them to stage a mock battle, which the entire fort, except for Annie, had turned out to watch. She'd already seen them fight—and not in feigned battle, but amidst gore and death. She did not want to see it again, nor did she have the time.

She was determined to use the reprieve the general's visit had bought her to show Lord William that she could be of service to him and his men—without being a wife or a camp follower. She'd cobbled together a list of tasks for herself, spending the day from dawn until dusk helping Dr. Blake. She tended soldiers, changed blankets and sheets, rolled bandages, mixed salves and poultices, ground herbs, cleaned the hospital and even emptied chamber pots.

Aye, it was tiring work and at times frightening—the piteous cries of pain, the blood, the ever present possibility of death. She hated seeing men suffer. Yet helping to ease their pain and despair gave her a feeling of fulfillment unlike any she'd known. For the first time in her life she was doing something that truly mattered.

She sat back on her heels, stretched the ache from her back. It was a beautiful day. The sun shone in a sky such as she'd never seen in gray, misty Scotland—wide as eternity and blue beyond imagining. The warm breeze carried smells that were new to her, the scents of the great forest awakening to spring. Honeybees, drowsy from their winter sleep, buzzed lazily about the garden, awaiting a feast of blossoms.

If only her spirits could be as bright as the sky.

She had not been herself lately, her feelings confusing even to herself. One moment she felt cross, the next near tears and the next she was lost in daydreams. Always at the center of her thoughts was Iain.

Why would he not speak to her? Why was he avoiding her?

It had been three weeks since the night she'd foolishly fallen in the river and nearly drowned, three weeks since Iain had held her in Joseph's sweat lodge, three weeks since he'd scorched her with his touch. In that time she'd scarce seen him but from afar.

He rarely came to check on her, but sent one of his brothers or Killy instead. When he did cross her path, his manner was gruff and cold, as if he barely knew her. After all the kindness he'd shown her—and the heat they'd shared in the sweat lodge—how could he treat her like this?

Annie forced her mind back to her work, determined yet again to put Iain from her thoughts. She worked her way down the rows, silently repeating what the doctor had told her about the each plant and its uses, her fingers busy in the rich soil.

The flowers of chamomile when boiled had a calming effect, soothed mild pains and agues and aided in stomach complaints. When crushed and mixed with poppy heads, a poultice of chamomile flowers could reduce swellings from sprains and bruises. Her mother had often taken chamomile tea after supper to aid her digestion.

A poultice of cabbage leaves was good for cleaning festering wounds, healing ulcers of the skin and treating burns—though it hadn't seemed to help Conall's powder burns nearly as much as the stinging salve she'd spread on him when Dr. Blake wasn't looking.

Why had she touched Iain like that, running her hands over his wet, bare skin? Had the cold river, lack of breath or her brush with death weakened her mind? What would Iain have done had he discovered her brand?

Pennyroyal. Pennyroyal tea was favored for use against fevers, colds, stomach pains and liver ailments. Dr. Blake had told her some women used it to poison babes that had not yet quickened in the womb, sometimes killing themselves, too. But she remembered Uncle Bain's physician giving her pennyroyal tea when as a child she'd had a bad cough.

Ragwort . . .

That night seemed like a dream to her now. Falling into the icy torrent, feeling Iain's strong arm encircle her and knowing then that she would live. Waking in his arms in the steamy darkness of the sweat lodge. Feeling his hard man's body beneath her hands. Shattering with the pleasure he'd drawn from her flesh.

Was that what it was supposed to be like between men and women—the sweet burning, the aching need, the surge of ecstasy that spilled over into every inch of mind, body and spirit?

Annie did not know.

Nor did she understand the change that had come over her. As if awakened to new life, her body seemed to have a mind of its own. All she had to do was think of Iain or glimpse him across the island and her blood felt thick, her breasts strangely heavy. Even the sound of his voice made her heart beat faster. And when she lay alone in his bed and the memory of his hands upon her was inescapable, her sex ached and grew wet for him.

But it was more than that. She longed to be held again as he'd held her afterwards, as if she were something precious. She'd felt safe then. She'd felt at home.

At least until he'd spoken of Albany.

What frightens you, Annie?

She hadn't been able to bear lying to him again, so she had told him nothing.

I cannae go to Albany.

You'll go where I deem you safe.

Rosemary. It helped heal sicknesses of the mind, including headaches. Dr. Blake said it also purified the air and prevented fevers from spreading from one patient to the next.

Och, nay, Annie! How could you do such a thing?

Her face burned with mortification any time she thought of that night. Joseph had been sitting nearby in the dark. Had he heard her? Had he known? If so, he'd shown no sign of it. He'd opened the flaps and stood aside while Iain, still naked, had wrapped her in the bearskin and carried her to a nearby lodge, where she'd dressed alone before a warm fire.

Then Iain, who'd dressed outside in the cold, had escorted her, bundled in the warm bearskin, back to his cabin, where he'd built up the fire and left her to sleep.

"Remember my words, lass," he'd said on his way out.

How could she forget?

If you stay here, you and I will lie together—as sure as the sun rises.

Something tickled in her belly at the memory, and she wasn't sure if his words scared her or whether what she felt was excitement. Either way, she knew he was trying to frighten her into leaving the fort. But there was something he did not understand.

She had no place else to go.

Ragwort. Ragwort. An infusion of ragwort flowers served to cleanse the eyes. The leaves in a poultice could relieve the pain of aching joints. It looked like the same herb Annie knew as staggerwort in Scotland, where it grew even in the high mountains.

Boneset. An infusion of boneset helped those with agues and other kinds of fevers to sweat. It also calmed the stomach and acted as a tonic. She had never heard of boneset and wondered why it had nothing to do with helping to set bones.

So much was new to her. So much had happened. Some days she felt like a straggler trying to keep up with her own life. One moment she was Lady Anne, living a life of comfort in Scotland, cherished by her mother, cosseted by her loving uncle. The next she was Annie Burns, living among rough Rangers and soldiers at a fort upon the American frontier.

Yet, as much as she missed Scotland and the comforts of the life she'd been born to, a part of her had begun to feel at home in Fort Elizabeth. She'd grown accustomed to the drums and trumpets and the crudeness of the Regulars. It was hard to fear them when she cared for their hurts and sicknesses and listened to their prayers each day. And although she lacked feminine company altogether, there were the Rangers. They treated her with respect and kindness, stacking firewood outside her door, fetching water for her, escorting her across the bateau bridge. Men of a sort she'd never have spoken with in Scotland, they reminded her of her brothers, and they made her laugh.

Dr. Blake's face appeared at the back door, a smile on his face. "Miss Burns, I've something you might want to see. 'Tis the rattle from the end of a rattlesnake's tail."

Annie wasn't so certain she wanted to see it, but she didn't say that. "I'll be right there."

"Most impressive, Major." General Abercrombie stared down the open field toward the shredded remains of a paper target, a smile of boyish excitement on his face. "I don't know when I've ever seen such bold marksmanship."

Iain said nothing.

Wentworth answered for him. "Major MacKinnon is unsurpassed at hitting marks, General, but survival on the frontier also depends on a man's ability to reload quickly, doesn't it, Major?"

Iain forced the anger out of his voice. "Aye, for certain."

Satan's hairy arse, how he hated this! For more than a fortnight, he and his men had been called on to perform like dancing bears for their supper, made to play at death for the amusement of a man who seemed to think war was a game.

Iain would have refused, rank be damned, but Wentworth had made it clear he had no choice.

"Do not make a mockery of this," Wentworth had warned him in private "General Abercrombie is not as convinced as I of the need for the Ranger corps."

Iain had laughed. "Will he send us home if we disappoint him?"

Wentworth's face had gone cold as ice. "What I mean to say, Major, is that you are still bound by your oath and I by mine. Do you understand?"

"Threatened wi' the noose again?" Hatred had flared in Iain's gut. He'd leaned forward, glared down into Wentworth's arrogant face. "One day this war will be over, and there will come a time for the settling of debts between us."

Wentworth had merely smiled. "Today is not that day."

At least his anger at Wentworth had helped him keep his mind off Annie—a bit.

He'd done everything he could to stay far away from her these past three weeks. He didn't trust himself to be near her, not after what had happened in the sweat lodge. The feminine feel of her soft body, the musky scent of her arousal, the sweet sound of her cries as she'd come against his hand—those memories drove him mad at night, made him burn for her as he'd burned for no other woman.

He would have pushed Wentworth to send her to Albany, except for her words that night.

I cannae go there. Please dinnae send me there. 'Tis no' safe for me.

He needed to find out what frightened her before he sent her onward. Of course, that meant spending time alone with her, talking with her, persuading her to trust him. How could he do that when he didn't trust himself?

The general slapped him on the back. "Don't you agree, Major?"

"Aye." Iain nodded. He had no notion what the general was talking about.

Today, Abercrombie had wanted to watch Iain and his men shoot at marks, so they had wasted God knew how much powder and shot destroying paper targets. To his great dismay, Iain seemed to have become an object of fascination for Abercrombie, who'd spent the past hour asking him to make one outlandish shot after the next. It wouldn't surprise him if next the general asked him to hit the moon while standing on his head.

His brothers stood with the men off to one side, rifles still in hand, mocking grins on their faces. Behind them, Regulars stood on the ramparts, watching him through spyglasses. Bastards, the lot of them!

"I've heard you are able to load while on your back, then fire while lying on your abdomen. I should like to see a demonstration. Shall we say four shots?"

Iain met Wentworth's amused gaze and silently wished him to hell.

Four paper targets with black circles at their centers were quickly set up far down the field, while Iain settled onto his back in the dirt with his powder horn and a pouch full of balls and smaller shot. He took a deep breath and waited for the general's word.

"Now, Major!"

His hands moving swiftly over the rifle, he loaded, flipped onto his belly and fired. He didn't have to look to ken he'd hit the target.

One. Two. Three.

He had just flipped over to fire the fourth shot when a man appeared on the road from Albany, shouting and screaming, his shirt stained with blood.

Iain shifted his aim to the dark forest beyond, waiting to see if anyone pursued the poor man, whom he recognized as one of the sutler's adult sons.

"Major?" The general was clearly waiting for that fourth shot and hadn't seen the lad.

But Wentworth had. "We have trouble, General."

*   *   *

"This doesna feel right." Connor's voice was barely a whisper as he crept forward through the trees beside Iain.

"Aye." Iain kept his gaze focused on the dark forest before them, misgiving prickling along his spine.

The sutler's son had told them a party of Abenaki had ambushed the supply train he'd been riding a scant two miles from the fort, and everyone but him had been slain. When asked how he'd managed to escape with his scalp, he'd said he'd hidden behind a slaughtered bullock and crept away on his belly until it was safe to run.

"They numbered no more than thirty, but they came at us of a sudden from the hills above," he told them between sobs. "They killed everything, even the chickens!"

Not wishing to give the war party more of a lead than it already had, Iain had immediately called out his men. "Turn out, lads! The Abenaki have come a-courtin'!"

But Abercrombie had delayed them with needless wavering. "Perhaps the Regulars are best suited to this particular task, Colonel. Or perhaps a complement of Regulars should join the Rangers. What say you?"

Mrs. Nanny Crombie, indeed.

Now Iain and his men, with Captain Joseph and a small band of his men guarding their left flank, moved swiftly and silently through the woods just off the road. The remains of the supply train could not be far ahead.

And then he saw it—six wagons laden with provisions and pierced by arrows. The sutler and his men lay scattered on the ground amid slaughtered livestock, scalped and lifeless. Two women—camp followers—lay naked and bloodied nearby, their bodies revealing just how cruelly they'd been used before they, too, had been killed and scalped.

Iain motioned for his men to move out. They would encircle the battle site to protect themselves from ambush before they moved any closer to the wagons.

He had taken but a few steps, when he heard Joseph's warning whistle.

"Take cover!"

In the next instant, the forest exploded in a hail of gunfire.

The Abenaki had been waiting for them—and there were far more than thirty.

Chapter Twenty

The wounded began trickling in just after supper—at first just minor bullet wounds, then more serious injuries, including Cam with an arrow lodged in his thigh. They all told the same story. A force of more than two hundred French and Abenaki had ambushed them near the site of the attack on the supply train, and Iain and his brothers were pinned down and under fire.

Annie tried to keep her mind on her work, cleaning the smaller wounds, offering strengthening drinks of rum and spoonfuls of laudanum, changing bloodied sheets, and providing two more willing hands when Dr. Blake needed them. But as the hours crept by and still more wounded arrived, she began to fear Iain and his brothers would not return.

Lord William and the general strode into the hospital just after sunset. Lord William did not deign to notice her in the general's presence but set about questioning the Rangers who were able to speak.

"The attack on the supply train was naugh' but bait, Colonel." Cam's words were slurred from laudanum. " 'Tis almost as if the bastards are puttin' all they have into killin' Mack."

Annie wiped blood from the floor, dread writhing in her belly like a snake.

"That's not too surprising, as there is a rather high price on the major's head, isn't there, sergeant?"

Lord William's words left her stunned, and she listened in secret horror and outrage as he coldly told the general how Iain's success against the French and their allies had led the French to put a price the equivalent of two thousand British pounds on Iain's scalp—more if he were brought in alive. He made no mention of the fact that he'd forced Iain to fight this war by threatening to bear false witness against him.

Annie loathed him.

Then she remembered what Iain had told her the French would do to him.

They'd have tried to break me, to pry secrets from my mind. Then they'd have given me to the Abenaki, who would have tortured me to death wi' great delight and merriment.

Her mouth went dry.

"The Abenaki in particular hate and fear Iain MacKinnon like the Romans hated and feared Hannibal. If you'll recall, the major struck deep into their territory two winters past to destroy an Abenaki village that had sent several raiding parties against British farmsteads. He slew most of the warriors, burnt their homes and left the women and children."

"Ah, yes, I recall hearing something about that mission." The general nodded and stroked his chin. "I heard he and his men nearly starved on the journey and were forced to boil and eat their own belts."

Annie remembered reading an account of that mission aloud to Brendan out of the *Boston Gazette*. It had seemed a nightmare. Yet Lord William and General Abercrombie spoke of it as if it were a mere curiosity.

"We boiled our belts and called it a feast." 'Twas Cam who spoke, his voice strangely flat. "We wanted to boil the leather strings in our snowshoes, but Mack wouldna let us, sayin' we needed them to get home. So we ate bark from the trees, frozen cattail roots, even boiled a pair of antlers we found along the way. We'd have perished had Mack not gone off on his own and brought down an old buck. How he did it, I dinnae ken. The rest of us could scarce stand."

Annie's dread grew, images of past suffering mixed with fears for what he might be enduring now. She couldn't bear to think of him lying lifeless on the cold earth, his scalp cut away, all that he was lost. Nor could she abide the thought that he might have already been captured and be on his way to a torturous death.

She busied her trembling hands with bandages, her back to Wentworth to hide her anger and distress from his watchful gaze, snatches of prayer flitting through her mind.

God, please bring him and his brothers back alive!

"Tell me, Sergeant, is it true that some of the men, mad from hunger, ate the flesh of their own dead?"

Annie heard the general's horrifying words, and Brendan's voice echoed in her mind.

Did you truly eat your belts, Private Kinney?

Aye, miss, and worse, but I willna speak of it to a lassie.

She remembered how hungry she'd been on the journey to the fort, and that had lasted only three days. She tried to imagine being stranded in freezing cold without food for weeks. The gnawing pain of hunger. Hopelessness. Desperation.

"Save your pryin' questions for me, General. Dinnae harry my men!"

Annie gasped, whirled about and saw Iain standing in the doorway.

He was alive!

Relief as heady as mulled wine rushed through her veins. She started toward him, then remembered that Lord William and General Abercrombie stood nearby. She halted in her steps—and she saw.

Iain's face was stained with sweat and gunpowder, his green-checked shirt dark with blood. Barely conscious, Connor leaned heavily against him. Behind them stood Morgan, bearing Killy upon his back much as Iain had carried her.

She met Iain's gaze and saw in his eyes deep anguish.

"You'll have to pardon Major MacKinnon, General," Lord William said, clearly displeased, as he led the general past

Iain and out the door. "The battle has obviously gotten the better of his tongue. Major, we await your report in my study."

Unable to break his gaze from Annie's, Iain ignored Wentworth.

Her wide green eyes hid nothing from him—her fear for his life, her joy at seeing him again, her worry for his men. She was a breath of life in a world filled with death, beauty in a landscape of ugliness and brutality.

"Over here, Major." Dr. Blake motioned toward two empty beds.

Iain bore Connor across the room and laid him back on the bed, while Morgan carried Killy to the other, then hurried off to secure Ranger camp for the night.

"Connor took a ball to the shoulder and lost much blood." Iain took hold of Connor's shirt and ripped it down the center, exposing his brother's chest. "Killy caught the edge of a French sword."

He knelt at Connor's bedside, feeling utterly useless, as Annie quickly washed the blood from Connor's chest and shoulder and then pressed a cloth against the wound to stanch the flow.

She took his hand, placed it on the cloth. "Press hard."

Iain did as she asked, while she coaxed laudanum down Connor's throat.

"Swallow, Connor." Her voice was soft, feminine, comforting. "That's it."

Dr. Blake gave the medicine a moment to work, then began to examine the wound, his poking and prodding causing Connor to groan and jerk awake. "The ball is lodged deep in the muscle. We shall have to cut it out, I'm afraid."

"Och, Jesus!" Connor's face twisted with pain and anger. "I bloody well ken that!"

Iain sat with his brother while Dr. Blake, with Annie beside him, moved to the next bed to gauge Killy's injuries. He saw how carefully Annie removed Killy's shirt, how caringly she bathed the gash in his belly, how tenderly she tried to wake the old Irishman to give him laudanum, and a warm sense of admiration crept over him.

The apron she wore was stained with blood—the blood of his men—but she showed no squeamishness. Instead she worked with skillful hands and did whatever the doctor asked without faltering, her brow knit as she bent her mind to the task. Only when she removed the makeshift bandages from Killy's head and saw he'd been scalped did she show shock. But in the next instant she was washing the wound, spreading a poultice over it and wrapping it in clean linen.

Iain's admiration grew stronger still as she knelt beside Connor and held his hand, murmuring reassurances in his ear, while Iain held him down and Dr. Blake went about the brutal business of digging lead from his shoulder.

"Squeeze my hand, Connor."

"I dinnae wish to hurt you, lass."

"You willna hurt me. I am stronger than I seem."

And when Connor finally lay asleep and bandaged against his pillow, she returned to Killy's side, seemingly without taking a breath, to help the doctor stitch his belly.

"She's a healer, your woman." Joseph spoke in his own tongue. He had entered the hospital silently and now stood beside Connor's bed.

Iain nodded. She was more than that.

"Why do you keep yourself from her? I watch you and see that you suffer."

How like Joseph to see straight through him—the bastard! "It is she who would suffer if I did not. I have nothing to give her—no home, no certain future, a tainted name."

"*Wastach-qua-am!*" It was Joseph's way of telling him he was stupid as a tree.

Iain felt his temper flare. "If I were to take her, I would have to wed her, for she is from the white world, and I would not shame her. But we both know there is little chance of my surviving this war."

"That is for the Creator to decide."

"I do not wish to leave her a widow to raise my children alone and unprotected!"

Anger sparked in Joseph's dark eyes. "Do you think we—your brothers, your people—would abandon her? I would take her as wife into my mother's lodge before I would see that happen! No, brother, I think you are afraid to love. But she is stronger than Jeannie, and her heart is true. Look at how she cares for these men—like a mother bear."

Blood pounded in Iain's ears, and he fought to rein in his temper, his control worn to a single thread by exhaustion and weeks of frustration. "You don't know what you're saying!"

"Don't I? Then perhaps you should listen to yourself. What was it you told her in the lodge? Yes, I overheard. 'If you stay here, you and I will lie together—as sure as the sun rises.' What use is there in fighting the sunrise?" Then Joseph reached down and touched Connor's brow. "How fares the cub?"

Joseph still used their nickname for Connor despite Connor's loathing of it—or perhaps for that very reason.

But Connor was in no shape to argue just now.

Rattled by Joseph's words, his blood still racing, Iain looked down at his youngest brother, felt the hitch of fear in his gut. "He's lost a lot of blood, but they were able to cut the ball out. If the wound doesn't fester . . ."

"He's strong, and if she watches over him the way she watched over you, he'll be back on his feet and bragging of his scar in a week."

Iain nodded. Then he brushed his anger aside and looked into Joseph's eyes. "None of us would be alive tonight if it weren't for you and your men. Once again, I owe you my life. *Wneeweh*."

Thank you.

"You've done the same for me many times. I promise not to keep count if you don't."

"How many men did you lose?"

"Sixteen wounded. Eight dead."

The weight on Iain's shoulders grew heavier. "I am sorry for them and their families."

"They died as warriors."

For a moment neither of them spoke.

Then Iain switched into English. "Wentworth is waitin' for me, aye?"

Joseph nodded. "Cooke is on his way to fetch you."

It was well past midnight by the time Wentworth and Abercrombie were finished with him. The general had asked him one foolish question after the next, proving how little he knew about forest combat. It had taken more patience than Iain knew he possessed to answer the man's tiresome queries and listen to his prattling.

Wentworth had finally brought it to an end. "It seems clear, Major, that this was an attempt to lure you and your men to your deaths. Once again your Stockbridge allies have proven their worth. I shall make a point of thanking Captain Joseph personally. You are dismissed."

Grateful for the feel of cool air on his face, Iain strode across the dark and silent parade ground back toward the hospital.

So far, he'd lost ten men. Lucas. Billy Maguire. Phinneus. Caleb. David Page. Charles Graham. Richard. Old Archi. Malcolm. James Hill. But more than twenty had been injured, seven of them gravely. How many would die still?

Weariness and grief pressed down upon Iain, an almost unbearable weight. His legs felt leaden, his soul barren. For three years he'd ordered men into harm's way. For three years he'd watched as good men were broken on the field of battle and perished. For three years he'd killed, sending other men's brothers to their graves.

What would it be like to feel earth on his hands once again instead of blood? To see crops newly sprung from the soil, not freshly dug graves? To hear the bleating of newborn lambs rather than the cries of the wounded and dying?

He'd agreed to fight this war to save his life and those of his brothers. Instead he'd consigned them all to a living hell. Would it have been so much worse to take the noose?

He quietly opened the hospital door and saw Annie at Killy's side, easing a spoon between his lips. She looked utterly worn, lines of fatigue on her face, dark circles beneath her eyes. He wished she'd never seen any of this, yet he couldn't deny she had a gift for nurturing the sick and the injured. Hadn't he kent she was a brave lass from the first moment he'd seen her?

Annie set the spoon aside, picked up a cup of cool chamomile tea, and held it to Killy's lips. The little Irishman had always been so kind to her, watching over her, telling her stories, making her laugh. Now he lay near death. His belly was cut so deeply she'd seen his entrails. The hair and skin from the top of his head had been sliced away, some warrior's grisly trophy.

She held his head as he drank, then laid it gently back on the pillow, ignoring her own weariness and the pounding in her skull. How could she give in to such weakness when so many brave men lay terribly injured and in need of comfort? Some of them might not live to see the dawn.

"Just rest now, Killy."

She heard the front door close and looked up to see Iain walking toward her. She forced herself to smile, gave Killy's hand a squeeze. "Look who's come to check on you."

She could feel Iain's soul-deep weariness from across the room. She saw the despair in his eyes, in the tight lines of his face, in the heaviness of his step.

And she thought she understood.

These were his men, his friends, his family. He'd lived with them, broken bread with them, fought side by side with them for three years. Now some were lost, while others were suffering, holding onto their lives by a thread. And like a true Highland laird, he felt responsible for them all.

Her heart ached for him.

He knelt first beside Connor, who was sleeping deeply.

She saw him pull the small wooden cross from inside his shirt and mutter a prayer, his brow furrowed with emotion. Then he kissed the cross, dropped it back inside his shirt, and crossed himself.

Strange that his Catholicism no longer made him seem an enemy. Certainly she hadn't forgotten his faith, but oddly such things seemed not to matter the way they had back in Scotland. What had changed?

He stood, felt his brother's forehead for fever, then strode over to her and crouched down beside Killy, a forced smile on his face. "Well, old man, now we ken what the Abenaki and the redcoats have in common—they cannae tell you from a dead man."

Annie was shocked by his words and might have pulled him aside to chide him had she not seen the weak smile on Killy's pale face.

"Some whoreson stole my scalp, Mack, and I'm after gettin' it back."

"You've got to get back on your feet first, aye?"

Dr. Blake emerged from the back room. "Major, I'm glad to see you. I was hoping you could escort Miss Burns to her cabin. I hate to see her walk through the fort in the dark alone, and I can't leave my patients."

Surprised that the doctor was trying to send her away, Annie was on her feet. "But you've so many wounded! You need my help tonight of all nights!"

Dr. Blake gave her an indulgent smile. "The colonel has assigned a couple of ensigns to assist me through the night. You've been very helpful, but you've done enough for one day. I would do you a disservice if I repaid your kindness by allowing you to exhaust yourself. Wash your hands, set aside your apron and go rest."

"But I know what the men need! I know their hurts! I've been wi' them since they came in! I am no' so tired I cannae—" She felt Iain's hand on her elbow.

"Come, Annie. The doctor's right. You're fallin' down on your feet. Let me get you home."

She tried not to feel slighted or hurt as Iain led her from the hospital and through the silent and sleeping fort, but she couldn't silence the petulant voice in her mind. If Dr. Blake planned to stay up all night to care for his patients, why couldn't she? Had she not proved to him she was capable of making a difference? How could a couple of ensigns who didn't know each man's needs comfort them as well as she?

But beneath her irritation, fear lurked, niggling at her belly. If Dr. Blake didn't see her help in the hospital as vital, how would she persuade Lord William not to send her to Albany?

When they reached Iain's cabin, they found it dark and the hearth cold. Annie lit candles, while Iain set about building a fire.

"Dinnae be fashed, lass." Iain's voice startled the silence. "He didna send you away because he doesna esteem your skills. He'd be a fool if he didna see you've a talent wi' the sick and wounded."

After three weeks of enduring the sharp edge of his tongue, it was the last thing she'd expected Iain to say. She looked over at him where he knelt adding another log to a small blaze. " 'Tis kind of you to say so."

"Nay, 'tis the truth. 'Tis grateful I am for your care. I've no doubt you've saved lives." The golden firelight made his face seem impossibly rugged and handsome, but when he turned his head to look at her, his eyes held deep weariness and sorrow.

Her heart sick for him, she dipped a cloth into the water left from this morning, squeezed it out and went to kneel beside him. " 'Tis naught compared to what you've done for me."

Then she pressed the cool cloth to his cheek and, wishing she could wash his anguish away, slowly wiped the sweat and gunpowder from his face.

His gaze met hers, and he spoke, his voice ragged. "Take heed, lass. Are you certain you ken what you're doin'?"

Chapter Twenty-one

It was her tenderness that broke him. He might have withstood a grenade attack. Or a blow from a tomahawk. Or a charge with fixed bayonets. But he could not hold out against the soft touch of her hands, her feminine gentleness, the simple compassion in her eyes.

What use is there in fighting the sunrise?

He raised a hand to her face, traced his thumb over the rosy apple of her cheek. Then he slipped a hand into her tresses, ducked down and took her lips with his.

It might have been weeks of unspent desire. It might have been the day's brush with death. But the moment his lips touched hers, his hunger for her flared like tinder. He crushed her against him, plundered her mouth with his tongue, kissed her until his lungs ached for breath.

With a little cry, she leaned against him, parted her lips to accept his invasion, answering the roughness of his passion not with a maid's shyness, but with a woman's need.

She was solace. She was beauty. She was life.

And he wanted her.

But not like this. Not on the dirty floor as if she were some tavern whore.

With experienced hands, he loosened first her gown, then her stays and petticoats, and he let them slide to the floor about her knees, leaving her clad only in her shift. Then, without breaking the kiss, he lifted her trembling body into his arms, carried her to the bed and stretched himself out above her.

She arched against him, whimpered, her hands sliding over his shirt as if seeking skin.

In one motion, he broke the kiss, sat back on his knees, pulled his shirt over his head and tossed it aside. Then, still wearing his breeches, he rested his weight on one arm, took both her hands in one of his and pressed them against his bare chest. "Take what you want, lass—whatever you want."

She met his gaze, her eyes filled with trepidation—and hunger.

Then he spoke the words he feared would one day consign her to grief. "As God is my witness, Annie, I swear I will marry you."

Her eyes widened with astonishment. "D-do you really mean that?"

"Aye, *mo ghràidh.* I willna forsake you. I ken 'tis against the law for a Catholic like me to wed a Protestant, but I promise I'll find a way."

With a little whimper, she shifted her gaze to his body and, with a look of longing on her sweet face, she slid her fingers through his chest hair, grazing his nipples with her thumbs, tracing the outline of his muscles with her palms.

He held himself still above her, gave her time to explore him. And just as it had in the sweat lodge, the feel of him seemed to inflame her. Her skin flushed pink. Her breasts rose and fell with each rapid breath, and her body trembled.

But if touching him stirred her, it almost killed him. Each brush of her fingers sent jagged bolts of heat to his already throbbing groin. He wanted to rip her shift from her body, spread her thighs wide and push past the barrier of her purity to claim her once and for all. But this was her first time, and he did not want to hurt her.

Unable to keep himself from her any longer, he lowered his head, kissed the satin swells of her breasts, nudging the cotton of her shift aside to reveal their puckered pink crests. And then he feasted, sucking her nipples into his mouth, teasing them with his tongue, tugging them to tight peaks with his lips. "Does that feel good, *a leannan?* Mmm, I can see it does."

She whimpered, arched her back to give her breasts more fully to him, her fingers digging into his shoulders. And he knew she burned as he burned.

He slid a hand down the curve of her waist, grasped her hips and pressed the thick ridge of his erection against her mound, a foretaste of heaven. "Och, lass, I've lain awake so many nights for the want of you!"

Her thighs parted, and she lifted her hips to meet his in a response that was pure female instinct. "Oh, Iain, touch me! Make it stop!"

He heard himself chuckle, even as the blood pounded through his veins, hot and thick, demanding union and release. "I'll no' put out the fire so quickly this time, *a leannan*. There is so much more."

He grabbed the fabric of her shift in his fist, drew the concealing cloth up her body, then brushed his hand over soft skin of her inner thigh, eager to touch and taste her sweetest flesh.

'Twas then he felt it—the raised flesh of a scar.

She gasped, bolted upright and jerked her legs together.

But not before he saw.

'Twas a brand in the shape of a *T*.

For thief.

Her heart slamming in her breast, her body shaking with fear, Annie saw the bewilderment on Iain's face turn to anger.

His eyes narrowed. "What is it, Annie? Tell me."

The blood drained from her head, left her dizzy and bereft of speech.

Before she could recover her tongue, he grabbed her ankles, pulled her flat onto her back, and forced her thighs apart. Then his fingers traced her scar. " 'Tis a brand, aye? And you are a convict, are you no'?"

"Please, Iain, stop!" She could not bear the shame of being held down like this, as her uncle had held her, and she struggled to free herself.

But he was so much stronger than she, and in the blink of an eye, he had captured her hands, stretched her arms over her head and restrained her body with the weight of his. He was still hard, the bulge of his sex pressing against hers from behind the leather of his breeches.

"Quit your strugglin' and answer me!" Fury darkened his face.

She met his gaze, forced herself to speak. "P-please, Iain, dinnae do this!"

For a moment he glared into her eyes. Then his gaze softened. He released her, rose and went to stand by the hearth. "I'm waitin' for your answer."

She scooted to the far side of the bed, hugged her arms around herself, scarce able to believe this was happening. How could she have forgotten?

"M-my name is Anne Burness Campbell, and I-I am no' a thief." Her voice wavered, but she forced herself to meet his gaze. "I am no' a convict. The brand is a punishment from . . . from my uncle."

Then, feeling strangely removed from her own body, she told him how her father and brothers had been killed at Prestonpans and how she and her mother had eventually been forced to seek shelter with her powerful uncle.

"My uncle saw to it that I wanted for naught. He treated me like a daughter, and he looked so like my father that sometimes I was able to fool myself into believing my father was still alive. I loved him."

She told him how once in a while a servant or guest would die in a strange accident. Though servants whispered in quiet corners, she'd never suspected her uncle. Not even after her mother had warned her not to trust him. Not until the night she'd gone after her misplaced book and heard her mother's cries.

"I looked through the crack in the doorway and saw her. He'd bound her to his bed. He was naked, and he was usin' her . . . in unnatural ways. His hands were wrapped round her throat. He was hurtin' her, and she was pleadin' wi' him to stop."

She repeated what she'd heard them say, felt her stomach turn.

Enough! Please, stop!

I say when it's enough. If you no longer wish to play my games, Mara, perhaps your lovely daughter can take your place. Does she have the same taste for pain as her mother?

Tears of grief spilled freely down her cheeks, but she did not feel them. "The next morn', she was dead, blue marks about her throat. My uncle lied, said she'd fallen down the stairs. He didna know I'd seen them."

Her body shaking uncontrollably, she recounted how she'd taken her mother's jewels and sewn them into the skirts she'd borrowed from her maid, hoping to make her way to Glasgow and her father's old solicitor.

"But Uncle Bain caught me. He'd beaten a confession out of my maid, Betsy, and come after me. He turned me over to the sheriff, denied that he knew me and saw to it the sheriff found the jewels. For three weeks he let me rot in gaol, where the men . . ." She could not speak of that.

"One day, Uncle Bain came to the gaol and gave me a choice—to come home wi' him or to be branded as a thief and sent over the sea. I wanted to go home! I wanted all to be as it had been before. I wanted to forget all I'd seen. But he had murdered my mother. I knew it would be only a matter of time before he did the same to me."

She swallowed, tried to still her stomach. "When . . . when I refused, he ordered the guards to hold me down, and he . . . he . . . he branded me himself. *And he enjoyed it.*"

At these last words, her stomach rebelled altogether. She leapt from the bed, grabbed the water pail and retched until she knelt weak and trembling, her body utterly purged.

She felt something touch her cheek.

The wet cloth.

He wiped her face, lifted her into his arms and laid her down on the bed.

She curled up against the soft bearskin, unable to cease her shaking, barely aware of Iain's cleaning up her mess or his pouring her a gill of rum.

He doesna believe you, Annie. No one will ever believe you.

Then he sat down beside her. "Drink, lass."

She sat up, took the cup with unsteady hands, swallowed, shuddered at the taste.

"Now finish it."

Uncle Bain's words echoed unbidden through her mind.

Any man you try to love shall find it—and discard you.

Fighting despair, she went on. "Master and Mistress Hawes bought and registered my indenture in Albany. I'd been wi' them for three months before the attack. Mistress Hawes hated me and thought me lazy because I didna ken how to milk a cow or darn socks or cook. She took my clothes and made me wear hers. She beat me wi' a leather strap. When I heard her scream, when I heard the Indians shout their wild cries, I . . . I ran."

Iain looked at the woman who sat beside him, pale and trembling, her golden hair in a tangled disarray about her shoulders, and fought the urge to comfort her. The lovely green eyes were the same, her creamy skin, her sweet, pouting mouth. But now she seemed a stranger.

She had lied to him. For weeks she had deceived him. She wasn't even Annie Burns! She was a cursed Argyll Campbell.

For a moment he said nothing; the only sound was the crackle of the fire.

"You lied to me."

"I am sorry! I didna know you! I told you as much of the truth as I dared!"

"You didna ken me?" The tumult inside him exploded into rage. "I've saved your life twice! I've bled for you! I've slept beside you, held you in my arms, and left your virtue intact! I told you the truth about my life! And yet in all these weeks did you no' think you could trust me wi' the truth about yours?"

She lifted her chin, her eyes glittering with tears. "I wanted to tell you! I wanted to trust you! I hated lyin' to you, but I didna think you'd believe me! No one else has. I couldna risk being sold again and findin' myself the chattel of someone else who would beat me—or worse. I wanted to forget. I wanted my life back. I wanted to be free!"

Her words struck at his heart, but he was too enraged to hear them. "The trouble wi' a liar, Miss *Campbell*, is that a man doesna ken what he can believe. Perhaps all is as you say. But perhaps you are a convict and a skilled storyteller doing all she can to avoid justly earned bondage. How am I to tell?"

"Iain, I am sorry! I didna mean to deceive or hurt you! You must believe me!"

The anguish on her face tore at him, but his anger was even stronger. "Must I?"

He turned his back on her, grabbed his shirt off the floor and strode toward the door.

Her voice, small and terrified, followed him. "W-will you tell Lord William?"

Without answering, he stepped out into the night and slammed the door behind him.

William stared at his chessboard, strangely unable to sleep. He'd moved the white queen out quickly and was now trying to ward off her attack with the black knight.

It had taken a damnable eternity to rid himself of the general. Abercrombie had insisted on questioning Major MacKinnon until well past midnight and then pretended to analyze the battle, while drinking the better part of a bottle of William's best cognac.

Thank heaven the general was leaving in the morning.

Abercrombie's presence had been disruptive and aggravating, but there was little William could do about it. The man was his commanding officer. William had never cried to his uncle or his grandsire for political favors, preferring to earn his way in the world so that he might merit whatever praise came his way. Yet he was hard pressed to see how he was going to tolerate much more of Abercrombie's foolishness in the waging of this war.

True, it had been entertaining to watch him put Major

MacKinnon through his paces shooting at marks, not only because it had angered the major so mightily, but also because Major MacKinnon was such an impressive shot. William would never admit it to anyone but himself, but he envied the major his skill in battle. Not that he himself wasn't deadly with a flintlock, but William was nowhere near the marksman that the major—like all his Rangers—was. Then again, he hadn't grown up firing a rifle to fill his belly.

He advanced the knight, checking the white queen's advance, then pondered the queen's next move.

What galled William most about Abercrombie's unexpected visit was the fact that he'd been able to spend no time on the question of Annie Burns—no more amusing dinners, no time to observe her. Still, she was ever in his mind. The more he thought about it, the more he was certain he'd seen her someplace before. Yet how could that be true? He certainly would have remembered meeting a woman as lovely as she. Nonetheless, the feeling remained.

He'd gotten daily reports from the surgeon, who'd taken a fatherly interest in her welfare, and what he'd heard had only served to intrigue him further—her quick mind, her ability to face sickness and injury without flinching, her apparent concern for the welfare of men she did not know. He'd seen these qualities himself just this evening, when he and Abercrombie had visited the wounded.

And he'd seen something else, too—her fear for Major MacKinnon's safety and her relief and joy when she saw he was still alive. She cared for him. Deeply. Why that should vex him, William knew not. They were both Highland Scots, both bound to the American frontier, both unmarried—a match, it would seem. But while Major MacKinnon was the grandson of a barbarian laird and descended from ancient Celtic kings, Miss Burns was ostensibly of common birth.

And yet she was not common at all. Rescued from squalor and death on the frontier, she'd read Shakespeare, pretended rather ineffectively *not* to know her table manners, and carried herself with a grace and poise more common among nobility than Scottish crofters. None of it fit. She was no mere husbandman's daughter—William would stake his life on that.

He also found it strange that she did not wish to leave Fort Elizabeth. He'd never met a woman who'd willingly chosen to live here—apart from camp followers, of course. Based on Dr. Blake's observations, William guessed Miss Burns was afraid of returning to Albany.

With any luck he'd soon know why. Shortly after Abercrombie had deposited his girth on William's doorstep, William had sent his man to Albany to seek information about her and the people with whom she'd been living. Surely they must have come into Albany for supplies now and again. A young woman as lovely as Miss Burns would be hard to forget.

Aye, someone would remember something.

Iain swung his claymore, felt his sword connect with Morgan's. The shock of steel striking steel traveled from his palms to his wrists to his shoulders. He deflected his brother's blade, lifted his own and sliced downward, narrowly missing his brother's skull.

Morgan thrust his blade into the earth, his face an angry scowl. "What the bloody hell is wrong wi' you this morn'? That's the second time you've come near to takin' my head off!"

Iain lowered his sword, caught his breath. "There's naugh' wrong wi' me. You're no' payin' heed!"

"The only reason your blade is no' lodged between my ears is that I *am* payin' heed!"

Iain knew Morgan was right. "Sorry, brother. I'm worried about Connor and the men."

"This is no' about Connor! 'Tis about her!"

Morgan's words cut deeper than any blade, and the rage Iain had carried with him through the night surged up from his gut. "Dinnae speak to me of her!"

"McHugh helped her across the bridge this morn'. He

said she looked as if she'd spent the whole night weepin'. Is that your doin'?"

Iain wanted to shout in his brother's face that Annie Burns was Annie Campbell—a liar and possibly a thief. Yet he found he could not shame her. Nor could he reveal her secret to Wentworth, who would surely see her sold again. As angry as he was, he could not bear to think of her in bondage. And so the truth festered inside him, mired in rage and anguish and his lingering desire for her.

"Shut your bloody gob, or I'll shut it for you!"

"So it's a fight you want, aye?" In the blink of an eye Morgan's claymore was back in his hands, and he drove hard at Iain, scarce giving Iain time to ward off blows that surely would have cleaved him apart had they met flesh.

But Iain had been sparring with Morgan since they were lads. He knew his brother's strengths and his weaknesses. He parried, struck hard at him, forced him backward and might have driven Morgan's blade from his grasp had Morgan not foreseen his move and countered with a blow of his own.

They fought like two men possessed, slashing at one another until Iain's arms ached, his heart hammered, and sweat poured down his face, the clash of steel against steel ringing through the bright morning. The Rangers gathered in a crowd around them, though Iain did not see them.

Then, abruptly, Iain's blade flew from his hands, and Morgan's fist connected with his jaw. He found himself on his back, dazed, the breath knocked from him, the tip of his brother's sword at his throat.

"You've been bested, brother." Sweat dripped from Morgan's brow, and his breath came fast and heavy. "You shouldna fight when you're so distraught. You'll wind up dead."

Iain knocked his brother's sword aside, drew air into his lungs and got to his feet, pain helping to clear his mind. He reached out, clapped Morgan on the shoulder. "You've a strong fist and a keen sword arm."

Then he went after his claymore and strode off toward the river to clean up, aware that his men were staring at him.

He would go see Wentworth and suggest another scouting expedition.

He needed to leave the fort.

Chapter Twenty-two

Annie stirred the embers and added wood to the fire. It was a warm spring day, but she needed to boil water to make herbal infusions for Dr. Blake, who had been called away by Lord William on a matter of some importance. The herbs had been cleaned and waited to steep in copper bowls on the nearby table.

Behind her, Connor and Killy slept, the last two Rangers to remain in the hospital. Both had been battling fevers, but Connor was now on the mend, thanks to his own infuriating stubbornness—and the little jar of stinging salve. Killy's belly wound, which luckily had not pierced his entrails, was healing, but the scalp wound on his head had festered badly.

Two more of Iain's men had died—Alban and Hamish—both of gunshot wounds that had pierced their bellies, spilling their own poisons into their blood. Annie had done all she could to relieve their suffering—given them laudanum, cooled their brows, held their hands—and had wept at their passing. The rest of the Rangers had recovered enough to move back to their wee cabins on the island, where they waited for their comrades to return from their latest mission.

Iain had been gone for six days now, and for each one of those six days, Annie had prayed for him—and feared for him. For all she knew, he lay hurt or was fighting for his life at this very moment. She remembered the endless leagues of their frightful journey through the forest and felt sick when she thought of him thrust into such danger once again.

He'd left the morning after the ambush, and Annie knew in her heart that he'd gone away at least in part because of her. Did he hate her so much he couldn't bear the sight of her?

Weighed down by the gloom of her own thoughts, she turned from the hearth, picked up a basket of linen strips, sat and began to roll them into bandages, her eyelids heavy. No matter how she had tried this past week, she could not sleep, at least not deeply. Plagued by unquiet dreams, consumed by regrets, she'd spent more time staring into the darkness and weeping than asleep.

She'd give anything if she could take that night back. She'd have halted his kisses and told him the truth before he could discover her lie himself. Perhaps then he'd have believed her. Perhaps he'd have found it in his heart to forgive her. Or perhaps it had always been too late.

He was willing to marry you, Annie.

And she would have accepted. No matter that he was a Catholic, the son of Jacobites, a man who despised her king. None of that seemed to matter now. Aye, she'd have married him—and thought herself the luckiest of women.

She loved him.

God save her, but she loved him.

She loved his strength, his courage. She loved his fairness, the protective way in which he led his men—a true son of Highland lairds. She loved his gentleness, the way his big hands, so fierce with rifle and blade, moved tenderly over her skin. She loved the deep blue of his eyes, the velvet of his voice, the exotic markings on his sun-browned skin. She loved his manly smell, the hardness of his body, the way his kisses set her aflame.

And he despised her.

Grief, bitter and sharp, stabbed at her breast, stealing her breath, robbing her day of light.

How could she have forgotten her brand? How could she have been so careless?

Time and again she'd asked herself that question, but she knew the answer. With his lips and hands upon her—and his promise to wed her fresh in her heart—she'd not been able to think of anything but him.

And now?

Now he thought her a thief. She had seen it in his eyes.

The trouble wi' a liar, Miss Campbell, *is that a man doesna ken what he can believe.*

She supposed she should be grateful he hadn't yet turned her over to Lord William or denounced her to his men. She was certain Lord William would send her to Albany to be resold if he knew. He might even clap her in irons—an ordeal Annie did not think she could endure again. But more painful than anything Lord William could do to her would be to see the kind light in the Rangers' eyes darken to loathing.

Water hissed and splashed as it boiled over onto the fire.

Annie set the basket of bandages aside, hurried to the hearth, wrapped her apron around her hand and lifted the pot of boiling water from its hook. Then, taking care not to burn herself, she poured it over the leaves in the copper bowls, covered the bowls with clean cloths and left the herbs to steep. She had just returned the kettle to its hook, when a voice startled her from behind.

"Can you get the doctor, miss? I've a bellyache."

She spun about to find a young soldier with a sunburned face standing only a few feet behind her. His blond hair was pulled back in a sloppy queue, his uniform unkempt. Even standing a few feet away she could smell he was in desperate need of a bath. "Dr. Blake is wi' the colonel just now. You can take one of the beds and wait for him to return, if you like."

His gaze raked over her, and he smiled. "Aye."

Feeling strangely ill at ease, she took a step back from him. "Shall I make you a cup of chamomile tea? It might help."

He nodded, his gaze fixed on her breasts.

She turned away from him and walked toward the hearth, grateful for an excuse to put distance between them.

He is just a soldier and young, Annie. Dinnae be a goose!

Rough hands grabbed her from behind, covered her mouth and cut off her scream.

His foul breath scorched her temple. " 'Tis not really me belly that aches—'tis me tadger. And I don't think a cup of tea will help me quite as much as your tight little cunnie."

Iain had set a relentless pace. They'd reached Ticonderoga in a quick three days. Iain had set up a guard, left Morgan in command and had then led a small party to the top of Rattlesnake Mountain. There they'd spied the beginnings of an abatis—a barrier of fallen trees that, when finished, would stretch from one end of the small Ticonderoga peninsula to the other. Clearly the French knew an attack was coming and were doing all they could to ready themselves.

"It doesna look so high," Dougie had said, squinting against the noon sun.

"That's because you're far above it," Iain had explained.

Joseph had pointed in the Indian way—with a jerk of his head. "Look how the soldiers reach up to throw more branches on the heap. It is taller than you are."

"Could we climb it?"

Iain had handed his spyglass to Joseph. "We'd be cut to ribbons by cannon and rifle fire from their ramparts. They've built it so that every foot is covered from above. If Abercrombie tries to send his troops over the top of that death trap, he'll lose them to a man."

They'd done their best to reckon troop strength. Then they'd come down off the mountain, taken turns getting some sleep and started the journey back to Fort Elizabeth.

If Iain had hoped the trek would take his mind off Annie, he'd been mistaken. Treading silently through the trees, he'd had far too much time to think, and there seemed to be reminders of her everywhere. The remains of the whaleboats he'd destroyed when the Abenaki had caught up with them. The hilltop where she'd slept in his arms. The prow of rock and earth that had hidden them from the French when the battle had overtaken them.

When he'd set out on this mission, he'd been certain Annie was naught but a liar and that his anger was more than justified. She had deceived him for weeks. She'd listened to him tell of the murder charge that hung over his head but kept her own life secret. She had looked into his eyes, heard his promise to wed her and she'd said nothing. She'd been ready to give herself to him—to yield her body, but not her true name: Campbell. Only after he'd discovered her brand had she spun her tale for him—and an unlikely tale it was.

But with each league that passed beneath his moccasins, his certainty crumbled until he now doubted himself as much as he doubted her.

How could she have concocted such a terrible story if it were not the truth? What virgin—and he knew women well enough to be certain she was a virgin—would ken anything of the sinister side of sex unless she had accidentally witnessed it, as she'd said she had? What court would have ordered her to be branded on her inner thigh instead of upon her thumb or wrist or cheek, where it could be seen as the symbol of shame it was meant to be?

So many things he'd always found oddish about her began to fit.

My uncle saw to it that I wanted for naught.

The new calluses on her hands and her baby-soft feet told of a pampered life, as did her skill with reading and the way she fit so well at Wentworth's dinner table. Iain had been raised in a laird's hall, after all, and even he didn't ken what all of that silver gibbletry was for.

He'd bound her to his bed. He was usin' her . . . in unnatural ways.

She'd gone pale when Iain had jested with her about tying him to his bed, fear making her green eyes go wide.

Mistress Hawes hated me and thought me lazy because I didna ken how to milk a cow or clean hides or cook. She beat me wi' a leather strap.

Hadn't he seen the yellow stripes upon her back?

I couldna risk being sold again. I wanted my life back. I wanted to be free!

If there was anything Iain understood, it was the yearning for freedom. Hadn't he and his brothers also been blamed for a crime they did not commit? Hadn't they been forced to fight for Wentworth simply because they knew no one would believe three Catholic Highlanders over the king's own grandson?

I hated lyin' to you, but I didna think you'd believe me! No one else has.

Most of all there was the way she'd told him—tears coursing down her cheeks, her body shaking, her stomach revolting. How could she have feigned such a response? Being forced to tell him had been hell on her, and he hadn't shown her the slightest bit of compassion.

Remorse gnawed at Iain's gut, and a dark sense of foreboding drove him forward.

"You can't get back to her any faster by walking into an ambush." Joseph spoke in Muhheconneok, his voice low enough that only Iain could hear him.

Or so Iain thought.

"You can't undo whatever stupid thing you've done by dying out here," Morgan agreed. "Slow down, and get your mind off Annie and back on the trail."

Iain felt a prick of irritation. "What makes you sure *I* did something stupid?"

"The regret on your face," Morgan said.

"Is it so plain to see?"

Joseph and Morgan answered as one. "Yes."

Then Joseph asked the question Iain had hoped to avoid.

"Are you going to tell us, or do we have to spend the rest of the journey guessing?"

He did not want to expose Annie, but he found himself telling them the story, certain they'd take his secrets to their graves. As he spoke, it became clear to him he'd done Annie a horrible wrong.

"Then I turned my back on her and walked away. I let her think I might turn her over to Wentworth to be sold again."

For a moment, neither Joseph nor Morgan spoke; the only sound was the whisper of moccasins against the forest floor.

Then Joseph let out a breath. "Have you always been this skilled with women?"

Morgan swore under his breath. "I can scarce fathom the horror of it—being betrayed and branded by her uncle, being sold to people who beat her, nearly being killed by the Abenaki. No woman should have to be so strong."

"No." It sickened Iain to think of Annie alone in gaol amid filth and stench and men so vile she feared to speak of them. It sickened him even more to think of her uncle forcing her legs apart and burning her with hot iron.

"So she's a Campbell." Morgan grinned. "I can see why in a camp of MacKinnons, Camerons, McDonalds and McHughs she'd want to keep that a secret."

"Campbell." Joseph spoke the name. "Is that an enemy tribe?"

"Yes." Iain didn't feel like explaining a century of Scottish history.

"I'll bet that's how she knows Wentworth," Morgan put in, "for I'm certain she knows who he is."

Iain didn't want to think about that. "The point is she lied to me."

"What would you have done in her place—a woman alone on the frontier?" Morgan tossed Iain a disapproving frown. "She was trying to survive."

Iain honestly couldn't say, and it bothered him all the more.

Then it was Joseph's turn to berate him. "Does she know what hangs over your head?"

"Yes."

"And how did she respond when she learned she'd been kissing a murderer?"

"But I am not really a murderer!"

Joseph met his gaze, his dark eyes unsympathetic. "How was she to know for certain? It is lucky for you she has more compassion in her heart than you have in yours, salmon brains."

Annie tried to pull away from her attacker, but he wrenched her arm painfully behind her back and shoved her toward the storage room.

"Do as I tell you, or I'll make it hurt worse!" He twisted her arm more as if to prove his point.

Brutal pain shot up through her shoulder, and for a moment she feared the bone would shatter. Unable to cry for help, unable to free herself, she stumbled before him, her mind racing for some way to fight back.

For a moment, she thought he would rape her on the storeroom floor. But he was in too much of a hurry for that. He forced her to bend over a heavy cask of rum, holding her in place with the wiry weight of his body.

Then he released her arm, lifted her skirts and kicked her feet apart, spreading her legs. Her fear thickened, turned to darkest dread. This could not be happening!

"What's this? A brand?" He chuckled. "So MacKinnon's woman is a convict. I'll bet you were a whore, right? Is that what it says?"

Desperate with panic, Annie kicked at his shins, clawed and bit at the hand that silenced her until she tasted blood.

"Ouch, bitch!" He jerked his hand away from her mouth. She screamed.

He drove his elbow into the back of her neck, leaving her stunned and dizzy. "Quiet, or I'll break your neck!"

She heard buttons snap off the fabric of his trousers, and tried to rise above her dizziness and pain to fight him. But he was heavier and much stronger than she. Pinned face-down, she could not reach him to strike at him.

"You might as well enjoy it, missy. I know I will."

"That might be hard wi' your brains splattered on the wall."

For a moment Annie thought it was Iain's voice she'd heard. But then her attacker jerked her upright and thrust her before him like a shield, his arm wrapped tightly around her throat.

Connor!

He stood wearing only his drawers, his right shoulder bound with bandages, a pistol clutched in his left hand and already cocked. He leaned against the doorway, barely strong enough to stand. But his aim was steady. "Get your hands off her, or I'll split your skull!"

"You'd risk killing your brother's whore?"

A muscle jumped in Connor's jaw, and his gaze darkened. "You Regulars have trouble hittin' marks, aye? We Rangers dinnae miss."

She felt her attacker's heart beat faster, felt his body tense, and her own pulse quickened.

With a mighty shove, the soldier thrust her away from him, sent her hurtling into Connor, and the two of them top-pled onto the floor. Connor broke her fall with his body, but the impact knocked the pistol from his hand. It clattered across the floor and slid beneath one of the empty beds, far beyond reach.

In a heartbeat, Connor was on his feet. The soldier drove into him, and they fell to the floor in a heap of flying fists. But Connor was already weak from fever and blood loss, and the soldier quickly had him on his back.

Glancing frantically about, Annie leapt up, grabbed a bottle of laudanum from the table and brought the heavy glass down on the soldier's head. He fell to the floor and lay still.

Weak with relief, Annie hurried to where Connor lay, knelt beside him. "Are you hurt?"

He sat up slowly, wiping blood from his lower lip. "Just my pride. 'Tis sorry I am I didna stop him sooner, lass. Forgi'e me."

She cupped his cheek in her palm, dabbed the blood from his face with her apron. "There is naught to forgi'e, Connor. If no' for you . . . Mercy!"

A deep shudder coursed through her.

Connor brushed a strand of hair from her cheek. " 'Tis best no' to think on that. But go now. Bring me my pistol, then fetch Wentworth. This bit of filth belongs to him."

As she hurried on unsteady legs to do as Connor asked, it came to her.

The soldier had seen her brand, and he would surely tell Lord William.

Knowing Annie would be at the hospital, Iain stopped to bathe in the river and stowed his gear in Morgan's cabin before entering the fort. He went to see Wentworth first to give his report and was admitted the moment he arrived. He delivered the intelligence he'd gathered quickly, impatient to be done so he could go to Annie. There was much he would say to her, much for them to discuss.

And then there was the matter of taking up where they'd left off—she on her back and bared to his kisses, he between her thighs.

"If they finish that abatis before we attack, there will be no way for troops to reach the fort over land. They've no more than three thousand men gathered now. The time to attack is soon, before the abatis is complete and their ranks increase."

Wentworth sat at his writing table and observed him coolly over a glass of wine. "General Abercrombie disagrees. He believes overwhelming force is the answer and wants to wait until he can amass and supply an army of fifteen thousand."

"Abercrombie is an idiot, and you ken it as well as I."

"Such decisions are not yours to make, Major."

"Nay, 'tis true. I dinnae choose how or when to do the fightin', but 'tis my men who do the dyin', aye?" Iain bent down and leaned in until his nose all but touched Wentworth's. "I tell you now, my wee German lairdie, I willna send a single Ranger over that abatis."

For a moment there was silence.

"Is that all, Major?" Wentworth's voice was as placid as a summer lake.

"Aye." Without waiting to be dismissed, Iain turned and strode toward the door.

Wentworth raised his voice a notch. "If you're looking for Miss Burns, you won't find her at the hospital."

Iain stopped in midstride and turned to face him, the sense of foreboding he'd felt all day returning full force. "Where is she?"

"She spent the better part of the afternoon upstairs—in my chamber." Wentworth brought something to his nostrils, closed his eyes and sniffed it, as if savoring its scent.

One of Annie's ribbons.

The sight of it—together with Wentworth's words—struck him like a fist. Annie had been in Wentworth's chamber? Had she left the ribbon as a token?

Even as he denied that she could have done any such thing, even as he reminded himself how Wentworth liked to bait him, a spark of jealous rage burned in his gut.

You turned your back on her and left her weeping, MacKinnon. Did you expect her to pine for you? Did you expect for her to wait for you? Did you no' learn that lesson wi' Jeannie?

He forced that voice out of his mind.

"Forget your bloody games, Wentworth. Where is she?"

"I'm afraid she's rather less innocent than when you left her."

Fury a buzzing sound in his ears, Iain crossed the room in three strides. It was all he could do not to grab the haughty bastard by the lace at his throat and throttle him. "If you have defiled her in any way, neither your rank nor your family crest will protect you from me! Where is she?"

Wentworth glanced at the ribbon in his fingers. "I believe she returned to your cabin, Major. She seemed spent."

From his window, William watched Major MacKinnon leave the fort with angry, determined strides, off to make what William hoped was a terrible mistake.

Most people were predictable. The major was far less so, which was what made him both an interesting and a worthwhile opponent. But today the major had responded to his words exactly as he'd hoped. William hadn't needed to exaggerate or even dissemble.

Miss Burns had, indeed, spent a part of the afternoon in his chamber, but only because he'd insisted she rest. And having endured a near rape, she was most certainly less innocent than she'd been when the major had left six days ago. That the ribbon had fallen from her hair was pure providence. But nothing had been able to persuade her to stay in his quarters, and William had known she was thinking of Major MacKinnon.

She'd been in a fragile state. How would she react to the fifteen stone of jealous, angry Highlander about to confront her? Would she endure him? Or would his anger break the bond between them, perhaps even drive her to seek William's protection?

William hoped for the latter.

Chapter Twenty-three

Annie sat before the fire in her shift, combing her nearly dry hair, trying to pull the pieces of herself together—or keep them from falling apart. Though she'd taken a bath—thanks to Brendan, who'd carried water for her—she could not seem to feel clean again. She could still mark the soldier's hands upon her, smell his rancid breath, hear his hate-filled voice in her mind.

I don't think a cup of tea will help me quite as much as your tight little cunnie.

She'd been through far worse, hadn't she? Aye, she had. But perhaps that was part of it. Since the night Uncle Bain had killed her mother, there'd been no solid ground beneath her feet, no safe haven. Nothing had been certain. There'd been nothing upon which she could depend.

Except for Iain and his Rangers.

She'd already lost Iain. And now she was going to lose the friendship of his men. Either the soldier who'd attacked her would reveal her secret to Lord William, or Iain would. Word of her true name would spread, and the same men who'd been so kind to her these past weeks would scorn her. She would lose the few friends she had. She would be alone again.

She'd been afraid Lord William would use the incident as an example of why she could not work in the hospital or stay at Fort Elizabeth. She'd been more afraid the redcoat who'd attacked her would immediately reveal what he'd seen, leading Lord William to question her or perhaps even call for Dr. Blake to examine her. But so far neither of these calamities had come to pass. Lord William had been the perfect gentleman, showing her every courtesy as she'd recounted the horrible ordeal to him, assuring her the soldier who'd attacked her would receive his just reward, even insisting she rest a while in the guest chambers upstairs. And, seemingly, her attacker had said nothing, perhaps because he didn't know her brand was a secret or perhaps because he knew admitting he'd seen it would confirm his guilt and lead to the gallows.

And so she'd gotten to the end of this day. But how was she to live with this for the rest of her life—this constant dread, this uncertainty, this loneliness? Could she truly hope to escape forever the fate Uncle Bain had thrust upon her?

It gave her some comfort to be in Iain's cabin, surrounded by his belongings, his scent. Brendan had told her that most scouting trips to Ticonderoga lasted six days. That meant there was a chance Iain would be back tonight. Though she knew she could not expect his affection, at least she would know he was safe.

The door flew open with a crash, swinging back so hard it hit the wall.

Annie gasped, leapt to her feet, heart thudding.

He filled the doorway.

"Iain!" The rush of joy she felt at seeing him alive and safe drove her fears and sorrows away. "You're back! You're safe!"

His hair was damp, his face clean shaven, his eyes dark as his gaze raked over her.

She shivered.

Without looking away, he shouted over his shoulder to a Ranger passing by. "McHugh, tell Morgan he's in command. There's a lead ball in my pistol for any man who disturbs me tonight!"

"Aye, Mack."

Then he shut the door behind him and drew in the string. 'Twas then she noticed the expression on his face—hard, brooding, angry.

A bolt of fear quivered through her. "I-Iain?"

Had six days in the wild not even taken the edge off his anger with her?

He strode slowly toward her, lifting his shirt over his head and tossing it aside as he walked. "Do you ken the ancient history of the Highlands, Annie?"

She felt a fluttering in her belly and took an involuntary step backward, afraid but helpless to tear her gaze away from his wine red nipples or the dark curls on his chest. "Aye."

His hands dropped to his waist, and quickly he removed his weapons—two pistols and a hunting knife—and set them on the table. "Then you've heard the stories of Highland lairds and what they did when the woman they wanted was claimed by another."

She looked into his eyes, wondered why he was saying this. "Aye."

"What did they do, lass?" He stood before her now, over-powering her with his presence.

"Iain, why . . . ?" But her words died when his hands moved to the fall of his breeches.

"They took the woman by force and claimed her for themselves."

In a single deft motion, he loosed the ties, peeled the soft leather from his hips and slid it down his corded thighs. His sex was huge, rising thick and hard from a nest of dark curls to stand against the ridges of his belly. Beneath, his stones hung full and heavy.

She had never seen that part of a man's body before, not in this state. And although his carnal beauty stirred her deeply, she was astonished to think anything that big could fit inside a woman without hurting her.

And then it struck her.

He intended to put that inside *her*.

Her heart tripped, and her mouth went dry.

By the time he'd kicked his moccasins aside, and his breeches with them, her breath was coming in pants, and she was trembling. "Y-you . . . you mean to . . . to bed me."

"Clever lass." He took a lock of her hair between his fingers, held it to his nostrils, inhaled. "You've washed his scent off you."

The soldier. He must be speaking of the soldier who'd tried to rape her. Somehow, despite the wild racing of her pulse and her breathlessness, she found the will to answer. "I-I tried."

"Good. I'll be damned before I share you wi' another man!"

She had just enough time to wonder how he could feel jealous of the man who'd attacked her before he crushed her against him, captured her lips with his and forced his tongue deep into her mouth.

This was no tender lover's kiss. It was urgent, rough, brutish.

Somehow it was perfect.

Oh, how she wanted him! How she needed him!

Annie moaned into his mouth and found herself kissing him back, the turmoil of the past six days and the lingering horror of the attack burning away and leaving her with a passion every bit as desperate and demanding as his.

Her tongue fought with his, claiming his mouth, even as he claimed hers. She stole his breath, even as he took hers. Her hands searched over him, feasting on the steel of his muscles and the velvet of his skin, even as his hands roamed over her.

"You're mine, Annie!" His voice was ragged, his breath hot against her throat, the nip of his teeth even hotter as he tasted the sensitive skin beneath her ear.

She reveled in the possessiveness of his words, gave up her throat to his bite, every feminine instinct inside her urging her to surrender. Then his fists bunched between her breasts. She felt a tug, heard the linen of her shift tear. The cloth fell away like a whisper, leaving her naked in his embrace.

"Oh!" She gasped, stunned by the sweet rasp of his chest hair against her nipples, by the searing heat of his sex pressed against her belly, by the rough caress of his callused palms on her shoulders, her back, the curve of her hips. Her knees turned to water, and she sagged against him, whimpering.

With a groan, he cupped her bare buttocks, lifted her hard against him and carried her the few steps to his bed, following her down onto the softness of the bearskin.

A voice in her mind wondered dimly why he was doing this now, but she brushed the question aside. She didn't care. He made her forget. He made her feel clean again. And as he trailed scorching kisses down her throat to her breasts, she was certain she'd waited for this moment her entire life.

Feeling every bit the Highland savage, Iain could not get enough of the woman who trembled and whimpered in his arms. He'd meant to punish her with his lust, to drive any

thoughts of Wentworth from her mind, to claim her once
and for all as his own. But she was more than his match. Her
ardent response provoked him. Her gentle acquiescence in-
flamed him. The musky scent of her need drove him mad.

He lifted his head, drank in the sight of her, and was
struck almost senseless by her beauty, his erection swelling
to painful fullness. Her eyes were squeezed shut, her golden
hair spread across the dark bearskin like sunlight. Her skin
glowed pink with arousal. Her nipples were drawn into
tight, pink crests—buds that, like the ripest fruit, demanded
his mouth.

With a hungry moan, he ducked his head, licked one,
cupping and molding the fullness of her breasts with his
hands. He heard her breath catch, felt her body jerk. Then
he lowered his head to feed in earnest, suckling one puckered crest and then the other.

"Oh, Iain!" Her fingers clenched in his hair, and she
arched beneath him.

He drew back his head, blew across her taut, wet buds,
watched them grow tighter still.

She gasped and shivered, and he saw her press her
creamy thighs tightly together, an attempt to soothe the
ache he'd caused there.

He slipped a hand between her knees, parted them,
denying her that respite. "Nay, *a leannan*. You'll have no relief that doesna come from me."

"Oh, Iain, please!" She arched her hips, unknowingly teasing him with her sweet scent.

He could not deny her without denying himself, and already his need for her was ripping him to pieces. Taking her
cries into his mouth, he slid his hand slowly up the silken
skin of her inner thighs. His fingers found her brand, and he
felt her stiffen.

"Easy, lass." He deepened the kiss, stroking the inside of
her mouth with his tongue even as his fingertips traced the *T*
so cruelly burned into her flesh.

But her scar was not what he was seeking.

He brushed his knuckles over the damp curls of her sex, parted her pouty outer lips, and tugged gently on the slick inner ones, letting his finger tease the tip of her swollen little bud. Then he parted her and slowly slipped a finger inside her slick heat.

Her startled cry became a long, rolling moan, and her fingers dug into the muscles of his shoulders. "Iain! Oh, Iain!"

"You're so wet, lass. So wet."

And tight.

Her maidenhead.

It was intact.

Whatever Wentworth had done, he hadn't taken her.

The surge of lust that flooded through Iain bordered on violence. He hadn't realized until that moment how much it meant to him that he be her first—and only.

Holding onto the tatters of his control, he stroked her, sliding first one finger, then two, in and out of her slippery core. Making her slick with her own dew, he rubbed circles over her swollen bud with his thumb, preparing her to take him, the thought of what her snug quim would do to his aching cock driving him insane. He could not wait much longer.

"Savor your last moments as a virgin, *mo leannan*, for I'll soon be inside you."

Both aroused and frightened by his words, Annie opened her eyes to find him looking down at her, his gaze gone dark, an almost feral expression on his face. "But, Iain—!"

"*Uist!* I warned you this would happen. Tonight you're mine." Then he lowered his hot, teasing mouth to her breast.

She heard a woman moaning in carnal abandon—and was surprised to realize the voice was hers. But then she'd never felt anything like the slick friction of his fingers inside her. Each thrust stretched her, filled her, promised to satisfy the throbbing ache inside her—but only made her more desperate. The way he teased that most sensitive part of her made her womb quiver, filled her belly with fire. Shame forgotten, she found herself spreading her thighs father apart, lifting her hips to meet him.

He groaned, nipped her earlobe. "Aye, *mo leannan*, open yourself to me!"

Frantic, desperate cries escaped her as he kept up a relentless rhythm, teasing her, penetrating her, driving her toward the edge.

But before her peak could claim her, he stretched out above her and settled himself between her legs, forcing her thighs farther apart with his own. Then she felt the thick head of his shaft press against her aching cleft.

She wanted him inside her, yearned for him inside her, yet she could not help the spark of fear that licked through her. "W-will it hurt?"

"My bonnie, sweet Annie! I will try to spare you, but, och, you are so . . ."

His voice trailed off into a rough moan. With a slight thrust of his hips, he nudged the hard tip of his sex inside her, then withdrew. Then he probed her again, and again he withdrew. Again and again he pushed into her, stretching her a bit more each time, opening her slowly, until his motions became an erotic torment.

She heard herself moan. "Iain, please!"

The next thrust felt tight, and she knew he'd reached her maidenhead.

"Oh, Annie!" For a moment, he stopped, poised on the brink of her innocence, his body rippling with tension, breath hissing from between his clenched teeth. Then with one agonizing, slow thrust, he breached her.

The pain was knife-sharp.

Annie bit back a cry, squeezed her eyes shut, instinctively trying to pull her hips away.

"It will soon pass, *mo leannan*." He held himself still inside her, raining tender kisses on her cheeks, her eyelids, on the pulse at her throat, whispering endearments in English, in Gaelic, in a language she didn't know, his body taut, his voice strained.

But even as the pain faded, she realized how much more

of him there was to receive. Only the head of his shaft was inside her. "Oh, Iain, I dinnae think I can—!"

"Easy, lass. You were made to take me. Feel how your body surrenders to mine." He withdrew and slowly, so slowly, entered her again.

This time instead of pain she felt an arousing sense of fullness. She whimpered with the pleasure of it, clenched her fingers against his chest.

"Holy Jesus God!" He groaned, withdrew again, then drove himself completely into her, punctuating his heated kisses with words. "You . . . are . . . heaven—so . . . perfect!"

She could feel him against her womb, his body joined fully to hers. It was too much, too much. It was not nearly enough. And then he began to move, his body sliding over her, against her, inside her in a sensual rhythm that scattered the last of her thoughts and set her soul aflame.

Iain forced himself to breathe, fought his body's urge to climax at once, determined to master himself and give her all the delight he could. He hadn't meant to hurt her, had tried hard not to hurt her. She had gifted him with her maidenhood, and now he would return the gift by showing her the fullness of a man's loving.

He moved in her with slow, silky strokes, allowing her to grow accustomed to the feel of him, letting her hunger build. Her eyes were half closed, her lips parted as she cried out in pleasure, the sound of his name mingled with throaty moans. He nibbled kisses along the column of her throat, whorled his tongue over her ear, bit down on her earlobe, muttering endearments against her fevered dewy skin.

"*Mo rùn-sa.*" My sweet darling.

"*Mo stòr.*" My treasure.

"*Mo ribhinn.*" My nymph.

Already she'd begun to tighten around him, gripping him like an eager fist. Lifting her hips, she met his thrusts, matched his rhythm stroke for stroke, her heat burning him alive. The claws of a climax dragged at his belly, drew him perilously close to the edge. But he would not let go. He would not. Not yet.

He thrust deep, held himself inside her, then ground the root of his cock against her mound. "Take from me, Annie! I want to watch you come!"

"Oh, God, Iain!" Her cries grew frantic, her nails biting into his shoulders.

And then her breath broke, and she arched against him—and shattered.

He caught her scream with his mouth, felt her clench down hard upon him, and almost lost what was left of his control.

Annie heard herself cry his name again and again as savage pleasure exploded inside her. Delight burned through her like a ravenous wildfire, the searing shock of it almost more than she could bear, as he fed the flames with deft, deep strokes. And then she was floating—nothing but velvety ashes on a warm breeze.

The sound of his breathing drew her back to awareness. She opened her eyes, saw him watching her, his chest expanding powerfully with each breath. He was slick with sweat, beads of perspiration gathered on his furrowed brow, strands of long dark hair sticking to his chest and cheeks. His lips were swollen from kissing her, his jaw clenched and dark with the day's growth of beard. His body almost shook with tension, muscles drawn tight across his chest, in his shoulders, beneath the Indian markings on his arms.

He seemed the very essence of primal male—fierce, potent, aggressive.

A warrior. A Highland barbarian.

Her barbarian.

And he was joined to her, his body still inside hers and still hard.

The breath left her lungs in a rush. "Iain!"

He began to move again, rekindling flames inside her she'd thought extinguished. But his rhythm was different this time, his thrusts more forceful. And even as her pleasure began to build anew, she realized how much he'd been holding back.

He had known her passion. Now she would know his.

"You'd drive a man mad, lass!" He shifted his weight to one arm, reached between them, found her sensitive bud, and caressed her.

In a heartbeat, she was on the brink again, bliss shivering inside her like sunlight on water. And then it spilled over, sensations too good to be real washing through her in wave after bright, trembling wave.

The sound of her cries seemed to push him over the edge. With a growl, he shifted, moved his hand to grasp her buttocks, and pulled her tight against him, angling her hips to receive him deeply. Then he drove into her with fast, powerful strokes, spearing her with his heat, his passion at last unleashed.

His pleasure feeding hers, Annie found herself clinging to him, gasping in surprise and delight, as another climax overtook her and sent her flying. But this time he went with her. She felt his body shudder, heard his deep groan, as he at last let himself go and spilled his seed deep inside her.

"Are you certain it's the same family?" William stared unseeing out his darkened window, disbelief warring with complete and utter surprise.

Annie Burns a *convict*?

"Aye, my lord, quite certain. The location of the cabin, the wife's advanced pregnancy and the description of the girl fit quite neatly."

"Was the sheriff aware of the massacre?"

"Aye, my lord. He told me Indians had most likely taken the girl back to their village to ravish, which he blamed on the Indian man's unnatural interest in white women and on her uncommon beauty."

Uncommon beauty.

A fitting, if inadequate, description of Miss Burns.

"So the sheriff met her in the flesh?"

"She was with Master Hawes when he registered her indenture. The sheriff seemed to remember her quite vividly, in part because of her beauty—"

William had no trouble believing that.

"—and in part because she insisted she was innocent, claiming to be the daughter of a Scottish earl and the victim of foul play."

Daughter of a Scottish earl.

William turned on his heel, feeling in his bones that he'd come to the truth. "Under what name was she registered?"

"Anne Campbell, my lord."

There were thousands of Campbells in Scotland, but not many of noble birth.

William poured himself a brandy and tried to recall the various branches of Clan Campbell. He was most familiar with the Argyll Campbells, as they—

The blood rushed from his head.

Anne Campbell.

Lady Anne Campbell.

Niece of Bain Campbell, Marquis of Bute, a hero of Prestonpans.

Daughter of the Earl of Rothesay, who'd died at Prestonpans.

The moment it came to him, he knew he was right. A memory flashed through his mind of a quiet girl, not yet old enough to have breasts but destined to be a beauty. Her hair was a darker shade of golden blond now, the face that of a woman and not a child. But the eyes—those stunning green eyes—were the same.

He'd met young Lady Anne while staying with Lord Bute on his way to visit the Duke of Argyll. He'd barely paid her any heed, despite her mother's cloying attempts to draw his eye, for the girl was neither old enough to merit his sexual interest nor wealthy and English enough to be a suitable prospect for a wife. He had considered bedding her mother, however, a pretty widow not much older than himself.

William swirled his cognac, recalled the night Miss

Burns—Lady Anne—had been led into his presence. The blood had rushed from her face the moment she'd seen him, and she'd curtsied like a lady at court.

"M-my lord."

The little minx had recognized him immediately. And yet she'd kept her identity secret, even though he was ideally placed in society to give her aid. In fact, she had lied to him. Why?

"Did the sheriff say what kind of foul play Miss Burns claimed to have endured?"

"Nay, my lord. He said only that he'd never met a guilty convict, as they all claim to be innocent."

"Of course." William set the snifter aside, opened the top drawer of his writing table, took a few sovereigns from the chest in which he kept his coin and dropped them in an out-stretched palm. "Excellent work. There's a meal waiting for you in the officer's mess. Speak of this to no one. Report to me first thing tomorrow. I'll have a letter waiting for you to carry to port. You are dismissed."

"I am your most humble servant, my lord."

But William, lost in his thoughts, didn't hear his man leave.

How had Campbell's niece come to be sold as a servant? Why had she not sought William's help, knowing he had more power than most men to redress whatever wrongs had been done her? Why had Campbell failed to protect her, and why had she not sought to contact her uncle? He had questions aplenty, but not a single answer.

Did Major MacKinnon know the woman he lusted after was both a convict and the daughter of a British peer? No, of course he didn't. He and his men would no more tolerate an Argyll Campbell among them than they would embrace the House of Hanover. If the major were to discover her true identity, it would enrage him—perhaps to the point of violence—leaving Lady Anne no one to turn to in this vast wilderness except William.

The very notion made William's groin tighten.

William would expose her, of course. And then he would offer her his protection. But before he could act, he needed to know her entire story. He didn't want to inadvertently set himself at odds with Lord Bute. Bain Campbell, though only a Scot, was not without his allies in the House of Lords, foremost among them his cousin, the Duke of Argyll. He was also reputed to be deadly with the broadsword.

William suspected Lady Anne would not willingly give him the truth about her situation, but he knew who would. He sat at his desk, set his brandy aside, and pulled out paper, ink and quill, his mind already crafting the strategically worded letter he would write to her uncle.

Chapter Twenty-four

Iain looked at the lass who slept in his arms and felt his chest swell with an emotion he'd thought never to feel again and was loath to name. When he'd heard Jeannie had married another man, he'd thought the rage and pain would be the end of him. When she'd been killed three months later, whatever had remained of his feelings and his dreams had been buried in the cold earth with her, leaving him empty. He'd resigned himself to war, certain he'd not live to see the farm restored or to take a wife and father children.

Now it seemed he would at least ken the pleasures of a wife. He ought to have been angry with himself, for 'twas not fair to Annie that she must now wed a soldier, a man with no home, a man who was not free. But as he held her, his body replete, his mind almost empty, all he could feel was deep contentment.

She stirred in her sleep, her sweet face like that of an angel. He brushed a lock of hair off her cheek, determined to do right by her for as long as God let him live.

But how would Annie, who'd been raised a Protestant amid wealth, her kin allied to royalty, feel about becoming the wife of an exiled Highlander, a Catholic, a man with nothing but the weapons and clothes upon his back? How would she feel about being wed by a priest and raising Catholic children? How would she feel about living her life on the frontier?

She'd lain with him, given herself to him with abandon, and had seemed willing enough to wed him a week ago. 'Twas clear in the way her body responded to his that she was attracted to him. But he suspected part of her attraction was owed to her plight. She had curbed her tongue in the wild for fear he might abandon her or do her harm. Was she drawn to him now because he offered her food, shelter and a man's protection? One thing was certain: Had the two of them met in Scotland, he the grandson of The MacKinnon, she the cosseted niece of a wealthy Argyll Campbell, she'd not so much as deigned to speak with him.

In the end it mattered not how she felt. Iain would have it no other way. He would not shame her, nor would he leave her unprotected in case their passion had gotten her with child.

And it had been passionate—beyond anything he'd known before. Certainly he'd taken pleasure in his share of women, but never had he felt anything like the rapture he'd found with Annie. Never had he been so aware of a woman's every breath, every heartbeat, every tremor as he'd been with her. When at last he'd let himself go, it had been *him*—his life, his very essence—that had spilled from his body and into her.

He had transformed her forever, taking her from maidenhood to womanhood, and yet it was he who was somehow changed.

With a little sigh, she snuggled deeper into his chest, and the bearskin slipped to reveal a slender, pale arm. And then he saw.

Bruises.

There were fresh bruises on her upper arms and on one wrist. Deep, purple bruises.

Holy Mary! Had he done that to her? He'd been angry, aye, and impatient in his need for her. But he hadn't hurt her—had he? He didn't remember seeing bruises on her when he'd undressed her, so this must be his doing.

She's right. You are a barbarian, MacKinnon.

He would have to be more careful of her from now on.

Sure she would wake hungry, he slid out from beneath her, careful not to rouse her. If he didn't get to the kitchens soon, there would be no supper left for the two of them. He washed the remnants of their union from his groin and saw flecks of blood on the cloth—her virgin's blood. She would be sore. He would see to it she got a hot bath tomorrow morning.

He dressed and quietly slipped out the door.

Outside, the sun had already set, but the air was still warm, the feel of spring on the breeze. From the kitchens came the smell of frying fish, roasted venison and corn bread. Dougie was tuning his fiddle to the sound of robust laughter as the men, their bellies finally full after six hard days on the trail, settled down with their rum.

Iain walked toward the kitchens feeling strangely at ease and satisfied. When had he last felt this way? He couldn't remember.

Up ahead, Morgan spotted him and fell in beside him, his face grave. "How is she?"

Beautiful, Iain wanted to say. *Well and truly bedded. Mine.*

He held back the words, but could not help the smile. "She's asleep."

"They're going try the bastard in a court martial tomorrow afternoon. I hope he hangs."

Iain stopped, confused. "You hope who hangs?"

Morgan stared at him as if he'd gone daft. "The redcoat who tried to rape her."

*   *   *

His fury building, Iain sat beside Connor's hospital bed and listened while his brother recounted the attack on Annie. 'Twas the second time he'd heard the tale—the first being from Morgan. He didn't know whom to hate most—the *neach dìolain* who'd hurt her, Wentworth for twisting the truth and driving him to a jealous rage or himself for permitting Wentworth to control him.

A redcoat had tried to rape Annie, and what she'd gotten from Iain instead of comfort was anger and lust. Sharp regret jabbed at his gut as he remembered his own words.

You've washed his scent off you.

I tried.

She hadn't been speaking of Wentworth, but of a man who'd tried to hurt her in the worst way a man could hurt a woman—and who had left her feeling tainted. And what had Iain said?

Good. I'll be damned before I share you wi' another man.

God, what must she have thought of that?

Well done, MacKinnon, you bloody arse!

And yet he did not wish to take back what he'd done after that—not for the world. He knew Annie hadn't been unwilling. She'd melted in his arms as if she belonged there. She'd met his kisses and caresses with her own, demanding from him as much as he'd forced her to give. She'd lost herself in their loving every bit as much as he.

"I am sorry I didna get to her sooner. If her scream hadna woken me . . ." The expression on Connor's face changed from regret to anger. "I wish I'd killed him—that son of evil!"

Iain put his hand on Connor's uninjured shoulder. "You've no cause to blame yourself. You did all you could. I'm grateful you were here."

Morgan gave Connor a jab. "Thank the Almighty for that French ball."

Then Connor frowned. "I find it strange she didna tell you this herself."

"I didna gi' her the chance." Iain took a deep breath then switched to Gaelic so Dr. Blake, who was puttering nearby, could not understand him. He did not wish to dishonor Annie with careless words. "Wentworth told me . . . I thought she'd been with Wentworth. I went to her to claim her."

"Holy Mary!" Morgan glared at him in disgust. "When McHugh told me you'd given the order not to be disturbed, I thought you'd gone to comfort her. What did you do?"

Iain looked at his brothers. "We need a priest."

"A priest?" His brothers spoke as one, still in Gaelic.

"Och, well, that's no problem. There are Catholic priests behind every bloody tree." Then Morgan grinned. "My brother is marryin' an Argyll Campbell."

"An Argyll Campbell?" Connor looked revolted, then stunned. "Our Annie?"

Iain rose, eager to return to her. She deserved all the tenderness he could give her tonight. "Morgan will tell you about it. I dinnae want her to wake and find me gone. But we've her safety to consider. She lives under penalty of bondage, and Wentworth intends some ill for her—I can feel it. Ask Joseph to call a warrior's council in two hours."

He thought of Annie lying naked beneath his bearskin.

"Best make it three."

Still on the threshold of dreams, Annie felt lips touch her cheek. She stretched, felt the soft caress of fur against her skin. Something smelled wonderful. She opened her eyes and found Iain stretched out beside her fully clothed, looking down at her, his gaze soft, a faint smile on his lips.

"My sweet Annie." He brushed his knuckles gently over her cheek.

"You've brought supper."

"That I have. Are you hungry?"

"Famished."

Then she met his gaze, and heat crept slowly into her cheeks as memories of what they'd shared filled her mind. Did other women behave as she had, so lost in pleasure they lacked all restraint and cried out with abandon? The sounds she'd made had been more animal than human, certainly not the sounds a lady should make. And the way her body had sweated and strained beneath his—

"You've no cause for shame, *mo ghràid*." He spoke as if he could read her thoughts. "What passed between us—'tis as it should be between a man and his lass."

"You dinnae think me wanton?"

He narrowed his eyes, bit his lower lip and pretended to study her until her face burned. Then he smiled. "Och, 'tis for certain you're a lusty creature when your blood runs hot—ardent, eager, radgie."

She gasped at the last word, torn between laughter and shock.

But he held his fingers to her lips, and his expression grew grave. "But there's naugh' of the wanton in you, lass. You came to me a maid, untouched and innocent. I willna forget that. I can only hope you dinnae come to regret it."

She saw the shadow of doubt in his eyes. Unwilling that he should suffer such uncertainty, she sat up, took his face between her palms and met his gaze. "I'd never imagined such pleasure could be found wi' a man. You were inside my body, but somehow 'tis my soul you touched, Iain MacKinnon."

Then she kissed him. She kissed him as he had once kissed her—first his upper lip, then his lower, then the fullness of his mouth.

He held himself still, the furrow of his brow and the catch of his breath the only sign that her words and her touch stirred him. "Oh, Annie!"

Wanting him, she ran the tip of her tongue over his lips, then slipped it into the slick heat of his mouth. He moaned, met her tongue with the velvet caress of his own, following her lead, allowing her the mastery.

When she at last broke the kiss, he lay on his back beside her. "I'm yours, *a leannan*. Do wi' me what you will."

At first she was taken aback and could do nothing but stare. Then, hungry for the feel of him, she found herself lifting the irritating cloth of his shirt over his head, baring his chest and shoulders to her touch. Remembering how he had pleased her, she sat up on her knees, leaned over him, and began to kiss his nipples as he had kissed hers.

To her delight, his muscles tensed. She looked up to find him wearing a grin.

"Aye, it feels good for a man, too."

Emboldened, she slid her fingers through the mat of dark curls on his chest and savored the feel of his muscles, laving his nipples with her tongue, tugging at them with her lips, feeling them harden in her mouth. She heard his breath rush from his lungs, felt his heartbeat quicken beneath her palm and knew the thrill of giving him pleasure.

When next she looked up, she found his eyes squeezed shut and his head turned to the side, exposing the corded muscles of his neck. One strong arm was thrown above his head, his fist clenched. His hair had fanned out across the dark bearskin, like the black of a raven's wing against the night sky.

He was so raw and braw, both fierce and bonnie. Her own pulse quickened, and heat flared deep in her belly, turning to cream between her thighs.

She wanted more of him.

With trembling hands, she sought to loose the ties of his breeches and was grateful when his big hands closed over hers to guide her. Then she sat back as he peeled the butter-soft leather away from his skin and tossed his breeches aside. He was completely naked now, just as she was, his shaft full and erect, his heavy sac with its dark curls drawn tight against his body. He lay back against the bearskin, his body an offering.

Hesitantly, she slid her hands up the hard muscles of his thighs, feeling the rasp of his body hair against her palms, her gaze fixed on the part of him that was so new to her.

His voice was a deep purr, urging her on. "Dinnae be afraid to touch me, *a leannan*. 'Tis time you came to ken my body, aye?"

Driven by curiosity and desire, she reached out, took the

weight of his sac in her palm, kneaded it gently, felt the round stones within. Then she took the length of him in her hand.

" 'Tis silky soft and yet so hard."

"The better to please you, lass." His voice was rough.

Slowly, she slid her hand up to the engorged crown, then ran her thumb over the bead of moisture that had emerged at the stretched and straining tip, rubbing it into his purplish skin.

Breath hissed from between his teeth, and the muscles of his belly tensed. His shaft leapt in her hand. He moaned, whispered her name.

Fascinated and excited to see she could arouse him so, she circled the tip with her thumb again and again, stroking the length of him to call forth more moisture. But when none appeared, she leaned down and licked him, circling him with her tongue to wet him.

"Sweet Jesus!" His entire body stiffened.

Eager to please him, she licked him again and yet again, until she was taking the entire salty tip into her mouth and suckling him.

"Stop!" His fingers threaded through her hair, gently forcing her head up. "Do you ken what you do to me, lass? Nay? I'll show you."

Then he wrested control from her, pulling her beneath him, plundering her mouth with his tongue and forcing her legs apart. She yielded gladly, more than willing to let him guide her through this sensual new world. But rather than entering her as he'd done before, he kissed a burning path over her breasts, down her belly, to her sex.

Feeling exposed, she fisted her hands in his hair to stop him. "Oh, Iain, dinnae think—!"

"Uist!" His fingers parted her, opening her to his gaze, to his touch, to the hot little gust of breath that left him at the sight of her. "You've had your taste of me. 'Tis my turn to feast."

With a shocking flick of his tongue, his mouth settled upon her, hot and insistent, making her gasp in surprise and delight. Just as she had licked and suckled him, so he licked and suckled her, drawing on her sensitive bud with his lips, teasing it with his tongue, sucking it with the heat of his mouth. It felt good beyond anything she could have imagined—desperate, blinding, savage pleasure.

"Iain!" She heard herself call his name, her breath coming in ragged pants, her fingers clutched in his hair, her body quivering uncontrollably as he made love to her with his mouth.

"You taste so sweet, Annie—like woman and wild honey." He moaned, the deep vibration only adding to the over-whelming torment.

Then he thrust his tongue inside her.

She came with a keening cry, breaking against his mouth, her fingers twined in his sweat-damp hair, her heart slam-ming in her chest.

And then he was kissing her, his lips wet with her juices, his tongue rich with her musky taste—and the fire inside her began to build anew.

Her climax had left her slick, and there was no pain this time as he slowly nudged himself into her, filling her, mak-ing her complete.

He made a sound like a growl as he settled there, cupping her bum, tilting her hips, penetrating her fully. "Och, Annie, lass! You are so wet, so tight!"

Already she was lost in the slow rhythm of his thrusts, the sweet stretch, the slick glide of him inside her. "Iain, oh, Iain!"

She lifted her hips to meet him, matching his thrusts mea-sure for measure, the passions of her flesh and those of her heart becoming one, even as her body and Iain's were one. And then it was upon her, scorching and sweet. She panted his name, wrapped her legs around him and pulled him closer as her inner muscles clenched around him in ecstasy.

He cried out for her, his breath hot against her temple. Then his body stiffened, and she felt his shaft jerk inside her as he found his release and emptied his seed against her womb.

* * *

By the time they remembered their supper, it had grown cold. They ate like ancient Romans, lying naked on their sides and sharing a single plate. Iain fed Annie slivers of succulent venison, licking the juices off her chin, while she licked his fingers. She asked him questions about his latest mission. He answered, well aware they had more important things to discuss.

He waited for a moment of silence. It was time. "Connor told me what happened today."

The joy fled her face, and her eyes filled with shadows. She looked away, hugged the bearskin close. 'Twas clear the attack had been far from her mind.

"Wentworth told me . . . He led me to think you'd been in his bed. Had I kent the truth, I'd no' have come to you thus. I'd no' have lain a hand upon you but to comfort you. I'm sorry, Annie."

"Lord William?" She looked at him, confusion in her eyes, and he could see she was puzzling it out. Then she did something he did not expect. She laughed. "You thought I'd lain wi' *him?* You daftie!"

Feeling like a fool, Iain recounted Wentworth's words. "The thought of you in his bed drove me to near madness. 'Tis ashamed I am. I let him play me like one of his pawns."

"I thought you knew. I thought you were angry wi' me for—"

His own words echoed in his mind.

I'll be damned before I share you wi' another man.

"Och, Annie, how could I be angry wi' you? 'Twas no' your fault. What a brute you must have thought me! Why did you no' stop me, lass?"

Her cheeks flushed, and she looked away. "The moment you touched me, I forgot. I . . . I wanted you."

The sweetness of her answer humbled him. He pulled her gently against his chest, kissed her hair, held her, offering her the comfort he'd denied her earlier. "Do you wish to tell me of it?"

She shook her head. But as the silence stretched on, the words began to spill from her. She told him how the redcoat had come to her complaining of a bellyache and how she'd offered to make tea for him while he waited for Dr. Blake to tend to him. She told him how he'd bent her arm behind her back and cut off her scream with his hand. She told him how he'd bent her over a cask, lifted her skirts, forced her legs apart—and discovered her brand.

"I tried to fight him! I tried!" Her body trembled.

He heard the desperation in her voice and wondered what it must be like to be a woman, to be smaller and so much weaker than men. He held her closer. "Dinnae blame yourself. You did all any wee lassie could do. He took you at unawares."

"I bit him, and he let go of my mouth long enough for me to scream. And then . . . When I heard Connor's voice, I-I thought it was you."

"I wish it had been." He fought to still his loathing for himself. "I'm sorry I wasna here when you needed me. I turned my back on you and walked away in anger, leavin' you alone wi' your sorrows. Can you forgi'e me, Annie?"

A shimmer of tears filled her eyes. "Y-you believe me?"

"Aye, lass, I believe you."

Understanding dawned on her face like the slow rise of the sun, and she looked up at him through astonished eyes. "Do you mean that?"

"Aye, *a leannan*. I was heartless that night. If I could take it back, I would."

Tears spilled onto her cheeks. "Oh, Iain! There is much I would change as well. I am sorry I deceived you!"

He wiped her tears away. "Though I dinnae like that you lied to me, you were tryin' to survive. I cannae blame you for that. Your uncle . . . he deserves a traitor's death."

Then her tears came in earnest, and Iain understood. She was weeping out the grief she'd held back all these lonely months as she'd fought to protect herself, to stay alive.

"Annie, *mo luaidh*, no man will hurt you again." Feeling utterly helpless, Iain held her trembling body, murmuring endearments, offering his strength as sanctuary, silently cursing her uncle and the redcoat who'd attacked her to the coldest, darkest circle of hell.

The redcoat would pay for his crime soon enough. And if that *mac-diolain* of an uncle ever crossed his path, Iain would gut him like the animal he was and feed his entrails to the crows.

Long moments passed. Annie's tears stilled.

Then Iain asked a question that had burned inside him for weeks. "You kent Wentworth when first you saw him, aye?"

She sniffed, nodded. "He stayed wi' us when I was but twelve. I was shocked to see him again and so afraid he would contact my uncle. But he doesna ken me."

Iain wasn't so certain. There was something in the way Wentworth acted toward her that said otherwise. "You must stay away from him, lass. He means you ill. I can feel it."

She shivered, snuggled more tightly against him.

He kissed her hair, held her tight. But there was one last thing Iain would ask her before he left her side for the warrior's council. He needed to hear her answer.

"Your uncle must be prosperous and powerful, indeed, if he plays host to Hanover. Tell me, Annie, is your uncle Argyll?"

She looked away, seemed to hesitate. "Nay. Argyll is his cousin."

Chapter Twenty-five

"I find the major's licentiousness appalling—to seduce an innocent under his protection! She is far above him and deserved better."

William stared out the window at the dawn and listened to Cooke's indignant condemnation of Major MacKinnon, wondering what the lieutenant would have to say if he knew the woman in question was a highborn lady. 'Twas a secret William had not yet shared with anyone. And although he was amused by the lieutenant's transparent jealousy, his own response confounded him. Much to his surprise, the thought of Lady Anne in the major's bed sickened him.

He kept his voice impassive, his words detached. "Come now, Cooke! They are both Scots—and he the grandson of a clan chieftain."

"A traitorous clan chieftain," Cooke muttered, brushing lint from William's jacket, which hung on its stand.

William had only himself to blame. He'd known from the first moment he'd seen Annie that she was no lowly daughter of the American frontier. Yet he'd done nothing to protect her virtue or to secure her for himself. Indeed, he'd known Major MacKinnon would eventually lose the war with his conscience and bed her—and he'd found the idea amusing.

He hadn't known she was Lady Anne, the daughter of an acquaintance and a peer. He hadn't even imagined such a thing, despite the bounty of clues that in hindsight made the truth seem obvious—that first formal curtsy, her knowledge of his title, her bearing at the dinner table, her near win at chess, her ability to read, her sense of duty toward the sick and wounded, her amusing naiveté about crude sexual matters. She'd been gently bred, intended to grace the arm of a gentleman, to run his household, to bear his heir.

But now she would do none of those things, for Major MacKinnon had clearly lost out to his baser nature and taken her. If it weren't made obvious by the fact that the major had been sleeping in his own cabin these past two weeks, the light in Lady Anne's lovely face would have given the truth away. There was a knowing sensuality about her, a feminine lushness, that hadn't been there before.

Aye, she'd been plucked. And not by William.

"Surely you don't hold the major responsible for the actions of his grandsire?"

"The major is little different—arrogant, disloyal, disrespect-

ful. You know better than anyone how little love he feels toward Britain, my lord. Surely you do not defend him!"

"I do not condone his actions, Lieutenant."

Though I'd have done the same myself.

How this had come about, William could not comprehend. He'd sent the major to her enraged, knowing Lady
Anne was in a delicate state and certain the major would ac-
quit himself terribly. Instead of driving them apart, the encounter had inexplicably had the opposite effect, winning
the major Lady Anne's maidenhead.

As commander of the fort, William could take action. He
could try the major in a court martial for conduct unbe-
coming an officer of the Crown. He could have the major
flogged—again. He could try and flog Lady Anne for forni-
cation. He could send her to Albany and turn her over to the
sheriff. He could force her to live within the walls of the fort
apart from the major, even under his own roof.

Though each of these actions had its justification—
military discipline, Christian morality, tradition, the letter of
law, propriety—each would be a strategic error on William's
part, serving to shame Lady Anne and to ensure her hatred,
not to mention the major's wrath. Nay, if William wished to
win Lady Anne to his own bed, if he wished to possess her,
he would have to be patient.

"If it weren't the worse for her, I'd think he should be
forced to take her to wife." The tone of Cooke's voice revealed just how little he truly thought of this idea.

Nor could William stand the notion. "Indeed, it would be
the honorable thing for him to do."

"Since when has the major cared for honor? He'll probably abandon her once he's got her with child. I would not
see her reduced to the wretchedness of a camp follower's
life." Cooke lifted the jacket from its stand, carried it over to
William, and held it up.

William slipped his arms into the sleeves. "I won't allow
that to happen."

Because I intend to have her.

"I still believe he was in some way responsible for the corporal's death."

William allowed his voice to take on a warning tone. "There is no evidence linking the major to the corporal's death—nothing at all to suggest foul play. Do not feed the rumors."

Cooke frowned. "Aye, my lord."

Oh, William knew Iain was somehow at the root of the soldier's demise. He simply couldn't prove it. They'd found the corporal who'd tried to ravish Lady Anne dead in his cell on the morning of his court martial without so much as a mark on his body. The guards on duty had sworn no one had entered the gaol, nor had William found any sign of struggle. And though the guard at the gate had reported seeing Captain Joseph and a few of his men enter the fort late that night, no one had witnessed them anywhere near the gaol. It seemed the corporal had simply lain down with a flask of rum and gone to sleep, never to wake up. The strangeness of it had prompted the Regulars to believe in their ignorance and superstition that the major and his Indian friends had put a curse on him and stolen his breath.

Not that the corporal's death was a loss, but there was discipline and British law to uphold. And William would have dearly liked to see the swine hang.

Still, the corporal's mysterious death had proved an effective deterrent. The Regulars seemed afraid even to look at Lady Anne, much less shout obscenities at her or touch her. And if fear of Indian witchery hadn't been enough, the armed Ranger who always seemed to be in her vicinity certainly was. Did she know the major had set his men to guard her? She never set foot across the bateau bridge without a Ranger shadowing her.

But the Rangers' ardor for her would last no longer than their commander's. She was an Argyll Campbell, daughter of a clan despised by every man among them. As soon as the major heard the truth about her, he would abandon her, and his men with him. Then William could step in and save her from utter ruin.

Iain leaned against the table dressed only in his breeches and felt the smooth scrape of the razor over his jaw. "We'll be married by a priest, and you'll go to live wi' Joseph's sister in Stockbridge until the war is over and I am free."

Annie lifted the razor from his skin and glared at him. Dressed only in her shift, her golden hair still tangled from sleep, she drove him to distraction just by standing there. "We'll be married by the chaplain, and I'll be stayin' right here wi' you. And dinnae talk, or the blade will slip, and I'll cut you."

'Twas a bit of an argy-bargy they'd found themselves in— Annie insisting on marrying within the Church of England, while he swore their union would be blessed in the Catholic manner. He could not blame her, for she had been raised Protestant and mistrusted the true Church. Nor was it a small matter. Under British law, Catholic marriages were not recognized, and children conceived under the blessing of Rome were held to be baseborn and misbegotten. But while she wanted a marriage that would be lawful in British eyes, he wanted vows made sacred in the eyes of God.

Iain had expected this difference of mind, but he would not bend. They'd be married by a priest, and the next morning Joseph and his men would take her to Stockbridge without Wentworth's knowledge. Although Iain was loath to be parted from her, she was not safe near the bastard lordling. If Wentworth should recognize her . . .

It was not the only plan Iain had made that would displease her. He'd talked over many things with his brothers and Joseph at their warriors' council the night he'd taken her innocence. They'd all agreed with Iain that he should tell his men her true name, for it was better they learn the truth from him than be surprised by it. They'd also agreed the soldier who'd tried to rape her must not live to testify.

Though there was a chance he would not admit to having seen her brand, none of them had wanted to take that chance. And although Iain had looked forward to killing the bastard himself, they'd insisted he have naught to do with it, as he would be the first person Wentworth would suspect.

"You stay with your woman tonight," Joseph had insisted. "Leave that son of a dog to me."

And so Iain had returned to Annie, crawled into bed beside her and held her while she slept. By the next morning the deed had been done, and he'd been able to speak truthfully when first Wentworth and then Annie had asked him if he was to blame for the soldier's death. Only when he'd heard the soldier had been found with an empty bottle of rum had he known how Joseph had accomplished it. Though he felt no remorse for what had been done, it had seemed to trouble Annie.

"I wouldna see you branded a murderer and hanged, Iain MacKinnon," she'd said.

Iain tried to ignore the ache he felt at the thought of leaving her, and watched as she went about the wifely duty of shaving him. It stirred him in a way he could not describe, the tender intimacy of this act, and he felt a kind of satisfaction he'd rarely known to think there would be other mornings like this—the scent of breakfast in the air, the fire burned to embers, perhaps a bairn or two sitting sleepy-eyed on the bearskin. And Annie.

Her brow was knit with attentiveness. Her breasts swayed enticingly beneath her shift, their crests dark against the white cloth. Her hair hung to her hips, a river of silk and sunlight. Unable to resist, he reached out, cupped a soft breast through the linen, and brushed her nipple with his thumb. He heard her breath catch, felt her nipple tighten, saw the pulse at her throat leap.

Her hands stilled. "The sun is already up, Iain. We cannae—no' now."

"Is that so?" He did not relent, flicking the eager bud, shaping her breast, feeling it grow heavy in his hand.

He could tell she was trying to ignore her body's response. She lifted his chin, shaved the right side of his throat, one stroke at a time, stopping to rinse the blade in a bowl of hot water. But her breathing was unsteady, and when he shifted his hand to cup her other breast, her lashes drifted to her cheeks, her head fell back and the razor clattered to the table.

His face still half covered with shaving soap, his blood burning, Iain pulled her against him and closed his mouth over hers. She pressed herself hard against him, her hot little tongue twisting with his, her fingers curling in his hair. When at long last he broke the kiss, he couldn't help chuckling. She had shaving soap on her face.

She smiled and wiped the soap away with the back of her hand, her laughter like the sweet fall of water. "So it's *my* beard you'll be shavin' now? You daftie!"

The idea struck him hard, made his blood run thick and hot. For a moment, all he could do was look down at her, staggered by the thrum of his own lust. Ignoring her surprised gasp, he lifted her, turned her, laid her back on the table, following her down to kiss a trail along the soft skin of her throat. Drawing up her shift in impatient fistfuls, he tore his lips from her skin, lifted the vexing garment over her head, and tossed it onto the bed behind him. Then he stood between her thighs, parting them, forcing her knees to bend.

She opened for him like a flower, her sex rosy, her scent wild and sweet—a blushing musk rose wreathed in golden curls. He savored the sight of her, the scent of her, his cock painfully hard and pushing eagerly against the leather of his breeches.

"Iain, wh-what—?

"I find I want you even more when the sun is up, *a leannan.*"

Annie felt his big hands close over hers, felt him draw her hands to her own thighs, forcing her to hold them back and apart. Heat suffused her cheeks as his gaze fixed upon her most intimate flesh and his eyes grew dark. His fingers ran lightly over her, parting her, brushing her most sensitive spot, the tip of one slipping inside her, making her moan. Then he reached for the shaving soap.

It was then she realized what he was about. It shocked her to her soul, drove the breath from her lungs, excited her beyond reason. "Nay, Iain! You cannae mean to—!"

"Aye, I do." Warm fingers slowly spread the soap over her mound and outer folds, kneading it into her, the pressure sending tremors of delight through her belly.

"Iain, nay, 'tis indecent, and . . . aah!" Her objection faded into a moan, and she found her hips lifting to meet his touch, shame forgotten.

"Hold still."

Those two words made her breath catch in her throat. Then she heard something swish in water. *The razor.*

At the first sharp touch of the cold blade against her mound, she whimpered, as much from arousal as from fear. "Oh, please, Iain, dinnae—!"

"*Uist, a leannan!* I willna hurt you." Brow furrowed, he slid the razor over her skin, one deft stroke after the next, pausing several times to rinse the blade in water.

'Twas like nothing Annie had ever felt before—the biting caress of the razor, the warm tingle that followed each stroke, the intimate touch of his hand as he held her for the blade. Her fingers dug into the flesh of her thighs as she fought not to move, both afraid and unable to breathe. She saw the heavy rise and fall of his chest and the midnight blue of his eyes and knew that he was just as stirred to passion as she.

He set the razor aside, then lifted the bowl of hot water, spilling a gentle stream over her to rinse her, water splashing unheeded on the floorboards below.

"Iain!" The breath Annie had been holding left her in a rush as the heat trickled over her vulnerable, sensitive flesh, flowing over her like the caress of hot silk. She closed her eyes, lost in unimaginable pleasure.

Then she felt only the brush of cool air.

She opened her eyes to find him staring down at what the blade had revealed.

"Och, lass!" He parted her, ran his fingers over her, slipped one inside her, drawing a moan from her throat. "You are bonnie beyond my dreams."

Eager to know what he saw, Annie glanced down and saw the mound of her sex stripped bare, the skin bright pink as if blushing to suddenly find itself exposed. "Mercy!"

And then she was beyond words, for Iain had dropped to his knees, settled her feet on his shoulders, and begun to taste her, his mouth hot and slick, his finger moving deep inside her. Though he often pleasured her with his mouth, the sensations his tongue conjured between her thighs this time were almost unbearable. Without her curls, every aching inch of her was free for him to tease and taste. He drew her puffy folds wholly into his mouth, laved the tender skin of her mound, suckled her aching bud, leaving her wet and slick and frantic for him.

Fingers clutched in his hair, she writhed and arched against his mouth, his name lost among cries and whimpers and moans, the heat in her belly a molten blaze. She wanted him. She needed him. "Iain, please! I need . . . ooh!"

He seemed to understand, for he stood and slowly unlaced his breeches, burning her with his gaze. His shaft sprang free, thick and hard. He grasped it, stroked it. "Is it my cock you're wantin', lass?"

"Now, Iain!" Aye, she *was* radgie, her hips lifting of their own accord, her body yearning for the invasion that would bring them both release.

He rested her calves against his shoulders, then pushed himself forward. But rather than entering her as she had expected, he slid the length of his shaft between the slick folds of her sex, pumping his hips, driving himself over her, teasing her aching bud with his hard, satiny head.

"What . . . ? Oh! Oh, God!" Helpless against the fire inside her, she reached for him with trembling hands and gave herself over to this new sensual torment.

Iain could not wait much longer. The sight of her bare sex, the musky taste and slick feel of her in his mouth, the rich scent of her, the erotic sound of her cries—'twas almost more than he could endure. But he wanted to prolong her pleasure, wanted to give her everything he had, for it would be long ere he made love to her again.

Her head thrashed from side to side in sexual abandon, her eyes closed, her cries desperate. Her nails dug into his forearms. Her breasts were swollen, her nipples pinched, her skin flushed pink.

God save him, but he loved her! Wanted her. Needed her.

Unable to wait any longer, he pulled back, guided the head of his cock to her glistening entrance, and buried himself inside her in one slow thrust. She closed around him, hot and slick and tight as a fist. "Sweet Jesus, Annie! You feel so good!"

His strained words were lost amid her cries as he thrust into her, bending down to meet her welcoming embrace, raining kisses on her face, her throat, her breasts. She wrapped her legs round his waist, drew him closer, her hips lifting to meet him. Then he felt the tension inside her peak—and break.

"Iain!" She sobbed out his name, her nails sharp against the skin of his back, her inner muscles clenching around him as she came, milking him to his own climax.

"Annie, *mo luaidh!*" He drove himself into her, three deep thrusts, shaking with the force of his release and spilling his soul against her womb.

They were still kissing, their heartbeats not yet slowed, when a knock came at the door.

"Iain, I dinnae wish to, um, wake you, but we've a problem." 'Twas Morgan. "Joseph's men have gone, and that whoreson of a lord is demandin' to speak wi' you."

"I'll be out in a bloody minute!" Iain shouted toward the door, realizing he had yet to finish shaving and getting dressed. He looked down, saw the worry in Annie's eyes, brushed a strand of hair from her cheeks. "Dinnae fret, *a leannan.*"

She reached up, held his face between her palms. "How can I help but fret? You live life wi' death on your heels."

"For your sake, lass, I promise to stay one step ahead."

Iain stood before Wentworth an hour later, spoke the words he and Joseph had agreed upon. " 'Tis I who wronged him. I must set it right."

Wentworth, a cup of tea held delicately in one hand, stared up at him through gray eyes that for once betrayed a hint of anger. "I am disappointed, to say the least. I would expect more from a man who knows their ways as well as you do."

"'Tis not uncommon for kin to bicker, is it, Your Holiness?"

Wentworth set his tea down and stood. "No, it's not uncommon. My noble uncle and His Majesty have upon occasion disagreed with one another, but His Grace never withdrew his army in a fit of ill will toward his father."

"Would that he had."

Wentworth seemed not to hear the treasonous comment and strode slowly across the room toward the window. "What do you propose?"

"Morgan and I should depart at once for Stockbridge, leaving Connor in command. Perhaps we can overtake them along the way. I am certain that, wi' the right words and gifts, I can persuade Joseph to return wi' his men."

"Just the two of you?"

"Few dangers lie between here and Stockbridge. There's no cause to spend my men's vigor on a task best accomplished by one or two alone."

"Very well. See that you return swiftly."

Then Iain got to the part of the plan that worried him most. "Miss Burns shall remain in Ranger camp under Connor's protection while I'm away. My men are under orders to see she doesna leave the island and to kill any man who tries to harm her."

"You know, of course, that I can countermand your orders where she is concerned."

"You can try." Iain turned and strode away.

But Wentworth's voice followed him out the door. "Let us hope they do a better job protecting her than you have, major."

With Wentworth's words planting misgivings in his heart, Iain returned to his cabin to fetch his gear and take his leave of Annie.

He held her close, wiped her tears away. "'Tis no' a dangerous mission, but it could be a long one. Dinnae fret."

She smiled, a forced smile that did not dispel the sadness in her eyes. "Go wi' God, Iain MacKinnon—and remember your promise."

He kissed her. "Always one step ahead, *a leannan*."

Chapter Twenty-six

It was only after Iain had gone that Annie discovered she was a near prisoner on the island. She tried to go to the hospital to help Dr. Blake, but Cam, who stood guard at the bridge, refused to let her cross.

"I'm vexed for you, miss. Truly, I am. But those are Mack's orders."

Her grief over saying farewell to Iain turned to fury. What right did Iain have to confine her thus? How was she to make herself useful if she could not work in the hospital? Why hadn't he discussed his orders with her before imposing them upon her as if she were his captive?

She went in search of Connor to set things aright. But Connor was on the other side of the river, drilling the men for the coming campaign against Ticonderoga. She could just see them in the great field between the fort and the forest, crawling on their bellies like boys playing in the dirt, rifles in hand, gear upon their backs.

But this was not a game. It was war.

And Iain had not confined her to the island to make her miserable, but because he thought it safest. As irritating as his orders might be, she would not waste anyone's time with a fit of childish temper. She was no longer the cosseted lady who'd needed a maid to help her dress, nor was she a lost child. Surely there was something else she could do to help, at least until she was able to speak with Connor.

Unsure where to begin but eager to keep her hands busy and her mind from worry, she went back to Iain's cabin and set about giving it the sort of thorough cleaning it'd likely never seen. She washed the bedding and hung it in the warm May sunshine to dry. She wiped dust from the windowsill and the mantle and polished the little crucifix. She stood on a chair and cleaned cobwebs from corners. But no matter how hard she worked, nothing pulled her mind off her fears.

What sort of mission would require Iain and Morgan to go off on their own? What had happened to make Joseph and his Stockbridge warriors withdraw? Was that where Iain had gone—to fetch them back? When she'd asked him, he'd told her he couldn't speak of it.

Bereft of answers, she took up the broom and began sweeping the floor. When the bristles brushed over the water-stained wood in front of the table, she stopped, knelt down, touched the dampness. Images of the passion they'd shared flooded her mind—the heat in his eyes as he'd lifted her shift over her head, the indescribable feel of his mouth upon her bared sex, the way his powerful body had seemed to shake apart in her arms as he'd climaxed and filled her with his seed. Just the memory of it made heat curl through her belly.

They'd been lovers for a little over two weeks now—two weeks so filled with joy they seemed to chase off the darkness that had come before. Every night, Iain had taught her something new about the ways of men and women, revealing the secrets of their bodies, bringing her pleasures she hadn't thought possible nor even imagined. And every night, she'd fallen asleep in his arms, feeling safe, her body, mind and heart content.

What miracle was it that had guided her to him through the vastness of the forest? It couldn't be mere chance that she had fallen down that embankment and landed at *his* feet. A man able to protect her. A man who could set her body on fire with a glance. A man who believed her.

She would thank God every day of her life for bringing her to Iain MacKinnon.

Now she was set to marry him—a Catholic, the son of Jacobites, a Highland barbarian. 'Twas not the match she'd dreamed of making as a young lass—a titled British gentleman with broad lands and an old and honored name. There would be no gown of French silk. No Burness emeralds gleaming at her throat. No tables groaning under roasted meats, wines and sugared cakes. No bright rooms filled with scented flowers. No chamber orchestra or quadrille to dance.

Instead, she'd wear a linen gown that had once belonged to someone else. Her throat and fingers would be bare. They'd feast on roasted venison, fish newly pulled from the river and boiled potatoes. Dougie would play his fiddle. And Annie would call herself blessed.

She stood and went back to her sweeping, a smile on her face.

Of course, they still had to resolve whether the wedding would be at the hands of a Catholic priest—an impossibility as there was none and because Annie didn't want her children to be considered fatherless—or the fort's chaplain, who would surely refuse to marry them unless Iain renounced his faith, which he would not do.

But they'd endured so much already. Surely there would be a way.

*   *   *

Iain moved his oar silently, the dark waters of Lake Champlain passing like a whisper beneath the canoe. He'd met Joseph at the rendezvous point a half day out of Fort Elizabeth, and he and most of Joseph's men had headed north, while Morgan and a small party of warriors had turned south toward Albany.

"Beannachd leat!" Morgan had called after him. *Blessings go with you!*

It would have been much simpler had Iain been able to ask for leave, but Wentworth would never allow a Catholic priest anywhere near the fort, especially not a French one. In these heretical times, priests were treated like criminals and spies. And so Iain and Joseph had concocted a disagreement between the two of them, giving Iain a reason to leave the fort.

Iain hadn't told Annie where he was going or why. He didn't want Wentworth to be able to hold her an accomplice if they were found out—'twas desertion to leave his post without his commander's consent. Nor did he want her to worry while he was gone or to blame herself if he was killed or captured. Although he'd told her it was not a dangerous mission, it was one of the most treacherous tasks he'd ever laid upon himself. Unwilling to risk anyone else's life, he'd planned to go alone, but Joseph had refused to be left behind.

Their errand was to journey north to Montréal through leagues of enemy territory, make their way past the gates painted like Wyandot warriors, find a priest and, without harming anyone, persuade him to come with them. Then they would retrace each perilous step, rendezvousing with Morgan at Stockbridge before returning with the priest—and Joseph's men—to Fort Elizabeth for a secret wedding. Then some of Joseph's most trusted warriors would guide the priest back to Ticonderoga. Wentworth would never ken he'd been there.

Provided nothing went wrong, it would be simple.

They made great speed. After four days on the trail, they

were already well to the north of Ticonderoga. But Lake
Champlain was heavy with French ships, not to mention
parties of Abenaki and Wyandot. They would soon have to
abandon the lake and travel overland.

In the next canoe, Joseph pointed at the western horizon.
The sun was low. They needed to make camp soon. Iain
spied a small inlet ahead of them to his left, indicated it with
a jerk of his head. Joseph nodded. They turned their bows
toward shore, dragged the small craft into the trees and hid
them in the underbrush. Then, senses attuned to the forest
around them, they scouted inland for a site to pass the
night.

They'd not gone far when they came to a rocky ridge.
With Joseph's men to guard their backs, Iain and Joseph
climbed to the top to get a view of the water and the surrounding forest. Iain took forth his spying glass and peered
out over the lake. To the north he saw a fleet of six ships and
a dozen bateaux gliding southward toward Ticonderoga. He
handed the spying glass to Joseph, pointed toward the
ships. Joseph looked through the glass, nodded in agreement with Iain's unspoken message: They would have to
wait until the ships passed tomorrow morning before setting
out on the lake again.

Then Joseph frowned. He lifted the glass to his eye once
again and pointed the lens toward the forest below. But Iain
didn't need the spying glass to see it.

Wagons. French soldiers.

A supply party.

It was headed westward—into Wyandot territory.

Joseph handed the spying glass back to Iain, jabbed him
in the shoulder with his elbow, a wide grin on his face.

Curious, Iain took the glass and looked down at the vulnerable little party. He counted perhaps fifty soldiers, nearly
thirty Wyandot—a sizeable escort for a journey so deep in
their own territory. They were guarding a dozen wagons,
each laden with supplies. There appeared to be no passen-
gers apart from—

Iain stared in amazement.

A priest!

Iain crept along on his belly, a knife between his teeth, with only the glow of the campfire to guide him. He'd waited and watched the French encampment until long past dark, when most of the supply party were asleep. Then he'd stripped down to his breeches and smeared his skin with bear fat and ashes to blacken it. Moving slowly and silently, he'd made it past the Wyandot sentries, nothing more than a passing shadow. The priest's tent stood just ahead, illuminated from within by candlelight.

He and Joseph had at first thought to waylay the supply train and take the priest that way, but Iain had deemed it too dangerous. He did not want to compound his sins by taking lives if he could help it, and there was every chance that the sudden appearance of a hundred Stockbridge warriors would sow panic among the French soldiers and their Wyandot allies and cause them to open fire. And although Iain would have been happy to wave a white flag of truce, reveal himself and ask the priest politely to come away with him, the price on his head was such that he'd never make it out alive. So he had chosen a path that was safer for everyone—except him. 'Twas his wedding, after all.

Not that he was alone. Joseph and his men had surrounded the encampment just beyond the sentries and were ready to intervene should the worst happen. Iain prayed the worst would not happen.

Using his forearms, he pulled himself forward inch by inch, listening for breathing, for footsteps, for the creak of leather, his gaze on the priest's tent just ahead of him. He was no more than two yards away from it and was considering how best to enter—whether to cut the back of the tent open with his knife or to tempt fate and use the flap—when a young French officer popped out of the tent beside it, strode past the fire to the priest's tent and ducked inside. There came a mutter of voices as the two fell into discussion.

Iain lay still in the shadows, watching, waiting.

The hoot of an owl. A cough. The shiver of wind through new leaves. Behind him, two Wyandot men argued in whispers about a woman. A log shifted in the fire pit, sending a shower of orange sparks skyward.

Iain had begun to wonder if the officer and priest were sharing the tent when the voices from within grew silent and the officer emerged again.

"Bonne nuit, Père Delavay. Dormez bien."

But the officer had taken perhaps three steps toward his own tent when he stopped, turned toward the shadows and seemed to look right at Iain.

His body coiled and ready to spring, Iain ignored animal instincts that told him to flee or fight, held his breath and prayed he would not have to kill.

Then the officer strode toward him, quick steps that showed no caution, one hand loosing his breeches.

Och, for God's sake! He's come to take a piss!

'Twas a poor reason for either of them to die.

Not daring to move a muscle, Iain could do nothing but watch as the officer, no more than three feet away from him, grasped his cock and drained it onto the soil near Iain's face. Then, humming a tune beneath his breath, the officer tucked himself back inside his breeches, turned and walked into his tent.

Seizing his moment, Iain stood and, moving as swiftly and silently as he could, made his way to the front of the priest's tent, lifted the flap and ducked inside.

The priest, an older man with a shock of gray hair, high cheekbones and an aristocratic nose, stared at him in utter shock and horror, his voice a dry whisper. *"Mon dieu!"*

"I am Iain MacKinnon, and I mean you no harm." Realizing the knife in his hand carried a different message, Iain sheathed it. Then he crossed himself. "Forgi'e me, Father, for I'm about to sin."

*   *   *

Annie listened to Killy's tale, taking care to keep her stitches even. The setting sun left her precious little light by which to finish mending Brendan's torn sleeve.

"But the supplies had been so long aboard ship that the biscuits were turned to stone! Even the weevils had gone."

The men erupted into good-natured laughter at this familiar story, their hard day of drills and shooting at marks eased by supper and their nightly ration of rum.

Despite her sorrows, she found herself smiling. "What did you do? Were you no' terribly hungry?"

"Aye, miss, and our bellies were makin' a terrible din. Mack ordered us to open the hogshead and set it beneath the fort wall." Killy, a born storyteller, paused for dramatic effect, a smile on his still-pale face. "Then he set us to droppin' cannon balls on the biscuits to soften them!"

The men guffawed.

She found herself laughing with them. "Cannon balls?"

"Aye, miss. We dropped a dozen six-pounders, and 'twas the hogshead broke first!"

The strains of Dougie's fiddle sang over the men's howls of laughter as he tuned it, his nimble fingers already slipping into a jig.

Annie set her mending on her lap. "'Tis grateful I am to have you back among us, Killy, for I love your stories."

A red flush stole into his face. "'Tis my Irish charm you cherish, miss."

"Aye, that too." She laughed, then rose from the tree stump that had served as her chair. "And now I'll bid you all a good night."

"Good night, miss."

"A pleasant sleep to you, miss."

She walked toward Iain's cabin through a warm breeze that promised summer, the cheerful sounds of men's banter and Dougie's fiddle behind her. A night heron flew with slow wing beats toward some hidden bog to fish. The western horizon blazed orange and pink, set aflame by the setting sun.

Could Iain see it, too? Was he sitting safe beside Morgan and Joseph with his flask of rum? Was he sharing stories with them and laughing just like his men? Was he thinking of her, just as she was thinking of him? Or was he in desperate peril, fighting for his life, perhaps even wounded—or worse?

You live life wi' death on your heels.

For your sake, lass, I promise to stay one step ahead.

Iain had been gone for twelve days—twelve long days and twelve longer nights. He'd said it wasn't a dangerous mission but that it might be a long one, and these past twelve days had seemed an eternity. She'd done her best to hide her fears, to show the same courage Iain always showed. But every night she'd lain awake praying that he and the others were safe, her mind haunted by her own memories of the forest—the sound of war cries, of rifles firing, of men dying upon the ground.

Keep your promise to me, Iain MacKinnon. God, help him keep his promise!

Connor and the men were doing their best to keep her spirits up, she knew. Despite the weight of his duties, Connor found time to talk with her each day, taking breakfast or supper with her, making certain she had all she needed. Killy was still too weak for physical labor, but his tongue was as strong as ever, and he used it ordering the men to bring her firewood and water. Like angels, Iain's men watched over her—rough angels who swore and liked their rum, but angels just the same.

It had astonished her to learn they knew she was a Campbell. Iain told her he'd revealed her real name to them not long after he'd learned the truth himself, judging it best for his men to hear it from him. She'd thought they would hate her, but if anything, they seemed more protective.

Three times Lord William had summoned her, and three times he had been drawn away by something urgent. The first time, a fire had started near the powder magazine. The second time, the drawbridge had collapsed. The third time, a band of Abenaki had appeared on the edge of the forest as if preparing for an attack, and the fort had been called to battle readiness.

Annie knew perfectly well the Rangers were behind these troubles. She'd heard McHugh and Cam laughing about the band of Abenaki with Brendan over breakfast.

"You make a bonnie Indian, but were you no' afraid they'd shoot?" Brendan had asked.

"They cannae shoot to save their hides, laddie," McHugh had answered.

"They're more like to hit themselves than their marks. Did you see their faces?" Cam had dissolved into laughter.

It had stunned her to think they'd take such measures to keep Lord William away from her. If they'd been caught, they'd have faced a court-martial and surely a flogging.

"You're one of them now, lass," Iain had told her before he'd departed. "There's no' a man among them who would betray your secret or let anyone harm you."

She'd come to realize that this ragtag band of men, these coarse Rangers, had become clan for one another, taking the place of kin left behind. Many of them had lost fathers at Culloden, and most had been driven into exile at the tip of an Argyll sword, but still they had accepted her. Even if their response was mostly out of love and loyalty to Iain, she was grateful.

Yet she knew they *did* care for her. And she knew something else about them—they were lonely, and she reminded them of all they'd left behind. She could see the longing in their eyes, hear the wistfulness in their voices when they spoke of home, or when Dougie played his fiddle. So many of them had sweethearts or wives and children they'd left far away in frontier villages, loved ones they hoped to protect by risking their own lives, battling the enemy of their enemy so they might have peace around their homes.

Most of them had been with Iain for three years, returning to their families only when given leave at Christmas. How did they endure it? How could they stand living so far away from those they loved? How could their wives and sweethearts bear the constant fear and doubt of wondering whether they were still alive or whether death had already separated them forever?

Tears pricked her eyes, spilled onto her cheeks. Did she weep for the men and their families or because she feared for Iain? She could not say.

But this she knew for certain: She would not allow Iain to send her away to Stockbridge.

She found Connor waiting for her at the door to the cabin. She tried to wipe her tears away, but he had already seen.

He frowned, his expression so like Iain's, and placed a re-assuring hand on her shoulder. "What is it, lass?"

She shrugged, tried to smile. "I try to be strong, but . . . I fear for him."

"Och, is that all?" He rolled his eyes. Then he grinned. "Perhaps this will help."

He held up his hand, and Annie realized he was holding a small wreath.

'Twas a wreath of pink, yellow and white forest wildflowers tied off with white ribbons.

She took it from him, stared at it in amazement. "Wh-what—?"

" 'Tis a gift for your hair from Iain. He bids you to trust him. He asks you to dress quickly and to come with me across the river to where he awaits you in the forest."

It took a moment for her mind to grasp what Connor was saying. "This is from Iain? Iain is back?"

Connor's grin became a wide smile. "Aye, and he's impatient to wed you. There's a gown for you on the bed. Hurry, lass, and dress! He's waitin'."

Chapter Twenty-seven

"Lie still, lass. We're almost there."

Annie, wrapped in a dark blanket to conceal her and protect her gown, lay on her belly in the canoe, while Connor, McHugh and Cam swam alongside the little craft, guiding it through the current to the far bank of the river. Over there, somewhere in the darkening forest, Iain waited for her.

Was she dreaming?

She touched the soft silk of her new gown, felt the wreath of flowers in her hair and her heart gave a leap. Iain was waiting to marry her.

Her mind whirled with questions. How could he hope to marry her when there was still no priest or vicar? If he had returned, why was he not in camp? Why was she being ferried across the river to meet him in secret? Where had he come upon so lovely a gown?

She had asked Connor all of these things, but he'd refused to answer, a big smile upon his face. "Och, quit hecklin' me wi' your wearisome questions, lass, and dress! It grows dark! Iain will tell you all you need to ken."

With trembling hands and barely able to breathe, she had removed her striped gown of green and rose linen and slipped into the new one. Cut from silk the color of dusty rose and trimmed with delicate ivory lace, it fit as if it had been made for her and looked as if it had never been worn before. Only after she'd finished tying the laces had she realized it was to be her wedding gown. She would marry in silk after all.

She felt the keel scrape sand, heard the splash of moccasins in water and lifted her head to find the three men bent double, dragging the canoe ashore, their clothes and hair sodden. Then powerful arms scooped her up, blanket and all, and Connor carried her quickly overland toward the distant line of trees.

" 'Tis no wonder he was able to bear you so long." Connor adjusted her weight in his arms. "You wecht no more than a bairn."

Soon the rushing of the river was replaced by the whisper of the breeze through the trees and the sleepy chatter of birds settling among the branches. Deep into the forest they went, until they came to a meadow of green grass and wild-flowers that opened to the sunset sky above.

And Iain was there in the gloaming, waiting for her, whole and safe and alive.

His long hair was damp, his face shaven, and she knew he'd had a bath in the river. He wore his leather breeches and leggings, but his shirt was of new linen. At his side was his claymore, the strip of MacKinnon plaid tied round its pommel.

"Iain!"

No sooner had she been placed on her feet than she was running toward him, aware of nothing but him. She leapt into his arms, felt his strength surround her, felt the warmth of his lips on her forehead, on her cheeks, on her mouth as he kissed her. And she kissed him back, parting her lips to taste him, twelve days and nights of fear and hunger melting away in the heat of his embrace.

She heard men's muffled laughter.

"First the wedding, aye?" 'Twas Morgan.

Slowly, she withdrew her lips from Iain's, found herself looking into his blue eyes, her mind still filled with questions, but her heart elated.

"You are the bonniest thing I've e'er seen, *a leannan*. Och, I have missed you!"

Then someone coughed and spoke with a distinct French accent. "Shall we begin?"

She turned her head, gasped.

Beside Morgan and Joseph stood a man in black robes, a

simple belt of rope round his waist, a rosary hanging from his hip.

A Catholic priest.

She stared up at Iain, stunned, angry, confused. "Wh-what . . . ?"

"Pardon me, Father, I need to speak wi' the bride." Iain's strong arm encircled her waist, and she found herself being led a short distance away. Then he lifted her chin, forced her to meet his gaze. "I ken this is not as you wished it, Annie. I can see you're angry wi' me, and I dinnae blame you, for I took this upon myself wi'out tellin' you. But what I have done could well be treason in the eyes of the *Sassenach*, and I would see you held blameless if I am discovered."

Furious and barely able to think, she glared at him. "What have you done, Iain MacKinnon?"

He brushed her cheek with his thumb. "I've deceived my commander, kidnapped a French priest and kept secrets from you because I wanted to protect you. Nay, listen to me, lass! Soon I'll be off to Ticonderoga, and there's a chance I willna return. What happens to you if I am slain and you begin to swell wi' my bairn? I wouldna see you bear a child penniless and in shame. Be angry if you like. Shout at me! Blame me! Strike me if you must! But marry me now, here, in this place—*while we still have time.*"

She sifted through his words, through the tempest of her feelings, her heart thrumming in her chest. She could see the concern in his blue eyes—and his uncertainty. And then it struck her: He had done all this—defied his commander, traveled hard leagues and put himself in grave danger—not knowing whether she would accept him in the end.

Then a strange stillness drifted over her, fury and confusion lifting from her heart and mind like a fog. Iain would be leaving for battle soon, and he might not return. What did any of the rest of it matter?

She glanced over at the priest, who watched her gravely, his face drawn with fatigue. Then she looked into Iain's eyes, her own filling with tears. "Aye, Iain MacKinnon. I'll marry you here, now, in this place—while we still have time."

He took her hand, gave it a reassuring squeeze, then led her back to the priest.

"Annie, this is Father Jean-Marie Delavay."

Unsure what to do—she had never met a Catholic priest before, nor a Frenchman—she released Iain's hand and sank into a full curtsy. "Father."

"Rise and tell me your name, child." His accent was thick, but his words were clear.

She stood, suddenly feeling nervous. "Lady Anne Burness Campbell."

"Lady?"

She heard Morgan's whisper of surprise, felt it pass like a shiver through Connor, McHugh and Cam, then glanced up to find Iain looking at her as if seeing her for the first time.

He raised her hand to his lips, kissed it. "Lady?"

Did he not know? Had he not been able to guess from her name? "Aye."

Then Father Delavay was speaking, asking them first to kneel, then to rise, his words drifting over her as if from a dream, a mixture of Latin, English and French. He bound their hands together with a strip of MacKinnon plaid, made the sign of the cross over them, speaking words of blessing both strangely familiar and utterly foreign to Annie.

But through it all she saw only Iain. Iain holding her trembling hands. Iain prompting her when it was time to speak her vows. Iain promising to love, honor and cherish her all the days of his life. Iain sliding a band of gold over her finger. Iain wiping tears of happiness from her face. Iain kissing her, lifting her off her feet.

And Annie called herself blessed.

Iain watched as Annie danced with Morgan to the sound of Dougie's fiddle and McHugh's forbidden pipes, her cheeks flushed with excitement, her unbound hair wreathed in flowers. She hadn't known the steps to the jig, so Morgan and Connor had taken it upon themselves to teach her, all the men in Ranger camp cheering her on. Graceful and light on her small feet, she had learnt quickly.

His blood ran warm with rum—and lust. Soon he would lift her off those dainty feet and carry her to his cabin and across the threshold and lay her upon his bed and take her as her husband. But he would not interrupt the celebration—not yet.

He'd ordered an extra ration of rum for every man except those on guard duty, and had managed to find a bottle of wine for Father Delavay, who, seeing Ranger camp from the far side of the river, had decided to stay for a few days.

"These are your men?" he'd asked.

"Those on the island, aye."

"Are they Catholic?"

"Aye, to a man. Most are sons of Culloden. The rest are from Ireland."

The priest had stood there, his hands tucked into the sleeves of his robes, his brown eyes reflecting firelight, his expression grave. "Now that I am here, I should hear their confessions—though from the looks of them, that might take some time. Can you bring me to them?"

"Aye, Father, and 'twould be most generous of you, but if you are found, you will most likely be hanged for a spy and I for a traitor."

Father Delavay had smiled. "I came to this land in search of adventure. It seems to have found me."

And so after talking it through with his brothers and Joseph, Iain had sent Annie back across the river with Father Delavay, Connor, McHugh and Cam, while he, Morgan, Joseph and Joseph's men trekked upriver and through the forest to arrive from the south as if returning from Stockbridge. He'd sent word to Wentworth that his mission had been successful; then he'd crossed the bateau bridge to find Annie waiting for him.

His men had cheered to hear the news of his marriage, but they had fallen into stunned silence when Father

Delavay had emerged from Connor's cabin to stand in the shadows. Some had crossed themselves. Others had gaped in disbelief.

"Why the solemn faces?" Father Delavay had raised his arms as if in exasperation. "This is a wedding celebration, *non?*"

Then Dougie had taken up his fiddle once more, and somberness had turned to merriment.

Now Killy was dancing with Annie, the old dog not much taller than she but just as nimble of foot. He whirled her about, drew an excited squeal from her throat, then stepped back and showed her his fastest Irish steps.

"Your men love her." Joseph stood beside Iain, a sip of rum left in his tin cup.

Wentworth did not allow the Stockbridge to drink rum, a rule that most ignored.

"Aye, they do." *And so do I.*

It amazed Iain to think Annie was now bound to him as his wife. Courageous, bonnie, bright, kind and passionate— aye, radgie—she was everything a man could hope for. She'd seemed so vulnerable in the forest, at first angry and taken aback by what he'd done, then frightened by the unfamiliar ceremony. Her willingness to set her anger aside and to trust him, turning to him to guide her through the sacred rite, had touched him deeply.

"I still don't understand what it means that she is a 'lady.' "

Iain had heard Morgan and Connor trying to explain the idea of nobility and peerage to Joseph and his men earlier—and failing. The idea that some were born more deserving or with better blood than others was strange to the Muhheconneok. "Think of her as being the daughter of a great sachem and 'lady' as a title of respect."

"Ah, then she has great knowledge passed to her by her ancestors."

Annie laughed as Cam stepped in and took the dance from Killy. "My turn, my lady."

Lady Anne.

Iain ought to have realized her father was a peer. If her uncle was cousin to the Duke of Argyll, almost certainly she'd been born to a lord and his lady. "Well, nay. In Britain, 'tis more about power, wealth and lands than knowledge."

"Europeans are strange."

"Aye, for certain." But Iain was done talking and watching other men dance with Annie. He stepped forward and gave Cam a good-natured shove. "Unhand my wife."

He'd just wrapped his arm round her waist and spun her about, when Annie gasped and the laughter and music died, the last notes leaving McHugh's pipes with a strangled wail.

And there, unannounced, stood Wentworth and Lieutenant Cooke with an escort of a dozen armed Regulars.

"It seems we have interrupted a celebration, Lieutenant." Wentworth glanced coldly at Iain, then shifted his gaze to Annie.

"Indeed, my lord." Lieutenant Cooke also looked at Annie, disapproval in his eyes.

Iain stepped forward, placing Annie behind him. "Morgan, did you forget to invite the German princeling to my wedding?"

"Och, it seems I did! Forgi'e me, Your Immensity."

While Cooke looked distraught, Wentworth merely smiled. "It seems felicitations are in order. Congratulations, Major. But how was this accomplished with no vicar or chaplain? For I'm certain I did not give the chaplain permission to join anyone in marriage."

Iain thought quickly, only too aware that Father Delavay was in Connor's cabin. If the priest were discovered, it would almost certainly mean the gallows for them both. " 'Twas by proxy at the hands of a priest I ken outside Albany."

For a moment, Wentworth looked startled; then the mask fell back over his face. "The Crown does not recognize Catholic marriages, as well you know."

"The Crown can bugger off!"

The shout came from somewhere behind him, and Iain found himself hoping the rum hadn't warmed his men's blood to the point of foolishness. He would not risk a battle with Annie in the middle.

"*Uist!*" he shouted at his men, then met Wentworth's gaze and spoke with deadly calm. "If you choose to view my bairns as bastards, that is of no concern to me. Annie is my wife, and she will remain wi' me as my wife, subject only to my rule. I will suffer no man to dishonor her or lay a hand upon her so long as I live."

Annie heard the strength in Iain's voice, felt the silence stretch dark and heavy between him and Lord William, the air thick with old hatred and unspoken threats. Did Lord William not know he was playing with fire? Already Captain Joseph's men had surrounded him and his escort. Many of the Rangers stood with knives unsheathed, and one or two had their rifles at hand. Wentworth and his men wouldn't make it out of Ranger camp alive if it came to fighting.

Then Lord William's gaze locked with hers. "Step forward, Miss Burns."

Annie felt her heart trip. She took a step, but Iain blocked her path with a raised arm.

"What do you want wi' her?"

But Lord William didn't answer. Instead he strode slowly forward until he stood just before her. Then he took her hand in his, bowed slightly and raised it to his lips.

"Forgive me, Lady Anne. I ought to have intervened sooner and protected you from this fate. If only you had trusted me . . ."

Annie felt the blood drain from her face. Her heart beat so hard it drowned out the rest of his words, and the ground seemed to shift beneath her feet. "*M-mercy!*"

She saw William reach for her, but Iain had already wrapped a strong arm round her waist and pulled her against him.

"Easy, *a leannan*. I willna let him harm you." His voice came as if from far away. "What is it you want, Wentworth?"

Annie saw William smile. "I would never harm her, Major, for your wife is more than she seems. Her real name is not

Annie Burns but Lady Anne Burness Campbell, and she is no frontier lass, but cousin to my friend the Duke of Argyll."

She heard someone laughing, heard the laughter spread until the men were lost in snorts and guffaws, but she could not laugh with them. If William knew who she was . . .

"I ken my wife's name." Iain's words sent the men into new spasms of mirth.

Lord William looked as if he'd been struck. She saw the astonishment on his face and beneath it the rage, and some part of her realized he'd meant to hurt Iain with this knowledge. But when he spoke again, his voice was cold and calm, and his words chilled her to her soul.

"Then, Major, you also know she is under penalty of indenture for fourteen years and that, with her rightful master slain in an Indian attack—a matter about which she was not truthful—her indenture remains to be resold."

"*I* am the rightful owner of her indenture!" Iain's shout seemed to silence the night.

Annie stared up at him in astonishment, wondering how he had managed such a thing, then back at Lord William, who for the second time in as many moments looked staggered.

A muscle jumped in William's cheek, and his nostrils flared. "Show me the papers."

Morgan reached inside his shirt, produced a bundle of parchment and handed it to Lord William, who broke the seal and read through the papers in obvious haste, tilting the pages toward the firelight.

When he lifted his gaze, all trace of anger had vanished, and there was a slight smile on his face. He handed the papers back to Morgan. "Everything seems to be in order. Well played, major. Very well played, indeed."

" 'Tis not a game, but my wife's life." Iain's voice carried an edge of loathing.

"Ah, just so." Lord William looked down at her, his gaze softening. "You have no further need for him, Lady Anne. If you wish it, I'll have this marriage annulled and lift you from squalor and shame back to a life of grace. Do you truly wish to be bound to this frontiersman, this *Catholic*, this man with no name, no title, no wealth?"

Fury pushed Annie's fear aside. "He has a name! He is Iain MacKinnon, grandson of Iain Og MacKinnon, chieftain of Clan MacKinnon. And I would be nowhere but at his side."

Lord William's gaze hardened. "I pray you do not regret your choice too soon."

As she watched him walk away, Annie felt a surge of relief so strong it made her tremble, but behind it came a swell of dread. Now that Lord William knew who she was, there was nothing to keep him from sending word to Uncle Bain.

She tried to reassure herself, told herself there was little Uncle Bain could do now that she was married and indentured to the same man. But even as the fiddle started up again, she could not shake the niggling fear that if Uncle Bain wished to harm her, he'd let nothing stand in his way.

"When would you have told me?"

Iain stroked the bare curve of Annie's hip, his mind empty, the heat of their mating cooling into sleep. "Told you what, *a leannan?*"

Her fingers played with the line of hair on his belly. "That you'd bought my indenture."

He'd wondered how she would react. "I hadn't decided. A part of me wanted to tell you tonight so you wouldna worry, but a part of me hoped never to tell you, to slip the papers into the fire fourteen years from now and watch them burn while you slept, never the wiser. 'Tis not befitting a woman's dignity to be owned by her husband."

She lifted her head and looked down at him with soft green eyes. "I willna lie and say it doesna feel strange to think you are by law my master. But I trust you, Iain. What you have done . . . you've saved my life again."

Iain remembered the look of shock and rage on Wentworth's face and felt a deep satisfaction. The bastard had hoped to force Annie to seek his protection by turning Iain and his men against her. 'Twas a heartless way to win a woman to one's bed.

"I told you I'd protect you, and I meant it." Then he told her how, knowing in his gut that Wentworth meant her harm, he and his brothers had met with Joseph and his best warriors to discuss how best to protect her and had come up with a plan. He and Joseph had pretended to argue, giving Joseph an excuse to withdraw and Iain a reason to follow. Then, once out of sight of the fort, they'd split up, Morgan heading to Albany to buy her indenture and a few wedding gifts, while Iain had gone north with Joseph and his men to kidnap a priest. He'd told her how they'd encountered Father Delavay a day's march north of Ticonderoga and how he'd persuaded the good father to come with him.

"I didna tell you because I didna want you to worry or to blame yourself if aught went amiss."

"Kidnapping a priest is—oh, Iain!" She glared at him. "And what would have happened had you been slain?"

"But I wasna slain, *a leannan,* and for my troubles I have a lovely new wife."

" 'Twas a chancy plan, Iain. At least you're safe. But, please, no more secrets. I am a woman, no' a bairn."

He cupped her soft backside and grinned. "Thank God for that."

She frowned, and her eyes narrowed.

He couldn't help but chuckle. "Och, very well, no more secrets."

"And dinnae think to spirit me away to Stockbridge in the mornin'. Aye, I know very well that is your plan, but I willna be parted from you."

" 'Tis for the best, Annie."

"Please, Iain, I cannae bear the thought of bein' so far away from you."

And because he felt the same way, he relented. "Very well. You can stay—for now."

She smiled, the kind of smile that made his belly knot up

and his groin grow heavy. Then she climbed on top him and ran her hands up his chest. "How might I serve you, master?"

He groaned, shocked by her willingness to play such a game. Hungry for her, he gripped her hips and drew her upward, until the musk and spice of her sex rested just above his mouth. A soft golden fuzz covered her pink flesh, a reminder of pleasures past. He parted her, heard her whimper.

"Feed me, wench."

William dashed his empty snifter on the cold hearthstones, the shattering glass but the merest expression of the rage that consumed him. He'd been outplayed and outmatched, and he hadn't seen it coming. Checkmate.

Clearly the major had taken advantage of the time he'd been away to do more than mend his differences with Captain Joseph—if, indeed, the two of them had truly quarreled. 'Twas tantamount to desertion and worthy of another flogging at the least, but William would never be able to prove it, just as he would never be able to prove the Rangers were behind the fire by the powder magazine, the broken drawbridge, or the "Abenaki" attack.

The major was too clever, too skilled, his men far too loyal.

Tonight William had expected to destroy whatever feelings the major had for Lady Anne by revealing her true name. He'd been certain the major and his men would turn against her, forcing her to turn to William for his help and protection. But the major had already known her name—and had already accepted her. And she had chosen him.

A MacKinnon and an Argyll Campbell?

It made no sense. Why had Lady Anne trusted the major with the truth but lied to him? The MacKinnon and Argyll Campbell clans were foes, whereas Lady Anne's family had long been aligned with the Crown. Why would she marry a man who had far less to offer her than William did? The major had purchased her indenture, but William would have been able to see her sentence abolished. How could she turn against her class? She'd chosen straw, bearskins and ale when William would have given her featherbeds, silks and the finest wines.

He stood and began to undress, tossing his wig carelessly onto his dressing table, trying to sort out the pieces. Like any puzzle, the state of affairs concerning Lady Anne could be put into order, and once ordered it could be controlled.

Perhaps being rescued by the major had sent her into flights of romantic fancy. Otherwise, William knew not how she, a woman who'd been gently bred, could find the major appealing. With his sun-browned skin, Indian markings and long hair, the man was scarcely more than a savage. But women were not always subject to logic when it came to sex.

He kicked off his shoes, slipped out of his stockings, and blew out the candles. Then he stripped off his breeches and drawers and lay down naked upon his bed to stare up at the ceiling in the dark. Outside his window the fort slept. Even Ranger camp had fallen silent.

He closed his eyes, tried not to imagine Lady Anne in the major's bed, failed. His cock stretched and filled with his want for her. He grasped himself and stroked lazily.

The trouble with this puzzle was that too many pieces were still missing. William needed answers, and there was only one person left who might give them to him—Bain Campbell, Lord Bute. William hoped to receive a reply from the marquis within the month, before leaving for the campaign at Ticonderoga. And then they would see.

A sense of restored calm settled over William.

The pieces were still moving.

The game was not over yet.

Chapter Twenty-eight

"My wife is a lady." Iain's words roused Annie from dreams, his voice a deep rumble, his breath warm against her neck. "And no proper lady would want a man to touch her like this."

His hand nudged its way between her thighs to cup her sex from behind, his fingertips pressing in slow circles right where she needed it most. Delight shivered through her, waking her fully. When he slipped his thumb inside her, she couldn't help moaning.

"Mmm, it seems the lady *does* like it." He stroked her inside and out, nibbling and nipping the skin beneath her ear, the heat of his erection pressing against her lower back.

"Oh, Iain!" Her peak came quickly, pleasure shuddering through her, silky and hot.

He carried her through it, prolonging her bliss with his practiced touch until the last tremors had faded to honeyed stillness. But he was not finished with her—not yet.

"What would my lady wife think if I were to draw her up onto her knees and take her from behind, wild and rough?"

She could feel his urgency, and her need for him flared anew. "Aye, Iain! Please!"

In a heartbeat she found herself on her hands and knees, her legs forced apart, his hands grasping her hips, the thick head of his cock prodding her. Her cry mixed with his deep groan as he buried himself in her slick heat.

"Och, Jesus, lass!" He thrust into her hard, filling her, stretching her, impaling her, his rhythm fierce, ruthless, perfect.

She felt his stones slap against her, his cock striking that sensitive place inside her, the slippery friction scorching and sweet. His fingers reached around to tease her tender, swollen bud, his lips hot against her shoulder as he kissed her and whispered against her skin. The combined delight was almost more than she could bear.

She called for him, cried for him, pleading for release. "Iain! Oh, God, Iain!"

And then it took her, frantic, violent pleasure pounding through her like a tide of fire. Her inner muscles quaked in ecstasy against his cock, clenching him again and again, until he cried out her name and came apart inside her.

They sank together to the bed, both breathless.

He rolled onto his back, pulled her against his sweat-slick chest and kissed her hair. "I think perhaps my lady wife is no' such a lady."

She lifted her head, fighting giggles. "Perhaps she's a bit of a . . . *radgie* lady."

The rich, golden sound of his laughter made her smile. He was no longer the battle-weary man who'd saved her from the Abenaki. In the month they'd been married, the tension that had lined his face had faded. He smiled easily and laughed more often, and at times she felt she was seeing him as he'd been before Lord William had forced him into war. His brothers and his men had noticed the difference, telling him that marriage agreed with him, teasing him whenever he was the last to show for muster, asking him with knowing grins whether he'd slept well.

"Aye, my wife is a radgie lady, but a lady just the same." He raised her hand to his lips, kissed it, the humor in his gaze turning to regret. "I must go, *a leannan*. They'll be waitin'."

From outside came the sounds of Ranger camp stirring to life as his men gathered for his inspection.

She forced herself to smile. "I know."

As she helped him shave and dress, she thanked God that today he was going only so far as the training grounds. Tomorrow he would leave for battle.

Fighting the sense of dread that threatened to overwhelm her, Annie took breakfast to Father Delavay, who despite grave danger to himself had chosen to remain in Ranger camp until he felt called to move onward. Annie suspected his reluctance to leave had more to do with his desire not to watch the Rangers he'd blessed and broken bread with kill and be killed by his fellow Frenchmen. She could not blame him.

Dressed in the garb of a Ranger so he could mingle among the men without standing out, he now had a small cabin to himself and spent his days in prayer and his evenings talking with the men, listening to their confessions and teaching them about a faith most knew poorly. He was nothing like she'd expected a Catholic priest or a Frenchman to be, but instead reminded her of her grandfather—though her grandfather had never complained about anything as much as Father Delavay complained about the meals and lack of wine at the fort.

"If I were British," he told her, looking askance at the sausage and biscuits she'd brought him, "I would surrender just for the food."

"It cannae be that bad!" She laughed, though she'd been unwilling to admit that even the smell of camp food turned her stomach these days.

After making certain he had all he needed, she went to the hospital, where she spent the morning making salves, rolling bandages and helping the doctor pack his medicines and instruments. He would be setting up a small tent hospital at the remains of Fort William Henry, where thousands of provincials and British Regulars were already encamped, preparing for the assault on Ticonderoga. Though she had asked to come with him and help, Iain had forbidden it.

"I didna send you away to Stockbridge, Annie, but dinnae think to sway me on this," he'd said, seeming almost angry that she should ask. "William Henry is blood-soaked ground, or have your forgotten? I'll have you nowhere near it!"

And so, able to do nothing but pray, she had resigned herself to wait out the battle here at the fort, left behind with the sick and injured and a small force of Regulars.

She arranged little jars in the leather pockets of a wooden chest, careful to make certain each was sealed. The heat made her gown stick to her skin, and sweat beaded at her nape and trickled between her breasts. She fought a wave of dizziness and found herself wondering how Iain and his men could train in the bright sun. Then she realized they were probably accustomed to the heat. After all, most of them had grown up here. While she'd been learning her table manners, practicing her needlework and studying her lessons in cool, rainy Scotland, Iain had been learning how to shoot and track and climb trees to steal honey from bees' nests—a skill he promised to put to good use for her when he returned.

And he would return.

He must return.

She could not imagine her life without him.

This past month had been the happiest she'd ever known. Never had she felt more alive. At times it was hard to believe such joy could be real. Each morning she awoke in his arms, and each night she fell asleep sated from his loving. And although they each had their duties during the day— he drilling his men for the coming battle, she caring for the sick and injured in the hospital—they'd found time in the evening to talk and love and dream.

She'd shared her memories of her mother, father and brothers and the beauty of their lands in Rothesay, while he'd told her of his clan and coming of age with Joseph and his brothers on the frontier. And late at night he'd spoken of his farm northeast of Albany and how one day, when the war was over and he was free again, he would reclaim it and build a home for her there.

But as happy as these weeks had been, the shadow of war hovered over them always, and Annie had known their joy was fragile. She'd done her best to push aside her fear for him, refusing to let it darken whatever time they had together. But now that the hour drew near, she found it impossible to hold her fears at bay.

What if he should be hurt or captured or killed?

She knew every precious inch of his body, and though he was strong beyond most men, skin and muscle could not halt a lead ball nor stand the blast of a grenade or the force of a cannon. She could not bear to think of him torn and broken upon the ground, dying as her father and brothers had died, in a pool of his own blood.

And what of Morgan, Connor and Joseph? Should one of them be grievously hurt or slain, Iain would blame himself and carry the crushing grief with him forever. What of the men? 'Twas impossible that they should all survive.

She felt tears prick her eyes and blinked them away. The least she could do was show the same courage as the men. They were risking their lives, not she.

"Mistress MacKinnon, I think these ought to go in that chest also," Dr. Blake called to her from across the hospital, pointing to a row of little pots.

She rose and took a step toward him. But the floor seemed to pull at her, the scrubbed boards rushing up at her, the room around her turning to shades of swirling gray. The last thing she saw was Dr. Blake's startled face.

Iain met General Abercrombie's gaze and wondered how many times he would have to repeat himself. "The abatis is at least six feet high, and brush and branches are piled waist-deep the length of fifteen paces afore it. We cannae hope to force their breastworks wi'out first layin' down heavy artillery fire. Men will become entangled in the branches and be cut down by the hundreds."

The general gave him an indulgent smile, smoothed his pale hands over the parchment map that lay on the table before them. "We have an army of almost sixteen thousand men, six thousand of which are trained British Regulars. I believe you underestimate their skill, major. Rangers are not the only fighting men of worth in His Majesty's army."

But Iain would not be silenced. "Not even British Regulars can fly, and when pierced by lead balls they die just as quickly as Rangers."

The other officers shifted uncomfortably around him, and the general looked at him through flat blue eyes, clearly angry.

Then Wentworth spoke. "I'm afraid I must agree with Major MacKinnon, General. Heavy artillery fire is the key to breaching their entrenchments without undue loss of men."

Iain met Wentworth's gaze. The two of them had barely spoken since the night of Iain's wedding. Wentworth had issued commands through Cooke or summoned Iain to his office only long enough to speak a few terse words before dismissing him. Clearly, the *mac-dìolain* wasn't accustomed to being bested and didn't like it. The fact that he was siding with Iain against Abercrombie proved only that he wasn't a fool as well as a bastard.

"Very well." Abercrombie gave an irritated snort. "We'll place the artillery here."

Iain watched as the general outlined his strategy in painstaking detail, and it became clear to him that, although Abercrombie was quite inventive when it came to transporting supplies and provisioning an army, he knew next to nothing about waging war. 'Twould be a miracle if they managed to take the fort.

For three years Iain had lived and breathed war, aware that each day might well be his last. He knew well the fear that besets a man in the last hours before the fray, knew the cold, dry taste of terror. But the thought of Ticonderoga filled him with some other kind of misgiving. This time something was different. And it was not hard to guess why.

Annie.

She was the last thing he'd expected. She'd taken him unawares with her apple green eyes, her golden hair and her sweet smile, restoring laughter, light and hope to his life though he'd not realized he'd lost them. She'd brought him back to himself.

Never had he been so intimate with a woman, her every thought and feeling as important to him as his own. Never had his heart and body and soul belonged so completely to anyone. Never had his dreams or the days ahead mattered more to him

Never had he felt so mortal.

"We'll make camp here before continuing northward," said the general, running his finger up Lake George to Sabbath Day Point.

Heads nodded.

Most of these officers had never been north of Fort William Henry, and Iain doubted whether they had any notion what they were facing. The forest alone might be enough to defeat them if they were not properly guided.

"The supply trains will—"

The door to Wentworth's office burst open, and Brendan limped through it, out of breath. He gave a little bow. "Forgi'e me, but I've a pressing message for Mack."

The general glared first at Brendan, then at Iain, but Wentworth nodded.

"The doc says Annie has swooned dead away!"

Iain didn't ask permission to leave.

Annie woke to find herself lying on one of the little hospital beds, Dr. Blake looking down at her, a worried frown on his face. "What . . . happened?"

"You fainted." He pressed a cool, wet cloth to her forehead.

"Fainted?" Her mind felt thick and slow.

"I must say you gave my old heart a fright. But you've no fever. How do you feel?"

"A wee bit dizzy. I fainted?" She'd never done such a thing in her life.

"Yes, indeed. Have you been eating well?"

"I've no' had the stomach for food of late. 'Tis far too hot."

"Any pain? Headaches?"

"Nay." She sat up slowly. "It must be the heat. I am no' accustomed to it."

"Perhaps." The doctor didn't sound convinced. "When was your last monthly?"

The question, asked so bluntly, brought heat rushing into her cheeks. She'd never spoken to a man of such things before. But as she tried to remember, she realized she was late—by a month. She pressed a hand to her belly in shock.

Could it be? So soon?

" 'Twas toward the end of April, I think."

"And now we've come to the end of June." The creases on his forehead smoothed, and he smiled. "I suspect, Mistress MacKinnon, that you are with child."

"A bairn?" Iain stood just inside the doorway, a look of complete astonishment on his braw face. Then his gaze met hers, worry and wonderment in his eyes. "Lass?"

Emotion swelled inside her, turning to a lump in her throat—amazement that she was already with child, joy to think Iain's baby was growing within her, tenderness at the look of naked longing in Iain's eyes. Never had she seen him so taken aback or so hopeful.

Beyond words, she reached for him, felt his big hand enclose hers.

Dr. Blake stood, smiled at Iain. "Your wife's confinement should come in midwinter."

Iain looked at her as if she were fragile and might break. "Is she—?"

"She is quite well. It is not uncommon for a woman in the early stages of breeding to feel dizzy or to have an unsettled stomach. She'll be fine with a bit of rest."

When Iain met her gaze again, the affection in his eyes made her breath catch. "You didna ken?"

Annie felt silly. How could she have missed the signs? "N-nay. I thought it was this dreadful heat."

He gave her hand a squeeze, smiled. "We shall have to cool you off."

"Mistress MacKinnon, I thank you for your help, but I believe your work here is finished for today. I recommend you spend the afternoon lying down."

She started to rise from the bed, but Iain scooped her into his arms.

"If the doc says you're to rest, that's what you'll be doin'. My thanks, Doctor."

It felt awkward to be carried through the fort past the curious stares of Regulars and Rangers alike, particularly as she didn't feel unwell, but Iain would not put her down.

" 'Twas only a fainting spell, you daftie. I feel quite well. There is no need to—"

"*Uist, a leannan.*" He pressed his lips to her temple, his voice gentle. "I like holdin' you. Let me savor it while I can."

She felt a hitch of fear in her belly, her joy turning bittersweet at his words as the terrible truth hit her. Tomorrow he was leaving for battle. He might not live to see his child born.

She laid her head on his shoulder and closed her eyes.

Iain had stayed with Annie until she'd fallen asleep, helping her to undress, running a damp cloth over her naked skin to cool her, letting his hand rest on the curve of her belly just above her womb. It amazed him to think his son or daughter was already growing inside her.

Her eyes closed, she'd smiled. "You are pleased?"

He'd struggled to put his feelings into words. "I hadna hoped for so rich a blessing as this, Annie."

Despite her protests that she was not in the least tired, she'd soon fallen fast asleep. He'd covered her with a linen sheet, kissed on her cheek and reluctantly left her side. Then, his thoughts filled with her and the new life she carried, he'd gone back to the work of war.

"Our battle plan is flawed, our leader a bletherin' fool and our enemy well prepared," Iain told his officers. "Our task is to carry out our orders—and to be ready with a better plan so that Nanny Crombie's strategy willna get us all killed."

He outlined Abercrombie's line of attack over the same

objections he himself had voiced. Why were the Rangers not being used to guide the army when they knew every inch of the forest around that fort? Why face the obstacle of the abatis when an attack from the La Chute River stood a much better chance of success? Why go ashore with the entire army in one place where the enemy could observe their movements?

Iain gave the only answer he could. "Because although Abercrombie delights in watching us shoot at marks, he doesna trust provincials to fight as well as Regulars."

Connor gave a snort of disgust. "Then he's as big an idiot as Braddock!"

They set to work, running through Abercrombie's plan, playing it out against the terrain and the layout of the fort, plotting what action to take should aught go amiss.

Only after the council was over and the other officers had left did Iain tell Morgan, Connor and Joseph the news.

"Annie is with child."

The three of them stared at him for a moment, then broke into broad grins.

Connor turned to Morgan. "Tell me, brother, do you think it's the quality of the farmer's seed and the strength of his spade that make the crop, or is it the richness of the field he's ploughin'?"

Morgan and Joseph broke into laughter.

Then Morgan answered, "Surely 'tis a bit of both, though in this case I'd have to say I've seen our brother's spade, and it's no' so strong nor so big as mine—"

"Nor mine," Connor added.

"—so it must be a fine field he's been ploughin', a fine field indeed."

Iain was about to curse them both for idiots, when Joseph laid a hand on his arm and spoke in Muhheconneok. "Don't let the cub's jesting bother you. I see the question in your eyes. You know we'll watch over her and the child if you don't return."

Iain nodded and let out the breath he hadn't realized he'd

been holding. Then he went off to exact a similar promise from Father Delavay. He didn't see the look his brothers shared with Joseph or overhear the vow they made to one another—that if any one of the four of them were to make it back from Ticonderoga, it would be Iain.

Chapter Twenty-nine

Annie awoke feeling muzzy-headed and more than a little queasy. She rose slowly, dressed and looked out over a subdued camp from the door of Iain's cabin, her heart sinking with the setting sun. Dougie was not tuning his fiddle tonight. Instead he was cleaning his musket. The others likewise cleaned their rifles, sharpened blades and bayonets, refilled their powder horns or packed their gear, talking quietly together.

Iain walked among them, speaking with each one of them in turn, checking their gear, answering their questions, jesting with them. She saw the confidence he inspired in his men, the way their faces brightened when he spoke with them. Like a Highland laird of old, he was showing them they mattered to him, sharing his strength.

And what would the wife of a Highland laird do?

She wouldna stand here weeping, Annie.

Fighting tears, she turned away from the door and began to lay his gear out on the bed, running her fingers over each item—his pistols, his powder horn, his claymore with its bit of tartan, his tumpline, his waterskin. It seemed so long ago now that she'd first drunk from the waterskin, first seen the MacKinnon colors tied round the pommel of his sword, first watched him dig through his pack.

Those had been dark days and terrifying, but they had brought her together with him. She would trade them for nothing.

Then, on sudden inspiration, she took one of his knives, grasped a lock of hair at her nape, and cut through it. Then she tied a knot in one end and slipped the strands into the pouch that held his flints and shot. A part of him would remain with her in her womb; now a part of her would go with him.

"Eager to see me go?"

Startled, her heart aching with sadness, she whirled about. "Dinnae say such a thing!"

He shut the door behind him, came to her and pulled her against him. "Och, Annie, forgi'e me. 'Tis but a soldier's wont to make light of leavin' for war."

"I find no humor in it!" Her grief made her sound shrewish and angry.

He kissed her forehead, held her closer. "We still have tonight, lass."

She pressed herself closer to him, held onto that hope. "Aye, we still have tonight."

She watched as Iain packed his gear—laughing with him when he found that she'd set out his snowshoes and bearskin coat.

"I dinnae think I'll be needin' these."

Then they shared a dinner of roasted beef and boiled potatoes, Iain coaxing her to eat, feeding her little bites over the objections of her wambly belly.

But though Annie longed to be alone with him, there were many things that seemed to require Iain's attention, and their meal was interrupted time and again.

First came Morgan. "The flints they've given us dinnae fit our rifles."

"Tell Abercrombie's whoreson of a quartermaster that you're under my orders to shoot him in the cods if he gets in your way, then take what we need."

Then came Connor. "McHugh got into a brawl with three Regulars, and they've thrown him in the guardhouse."

"Oh, for God's sake! Leave him there to stew awhile. They'll let him out ere morn'."

Then came Brendan and Killy, looking furious. Killy spoke for the two of them. "We've been told we're to stay behind, Mack. You can't mean to be leavin' us here!"

Iain gave Annie's hand a squeeze. "It's true you willna be headin' north to Ticonderoga wi' us, but it's no' because I find you weak and dinnae trust you to fight. I've a different mission for you. I need you to watch over Father Delavay and Annie for me. 'Tis yet a secret, but Annie is wi' child."

The two Rangers' frowns turned to grins, and they listened as Iain told them how there were only a handful of men he would trust with this mission and how Annie needed not only protection, but extra help about the cabin now that she was in a delicate way.

"Can I rely on you?"

Brendan nodded fiercely, his young face grave. "Aye, Mack."

Killy grinned. "You'll name the babe after me, of course."

Iain dismissed them with a wave of his hand. "Daft bloody Irishman!"

Annie waited until the men had gone to speak. "You are kind to spare their feelings."

"I wasna tryin' to spare them, Annie." He looked at her gravely for a moment, then grinned. "But watch now—I asked them to keep the bairn a secret, which means all of Ranger camp will ken afore you can blink. They'd tell the redcoats and the French nothin', even under torture, but no Ranger seems to be able to keep a secret from another."

And true enough, by the time Iain was finished with his meal—Annie had refused to swallow another bite—there were calls from outside for the two of them to come forth.

Iain led her out the door, and sensing her shyness, wrapped an arm about her shoulder.

His men cheered. Then one by one they stepped forward, filing past Annie, doffing their caps, bestowing their kindest benisons upon her and the bairn.

"A long life and happiness."

"Thank you, Cam."

"A long life and good health to you and the bairn."

"Thank you, Forbes."

"If it's a lass, may she have your beauty, and if it's a wee laddie, his father's courage."

"Thank you, Dougie."

Iain watched as his men poured out their humble blessings upon Annie and their unborn child. He'd known they cherished her, but he'd not foreseen this. Something twisted in his gut to realize that not all of them would return. And then he understood. On the eve of ugliness and death, his men were paying reverence to beauty and new life.

Annie looked every bit the high-born lady, receiving their attention with grace and gratefulness despite her own grief and worry, answering their words with her sweet smile, though Iain could tell she was near tears. Yet, although she brought happiness to his men, he wanted her for himself.

As the last of his men filed past her, Iain took Morgan aside. "I'm putting you—"

"In command, aye, I ken. Go to her, Iain."

Bidding his men to rest well, Iain led Annie back inside and closed the door behind them, shutting out the night. At last they were alone.

She stood with her face downcast in the flickering candlelight, her arms hugged round her, looking small and fragile and frightened. She drew a shaky breath, and he realized she was trying not to cry.

He drew her into his arms, kissed her hair. "Come, Annie."

"I-I want to be strong like you, but—" Her voice broke.

"The Muhheconneok believe part of a woman's strength lies in her tears. Dinnae be ashamed to weep, *a leannan*. You willna seem less in my eyes."

She lifted her gaze to his, her green eyes glittering, wetness upon her cheeks. "I cannae bear the thought of losin' you, Iain MacKinnon."

He understood her anguish, for he could not stand the thought of leaving her to bear his child without him near. But he did not tell her that. "I've no intention of dyin', Annie."

"Make me forget, Iain! I need to forget—even if just for a while."

"Aye, lass."

He kissed her face, tasting the salt of her tears, intending to comfort her. But the moment his lips touched hers, need overwhelmed him. Gentleness gave way to a fierceness that shattered his restraint. He fisted a hand in her hair, angled her mouth to receive him and kissed her with the roughness and desperation of a man facing the gallows. And she kissed him back, melting against him with a whimper, her fervor every bit a match for his.

They knew each other well, their hands tugging at lacings, pushing aside leather and linen, seeking the fastest path to skin, the truest ways to please. Then, naked, they fell upon the bed, limbs entwined, bodies impatient for union and release. He pushed her thighs apart and felt her hand close around his cock as she guided him eagerly into her welcoming heat.

"Annie, *mo luaidh!*" The slick, tight feel of her forced the breath from his lungs, sent fire spearing through his gut, making his cock jerk and his stones draw tight.

She called out for him, wrapped her legs around his waist, her hands sliding over the shifting muscles of his back and buttocks, gripping and kneading him as he drove himself into her. "Oh, Iain, I need you!"

Already on the brink, he buried himself deep inside her, grinding the thick root of his cock against her slick and swollen sex, determined not to find pleasure without her. She gave a long, throaty moan, her head tossing from side to side as he kept up a relentless rhythm, her inner muscles constricting around him.

He whispered nonsense against her cheeks, her lips, the throat, murmuring endearments in English, in Gaelic, in Muhheconneok. "Come for me, *mo luaidh! Tha gràdh agam ort! Nia ktachwahnen!*"

Then her breath caught in her throat, and she came, arching off the bed, her nails biting into his shoulders, fresh tears spilling down her temples. "Iain!"

She was the bonniest thing he'd ever seen, ecstasy mingled with sorrow on her lovely face as oblivion claimed her. The sight of her bliss stripped away his control, and, with her name on his lips, he joined her in sweet forgetfulness.

"Iain?"

"Mmm?"

"If the bairn is a lass, I'd like to name her after our mothers—Mara Elasaid."

" 'Tis a bonnie name. And if 'tis a laddie?"

"Then we shall name him after his father."

"Och, well, 'tis a grand idea. And what name would that be?"

"You daftie!"

Long into the night, Annie lay with her head against Iain's chest, fighting to stay awake, knowing that if she slept, dawn would overtake her and Iain would leave. She listened to his slow breathing and the steady beat of his heart, savored the silky warmth of his skin, the firmness of his muscles, the rasp of his chest hair against her cheek. He felt so strong and alive, so vital, and she found it both cruel and terrible that anything should rob him of life now.

They'd made love twice again, taking time for tenderness, lingering over the smallest pleasures. She had reveled in the feel of him, in his scent, in the bliss his body conjured from hers, committing every inch of him to her memory by touch, taste, sight and scent. She had taken all he offered and denied him nothing.

Was it truly possible for the heart to withstand such a tempest of feelings—equal parts grief and joy, fear and hope? She hadn't known love could be so sorrowful, nor joy such a source of sadness. Yet if this tumult was what it meant to love Iain with her entire being—body, mind and soul—she would accept it.

"Annie?" Iain's lips pressed against her cheek.

Her eyes flew open.

He stood beside the bed, already clad in his breeches, the sunrise glowing pink against the parchment window behind him.

She sat up with a start. "Nay!"

He brushed a strand of hair from her face. " 'Tis well you slept. Dinnae blame yourself."

She rose, feeling as if she were made of wood, and dressed. Then, as she had done so many times, she helped him to shave and dress, handing him his belt, his pistols, his knives, until he stood before her, not her husband, but a warrior bound for battle. Tears scorching her throat, she walked with him out the door.

Outside stood Morgan, Connor and Joseph.

Beyond the cabins, his men waited.

Joseph stepped forward and embraced her. "I'll keep you and your baby in my prayers."

"And you'll be in mine."

Then Connor pulled her against him and kissed her cheek. "Be well, lassie, and dinnae fret. We'll watch over him."

"Watch over yourself, Connor MacKinnon." She smiled through her tears. "My baby will need uncles."

"Fear not, Annie. All will be well." Morgan took her, held her tight, kissing her temple. Then he whispered, "I'll bring him back to you."

"Be safe, Morgan. Please, be safe!"

Then the three of them turned and walked away, leaving her with Iain.

He turned to her, pulled her against him for one last embrace. *"Tha móran ghràdh agam ort, dh'Annaidh."* *My love lies upon you, Annie, and it always will.*

Then he did something she never would have expected. He dropped to his knees, grasped her hips, and pressed his lips to her belly over her womb.

She twined her fingers in his hair, stifling a sob. *"Tha móran ghràdh agam ort, a luaidh."*

Then he rose to his feet, gave her hand one last squeeze

and walked away, his fingers releasing hers one at a time, until her hand was empty.

"Bain Campbell, Marquis of Bute? On his way here? Are you certain?"

"Aye, my lord. If he hadn't been detained by some unfortunate business in New York, he'd be here already. He should arrive tomorrow."

William had been expecting some kind of reply from Campbell any day now, but not Campbell himself. "How extraordinary."

"He must care deeply for his niece, my lord."

"So it would seem." He pressed a sovereign into his man's hand. "Thank you. You are dismissed."

"Aye, my lord."

"Oh, one last thing. You said he was detained by some unfortunate business. What sort of unfortunate business would that be?"

"It seems someone strangled a kitchen maid at the inn where the marquis was staying, and another maid accused him of the deed. He was questioned, an inconvenience that delayed his travel by several days."

"I see. Thank you."

With Lieutenant Cooke gone to battle this past week, William had become accustomed to performing his own wardrobe and morning toilette. He brushed yesterday's powder off his jacket, slipped it on, then played with the lace at his throat, striving for symmetry.

He'd bitterly resented General Abercrombie's decision to leave him in command of Fort Elizabeth, knowing full well he'd earned Abercrombie's disfavor by repeatedly challenging the general's strategy. Yet Abercrombie seemed to have as little talent for influencing minds as he did for planning battles.

William had sent a missive to London last week before his Regulars marched north, describing his misgivings about the general's plans for Ticonderoga, with instructions to present it to His Majesty should the effort at Ticonderoga fail. The letter would be proof not only that William was a more competent strategist than Abercrombie, but that he'd tried to save the day—and had been held back for doing so. His grandfather would be furious.

Unless Abercrombie won a clear victory at Ticonderoga, his days as a general were over. William would make certain of it.

William adjusted his wig on its stand and began to powder it.

Yet now it seemed Abercrombie had done William a favor, for William was about to have all of his questions regarding Lady Anne answered—and at a time when Major MacKinnon and the bulk of his men were occupied elsewhere. The handful of sick and injured Rangers and the dozen or so Stockbridge warriors MacKinnon had left behind would not hinder Lord Bute, who was still Lady Anne's legal guardian. If Campbell wished to have her illegitimate marriage annulled and to take her back to Scotland, no one had the authority to stop him.

Of course, William hoped he would choose a different course of action, one that left her in William's keeping.

William had prepared his own story, which had the virtue of being largely true. Lady Anne had been rescued from slaughter on the frontier, but had declined to reveal her true name. William had unfortunately not recognized her until it was too late to halt her disastrous marriage with Major MacKinnon. William would apologize, though Campbell could hardly hold him accountable, as his niece had lied to him.

Then William would ask his questions. How had Lady Anne come to be on the frontier? How had she become indentured? Why might she wish to keep her identity secret?

The answers, together with the reunion of uncle and niece, would doubtless make for quite a diverting afternoon.

William brushed the powder from his hands, tapped his wig to remove the excess, then put it on, using the looking glass to guide him. When he was satisfied with his appearance, he strode downstairs to his office and began to sort through the many missives sent from the front. The most recent, dated the evening of July fifth, announced the army's arrival at Sabbath Day Point.

That was two days ago. With any luck, the battle for Ticonderoga had finally begun.

Iain lay on his belly on the mountain top watching the British advance—such as it was. "Who wants to help me round up lost red sheep?"

Below and behind them to their right, a battalion of redcoats blundered blindly through the forest on a heading that would lead them west of the Ticonderoga Peninsula.

Morgan took the glass from Iain, gazed through it, then shook his head. "Where the bloody hell do they think they're goin'?"

Iain ordered his men to move out quietly, cursing Abercrombie for a fool. Rather than choosing the Rangers to guide the army, he'd sent Iain and his men off to guard their left flank and to hold the high ground against ambush. Now redcoats were scattered through the forest in small detachments—easy prey for Montcalm should he find them.

The mountainside was steep and heavily wooded, offering both plentiful cover and many opportunities for ambush. Still, Iain led his men swiftly, hoping to prevent the first massacre of this campaign.

They'd been out for a week now, having spent several days at the ruins of William Henry building a fleet of whaleboats and bateaux to carry their entire force—the largest army Iain had ever seen—up Lake George. When they'd finally struck out on the water on July fourth, the sight of the fleet had been awe-inspiring. Even Connor had gaped in amazement.

"Nanny Crombie kens how to launch ships, I'll give him that."

Landing was another thing. Already in their second day

ashore, they had yet to approach the fort, which stood at battle readiness, its troops well aware a British army was coming. There would be no element of surprise.

Iain reached inside his shirt, clasped the little medicine pouch Joseph had made for him yesterday. Inside was the silky lock of Annie's hair. He'd discovered it as soon as he'd reached William Henry, had taken it out and held it to his nose. It still smelled of her—musk and honey. How like Annie to surprise him in such a way.

Saying farewell to her was one of the hardest things he'd ever had to do. Had she not been with child, it might have been easier. Women died in childbed every day, and many bairns did not live to take their first breath. Iain wanted to be with Annie when her time came. Yet he'd found peace to think that no matter what happened to him, their love would—God willing—take the shape of a child to bring her joy and to comfort her. He'd found greater peace still in Father Delavay's solemn promise to baptize the bairn at birth—and to grant Annie baptism and Last Rites should the worst happen.

Iain had just turned their course in a more southerly direction when there came the popping sound of gunfire from directly ahead. "It seems the wolves have found our sheep. Come!"

They moved through the trees as quickly as they could, keeping in formation, and found they'd already outflanked the French, who stood with their backs to them, firing upon the Regulars, who were racing musket balls for cover.

Without needing a command, the Rangers took cover as one, aimed, fired.

Iain reloaded, aimed and spotted a British officer trying valiantly to rally his men, unaware that the French were thick behind him. The officer shouted to his men, steadied them, bringing order to the chaos. But the French were reloading. If the officer didn't take cover quickly, he was going to be full of holes.

And then Iain saw his face.

Lieutenant Cooke.

Iain knew he had just a few seconds. Motioning for Cam and Morgan to cover him, he ran into the fray, driving himself into Cooke's back and knocking him to the ground just as the French launched a salvo of lead.

Cooke lay facedown beneath him, stunned, the breath knocked from his lungs.

Iain rolled onto his back, choosing his target, then flipped onto his belly, took aim, and fired. Ranger gunfire exploded from the trees all around him, scattering the French lines.

Beside him, Cooke gasped, coughed, then gaped at Iain in astonishment.

"Good day, Lieutenant." Iain grinned. "Miss me?"

Chapter Thirty

It was late morning of the next day when William welcomed Bain Campbell, Lord Bute, to Fort Elizabeth, and with him a young woman he claimed was Lady Anne's former maid. He seemed most anxious for William to understand how his niece had come to be indentured and insisted the maid give her account of it.

"She was there and abetted Annie," he said.

But as William listened to the young maid's faltering explanation, he knew it for a lie. No British court would transport a young woman of noble birth for stealing jewels from her uncle's house. It simply would not happen.

Ever.

Nor did William believe Lady Anne capable of the schemes Campbell attributed to her—deceiving him, defying him to run off with a wealthy merchant's son, stitching stolen jewels into her skirts as an ill-gotten dowry. Though she had lied to William, he knew she was not a practiced liar. She couldn't even feign poor table manners with any consistency. Nor was she the sort of woman who used men to acquire wealth. Otherwise she'd have made her way into William's bed and not Major MacKinnon's.

"I begged her no' to do it, my lord, but she didna listen to me. She left me no choice but to find my lord Bute to stop her, my lord." The maid's voice quavered with unshed tears and audible regret.

No choice.

Unless William was very much mistaken, the young maid had been coerced into offering him this account. If her bowed head and trembling hands hadn't told him that, Bain Campbell's bullying manner and hovering presence would have. He stood over her, his gaze fixed hard upon her, as if speaking his words through her.

Rather than getting answers, William found himself with still more questions—and the niggling feeling that Campbell himself was in some way accountable for his niece's plight. He had no doubt the young woman—Lady Anne's former maid—knew the truth. Perhaps he could find a way to spend a few moments alone with her.

"You cannae imagine how hard these past months have been, wonderin' where she was, hopin' she was alive and in good health. I cannae thank you enough for your letter." Campbell stood in his shirtsleeves and breeches without even a wig upon his head. He was a large man, outweighing William by easily three stone, his arms thick from a lifetime of brandishing a broadsword.

William smiled and gave a courtly bow of his head, wondering if Campbell knew how transparent his lie was. If he'd wanted to know where Lady Anne was living, he might easily have traced her path as far as Albany and then to the cabin of her first master. And yet it was clear from Campbell's disheveled appearance and his manner that he was truly distressed—whether for Lady Anne's sake or for some other reason, William could not yet discern.

"I am grateful to have been of service. But I'm afraid her

circumstances have changed since I penned that missive. Your niece is married."

Campbell looked thunderstruck, his mouth hanging open, his eyes wide. "Married?"

"Aye. The officer who rescued her married her in secret. He also owns her indenture. I'm afraid it may be difficult to remove her to Scotland, if that is your aim."

Campbell laughed, then sat, burying his face in his enormous hands. When he lifted his head and met William's gaze, he was still smiling, but his rage was palpable. "Who is this officer?"

"Major Iain MacKinnon, commander of MacKinnon's Rangers."

Campbell leapt to his feet. "A MacKinnon? From Skye?"

William nodded. "Major MacKinnon is the grandson of Iain Og MacKinnon."

"An exiled Jacobite? A Catholic?" He spat the words in obvious distaste.

"Unfortunately I did not recognize her soon enough to prevent the two of them from becoming infatuated, nor did I know of the union until it had been consummated." If he'd known who she was, he'd have taken her himself.

Campbell began to pace. "You are no' to blame. The fault lies solely with this MacKinnon. 'Twas a Catholic wedding, you say? Then it matters not. She'll return with me to Scotland, and that will be the end of it. Take me to her."

As William led Campbell through the fort toward Ranger camp, he wondered whether writing to his old acquaintance had been a terrible misstep.

"Well, 'tis a grand day for Britain. We've reached the fort." Iain took position behind a wide trunk, his rifle loaded and ready, his body taut with the anticipation of battle.

His men's quiet sniggers passed like a whisper through the forest.

The Rangers were ready.

Ahead through the trees lay the barrier of the abatis and

behind it the hastily built breastworks, little more than a high wooden wall padded with soil. Along the entrenchments, the hats and musket barrels of French soldiers bobbed as they rushed to their posts.

The enemy was ready, as well.

Iain could see why Abercrombie thought his army could make short work of Ticonderoga. The breastworks themselves could be easily blasted to bits with cannon. But it was not the breastworks that worried Iain—it was the abatis. A thick snarl of branches skirted a chin-high wall of tree trunks, rendering the ground all but impassable. Any soldier who tried to cross it would find himself entangled and stopped short, an easy mark for the French sharpshooters.

Iain gauged the distance between his position and the French guns, sweat trickling down his temples, his chest, his back. 'Twas a hot day. "We're in range of their marksmen. Keep your heads down, lads."

The sound of the drums drew near, marking the approach of the artillery and the infantry. Humiliated by yesterday's wandering in the wilderness, Abercrombie had seen to it that the army had gotten off on the right path this morning. Not that he'd used the Rangers as guides, nor even thanked them for rescuing his lost companies the day before. In truth, he seemed to resent the Rangers' help and had shouted in Iain's face when Iain had led Lieutenant Cooke and the lost Regulars back into camp—together with more than 150 French prisoners.

"You've exceeded your orders, Major! You were commanded to take and hold the high ground for the army's advance, not to guide or take captives!"

Iain had shouted back. "The army wasna advancin'! Would you rather I'd let your men be cut down afore the battle was even joined?"

At least Lieutenant Cooke had been grateful. "I may have underestimated you and your men. I see now why Colonel Wentworth tolerates your insubordination. Your woodcraft is unmatched. You saved my life. You saved the lives of my men. Thank you, sir."

'Twas the first time Cooke had called him sir.

The sound of the drums drew near, the beat counting off the last moments of men's lives. 'Twas a cadence Iain had heard too many times, one usually followed by gunshots, the deep roar of cannon, the screams of the dying.

He reached for the medicine pouch inside his shirt, lifted it to his lips and kissed it.

Dinnae fret, lass. I'll be home soon.

Then Connor spoke in a loud voice. "It occurs to me that it makes no sense for us to whisper and sneak about when the British army announces its arrival wi' drums and bright red uniforms."

The men howled with laughter.

But something was wrong. Though Iain could see those telltale red uniforms through the trees to his right, there came no squeak and scrape of wheels. And that meant . . . *no artillery.*

At a shouted command, the rhythm of the drums changed, ordering the Regulars into attack columns. Men hurried into formation, their boots a dull thud on the forest floor, their buckles and bayonets rattling, their breathing heavy.

"Och, for the love of God, nay!"

But it was too late, and there was nothing Iain could do. The orders had been given.

Morgan took aim. "Abercrombie will rot in hell for this!"

His heart pounding hot with rage, Iain raised his rifle to his shoulder. "God be wi' you, lads. God be wi' us all."

Annie made careful stitches in the linen, the wee bedgown almost finished after two afternoons of sewing. The cloth, needle and thread had been a gift from Iain. He'd left them wrapped in canvas beside the hearth when she'd not been looking, together with a letter asking her not to worry and assuring her he'd be home as soon as he could. Though it was perhaps a bit early to be stitching baby clothes—the bairn had not yet quickened—the work helped to keep her mind off her fears, which had surely been Iain's purpose.

In the shade of Killy's cabin, Father Delavay was trying to explain the Immaculate Conception to a handful of Rangers.

"The words 'Immaculate Conception' betoken not Christ, but the Virgin," he said, his French accent curling around the words in a way Annie found pleasing.

" 'Tis because she got a big belly wi'out the mess of a man's spunk," offered Brendan.

Annie felt herself blush to the roots of her hair and bent her gaze upon her sewing.

"*Non, mon dieu!* It is because she was born free of sin, you silly Scotsman!"

And for the first time in more than a week, Annie found herself smiling.

Iain had been gone eight long days, each harder to endure than the one that came before. During the day, she moved about as if in a fog, her body in Ranger camp, her heart and mind with Iain. At night she lay awake in the dark and prayed.

God, watch over them. Keep them safe.
Bring him back to me whole and alive!

How strange that she was sitting under a cheerful blue sky, listening to the sweet songs of birds around her, when a few days' march to the north armies were killing and dying. It seemed nature paid little heed to the struggles of men—or the heartaches of women.

Was this how her mother had felt when her father and brothers had marched away to fight at Prestonpans? Annie remembered the morning well. Her mother's tears. Her father's crushing hug. Her brothers' boisterous teasing. The mist. The scent of autumn. The cold floor against her bare feet.

Her father and brothers had departed for war looking braw and invincible to her six-year-old eyes, though her thoughts had been more on her hungry belly and the porridge she had yet to eat than on what might betide them.

Four days later Uncle Bain, stained with gore, had brought the news.

"They're lost, Mara. All of them."

Her mother had fallen to the floor with a heartrending wail and had lain there sobbing, the sound of her cries terrifying to Annie, who hadn't understood—not yet.

O, Mamaidh!

Lost in her memories, Annie didn't realize she was weeping until a tear fell upon the linen. She quickly wiped her tears away, her mother's sobs still raw in her heart.

Nearby the men were laughing about something—Annie hadn't heard what.

Then came the warning whistle, a sound Annie had learned to recognize.

The laughter died, and the men rose to their feet.

"You'd best be gettin' inside, Father." A pistol had appeared in Killy's hand. "You, too, mistress."

As Father Delavay hurried away, Brendan peeked round the cabin toward the river. "Wentworth's crossin' the river. He's got six redcoats and two people wi' him—a big man I've no' seen afore and . . . a young lassie!"

"A lassie?"

Men scurried to have a look, jostled to see, murmuring their appreciation.

"Och, she's a bonnie thing."

Annie joined them, hazarding a curious glance round the corner, her spirits lifting at the thought of another woman's company.

And she saw.

She took a panicked step backwards, bumping into Killy. The blood rushed from her head, and her mouth went dry, her heart knocking against lungs bereft of breath. Even from a distance, she recognized them—his long stride, his broad shoulders, her pale blond hair and willowy form.

Uncle Bain. And Betsy!

Dear God, poor Betsy!

"N-nay!"

"Who are they, mistress?" Killy stood before her, pistol in hand.

"H-he is Bain Campbell, Marquis of Bute—my uncle." Her voice was a whisper, her tongue barely able to speak his name. "And she is . . . was my lady's maid."

"We'll no' let him hurt you." Brendan put himself between her and the approaching party, knife in one hand, pistol in the other. "Form up, lads. Annie, get inside!"

The men leapt to their feet, rifles at the ready, knives and tomahawks in hand.

But Annie knew she could not hide behind the Rangers—not this time. Uncle Bain would not hesitate to kill should they confront him, nor would the Rangers let him take her against her will. Men would die. And if her uncle were among them, these brave men would pay with their lives.

She had no choice but to face Uncle Bain without them.

With trembling hands, she clutched the tiny bedgown to her stomach, felt the warm weight of Iain's gold band on her finger. She was no longer the vulnerable and innocent lass her uncle had branded and sent away. She'd known the love of a good man. She'd seen the horrors of war. She'd even killed.

She would not let him hurt her—not again.

Nor would she let him harm any of the Rangers or sweet Betsy.

Her mind raced, seeking a way out. "Killy, Brendan, please dinnae fight him! If you do, you will surely be put to death, and I cannae bear to see any more Rangers perish for my sake! I must go to him."

Brendan shook his head. "I dinnae like this. Mack asked us to watch over you, and that's what we should be doin'!"

"She's right, Brendan. Kill that bastard, and you'll either be hanged outright or spend the rest of your life hidin'. Have you got a plan, mistress?"

"I'll go speak wi' him. Let him think you mean to defend me. But dinnae fight him."

"Why is he here?"

"I dinnae ken, Killy. I suspect he means to take me back to Scotland or . . ."

Or kill me so that he can bury the truth about my mother wi' me.

"You cannae mean to go wi' him!"

"Nay, Brendan. But someone must get word to Iain. If he doesna come quickly . . ."

Uncle Bain could not simply murder her beneath Lord William's roof. Nor could he take her from the fort against her will. She was a married woman and carried her husband's child.

But your marriage was Catholic. He willna honor it.

Nay, he would not honor it. But there was something he couldn't brush aside. She was indentured. Not only did the bairn inside her belong to Iain, but by law, so did she. Uncle Bain would have to buy her from him, and Iain would not sell her—if he yet lived.

And what if Uncle Bain challenged Iain to fight?

The question struck her like a blow, stirring the fear in her belly. Uncle Bain was known for his prowess with the claymore. But she could not think of that now. She must keep her wits about her.

"We'll see to it, mistress." Killy pressed the smooth handle of a small knife into her hand. "You take this. We'll be keepin' a watch on you as much as we're able."

The escort drew near.

She tucked the blade into her skirts. "I must go to him."

"God be wi' you, lass!"

Annie lifted her chin and willed herself to walk on legs gone coggly with fear toward the man who had tried to destroy her life. But with each step, her fear lessened, turning to fury. By the time she stood before him, it was not fright that made her tremble.

"Annie." Uncle Bain's gaze traveled over her, distaste flickering through his eyes at the sight of her clothes and the almost finished bedgown in her hand. "Och, lass, you cannae be breedin' by that—"

"You *mac an uilc!*" She took a step back. "Why have you come? Have you no' done enough to hurt me?"

Before she could react, he pulled her into his embrace, his arms steel, his voice menacing. "Do aught to shame me, Annie, and your wee maid will pay the price, just as she did the night you tried to flee."

Annie heard the heavy clicks of a dozen rifles being cocked. "Do aught to harm me or Betsy, and the men behind me will kill you."

He stiffened, gave a snort. "They wouldna dare!"

"They are my husband's men and have sworn to live or die at his command, no' Lord William's. They care neither for Britain nor for nobility. They know what you did and hold their fire now only because I asked it of them."

Slowly he released her and stepped back, his gaze fixed on the Rangers behind her. "I'll have them flogged."

"You are no' in command on this island. My husband is. And if he returns from Ticonderoga to find you here, you'll ne'er see Scotland again."

Uncle Bain looked down at her and laughed, his eyes those of a stranger. "By the time MacKinnon returns, you'll be gone."

Iain heard the drums beating retreat, caught sight of a French soldier aiming a musket over the breastworks, and fired. The soldier jerked and fell out of sight, his shot unfired, his cry lost amid the moans of the dying. Iain reloaded and aimed again as the redcoats pulled back into the cover of the forest, but the attack was over.

He closed his eyes and sank back against the tree trunk, his throat parched, his mouth bitter with the taste of gunpowder, his nostrils full of the stench of blood. His left shoulder ached where a ball had pierced it. His cheek still trickled blood, cut by woody shards from a tree blown apart by French cannon. A shell fragment from a cannonball had cut a groove across his thigh. Still, his wounds were small—though they might not have been had Morgan not jerked him out of the way of a falling branch. It had been large enough to crush a man.

All around him were the cries and moans of the injured and dying. Regulars lay by the hundreds before the abatis like broken toy soldiers, their bodies mangled, the grass beneath them stained with blood. Six times Abercrombie had ordered them to attack, and six times the redcoat officers had dutifully led their men across the field toward death, valiant victims of their own loyalty and their commander's arrogance. Beyond the mangled bodies stood the French breastworks, defiant and intact.

Never had Iain seen anything like it—such senseless death. He and his men had done their best to pick off the French soldiers, killing them by the scores. But there were not enough Rangers to cover the entire length of the breastworks, and without artillery there was no way to deprive the French of their cover. And although the Rangers were not out in the open, they'd paid a high price as well. When the French had realized where the deadly gunfire was coming from, they'd turned their artillery toward the trees and tried to pound the Rangers into the ground.

Iain supposed he and Joseph had lost nearly thirty men between them, with just as many badly injured. They'd had only enough time between attacks to see to their dead and wounded before Abercrombie had ordered the fray to begin anew.

"I didna ken one man could be both so stupid and so stubborn!" Morgan sat down beside Iain, his face black with gunpowder and beaded with sweat, his eyes dark with the weariness of battle. "He doesna change the plan of attack but sends more men out to die! The bastard is no' fit to command! Let me see your shoulder."

"Quit hoverin' over me. Aye, I ken that's what the three of

you are doin'." Iain pushed his hand away. "See to Cam. He took a ball to the chest."

"There's naugh' to see to." Morgan handed Iain a water-skin, then began to dress his shoulder. "He died sometime during the last attack, may God rest his soul. Charlie Gordon lost his head to a cannonball."

Morgan's words struck Iain like a fist. He crossed himself, sadness and rage twined in his gut.

Cam had been a brave man—among the best. He'd been with Iain since the beginning. Charlie had been but eighteen.

Iain felt sick—sick of death, sick of killing, sick of war. "Have you seen Connor?"

"He went after more powder, balls and flints."

Iain drank, then tossed the skin to Dougie, who sat in stunned silence behind a nearby tree. Cam had been Dougie's best friend.

Iain stood, slung his rifle over his back. "Let's get our wounded out of here."

Aware that the French marksman were still watching, they kept low, tending those whose injuries, like Iain's, were light, and sending those who needed care on to the surgeons' tents. Not twenty minutes had gone by when Iain heard the drums beat again—but this time they were ordering the army to withdraw.

Iain heard his men cheer, heard the relieved shouts of Regulars whose lives had been reprieved. But he heard something else as well—the calls of French officers organizing their men into columns. Montcalm was going to return the favor of their visit with a counterattack.

Connor dashed up to him, face blackened with war paint and gunpowder, hair slick with sweat. "Abercrombie sends word we're to cover the retreat."

Morgan spat on the ground. "He stirs up the hornet's nest and then runs, leavin' us to deal wi' the sting!"

" 'Tis the first wise thing he's done all day." Then Iain called to his men, "Form up, laddies. Montcalm is sendin' his men to bid us farewell."

He thought of the miles of forest that lay between them and their whaleboats. He thought of the redcoats, limping their way over unfamiliar territory. He saw the fatigue on his men's blackened faces, not a man among them unscathed.

Then he loaded his rifle.

Chapter Thirty-one

It was for Betsy's sake that Annie went with Uncle Bain and Lord William into the fort. Though she'd planned to remain in the cabin, she'd refused to leave Betsy alone with Uncle Bain. She'd rushed forward to embrace Betsy and had seen the haunted look in her maid's eyes. In that instant she'd known that whatever Betsy had survived these past months was far more terrifying than what she herself had endured.

Uncle Bain had tried to separate them, to have Betsy billeted in his quarters, but Annie had stopped him. " 'Twould be most unseemly. Would you shame your host?" she'd said in her haughtiest voice. "Betsy shall stay with me and attend me as she used to do."

Lord William had placed them in a room beside his own quarters, which he'd yielded to her uncle in a gesture of hospitality. Annie didn't like being so close to Uncle Bain, but at least the door to their room had a lock—which she'd used as soon as Betsy's trunk had been delivered. Then she'd gone to the window and thrown it open, leaning out so that Iain's men would see her and know where she was. She'd spotted two Stockbridge standing nearby. One of them nodded in acknowledgment, and some of the fear in her belly had eased.

She was not a prisoner.

Then she'd turned to Betsy. The two of them had held one another and wept.

"I'd despaired of e'er seein' you again, my lady. He told us you'd been waylaid and killed, but I kent in my heart he'd found you. I feared the worst. 'Tis my fault! I told him where you'd gone. I am so sorry!"

" 'Tis I who am sorry! I should never have left you wi' him. He told me he'd beaten you and—"

Betsy squeezed her eyes shut. "Please dinnae speak of it! It lies behind us now. But you must tell me how you came to be here in the wilderness."

And so Annie did, starting from the terrible moment Uncle Bain had found her to the day Iain had departed for Ticonderoga. She told Betsy of the brand her uncle had given her, of the long journey over the sea, of the humiliation of being sold and stripped of her clothing. She told of the Abenaki attack and her flight through the forest and awakening in Iain's bearskin coat. She told how Iain had gotten her safely back to the fort and taken a hundred lashes for disobeying orders to save her. She told how she'd fallen in love with him and had married him in the forest and now carried his child. She told how she feared for Iain and his men and longed to see them all safely home again.

"Is he a bonnie man?" Betsy asked, a shy smile on her lips.

"Aye, he is bonnie. And braw. And he willna let Lord Bute harm us."

If he yet lives.

Then Betsy stood, crossed the room to her trunk, and opened it. From within she retrieved a silver-handled brush, a delicate porcelain doll in a pink silk gown and something small wrapped in parchment.

The silver-handled brush that had belonged to her grandmother. The porcelain doll her father had given her for Christmas so long ago. Rose soap.

Annie held the soap to her nose, felt a hot rush of tears at the treasures that lay in her lap. "Oh, Betsy, you are far too kind!"

"I thought if you truly were alive, you might be missin' a bit of home."

Then Annie said what she'd wanted to say for months. "If

ever I caused you unhappiness as your mistress, I ask you to forgi'e me. I didna understand what it means to wait hand and foot upon others until—"

But Betsy pressed her fingers to Annie's lips, tears filling her blue eyes afresh. "You were ne'er a burden, my lady."

Annie felt a weight she hadn't realized she was carrying lift from her shoulders.

William sat in the dark of his study and sipped his cognac, chess of no interest to him, Campbell's heavy snores sounded from the floor above him. He'd insisted Campbell take his room and that Lady Anne and her maid be billeted in the guest quarters beside it. Not that he'd wanted to give up his feather bed in favor of a stiff pallet in his drawing room, but it had been the only way to keep an eye on Lady Anne's safety. Campbell had agreed with obvious reluctance, no doubt hoping to avoid the suspicion he would have aroused if he'd insisted on staying in the more austere barracks.

William knew Campbell was trying to keep him away from Lady Anne. He never left her alone with him, not even for a moment. Whatever the truth was about his niece's plight, Campbell didn't want William to hear it. And that made William wish to hear it all the more.

But no one would tell him anything. When he was nearby, Lady Anne lapsed into silence, and Lord Bute brooded or prattled on about unimportant matters. William's lone attempt to question the maid in private had so terrified her that for pity's sake William had ceased his interrogation and left her in peace—but not before he'd seen the dark bruises round her neck.

There was only one thing he knew for certain: Annie feared and hated her uncle and did not wish to return with him to Scotland. He'd seen the shock and horror on her face when she'd first spied Campbell. He'd watched as she'd walked to meet them, head held high despite her fear, and he'd admired her courage.

William did not wish to see her leave for Scotland, either, yet why he should even consider interfering was beyond him. If Lady Anne stayed, it would not be to warm his bed but Major MacKinnon's. William had little to gain and much at stake should he anger Campbell. While William was of royal blood and had his grandfather's ear, Campbell was a peer and sat in Lords. His political influence and the fact that he was a Scot made him a valuable ally for His Majesty. Earning Campbell's wrath might set William at odds with his grandfather, putting at risk any hopes he had of earning a real title and lands of his own.

If only he had a clear and legal reason to intervene . . .

Campbell had wanted him to intercede, but in an altogether different fashion.

"Is there no way you can order this MacKinnon to the front of the battle and see to it he dies?" he'd asked.

Never having been asked to commit outright murder, William had been taken aback, though he'd done his best not to shout it. "Major MacKinnon is most often in the forefront of the battle and has survived three years of the worst fighting. However, if you think it would help, I should be glad to offer Lady Anne my counsel."

Campbell had laughed, a nervous sound. "That willna be necessary. She'll no' have her way in this, but will be guided by me. We'll leave in the mornin'."

William wasn't so certain. He sipped the last of his cognac and stretched his legs out before him. Then he heard the soft click of the knob turning, knew his man had arrived.

"My lord."

"Is it as I suspected?"

"Aye, my lord. Two Rangers left shortly after the lady was brought here. They headed north."

"To fetch Major MacKinnon."

"I believe so, sir."

"Excellent." William stood, walked to the chest where he kept his coin, and retrieved a small purse of sovereigns. "I have another assignment for you—two. First, find whoever is in command of the remaining Stockbridge and bring him to me."

"Aye, my lord."

"Second, I need you to spy on a household, to hear all that is said within its walls without being seen and to report back to me all that you hear."

"I am your humble servant, my lord. Whose household?"

William turned and tossed the purse to him. "Mine."

Annie awoke to the startling and wonderful news that Abenaki warriors had been sighted in the forest around the fort, wearing war paint and shouting their battle cries. They had yet to do more than fire a few harmless arrows at the walls, but their presence was enough for Lord William to insist that her uncle not leave for Albany for another day or two.

"They will slaughter and scalp any British subject who crosses their path," Lord William explained as they finished their breakfasts. "To set out while they command the forest would be an act of suicide."

Uncle Bain was not pleased. "Why do you no' send your troops out and drive them away? 'Tis a strange way to win a war."

"They're hoping to lure us outside the walls into an ambuscade. Though we see but a dozen among the trees, there are likely hundreds more waiting to attack from hiding. With most of my troops at Ticonderoga, I cannot risk an attack. If we amuse ourselves by not responding, as we did just six weeks past, they'll eventually lose interest and go back to their villages. Isn't that right, Lady Anne?"

She met Lord William's gaze, found him looking at her with a strange intensity. "Aye."

Six weeks past it had been Rangers pretending to be Abenaki in order to keep Lord William occupied and away from her. But Lord William knew that, or at least suspected it—she could see it in his eyes. Was he perhaps trying to tell her the same ruse was being used now? Could he be trying to help her?

She stared into his gray eyes, then looked quickly away, not wanting to arouse her uncle's suspicions. But inside her belly, hope blossomed.

After breakfast she settled herself in the drawing room with her sewing, hoping to get a chance to speak with Lord William privately. Surely Uncle Bain would need to use the privy sometime. But her uncle seemed to recognize her aim and did not leave the room, making idle chatter with Lord William until Annie thought she would go mad.

Then a soldier rushed through the door and drew Lord William away on a matter of some urgency, and Annie found herself alone not with Lord William but with Uncle Bain. She rose, walked toward the door, certain no good could come of this, but he blocked her path.

" 'Tis past time you and I spoke, Annie." He cupped her shoulders in his big hands.

She shrugged off his touch, pushed past him. "I've naught to say to you. You're a murderer and a betrayer of kin!"

His voice followed her. "Your mother came to my bed of her own accord."

Annie whirled about, her heart hot with rage. "You lie!"

He stood looking out the window, and Annie knew he was watching for Lord William's return. "I speak the truth. I reminded her of your da', just as I reminded you of him. She was a woman at the height of her beauty and very lonely."

"She warned me about you! She told me no' to trust you!"

But he wasn't listening. "At first she enjoyed our little games. Aye, she enjoyed a bit of pain, your mother did."

"*Uist!* I willna hear you speak of her thus!"

"But then I wanted more."

"You killed her just like you killed the others! I heard her weepin'. I saw you! Your hands were round her throat!"

He spun about to face her. "You didna see what you think you saw! I tell you this, little Annie. Your mother came ere she died!"

"Nay!" Annie screamed the word, tears sliding down her

cheeks, her sewing clutched to her breast. "You are vile beyond imagining!"

But he had turned back toward the window. "Aye, perhaps so. But the needs and desires of great men are different from those of other men. I need to feel my lovers' lives in my hands, to feel the power I have over them, in order to spend. You wouldna understand."

She took a step back from him, cold chills running down her spine. Listening to him was like getting a glimpse through the doorway to hell. "You think you're a great man—you, who find pleasure in the pain of others? You branded me, burnt me with iron, and you enjoyed it! That is no' the action of a great man, but a demon or a madman!"

He didn't seem to hear her. "Most of the time, they recover and start to breathe again. But sometimes . . ."

"You're depraved!"

"I thought by sendin' you over the water, I could silence you, yet keep you alive—my own dear brother's child. But then I got the letter from Lord William." He laughed. "Quite the coincidence that you should find your way to him. And then I knew I had to have you wi' me."

He turned to face her, his gaze hard. "You'll come wi' me to Scotland, Annie, and that's the end of it!"

"Why can you no' leave me in peace? I've no' told Lord William a thing! I love Iain, and I willna be separated from him!"

"You'll forsake that traitor MacKinnon and come wi' me to Scotland, or you'll be buried with that bastard you're carryin' still inside your womb!"

She pressed a hand to her belly, instinctively shielding her baby. "Iain will kill you for this!"

Then she turned and fled.

Iain crossed himself, closed Lemuel's eyes, pulled the woolen blanket over the young man's ashen face. Twenty-six Rangers, eighteen Stockbridge and more than thirteen hundred redcoats and provincials dead—for nothing. Fort Ticonderoga stood exactly as it had before the British army had arrived. Iain doubted French losses topped five hundred.

It would be one thing had the French defeated them in a cleverly planned ambuscade or slain them by virtue of overwhelming numbers. But Abercrombie had known the abatis was there. He'd been warned about the need for artillery, and yet he'd sent his men against the barrer time and again, forcing his troops to founder through branches and tree trunks while the French cut them down at their leisure.

The *neach diolain* deserved to be shot.

At least the retreat had not been as bitter as he'd feared; Montcalm was too clever a strategist to allow himself to be drawn far from the protection of the fort. Abercrombie's stupidity had saved the day for the French, and Montcalm had seemed not to wish to tempt fate.

Iain stood and made his way out of the hospital tent at Sabbath Day Point toward the place where his men were encamped for the night. His left shoulder ached fiercely where the surgeon had cut it to remove the musket ball. His body longed for sleep, his mind for the forgetfulness of dreams. But before he could seek his own comfort, he needed to see to his men.

He strode among them, checking their injuries, praising their courage, offering what assurances he could.

"Mack." Dougie's eyes were filled with grief for Cam.

Iain clapped his right hand on Dougie's shoulder, gave him a squeeze, sharing his sorrow. "He fought well. Sweet Jesus, I shall miss him."

Dougie nodded, tears on his stubbly cheeks. "He was a brave man and a good friend."

Moving on, Iain asked, "How's that eye, McHugh?"

"I can still see wi' it."

"Och, well, then. You get first watch."

After making certain his men were settled, he sought out his brothers and set up his pallet beside theirs—pine boughs with a woolen blanket for warmth. He sat, accepted the flask Morgan shoved under his nose and took a deep drink of rum. Then he passed the flask on to Connor, who had an impressive black eye and a row of stitches on his cheek.

"You look bonnie."

"And you." Connor grinned, raised the flask and drank.

" 'Tis clear out of the three of us whose face God favors most." Morgan took the flask back, his smile flashing white in the gloaming. "Not a scratch."

Connor gave a snort. "I think the Almighty confused your face for your arse and wanted you to be able to sit."

Iain lay back on his pallet, stared up at the stars and thanked God that his brothers had made it through the battle alive and whole. So many had not. Then he pulled the medicine pouch from his shirt and kissed it. Tomorrow would take him home to Annie.

Trying to ignore the throbbing pain in his shoulder, he closed his eyes.

'Twas the middle of the night when Joseph awoke him. "You have guests."

Killy and Brendan.

Iain sat bolt upright, a knot of fear in his gut. "Annie."

Killy nodded, his old face lined with fatigue. "Her uncle has come for her. He arrived yesterday. We came as fast as we could."

Iain was packing his gear before Killy finished speaking, anger burning away his pain and weariness, his blood pumping hard in his chest. "Did he say why he'd come?"

The men shook their heads.

"What the bloody hell?" Connor sat up, blade in hand.

Beside him Morgan awoke.

"She fears he means to take her back to Scotland," Brendan answered. "She wouldna let us fight him, Mack. She asked us not to shoot, not even when he took her from the island. She said he'd make us pay and she didn't want to see more Rangers die for her sake."

So Bain Campbell had Annie. Wentworth must have written to him. The bastard!

"We set a watch on Wentworth's quarters—that's where he's got her stayin'—then we set off to fetch you."

"You've done well. Stay and get some rest." He slipped into his tumpline pack, adjusted the pistols in his waistband. Then he turned to his brothers. "Morgan, you're . . . What the bloody hell do you two think you're doin'?"

"We're comin' wi' you." Morgan stuffed his gear into his pack and stood, powder horn slung over his forearm.

Connor slipped into his pack, adjusted its weight. "Do you think we'd let you face this whoreson of a Campbell alone?"

He looked into his brothers' eyes. "Abercrombie will call this desertion. If we're caught, we'll be shot. I cannae ask this of you."

Then Morgan stepped forward. "If I'd been in command on that snowy March morn, I'd have done my duty. To my everlasting shame, I'd have left the lass to be raped and murdered. But you took the risk and paid the price, and now you've got a bonnie, sweet wife and a bairn on the way. I'll no' let you lose that. Nor will I suffer any man to harm Annie again."

Connor nodded. "I swore to watch over her for you. How do you ken you'll come back through the forest alive? If aught should befall you, someone will still need to go after Annie."

It made sense, but they were taking a terrible risk.

Joseph leaned his head in between them. "If you women are done blathering, my men and I have canoes waiting."

Iain turned to Killy and Brendan. "My thanks, men, for your aid. Killy, tell McHugh he's in command now. If Nanny Crombie sends for us, tell him we've gone berry pickin'."

Then Iain followed Joseph off toward Lake George, with Morgan and Connor behind him.

Annie looked up from her sewing, saw Uncle Bain's head lolling, his eyes closed. Lord William sat at his desk, reading through seemingly endless piles of correspondence. If only Uncle Bain would begin to snore. Then Annie would know it was safe to speak.

Shaken by her encounter with her uncle, horrified by what he'd said, she'd spent most of the afternoon locked in the bedroom with Betsy. Only when Lord William had returned again had she ventured forth, desperate to speak with him in private. But Uncle Bain hadn't left her side once.

She was about to give up and seek her bed, when a knock came at the door and a courier entered, bearing dispatches from Ticonderoga. One look at his face and Annie knew the battle had not gone well.

Lord William took the letters and read through them one at a time, his face impassive. "Thank you, Lieutenant. Any idea when I can expect the army's arrival?"

"The general expects to reach William Henry by tomorrow. With so many wounded, the journey overland is likely to take another full day, Colonel."

"Very well. Dismissed."

The courier saluted and was gone.

Barely able to breathe, Annie stood, waited.

Lord William arose and walked to his window, his fists clenched behind his back. But when he spoke his voice was utterly devoid of emotion. "His Majesty's companies have suffered a resounding defeat. Losses are high. Nearly all of the officers are either injured or slain. The general attacked without artillery. Our columns never breached Montcalm's breastworks."

Annie's knees turned to water, and she sank back into her chair. "Wh-what of the Rangers, my lord?"

He turned to face her, picked up one of the dispatches, glanced at it. "The reports say the Rangers also sustained heavy losses, though it seems Major MacKinnon survived the battle. He and his remaining men covered the retreat. No word after that."

She released the breath she'd been holding, her heart holding to one fact.

Iain had survived the battle.

"I am deeply grieved for our losses, my lord. Good night—and thank you, my lord."

She was halfway up the stairs when she heard her uncle speak.

"Prepare an escort. I leave with my niece in the morning."

Chapter Thirty-two

Annie held tight to Betsy, who trembled with fear.

"He'll kill us, he will!"

"He's no' goin' to hurt anyone—no' again." Annie wished she were sure of that. She felt the press of the knife against her hip, resolved to use it if her uncle tried to harm them.

Out in the hallway, Uncle Bain shouted once more for her to unlock the door. "If you dinnae open it now, lass, I'll take it out on your backside wi' my belt!"

"You may speak wi' my husband when he arrives! Until then I'll no' leave this room!"

It happened all at once. A crash as the door flew open. Betsy's terrified scream. Uncle Bain's fist in her hair, yanking her painfully to her feet.

"Get downstairs! The carriage is waitin'!"

Then Lord William was there. "Control your temper, Campbell. Do as you like later, but do not strike her under my roof. Might I escort you, my lady?"

"Mind your own affairs, Wentworth." Uncle Bain released her with an angry grunt.

Fighting tears of desperation and rage, Annie accepted Lord William's arm. "Come, Betsy. Iain will find us along the way."

Clinging to that hope, she let Lord William lead her down the stairs and outside to the waiting carriage. "The Stockbridge will escort you as far as Albany," he told her, as if he was sending her on a pleasant outing with a chaperone.

"My husband willna like it that you've allowed me to be taken from your own home against my will. I belong to him, as does the bairn I'm carryin'."

"Lady Anne, your marriage was outside the established church and is therefore invalid. According to British law, you have no husband, and your child has no father."

"Then British law is unjust!" Her voice quavered with rage and unshed tears.

"Perhaps." Lord William helped her into the carriage. "As for the matter of your indenture, your uncle left a goodly sum to compensate Major MacKinnon for his purchase of you."

She sat, adjusting her skirts, tears spilling down her cheeks. "How can anyone buy that which is not for sale? 'Tis theft!"

Lord William closed the carriage door. "I suspect the courts would honor the sale if the major chooses to contest it, as it places you in the care of your noble uncle."

"There is naught that is noble about him." She spoke the words not caring if Uncle Bain heard her.

Lord William took her left hand, lifted it to his lips in farewell. "I wish we had become reacquainted under different circumstances, my lady. You are a most remarkable woman."

Then, in one swift move, he slid Iain's golden wedding band from her finger.

Annie cried out in dismay, reached for it, the loss of it like a blade to her heart. "Nay, you cannae—!"

"That bit of gold belongs to MacKinnon. Lord William will see that he receives it." Her uncle chuckled as he settled in across from her, Betsy pale and shaking beside him.

"You bastard! You would take from me something so precious?" She spat the words at Lord William, her cry becoming a sob as she realized she was truly being taken from the fort.

Uncle Bain's gaze met hers, and in his eyes, blue eyes so

like her father's she saw her own death—and Betsy's. "Where you're goin', you'll have no need for gold rings."

A chill crept up Annie's spine, and she reassured herself with the pressure of the knife against her hip.

Iain will come for you, Annie. You know he will.

She looked at Lord William, wondering if he'd heard her uncle's threat.

Lord William glanced furtively toward her uncle, then his lips moved.

As the carriage lurched forward, Annie could have sworn he'd said, "Be ready for anything."

Iain and his brothers arrived with Joseph at Fort Elizabeth just before noon and made straight for Wentworth's quarters. They shoved the guards aside and interrupted Wentworth in the midst of a conversation with one of his aides.

Wentworth dismissed the young officer at once. "What took you so long, Major?"

Iain reached down, grabbed Wentworth by the lace at his throat and yanked him to his feet. "Where's my wife?"

Wentworth met his gaze, his gray eyes cool. "She left with her uncle two hours ago."

"If aught should happen to her—"

"Let me guess. You'll kill me. Now that you've made that clear, why don't the four of you do what you can to refresh yourselves? I've got horses waiting for us. Captain Joseph's men agreed to dawdle on the trail and to watch over Lady Anne. We ought to be able to catch them long before they near Albany."

Astonished, Iain released him. "What are you sayin'?"

"I'm telling you there's still time to save Lady Anne."

They set out almost immediately, Iain taking time only to spread salve on his aching shoulder and to array himself for a different sort of battle. While he dressed, Joseph and his brothers sang the war songs, Joseph fanning smoke against him with an eagle feather, his brothers sharpening his claymore and dagger. Iain closed his mind to fear, to any imaginings of Annie's despair, to any emotion that might weaken him.

Be strong, a leannan. *I've no' forsaken you.*

The Regulars at the fort stared at him, most with wide, frightened eyes.

Wentworth merely nodded. "I see we are ready."

Soon Iain was sitting astride one of the cavalry horses, riding down the road for Albany, his brothers, Joseph and Wentworth beside him, his claymore hanging heavy against his back. He asked the question he'd wanted to ask since they'd left the fort. "Why do you aid us? Is Campbell no' one of your kind? Was it no' you who brought him down upon us?"

"Bain Campbell is a depraved murderer, as I'm sure you're aware." Wentworth's voice dripped with disgust. "I'd never have contacted him had I known the truth of the matter."

"And how did you learn the truth?"

"I have my means."

Iain had no doubt that was true.

"You must remember that you are injured and fatigued from battle and from your forced night march, while Campbell is well rested," Wentworth warned him. "He is a formidable opponent with the broadsword and played a significant role in helping His Grace, the Duke of Cumberland, devise a method to counter the Highlanders' charge at Culloden."

Iain knew well the story of that battle. He knew how each British soldier had been drilled to attack not the warrior before him, but the unprotected left side of the next man down. Campbell deserved to die for that reason alone. Yet, although many a Highlander had been cut down that way, it had been musket balls that had won the day for Cumberland; a claymore was no match for a weapon fired at a distance.

"Don't tell me you fear for my safety."

"I am risking much, Major."

"Aye, that's true." Iain turned to his brothers. "Lads, keep a watch on the wee princeling so that he doesna scratch himself on a branch or lose a button."

"I cannot afford for you to be killed." Wentworth sounded vexed.

"Och, well, I wouldna want to die and leave you with a bunch of thorny questions to answer." Iain hadn't been able to keep himself from laughing, his brothers and Joseph with him. "Dinnae fret, Your Gracefulness. Bain Campbell will not survive this day."

Annie bit back a moan, the jostling of the carriage and the stifling heat making her unsettled stomach worse. How she was going to make it all the way to Albany without being sick, she did not know. She held Betsy's hand tighter, breathed slowly, tried to still her queasiness. Then again, her sick belly was the least of her worries. If Uncle Bain had his way, she'd never reach Scotland alive. But he wouldn't kill here. It was too close to Lord William, too close to Iain and the fort. He would wait until he was alone with her.

Be ready for anything.

As soon as they'd gotten outside of the fort, Annie had re- alized something was afoot. 'Twas a small group of Joseph's men that had been sent as their escort, not British Regulars. She'd been too upset to think on it before.

"They know I'm Iain's wife," she'd whispered to Betsy when Uncle Bain had stopped the carriage to relieve him- self. "They are as kin to him. See how a warrior walks close to each door where he can see us? They willna let my uncle harm us. You must be prepared."

Annie knew the Stockbridge were looking for ways to slow the journey. If the false ambush hadn't told her that, the two fallen trees that blocked the road certainly had. But still the carriage moved forward, wheels creaking, as leagues of lush green forest passed by her. Albany was growing ever nearer.

What if Iain was killed in the retreat? What if he was in- jured and cannae come for you?

The questions struck at her like blows. A wave of nausea rolled through her, and this time she couldn't help moaning.

" 'Tis no more than you deserve, spreadin' your thighs for

a Catholic, a mere soldier. How ashamed your father would be." Her uncle looked at her with revulsion. "Tell me—what did MacKinnon say when he saw your bonnie brand?"

Annie opened her eyes, met his gaze, smiled. "He swore one day to kill you."

Uncle Bain laughed, but not before Annie saw the fear in his eyes.

And then she heard it—the birdcall that wasn't a bird.

The carriage rolled slowly to a stop.

"What in God's name is it now? I wish Wentworth had sent us off wi' disciplined British Regulars instead of these—"

The doors of the carriage were jerked open. She felt strong arms seize her about the waist, heard Betsy scream and thought she saw someone press the point of a bayonet against Uncle Bain's throat.

Then she found herself looking into Morgan's face as he pulled her from the carriage and led her to a safe distance. "I've got you, lass."

"Oh, Morgan!" Annie wrapped her arms about him, relief to know she was safe adding to her joy at seeing him alive and unhurt.

She looked about her, seeking Iain. Beside her stood Betsy, her hands over her mouth, her eyes wide. Over by the carriage, Connor, his eye blackened and stitches upon his cheek, took the reins from the unconscious wagoner. Rifles at the ready, the Stockbridge stood among the trees, surrounding the carriage and blocking the road.

"Where is—?"

Morgan gestured with a nod of his head.

She looked, and the sight of Iain drove the breath from her lungs.

He stood in the middle of the road twenty paces before the carriage. Like a Highlander of old, he wore the MacKinnon plaid, his right shoulder bare, his claymore clasped powerfully in his right hand. The long hair at his temples was done in thick warrior's braids, the rest hanging dark down his back. But the top half of his face was painted not in Gaelic blue but with Indian vermillion, and Indian markings decorated his arms instead of armbands.

"Bain Campbell! Stand forth, and draw your blade!" Iain's challenge echoed through the forest.

And she knew. Iain meant to fight Uncle Bain to the death, not as a Ranger with his rifle, but as a Highland man, blade to blade.

Fear uncoiled like a serpent in her belly.

Few could best her uncle at swordcraft.

The Stockbridge moved away from the carriage, weapons still at the ready.

Looking outraged, Uncle Bain stepped down. He removed first his wig, then his jacket, and tossed them both in the carriage. Then he reached inside the carriage and drew his claymore from beneath his seat. Slowly, confidently, he walked around the carriage, his boots crunching against the dirt.

When he saw Iain, he laughed. "You think to judge me, MacKinnon? I've littered the ground wi' the corpses of men like you."

Iain raised his blade and smiled. "You've never met a man like me."

Unable to breathe, Annie watched as Uncle Bain sprang forward, driving at Iain with blows that could cleave bone. But Iain blocked his blows with seeming ease and came back at him hard, driving Uncle Bain almost back against the horses. Then the edge of his blade caught Uncle Bain's left arm.

Uncle Bain gasped as a ribbon of red welled up against the linen of his shirt.

Iain stepped back, his chest rising and falling heavily. "That's for every Highland laddie you betrayed at Culloden."

Uncle Bain made a sound like a growl, rage terrible upon his face. He raised his blade and rained deadly blows down upon Iain, trying to force him to his knees or knock his blade from his hands. But Iain parried and countered with strikes of his own, the clash of steel against steel ringing through the forest.

"Your strength is fading, MacKinnon. And your left arm— no' so strong, is it?"

Then Annie saw what she hadn't seen before. Iain seemed to be struggling to hold on to his sword with both hands, and beneath his plaid she thought she saw bandages. He was wounded.

Morgan held her tighter. "Easy, Annie."

"That only makes us even, old man. I've strength enough to finish you." With no warning, he leapt forward, drove Uncle Bain's sword aside and thrust the tip of his blade into Uncle Bain's left thigh. "That's for Lady Mara Burness Campbell."

And so her mother was avenged.

Tears stung Annie's eyes.

Uncle Bain cried out, staggered back and dropped to one knee, blood soaking the front of his breeches. But when he came up again, there was a small pistol in his hand.

Annie's heart lurched.

She screamed. "Iain!"

The pistol fired.

Iain dropped to his knees, a look of astonishment on his face, blood blossoming against the right side of his ribs. He touched his fingers to his own blood, his brow furrowed in obvious pain. "It willna end wi' me, Campbell. Slay me, and you'll face my brothers and after them, my Muhheconneok kin. You cannae possibly kill us all."

"Nay, but I can kill you and know that I leave my niece in misery."

Tears streaming unnoticed down her cheeks, Annie watched in horror as Uncle Bain raised his blade and moved in for the deathblow.

Morgan forced her gaze from the battle, pressed her face against his chest, and held her fast. "Dinnae watch, lass."

She fisted her hands in the cloth of Morgan's shirt, her body trembling, Iain's name a whisper on her lips.

Then she heard it—the grunt of impact as flesh yielded to steel, the rattling of lungs as breath fled the body, a long animal groan. And silence.

"And that's for my Annie!"

'Twas Iain's voice.

Annie whirled about and saw Iain standing over Uncle Bain's lifeless body, blood staining his side, his face lined with weariness and pain, his bloodied sword thrust into the ground. The air around her erupted into victory whoops, Morgan and Connor joining Joseph and his men in their strange cries.

"Iain!" She ran to him, relief that he was still alive mingled with fear that he might be mortally wounded. She wrapped her arms around him, careful not to hurt him.

"You shouldna see this. 'Tis no' fittin' for a lady." He kissed her hair, pulled her close with his weakened left arm and led her with unsteady steps away from her uncle's cleaved body. "Did he hurt you, *a leannan?*"

"Nay, thanks to you and to Joseph's men—"

Then, before her, Lord William rode out of the trees.

So he *had* been aiding her.

"—and Lord William."

Then Iain moaned and leaned more heavily against her. "I dinnae think I can stay upon my feet much longer, lass. Help me to the carriage."

In the next instant, Connor was beside her, taking Iain's weight, helping her to settle him in the carriage. "Let's get him to the surgeon."

As the carriage turned back toward the fort, Annie pressed a cloth to his side to stanch his bleeding, stroked his hair and prayed.

God, dinnae let me lose him now!

Iain drifted back and forth between pain and oblivion. He knew when they reached the fort and took him from the carriage. He knew when they gave him laudanum and put a leather strap between his teeth for him to bite. He knew when they pulled the ball from his side in a moment of shattering pain. And he felt Annie beside him, stroking his brow, whispering to him, holding his hand, her fingers small and warm.

He heard Dr. Blake's voice. "Lucky for him, the ball hit in a rib, shattering the rib but sparing his organs. If we can keep the wound from festering, he'll recover."

He heard Annie weeping, felt her head resting against his chest, and tried to reassure her.

But he was so tired, and before he could say more than her name, darkness claimed him.

Chapter Thirty-three

William stared out his window, watched for her, feeling strangely ill at ease in his own skin. Today he had looked on as one of his men—a Catholic with no reverence for the Crown—had slain a peer and a political ally. He'd seen a man of dubious birth fight with valor and honor, and a nobleman—a man of his own class—disgrace himself with cowardice. And he'd felt both relief and joy when the death-blow had been struck and the nobleman slain.

Not only had he watched the battle, but he'd worked hard to arrange it. Campbell would have had a two-day lead on MacKinnon had William not interfered—two days in which he might easily have abused or murdered Lady Anne. Nor would it have been so simple a thing to waylay the wagon had he not set the Stockbridge to escort it instead of British Regulars.

Aye, he'd played a significant role in Cambell's demise, and he'd been happy to do so.

And why?

He told himself Campbell was a depraved criminal who had eluded justice and would have continued to do so if someone hadn't acted. He told himself what he'd done was in the interests of society, of decency, of morality. But he was lying to himself. He didn't care about any of those things.

The real answer walked across the parade grounds, her lovely face lined with fatigue, her skirts stained with blood.

Lady Anne.

Before he'd met her, he'd never have interfered in the private life of a fellow nobleman, no matter how depraved the bastard was.

He heard her light footsteps on his porch, listened as the guards admitted her, turned to watch as she entered his study.

She curtsied. "You sent for me, my lord?"

William found himself uncharacteristically at a loss for words. "I understand Major MacKinnon is expected to recover."

She looked pale, and he wondered if it was due to the day's ordeal or her condition. "Aye, my lord."

He picked up a dispatch off his desk. "General Abercrombie has accused him and his brothers of desertion. I have already responded with my own missive, explaining that I recalled them for an important and clandestine mission. Also, I have informed the authorities of your uncle's tragic death at the hands of the enemy. If only he'd taken my advice and remained until the forest was secure."

Her eyes betrayed her every emotion—alarm, relief, gratitude. "Thank you, my lord."

Oddly affected by the thawing in her eyes, he began to ramble, turning his back to her. "The major and his men have quite a supporter in Lieutenant Cooke. It seems the Rangers saved his life and those of a great number of Regulars who had gotten lost in the forest on their way to the battle."

"I'm glad to know the lieutenant was spared, my lord."

"Is your maid settling in?" William couldn't remember the girl's name.

"Aye. Morgan and Connor are sharing a cabin to make room for her."

Then he turned to face her, irritated with himself for faltering. "Let me come to it. Now that your uncle is no longer a danger to you, you are free to return to Britain. I would be honored to aid you, offering you my protection and a gentle reintroduction to society, as well as whatever funds you might need. Until the war is over, you would have to stay in my home in Albany, of course, but once the war is ended, we would repair to London."

For a moment she looked utterly taken aback. "Are you offering me a place as your mistress, my lord?"

He tried to explain, the words spilling forth. "Had I known who you were, Lady Anne, I'd have insisted you stay in my home under my protection. Because I knew your uncle, you did not trust me—I understand now. Needing a man's protection, you chose to ally yourself with Major MacKinnon. But you no longer need to hide. You no longer need his protection. You are free to leave this illegitimate union and reclaim the honor of your station. Because you bring nothing of value to our joining, I cannot marry you, but I can offer you a life of ease, far from the frontier, where you need not toil or fear for your safety."

"And what of the bairn I carry?" She placed her hand protectively over her belly.

Feeling more confident, he continued. "Certainly, I do not relish the thought of raising another man's child, but I've left enough chicks in other men's nests to see it as a kind of just comeuppance. I would not stop you if you chose to relinquish the child, but I will not force you to do so."

She smiled. Then she laughed. "You have aided me today beyond all hope and expectation, my lord, and I am grateful. And although I know I should be honored by your offer, my answer is nay. I didna marry Iain simply because I needed a man's protection and he was at hand. I married him because I love him."

William felt a stab of bitterness to hear her speak such nonsense. "I do not understand what you as a noblewoman see in a man like him."

"Oh, but you do. You know how honorable he is, how strong and courageous. You knew he would come for me. You knew he would sacrifice all he had to save me. But just so there will be no misunderstandin', here is the difference between you and Iain MacKinnon: It didna matter to Iain whether I was a penniless crofter lass, or a Campbell and the daughter of an earl. He treated me wi' honor and respect, risking his life for me, even when I was a stranger."

William felt as if he'd been reprimanded and found himself staring at his feet.

Then she moved on, dropping his proposal as if he'd never offered it. "Now that I am here, my lord, I wonder if I might ask for three favors of you."

He swallowed, tried not to act as wounded as he felt. "If it is in my power to grant them, my lady, I should gladly do so."

"First, I should like my ring."

"Of course." William pulled it from his pocket and placed it in her palm.

"The second is more difficult. My uncle was in possession of my inheritance at the time of his death—the Burness jewels, as well as certain personal effects. I should like to retrieve them and place them in my husband's keepin'."

The word "husband" felt like a blow. "Certainly, my lady. I shall be glad to help you win back what is yours."

"Thank you, my lord." She smoothed her skirts and clasped her hands together, suddenly seeming nervous. But her gaze met and held his. "I should also very much appreciate it if you would release my husband and his brothers from His Majesty's service."

Anger stirred in William's gut. "That is out of the question."

"They have fought for three long years, my lord, longer than most volunteers. How many times have they killed for you? How many times have they nearly lost their lives?"

"The war is not over, and men with their skills are badly needed, as the defeat at Ticonderoga shows only too well."

"Is that why you entrapped them? Oh, aye, I know the truth. Like my uncle, you exact a punishment where no crime has been committed." Her voice quavered, and he could tell she was furious.

But so was he. "If they had joined of their own volition, they would be free to go. But their refusal to offer the Crown due reverence, together with Britain's extreme need, justifies my pressing them into service!"

She glared at him, then reached down and picked up a white pawn from his chess board. "You envy my husband, and no' only because I willingly lie beneath him at night. You envy him because he is a true leader of men. Unlike you, he knows that men are no' just pawns to be trifled with, pieces to be shifted according to whim. His men fight for him because they love him. Your soldiers fight because they must."

She placed the pawn back on the board. "I beg of you, my lord, release them!"

Cut by her words, he fought to speak. "I cannot."

"You mean you *will* not!" She took the chess board and flung it from its stand, scattering the carved marble pieces about the room. "There is more honor in each drop of my husband's precious blood than you possess in your soul!"

And then she was gone.

William stood for a moment, his thoughts as scattered as his chess pieces. He reached down with a trembling hand, picked up the black king, saw that it had cracked. Then, broken king still in hand, he watched through the window as Lady Anne hurried back to the man she claimed to love. He felt not enraged but strangely empty.

Iain opened his eyes, saw the log wall of his own cabin. His mouth was heavy with the taste of laudanum, but his mind was clear. His left shoulder ached, and his right side hurt fiercely with each breath, a sure sign the effects of the poppy had worn off. He shifted, seeking comfort, and felt a warm weight beside him.

Annie.

Still clothed, she slept deeply, her breathing soft and

even, her body pressed against his, her hair spilling over her face. She'd been through a terrible ordeal and was surely worn out. He brushed the hair off her cheek, wanting only to see her face.

She lifted her head with a start, looked at him through worried eyes. "Iain?"

"I didna mean to wake you."

She sat up. "Are you thirsty?"

"Aye."

In short order, she'd gotten him water, felt his forehead for fever, checked his bandages and tried to give him more laudanum.

"Nay, lass. Set the bottle aside."

She looked at him in confusion. "Are you no' in pain?"

"Aye, but let me bide wi' you a wee ere you send me floatin' again. Come and lie beside me as you were."

She did as he asked, looking down at him, her hand resting lightly on his chest. Then her eyes filled with tears. "It feels like a miracle to lie wi' you when so many times these past days I've feared you lost."

He wiped a single tear from her cheek. "I promised to stay alive, aye?"

She nodded, her lips curving in a smile that vanished as quickly as it appeared. "I'm grieved at the loss of so many of your men. I shall miss them, especially Cam."

And Iain found himself recounting the defeat at Ticonderoga, sparing her the full horror of it. "By the time Abercrombie sounded the retreat, I'd begun to wonder if any of us would survive. 'Twas as close to hell as I hope to come."

Fresh tears streamed down her cheeks. "I regret that so many should suffer. Think of the wives and children . . ."

"All I'm thinkin', *mo luaidh,* is how grateful I am to be here wi' you." He stroked her hair, reveling in the feel of her. "When Killy and Brendan told me your uncle had come, I feared I'd never see you alive again. The journey back was the longest night of my life, wonderin' each moment what torment he was forcin' upon you. I'm sorry I wasna here when he arrived. He'd ne'er have set foot upon the island."

Annie looked into the eyes of the man she loved and, despite her desire to forget, told him all that had happened from the moment she'd first spied her uncle with Lord William and Betsy. She told him how she'd gone with Uncle Bain to protect Betsy. She told him the terrible things Uncle Bain had said about her mother. She told him how Lord William had kept Uncle Bain from hurting her when she'd locked Uncle Bain out of the room. She told him of her fear that he was dead or injured and that she might never see him again.

"I was terrified!"

"You were uncommonly courageous."

Then she told him of the journey through the forest—how she'd known something was about to happen, how she'd warned Betsy, how her heart had fairly skipped a beat when she'd seen him standing in the middle of the road dressed as a true Highland warrior.

"If I hadna been in love wi' you already, I'd have fallen in love wi' you then."

He grinned, his whiskery face unbearably bonnie even with its cuts and bruises. "So you like the sight of me in a plaidie, aye?"

"Aye—and wi' braids in your hair." She leaned down and kissed him. "But I think red paint looks silly."

"Dinnae let Joseph hear you say that. The Muhheconneok are quite fond of vermillion."

She ran her hand over his chest, pressed her palm against his heartbeat. "When Uncle Bain stood wi' that pistol in his hand and fired—"

"Dinnae think on it, *a leannan*."

But she couldn't help it. "Morgan turned my head away so I couldna see, but I heard. I heard . . . and I thought you were gone."

"An old swordsman's trick—let the enemy close in for the deathblow and get under his blade. He went quickly."

She closed her eyes, tried to forget the fear of that moment. "How strange it is to think we're together tonight because of lord William."

"Aye, strange, indeed. Though I'd like to say I think better of him, 'tis no' true. He's proved himself capable of great and deadly deception. He wanted your uncle's death as much as I, and for much the same reason. He wanted you."

Annie looked away, her mind shifting to her encounter with Lord William.

"What is it, Annie?" Iain's voice grew grave. "Tell me."

"This evening, Lord William offered to make me his mistress." She recounted Lord William's proposal, telling Iain everything except for the fact she'd pleaded for his release. "He even offered to let me keep the bairn, saying that raisin' another man's child would be a 'just comeuppance.'"

Iain looked gravely into her eyes, his knuckles caressing her cheek. "He's right. You could return to Scotland and live a life of free of worryin' that your husband has been shot or taken by Indians, free of the fear of hunger, free of toil. You could wear silk gowns, be pampered by servants and find a wealthy man to marry you in the accepted church. But I am no' so selfless a man as to let you go, Annie."

She turned her head, kissed his palm. "And I am far too selfish a woman to want to leave. I want to live my life beside you, no matter what may come. My love lies upon you, Iain MacKinnon."

"As mine lies upon you."

Epilogue

Ian awoke to the sweet sound of Annie's singing.

"As I cam in by Strichen town one misty mornin' early, I heard a lassie sair lament for her true love nae returnin'."

He opened his eyes and watched as she rocked the baby and held him to her breast. Her gaze was fixed on little Iain's face, one of her fingers gripped tightly in his wee fist, a look of contentment on her bonnie face. Her golden hair spilled in a silken tangle over her shoulder, a contrast to their son's downy dark curls.

A feeling as warm as sunlight swelled in Ian's chest. He could have watched the two of them forever. He was the luckiest man alive and well he knew it.

The baby would be three months old next week. Born on a frosty January morning, he still seemed a miracle to Iain. Annie's pains had started in the evening, quickly growing fierce. Iain had paced outside the cabin in the dark while

Joseph's sister, Rebecca, and Betsy had tended her. His brothers, Joseph and a company of worried Rangers waited through the long, cold night with him, gathered round the fires with their flasks and furs.

Rebecca had tried to reassure him. "The first time is always the hardest. Her cries do not mean she is dying. Yes, it hurts, but it will not kill her."

But as the sun had risen and Annie's cries had grown more desperate, Iain had begun to fear in earnest, her suffering tearing at him, in no small part because he'd caused it. And for the first time in his life, he'd felt truly helpless. Though he'd have borne any anguish to protect her, he could not spare her this.

Then Rebecca had opened the cabin door. "She wants you beside her."

Fearing the worst, Iain had entered to find Annie dozing on the birthing stool, naked apart from a blanket round her shoulders, her face beaded with sweat and lined with pain and fatigue.

He'd knelt beside her, taken her hand and caressed her cheek. "Annie?"

She'd opened her eyes, given him a weak smile and whispered. "You've seen so much death, Iain. Now see life."

Astonished that she should allow him to penetrate this most womanly of moments, he'd supported her head against his shoulder as the next pang began, felt her grip on his hand tighten as her entire body arched and trembled. And he'd watched, unable to breathe as she'd endured the last agonizing minutes of birth, pushing his son from her body with a scream.

When Iain at last had opened the cabin door, raised the swaddled babe for his men to see and proclaimed that he was the father of a strong son, the Ranger Camp had exploded with cheers. A week later, with Father Delavay to speak the blessings, they'd baptized the baby Iain Cameron MacKinnon in memory of Cam.

Iain would never know why Wentworth had suddenly released him, passing the command of the Rangers to Morgan, though he suspected it had something to do with the bastard's lingering affection for Annie. Wentworth had summoned him a few days after little Iain's birth, thanked him for his service and dismissed him from the army on the condition that he agree to return if the Rangers should have dire need for him. Though Iain had at first refused to part from his brothers or his men, Morgan and Connor had insisted.

"Each time we go on a mission, I see the fear in Annie's eyes, and I pray to God I dinnae ever have to tell her you've been killed or taken," Morgan had said. "I dinnae think I have the courage for that."

"You've got a bonnie wife and a wee son," Connor had said. "They need you. Now you can go back to the farm and build a home for all of us. This war cannae last forever."

And so Iain had waited until Annie had healed and the snow had melted. Then he'd packed their worldly goods, including the small chest that held Annie's inheritance, into a wagon and hooked the wagon to a sturdy team of oxen.

"God go wi' you, my lady!" Betsy, who had married Brendan just before Christmas, had wept openly at being separated from her former mistress. "I shall miss you!"

Annie had smiled through her tears. "We shall see each other again. I promise."

With Joseph and his men to escort them through the forest, Iain had taken up the reins and left Fort Elizabeth behind, Annie and baby Iain beside him.

"*Beannachd leat!*" Morgan had called after them. *Blessings go with you!*

Connor had waved. "And keep a warm meal ready!"

Though his brothers had bid them farewell and even Wentworth and Cooke had watched them depart from the walls, the Rangers, busy preparing for their next mission, hadn't turned out to see them off. That more than anything had made him realize he was no longer one of them. He was no longer a Ranger. Though he'd wished to take his leave of them in some fitting way, perhaps it had been for the best, for they were still bound to war, while his life lay elsewhere. Still, their seeming indifference to his going had left a strange emptiness in his gut.

He would never forget them—those living and those he'd watched die.

He and Annie had been in Albany for a week now. Iain had used the time to buy livestock, feed and supplies and to hire the wagons needed to haul it all out to the farm. 'Twould take a year's hard labor to win the land back from the forest, but first he would have to rebuild the cabin and barns. He'd promised Annie a roof over her head and a fire in the hearth within a week, and he meant to keep that promise.

"*So I'll gang back tae Strichen town, for I was bred and born in, and I'll get me anither lad tae marry me in the mornin'.*"

She looked up, caught him watching her and smiled. "Do you know, little Iain, that your da is a braw man? Aye, he is. And an honorable one."

Iain rose, crossed the room and pressed a kiss to Annie's cheek. "A good morn' to you, *a leannan*. And to you, young laddie."

Then he set about washing and getting dressed. The wagons would be loaded and waiting for them, and he wanted to depart within an hour.

Today, after nearly four years of war, he was going home.

Annie shifted the baby's weight in her arms and watched field and forest roll by. At first they'd traveled a well-worn road past farms with cattle and bleating sheep. Then the farms had grown sparse, gradually giving way to forest. Now the road was thick with grass, and they rarely passed a cabin or haycock, the only sound the creaking of the wagons, the clucks and lowing of their livestock, and the occasional word from one of the wagoners behind them.

She would never tell Iain, but she'd been sad to leave Albany. It had been exciting to see shops and churches again, to read newspapers, to mingle with throngs of people in the street and speak with other women. Iain had bought three lovely new gowns for her, together with cloth, needle and thread so that she might stitch clothes for the baby.

Wherever she'd gone, she'd been treated with as much deference as the wife of Iain MacKinnon as she'd known as Lady Anne, daughter of the Earl of Rothesay. Everyone in Albany seemed to have heard of her husband and read of his exploits in the papers. And though some seemed leery of him—perhaps because Lord William had yet refused to clear Iain and his brothers of murder—it was plain that most people felt they owed him a personal debt for keeping the French and their Indian allies at bay. Some had even refused his coin.

And Annie had come to realize she was the wife of a living legend.

Though it had been hard to leave Albany behind, she knew how much it meant to Iain to return to his home. But she also knew what to expect. Iain had told her the cabin and barns had been burned to the ground. Weeds and underbrush choked the fields. The orchard was overgrown with saplings. They would have to sleep in a lean-to for a time, just as they'd done in the wild when they'd first met, but even after the cabin had been rebuilt, life would be a struggle.

"It willna be easy, Annie," Iain had warned her. "At first we'll depend on what I bring in with my rifle and traps for food, but by next year's harvest, the land will begin to yield for us again, and there will be plenty. I promise you'll ne'er go hungry."

But even had he told her they would live on nothing but dry cornmeal and river water, Annie could not have denied him this nor tainted his excitement with worries. She knew how he longed to rebuild what had been lost. Even now she could see the anticipation on his face.

"We're almost on MacKinnon land." He glanced down at her and smiled.

Annie looked about for a cairn or landmark. "How can you tell?"

His hands busy with the reins, he pointed with a nod of his head. "That wee burn marks our southern bounds."

They crossed the little creek, wheels splashing through water and jarring over stone, and then started round a bend in the road.

Iain frowned.

"What is it?"

"Smoke."

And then Annie smelled it, too—just the faintest hint of woodsmoke carried on the breeze. With it came the sound of knocking, a distant beating sound. Iain had warned her they might find squatters on the land—perhaps Indians, perhaps deserters—and that he might have to shed blood to free it again.

"If that happens, keep hidden," he'd warned her. "If they're Indians, chances are they're Stockbridge or Six Nations and willna seek to harm us, but deserters are no' likely to welcome us or to treat a woman well."

Suddenly Annie found herself wishing Joseph and his warriors were still with them. Once they'd reached Albany, Joseph had turned back to the fort so that he'd be able to accompany Morgan and the men on their mission. Now it was just Iain and the five wagoners behind them—hired men who, though in awe of Iain, might flee to safety rather than fight.

Iain took up his rifle and laid it across his lap, slowing the oxen as they rounded the bend.

And then they heard it.

The Rangers' warning whistle.

Annie saw the surprise and confusion on Iain's face and wondered, too, how this could be. Had Morgan and Connor encountered trouble and sought refuge here? Had someone learned the call and decided to use it to deceive and waylay Iain?

She held the baby close, her gaze fixed ahead.

Then the road grew straight again, and the forest fell back to reveal fields of dark, tilled earth, a house and a barn standing in the distance. Men worked everywhere—plowing the fields, tending the orchard, hammering upon the barn and cabin.

For a fleeting moment, Annie thought the land had been taken over by squatters—a whole clan of them. But then one of the men in the fields raised his head and grinned.

"It's about time you were gettin' here, Mack. Would you leave all the toil for us?"

Killy!

Breath left her lungs in a rush, and a hard lump formed in her throat. "M-mercy!"

The Rangers hadn't gone on a mission with Joseph and his men at all. They'd come to the farm and had put their backs into reclaiming it.

"Holy Mother of God!"

Annie looked up and saw a look of utter amazement on Iain's face.

A shout went up from the men working in the fields, and someone on top of the house stood and waved. 'Twas Morgan.

Annie waved back. "Oh, Iain, look what they have done!"

"I'm lookin', but I cannae fathom it."

He urged the oxen forward, drawing the team to a halt before the cabin. All around them, Rangers sized logs, sawed shingles, plied the hammer and dug the earth. Joseph and his men tended little fires built to burn out stubborn trees and brush. Morgan shouted for more nails, while Connor worked to hang the front door.

Annie gaped in disbelief at all they had accomplished, the scent of sawdust and new-tilled soil tickling her nose. She felt Iain's hands close about her waist and met his gaze as he lifted her and the baby to the ground. His blue eyes mirrored her own tangled emotions—astonishment, gratitude and something so raw it almost hurt.

He kissed her forehead. "Stay by the wagons, lass. I

wouldna want something to fall and strike you or the baby."

Connor glanced at them over his shoulder. "Are you goin' to stand there starin' wi' your mouth hangin' open, brother, or are you goin' to help me wi' this?"

That made Iain grin. Annie watched as he lifted one side of the door and held it while Connor tried to fit it to its hinges.

" 'Tis a strong and sturdy door."

"You've McHugh to thank for that." Connor raised his side with a grunt. "He's a carpenter by trade."

By the time the door was hung straight—a task that seemed to involve a certain amount of cursing—Morgan had finished with the roof and climbed down to join them. "Would you like to look about your new home, Annie?"

As Rangers unloaded the wagons and sent the wagoners back to Albany, Morgan guided Annie and Iain through the house, accompanied by Connor and Joseph. He led them across the smooth puncheon floors, past the wide hearth and through the spacious front room to the three bedrooms, each with its own fireplace, and then to the broad loft above stairs.

" 'Tis a big house." Annie looked from one end of the loft to the other.

"We were all thinkin' the two of you are likely to have many wee ones." Connor winked, and Annie felt her face burn.

"Besides, where am I going to sleep?" Joseph grinned. "Your home is my home. Is that not so, brother?"

Iain frowned. "Och, aye, I suppose."

Next, Morgan showed them the secret chamber built beneath the floor of the main bedroom. Then he took them out the back door, past the privy house, the large stone oven and the smokehouse to the barn, where their livestock had already been settled with hay and corn, chickens pecking at the straw.

Annie shifted the baby in her arms and watched as Iain tested the stall doors, climbed to the hayloft, and ran his hands over the smooth planks of the walls, the look on his handsome face like that of a man lost in a dream. It seemed a dream to her, as well, her worries about sleeping with the baby in the cold night air and of Iain breaking his back in the fields vanishing.

By the time Morgan had finished showing them around, the men had gathered between the house and the barn and stood covered with dirt and sweat, grins upon their faces.

Iain seemed to search for words. "What you have done here, 'tis beyond all hope or imaginin'. You have my abidin' gratitude. But are you no' supposed to be spyin' on Montcalm?"

The men chuckled.

"You're no' the only one who can find ways to outwit Wentworth, brother." Morgan clapped Iain on the shoulder. "Montcalm can bide a wee, but this couldna. What one man cannae do alone in a year, two hundred men can do in a matter of days. There wasna a soul among us who wanted you and Annie to start your new life wi' such toil and hardship."

Annie tried to speak around the lump in her throat. "However can we repay such kindness?"

" 'Tis us doin' the repayin', mistress." Brendan stepped forward. "You've cared for us when we were sick and injured, and there is scarce a man here who doesna owe Iain MacKinnon his life."

Then Annie listened, tears pricking her eyes, as one by one they spoke.

Brendan told how he'd frozen with fear in his first battle, unable to reload as two French soldiers closed in on him with bayonets, only to find Iain beside him, rifle at the ready. Joseph told how he'd surprised a bear in the wild and how Iain, only seventeen, had fought the enraged animal off him. McHugh told how Iain had carried him back to camp when he'd caught his ankle in a mislaid trap and hadn't been able to outrun the Abenaki.

And so it went, tale after tale, until Dougie told how he'd

been captured by an Abenaki war party, stripped and tied to a tree to be tortured. "I thought it was my end, and a grisly one at that. But then I heard a rifle fire, and one by one the Abenaki fell, pierced clean through their hearts. They couldna tell where the shots were coming from—one from here, one from there. And I kent it could only be Iain Mac-Kinnon riskin' his own fool neck to save me."

It was Dougie who started it, his voice strong and clear, until the chant was picked up and the Rangers and Muhhe-conneok shouted in unison, fists raised against the sky.

"MacKinnon! MacKinnon! MacKinnon! MacKinnon! Mac-Kinnon!"

Tears streamed down Annie's cheeks, her heart so swollen it ached, and she knew she would tell her grand-children of this moment. This was the men's way of doing what they had not done at the fort—'twas their way of say-ing farewell.

Iain's head was high, his expression that of a seasoned warrior, as he took in this tribute. But she could see the sheen of tears in his eyes. He slipped his arm around her waist, drew her closer to him as the shouting died down.

"No commander has ever been more proud of his men than I am of you. You're the best—aye, and the bravest." His voice dropped to a ragged whisper. "I'll ne'er forget you."

For a moment there was silence.

Then Connor turned to Morgan. "*Major* Mackinnon, is it no' time we headed north?"

"Aye, it is, *Captain*."

Annie could not bear to see them leave, not so quickly. "But you cannae go! Stay and rest awhile! Join us for supper!"

Morgan gave her a grin. "I wish we could stay, Annie, but we cannae let Montcalm grow lonely. General Amherst has his sights set on Ticonderoga, and he might have the wits and the mettle to do what old Nanny Crombie could not. But you'll see us again, lass—and soon."

Then he turned to the men. "Fall out, Rangers!"

And with whoops and shouts, the Rangers and the Muhheconneok took up their tools and weapons, said farewell and disappeared into the forest.

Annie turned to her husband, lifted her gaze to his. "Since I met you, Iain MacKinnon, I seem always to be feelin' both sadness and great joy at once."

"Aye, lass, 'tis much the same for me." He kissed the top of her head, wiped the tears from her cheeks, his blue eyes filled with tenderness. "But my Muhheconneok grannies would say you cannae open your heart to one wi'out riskin' the other, and I would rather chance the deepest sorrows of hell, Annie, than surrender the joy you and little Iain bring me each day."

Then he scooped her into his arms and bore her and the baby across the threshold into their new home and a new beginning.

RIDE THE FIRE

PAMELA CLARE

There is only one rule on the frontier—survival. So when a wounded, buckskin-clad stranger appears at the door of her isolated cabin, Elspeth Stewart feels no qualms about disarming him and then tying him to her bed. Nicholas Kenleigh threatens not only her safety, but her peace of mind. Bethie has every reason in the world to distrust men; the cruelty she has suffered at their hands has marked her soul, though her blonde beauty shows no sign of it. But she finds herself believing in Nicholas, in his honor, his strength. As he brings her baby into the world, then takes both mother and daughter into his care, she realizes this scarred survivor can heal her wounded spirit, and together they will…

CARNAL GIFT

PAMELA CLARE

Her body and her virginity are to be offered up to a stranger in exchange for her brother's life. Possessing nothing but her innocence and her fierce Irish pride, Bríghid has no choice but to comply.

But the handsome man she faces in the darkened bedchamber is not at all the monster she expected. His tender touch calms her fears while he swears he will protect her by merely pretending to claim her. And as the long hours of the night pass by, as her senses ignite at the heat of their naked flesh, Bríghid makes a startling discovery: Sometimes the line between hate and love can be dangerously thin.

ATTENTION
BOOK LOVERS!

Can't get enough of your favorite **ROMANCE**?

Call **1-800-481-9191** to:

✳ order books.

2/8 11/11